DYA.

3

A CORRUPTIBLE CROWN

A CORRUPTIBLE CROWN

Gillian Bradshaw

This first world edition published 2011
in Great Britain and the USA by
SEVERN HOUSE PUBLISHERS LTD of
9–15 High Street, Sutton, Surrey, England, SM1 1DF.
Trade paperback edition first published
in Great Britain and the USA 2011 by
SEVERN HOUSE PUBLISHERS LTD.

British Library Cataloguing in Publication Data

Bradshaw, Gillian, 1956-
   A corruptible crown.
   1. Great Britain–History–Civil War, 1642-1649–
   Fiction. 2. Blacksmiths–Fiction. 3. Publishers and
   Publishing–Political aspects–England–London–
   History–17th century–Fiction. 4. Levellers–Fiction.
   5. Historical fiction.
   I. Title
   813.5'4-dc22

ISBN-13: 978-0-7278-8021-5 (cased)
ISBN-13: 978-1-84751-349-6 (trade paper)

All Severn House titles are printed on acid-free paper.

Severn House Publishers support The Forest Stewardship Council [FSC],
the leading international forest certification organisation. All our titles that
are printed on Greenpeace-approved FSC-certified paper carry the FSC logo.

Typeset by Palimpsest Book Production Ltd.,
Falkirk, Stirlingshire, Scotland.
Printed and bound in Great Britain by the
MPG Books Group, Bodmin, Cornwall.

'I go from a corruptible to an incorruptible crown, where no disturbances can be, no disturbances in the world.'

Charles I, 30th January, 1649

'I see that though liberty were our end, there is a degeneration from it. We have engaged in this kingdom and ventured our lives, and it was all for this: to recover our birthrights and privileges as Englishmen; and by the arguments urged there are none.

Do you not think it were a sad and miserable condition, that we have fought all this time for nothing?'

Edward Sexby, in the Putney Debates

One

The tide was out, and the mud-flats of the Severn estuary shimmered with heat-haze under the June sun. The ships driven aground by the storm earlier in the month seemed to float on the heavy air, and the men struggling to salvage their cargo appeared and disappeared in the haze, ant-sized, grey with mud.

Jamie Hudson, a blacksmith, stared wearily at the scene and wished himself out in the mud along with the others. The makeshift smithy behind him was hot and close as a baker's oven, and the poor quality coal he'd been given filled it with acrid smoke. He'd been working with a damp cloth over his mouth and nose, but even so he'd had to come outside to ease his sore eye and aching lungs.

He dipped his cloth in the water butt beside the smithy, wiped his face, then wrapped it around his head again and went back inside to pump the bellows. The salvage team wanted braces for a cradle strong enough to take off the great guns; they wanted a mattock and three crowbars mended; they wanted two lengths of chain joined together – in short, there was plenty of work waiting for him.

When the two visitors arrived he at first paid no attention to them. He was busy punching a hole in a glowing piece of iron and drifting it to fit a grapple – tricky work, particularly since the sulphurous vapours from the coal were making the iron brittle. He couldn't use solid strikes of the hammer; he had to coax the hot metal with a gentle *rap-rap-rap* that was not only slow but required close attention.

The metal cooled quickly, though, and stiffened as it did so. When its glow had faded to a dull orange, Jamie returned it to the fire and turned to face the visitors. He'd expected someone from the camp – the carpenter, perhaps, come to ask whether the braces were ready. Instead he found himself facing his elder brother – a man he'd believed to be comfortably the other side of the kingdom. He stared in shocked disbelief.

The other stared back uncertainly, and Jamie became aware of himself as a shrouded figure, standing in the smoky darkness, hammer in hand. He wished he could stay that way. He had not spoken to anyone in his family since his furious departure from home, six years and a lifetime before. He was altogether unprepared for this meeting.

'Jamie?' his brother asked at last – then coughed. The other visitor, meanwhile, had a hand cupped over his mouth and nose to protect them from the fumes: in the dim light of the smithy Jamie couldn't even tell whether or not it was someone he knew.

'Robert,' Jamie said hoarsely. He swallowed. 'Aye. We can speak outside.'

The sunlight was painfully bright after the darkness of the forge. Jamie squinted through it. His brother Robert seemed much the same as ever: a big man in his thirties, with a handsome high-coloured face and long brown hair tied back under his wide-brimmed hat. His chin was stubbled and his clothes were travel-stained; his riding boots were spattered with fresh mud from the road. His companion was vaguely familiar, though Jamie couldn't put a name to him: a dark, sneering fellow in the red coat of the New Model Army, similarly travel-worn.

The air, muggy as it was, felt deliciously cool and fresh after the smithy. Jamie unwrapped the damp cloth and wiped his face with it. Robert flinched and exclaimed loudly, 'Jesu!' Jamie winced.

'Your face looks like a soused hog's cheek!' Robert said, with a mixture of reproach and disgust. 'Lord a' mercy!'

Jamie said nothing. He'd known that his family would be horrified by the ruin of the right side of his face: it was one of the reasons he'd stayed away from them. The war had eaten the handsome young man who'd stormed out their door, and spat out a grim, hulking, one-eyed ogre. Strangers looked at him with real fear; small children hid behind their mothers at the sight of him. Deliberately he called up the memory of his young wife stroking his scarred cheek and smiling up at him, her beautiful dark eyes alight with love. If his face could inspire that, he could live with it.

'Your friend that writ us said you'd lost an eye,' Robert went on, 'and some part of your hand . . .'

Jamie held up his right hand, with the iron brace that now stood for his missing fingers. 'Aye. As you see, I've learned to do without it. Brother, I . . . I'm surprised to see you.'

Robert snorted. 'Aye, for you've sent us no word these three years, to say where you were and what you were about – apart from that last January to say that you were wed. It were better to have sent no word than that one! Father was in a rage for a week.'

Jamie sighed. He'd guessed that his father was very angry. There'd been no word from the old man — but the regular instalments of money that had been coming ever since he was wounded had stopped. 'I meant him no disrespect. I would have waited for his blessing, but . . .'

'. . . but you had only a brief while, aye, so you said, to settle your affairs before you were obliged to rejoin the Army — but *that* begged more questions. Such as, why you couldn't wait til you were clear of the Army before you wed, and why you were *obliged* to rejoin it in the first place. God have mercy, I learned the answer to *that* when I went to the Commissary-General to ask what had become of you. Arrested and sent to prison! Locked up like a common vagrant for brawling, and released only because the Army had need of a blacksmith! I haven't yet dared tell Father!'

Jamie looked at him sharply. 'Ireton told you I was arrested for brawling?'

'Ireton?' repeated Robert, momentarily distracted.

'You said you went to the Commissary-General.'

Robert shrugged, his lips jutting dismissively. 'To his office. To his staff. Do you tell me they lied?'

'Aye,' Jamie said, with quiet intensity. He glanced at Robert's companion, remembering now where he'd seen the man before: Ireton's office. The memory was not a pleasant one.

Robert paused, staring at his brother in surprise. The companion snorted in contempt. 'You prefer to plead guilty to mutiny and striking an officer?' he asked.

Jamie stared at him a long moment. Once he would have contradicted the man immediately, but Time with its many humiliations had taught him to be more careful — and Commissary-General Ireton's name had come up, which called for a double measure of caution. He asked mildly, 'What is your name, sir?'

The other sneered. 'Lieutenant Isaiah Barker.' He did not say what he was doing here, in Robert's company.

'You are mistaken, Lieutenant Barker,' Jamie said evenly. 'I am guilty neither of brawling nor of mutiny.'

'You were arrested at Ware!' replied Barker with sudden vehemence.

'Aye,' Jamie agreed. 'But I never heard that a private gentleman was forbidden the place, and I was not a soldier then – as I think you know, sir, for the matter was discussed in your presence. And it's true that I struck an officer, but I saw him set upon a friend of mine to rob him. I had no duty to stand aside. I went to my friend's help.' He looked back to his brother, met and held his eyes. 'Judge for yourself, Rob! Is it right to stand aside when a friend is being robbed?'

Neither Robert nor Barker objected that an officer wouldn't engage in robbery. Most of England had experience to the contrary.

'If this be true, why were you arrested?' Robert asked suspiciously. 'Or why could you not trust the law to set you free again?'

The answer to that was long and complicated, and Jamie was grimly certain that Robert wouldn't like it. While he hesitated, desperately trying to think how to begin, Barker waded in with the blunt truth. 'Because he's a damned Leveller! This "robbery" he speaks of was no such thing! Lieutenant Greenly had been ordered to seize the mutineers' printing press, but . . .'

'Those were no lawful orders!' interrupted Jamie. 'The press belonged to John Harris, his own property and . . .'

'Another damned Leveller!' replied Barker.

'To be a Leveller is no crime,' said Jamie, 'much as some might wish it otherwise! It was John's press. What right had Oliver Cromwell to take it from him? Last I heard, he was Lieutenant General, not Licensor! And for all you say there was no robbery, your friend Greenly's man was seizing everything he could lay hands on!'

'Why should he respect your friend's property?' sneered Barker. 'You Levellers have no respect for *any* man's property. You'd do away with property altogether!'

'That's a lie!' Jamie said forcefully.

Barker merely sneered again, then slapped Robert's shoulder. 'Well, you've found your levelling brother: I wish you joy of him! I must be off about my business.' He strolled off in the direction of the camp headquarters down the hill.

'It's a lie,' Jamie repeated.

Robert, though, was looking troubled and unhappy, just as Jamie had feared. The Hudson family had been divided even over whether Parliament was right to stand against the King; what they'd heard of the beliefs of the Levellers would horrify them. Jamie had imagined their horror many times, just as he'd imagined their reaction to his scars – and here it was, staring him in the face. He would have to try to make Robert understand, but he dreaded the task. He had never been good with words.

'Brother,' he said to Robert urgently, 'I know not what that man has been telling you, but you should not believe him.'

Robert shook his head unhappily. 'I have heard of this levelling faction from others besides him. I am sorry to hear that you number yourself among them.'

'What you have heard is lies,' said Jamie. 'Surely you know how thick and fast lies grow these days! I pray you, do not condemn us without even a hearing!'

Robert was unconvinced, but he grimaced and nodded. 'I will hear you out, brother. I can hardly do less, after coming all this long way to find you.' He sighed. 'You have not asked what brings me here.'

He had not: he had been too shaken and defensive even to think of it. Looking at Robert now, he realized that it was bad news. He didn't want to hear it, and wished again that Robert had stayed in Lincolnshire.

'Our brother is dead,' said Robert.

Jamie stared at him, shocked speechless. They'd been three boys in the family, and four girls. Robert was the eldest; Nick and Jamie, born only a year apart, had followed three girls, and had grown up inseparable. There had been constant squabbles, with Nick trying to be master and Jamie stubbornly refusing to submit – but they had been allies against all the world else.

Then came the war. Nick went to fight for the King, Jamie enlisted for Parliament, and they had not spoken since. Something in the back of Jamie's mind shouted in anguish, *He can't be dead. We haven't been reconciled!*

'Your Army killed him,' Robert said. His voice was flat, but that *your* had an edge. Their father George Hudson had abhorred the very notion of rebellion, though he'd been unwilling to risk the family estates by espousing Royalism when all his Lincolnshire neighbours supported Parliament. He had complied with the demands of the county authorities only when he couldn't wriggle out of them. When Nick went off to fight for the King, he'd tut-tutted in public but had been privately proud; Jamie's choice had been another matter. Robert had always cast his own opinions and conduct in their father's mould.

Jamie started to ask what had happened, but his voice caught. He cleared his throat.

Robert gave him a long look of appraisal, then nodded. 'So you haven't forgotten how dearly you loved him once.'

Jamie shook his head dumbly. 'How . . . ?' he whispered.

'When he heard of the rising in Kent, he went there directly. He joined up with the rebels and marched with them as far as Maidstone. He was killed in the battle there.'

News of the battle at Maidstone had arrived in the camp by the Severn a few days earlier. Jamie, like the rest of the men, had cheered the victory; like the rest, he'd felt only hatred for those who'd refused to accept defeat, and had started the cruel and bloody war all over again.

The awful realization struck: he'd cheered his brother's death.

Shaking, he cleared his throat again. 'Do you know how . . .'

'He took a musket-ball in the stomach.'

'Oh, Christ!' Jamie had seen men die that way. Tears burned his working eye; the empty socket ached.

'He lived long enough to tell the surgeons his name and kin, and one of them sent a letter.' Robert was silent a moment, then shook his head. 'I rode down to Maidstone to fetch him home. Father wanted him laid to rest in Bourne churchyard. But by the time I arrived, he'd already been buried. No one could even tell me which was his grave.'

Of course not – but Robert, Jamie remembered, hadn't fought in the war, and didn't know what things were like after a battle. A corpse with ruptured guts, in summer? It had been put in the ground as fast as possible, to keep its stench from the nostrils of the living. Probably it had gone into a common pit. The men who dug the graves wouldn't even have known the names of those they buried, let alone remember where they put them all.

'I searched for his things,' Robert went on, his voice suddenly rough with anger. 'I spoke to the surgeons, and begged for anything that had been his, so that I could take it back to Father, but I was told I'd more hope of finding a particular coin from a purse cut last winter. It seems looters will strip any fallen man to his shirt, and if they miss anything, the hospital attendants make off with it!'

Jamie nodded. Yes, that was what happened. He imagined Nick lying in the filthy street at Maidstone, curled up round his torn guts, heard him cry out when the looters turned him over, saw him carried half-naked to the surgeons, saw him buried in an unmarked grave. He was still holding his damp cloth, and he pressed it to his face. His throat worked, choking him. He had *cheered*.

He would not see Nick again. They would never be reconciled, not on this Earth.

'I did find the surgeon who'd tended him,' Robert said, anger ebbing into weariness, 'the one that writ us with the news. He said Nick died well, calling upon Christ to receive him.'

The surgeon might have lied, of course – but he must be a conscientious man, to have taken the trouble to write to the family of a defeated enemy. It was likely enough that he'd told the truth. Men dying of stomach wounds did call upon Christ. They called on anything that might help them!

There was a silence. Jamie knew that he was expected to utter some pious hope that Nick was now in Heaven. He did hope it, but couldn't make his voice work to say so. At last Robert went on, 'Since I had dealt with the Army so far, I decided to ask after you. At the Commissary-General's office I met Lieutenant Barker, who said he was bound this way with dispatches, and offered to escort me.'

Jamie wiped his face again.

'I thought you should hear this from kin,' said Robert, 'and not months hence from a stranger.'

'Best if I never heard at all,' Jamie croaked, 'but – thank you, Rob.'

Robert's shoulders slumped, and he sighed deeply. 'There is much we need to speak of, Jamie, but I'm hungry and weary to the bone. Barker rode hard. Have you lodgings?'

Jamie had a place in a nearby farmhouse. He led Robert there, agreed with the farmwife for some food for his brother, then went back to the camp to fetch Robert's horse. It seemed that Robert had arranged for it to be stabled along with that of his travelling companion Barker, but Jamie had no confidence that the Army would respect the property of a civilian visitor. Horses were always in short supply, and Robert's mare was a fine beast. The salvage teams were straggling back to camp now that the tide was coming in: he wanted to get the mare out of the Army picket line before anyone took a fancy to her.

He was leading the mare back through the camp when the captain spotted him. 'Ah, Cyclops!' he shouted.

Jamie stopped. The nickname 'Cyclops' hadn't been the captain's

invention, but a witticism of the Commissary-General's staff, passed
on down the line, like Jamie himself. Jamie didn't know Latin, but
he'd gathered that one of the pagan gods had had a smithy manned
by one-eyed monsters. He hated the nickname, but answered to it.

The captain came over. He was a short, round-faced man a little
younger than Jamie, energetic and competent. 'I hear you've suffered
a loss,' he said, peering up at him doubtfully.

Barker must have told him. Jamie glanced around for the lieutenant,
but didn't see him. 'Aye,' he agreed heavily. 'My brother Nicholas is
dead.'

'Fighting for the malignants!' the captain said wonderingly. 'Strange,
that.'

'Not so strange,' Jamie said wearily. 'Sir. There must be a score of
others even in this camp with one kinsman or other who sided with
the King.'

The captain shrugged: yes, but they weren't Levellers. The gulf
between King and Parliament might be deep, but that between the
King and *The Agreement of the People* had become unbridgeable. 'I'd
give you space to mourn,' he said, 'only we're pressed for time. This
messenger, Lieutenant Barker – he tells me he means to go on to
Pembroke and be back within the week. He says that when he returns
to General Ireton, he wants to report that the great guns have been
salvaged and are on their way. You truly grieve for this malignant
brother?' he added in surprise.

'Aye,' Jamie said shortly.

The captain grimaced. 'Well. Blood binds, I suppose, even where
spirit sunders. Grieving or not, Mr Hudson, you must back to work.
What are you doing with that horse?'

Jamie patted the mare's sweaty neck. 'Stabling her. She's my
brother's.'

'And you've inherited her? She's a fine animal!'

Jamie shook his head. 'My other brother. Who came to me with
the news. He's weary from the journey, so I said I would see her
stabled.'

'Ah.' The captain appraised him a moment, then decided not to
make an issue of it. He, too, patted the mare, then ran an appreciative hand down her foreleg. 'A fine horse!' He looked up, frowning
a little: it was a better horse than he'd expect of a blacksmith's brother.
Jamie understood his surprise, but didn't explain. If his fellows in

the camp knew that he was a gentleman's son they'd expect him to be generous with money – and he didn't have any.

'Well, see to her, and then go to your work!' ordered the captain. 'Barker also said that when he goes back to the Commissary-General, he means to take you with him. He says by the time he returns from Pembroke we'll have no more need of your services. I hope he may be right!'

That was unexpected. The image of his beautiful young wife smiled up into his mind's eye, and suddenly his heart was racing. 'Will he go through London?' he asked eagerly.

The captain shrugged. 'He said that he left General Ireton in Canterbury – the rebels there have surrendered to him, God be praised! But where Ireton will be when you reach him, who knows? This new war blows about like sparks in the wind. Who knows where it will flare up next?'

He left the mare at the farmhouse, promising the farmwife that Robert would pay for her fodder, then went back to the smithy. Without the need to concentrate on the hot iron, he would have had to contemplate the horror of Nick's death – that, and struggle to damp down the hope of seeing his wife soon. If he could tell *her* about Nick, the horror would be bearable – but he doubted very much that General Ireton would be in London.

He drew a glowing brace out of the fire and began to punch another hole in it. The sooner he and the Army did their work, the sooner this bloody, unnatural war would be over – and the sooner Jamie Hudson could go home to his wife.

'Your hosts tell me that you are the best of a bad lot,' Robert told Jamie.

It was dusk – a slow June twilight – and they were sitting in the farmyard after supper. The two other soldiers billeted at the house were playing nine-men's morris with stones on a board scratched into the mud the other side of the yard. Jamie glanced to see whether they'd overheard, but neither of them looked up.

'It's the free quarter,' he replied softly. 'The fellows here are good enough men – better than many – but our hosts aren't rich. Three extra mouths to feed are a burden. They feel we ought to be working for our keep. They object to me least, because I mend tools for them.'

Robert grunted. The Army's use of 'free quarter' – billeting men in civilian households without payment – was a source of ill feeling in most parts of England, but not of immediate interest. His attention was caught more by his brother's mending of tools. 'I was surprised when I heard you were a blacksmith again,' he said. 'Your friend that writ us said you'd lost your trade together with your fingers. He begged us to send money.'

Robert's voice was flat. The family *had* sent money – that now-stopped allowance – and now he was wondering if they'd been tricked. Jamie looked down at his hands – the good left and the half-iron right. Then he undid the catch on the iron brace and slipped the half-hand out. He showed his brother the mutilated thumb and two missing fingers. Robert's nose wrinkled in revulsion, and Jamie dropped the hand in his lap again. 'I thought I had lost my trade,' he said quietly. 'I lived on your money for more than a year. But last winter Lucy pointed out I still had the better part of the hand.' He moved the stump of his thumb back and forth. 'She told me I could make myself some device to supply my lack, if I would but give over wallowing in brandy and self-pity.' He smiled at the memory. 'What could I do after that but try again?'

Robert frowned. '*Lucy*,' he repeated, with distaste. 'The woman you married.'

'Aye.'

'And the wench is with child?'

Jamie sat up straight. '*What*? When did you hear that? I've heard nothing of it! Did you visit her in London?'

Robert made an impatient gesture. 'Why should you have made such haste to marry the slut, if you *hadn't* got her with child? Our sisters have all been weeping to think what sort of creature they must call "sister".'

Jamie stared, then said with quiet ferocity, 'My *wife* is no *slut*! She is a brave honest woman, daughter of a freehold farmer from Leicestershire and niece of a London mercer! I was in haste to marry her because I feared that some other might seize on her if I did not.'

Robert gave a 'Huh!' of surprise. After a moment, he added, 'But your letter said nothing of a dowry!'

Jamie grimaced. 'Her family suffered great losses in the war. Most of her dowry was spent to mend them.'

Robert frowned in puzzlement. 'She's an heiress, then?'

'Nay!' Jamie exclaimed, impatiently now. 'Even if you have no use for beauty or wits, Rob, you must be aware that others do! Mistress Wentnor had already refused one proposal of marriage, and that from a man with property, two good hands and a handsome face. I have no doubt there would have been more, for she's a bright light men love to look upon. Her father chanced to be in London when I was released and he was willing to give his consent, so I seized my opportunity. I was afraid that if I let it slip, she'd change her mind. I'm no great catch, Rob, with this face and hand and not money enough to buy a ring for her finger at the wedding.'

He remembered his wife on their wedding day. It had been a dark day early in January, with no flowers to be had, and the church had been a Puritan one her family favoured, bare and austere. Her ordinary russet gown had been tricked out with a few snippets of pink silk, and her dark hair crowned only with a chaplet of rosemary. She had shone, he thought, like the sun in winter, more dazzling in the world's bleakness.

'She could have done much better,' he said, with a pang of shame. 'I could not, though I wed the richest maid in England.'

'And she's not with child?' asked Robert in confusion.

Jamie reviewed the conversation in his mind, and reluctantly gave up the idea that Robert had any information at all about Lucy. He told himself he was relieved – what would his wife do, on her own in London with a new baby? – and pushed aside the way his heart had stuttered at the prospect of a child smiling up at him from his wife's arms.

'She would certainly have writ to tell me if she was,' he told Robert coldly.

'She can write?' Robert asked in surprise.

'Rob,' Jamie said in exasperation, 'I met her working on a printing press! Her father's a yeoman with forty acres freehold. He's a godly man: of course he had his daughter taught to read her Bible!'

This, he could see, impressed Robert. A yeoman wasn't a gentleman – of course not! – but freehold property was the next best thing, and forty acres was a big freeholding. 'Well,' said Robert, after a reflective pause. 'This is better than we feared!'

Jamie gave him a look of dislike. 'What, you thought I'd pledged myself to some slut I met while drunk in the London gutter?'

Robert didn't reply, which meant *yes*. 'You should not have married without Father's blessing, but it's better than we feared,' he said instead. He studied Jamie thoughtfully. 'I gathered from the Commissary-General's staff that the Army thinks highly of your skill, too.'

Jamie wished the Army thought less of his skill: he could have hoped then for release.

'That's to your credit,' Robert decided. 'Though blacksmithing's no trade for a gentleman.'

'Good enough for a gentleman's third son,' Jamie replied sourly. 'Or so everyone said at the time.' His father had been unwilling to spend what was needed to get him into a more gentlemanly profession. Robert had been to Cambridge, and Nick had been apprenticed to a merchant, but a smithy had been reckoned good enough for George Hudson's rebellious third son. That still rankled – even though Jamie liked his trade.

'You're a gentleman's second son now,' Robert said quietly. 'And likely heir to the estate.'

Shocked, Jamie inspected his brother's face. 'You're the heir, Rob, and you've a fine son of your own!'

'Georgie died two years ago,' Robert said flatly.

Jamie gulped. Georgie had been a noisy five-year-old when he saw him last; he'd assumed the boy was now ten or eleven and at school. 'God have mercy!' he said. 'Rob, I'm sorry; I didn't know.'

'He was fishing at Carr Dyke,' Robert said slowly, 'and his line caught on a snag. He waded out to free it and cut his foot on something in the water. He came home limping but happy enough – proud of his catch, in fact; we all ate fish for supper. The cut, though, the cut on his foot – it went bad. It swelled, and he took a fever from it. By the time we called the surgeon it was too late: the infection had gone up his leg to his groin. He died in his mother's arms. She shut up the nursery after.'

'I'm sorry!' Jamie said again helplessly. 'I didn't know!'

'Aye, for you've had naught to do with us for *three years*, Jamie!' Robert said, with sudden anger. '*Six years*, I might say, since we've had precious little news of you ever since you joined the rebels! A most unbrotherly silence!'

Jamie raised his hands, the good one and the bad. 'I'm sorry, Rob! But I would have wrote more, if I'd dared! Surely you remember that Father forbade me to write to him or to enter his

presence again unless it was to tell him that I'd returned to what
he called my "duty"?'

Robert glared. 'Aye. And why shouldn't you have yielded to him?
What have you gained from your soldiering for Parliament? Scars and
maiming and the need to serve or go to prison! It was a bad cause
from the beginning!'

'I thought the liberty of freeborn men a good cause.'

Robert made a noise of disgust. 'The King was high-handed, I'll
grant it! He pushed his prerogative too far. But he'd already conceded
most of what Parliament wanted before the war broke out!'

'He never "conceded" any power that would let Parliament hold
him to his promises, though! That he refused absolutely!'

'He is God's anointed! Such rebellion cannot be justified in the
eyes of Heaven! And look, your *Parliament*' – Robert spat the word
with disgust – 'has become more high-handed and tyrannical than
ever King Charles was!'

'Hush!' said Jamie, with another glance at his fellow-soldiers. It
was growing too dark now for them to play their game, and they
were getting ready to go in.

'He can rail against Parliament as much as he likes!' one of them
called back cheerfully. He dusted off his knees, grinning. 'Greedy
rogues and lying knaves, all of them! God keep you!'

He and his friend went into the farmhouse. 'You're in luck that
he missed your praise of the King,' Jamie said soberly. 'He would
have taken it as licence to plunder you. He's one of those who want
the King's head.'

The King had been Parliament's prisoner for nearly three years
now. There had at first been hopes that he would agree to one of the
new constitutional settlements offered to him. Parliament still hoped
for that, even though the King had raised up a second war.

Robert peered at him through the dusk. 'I'd heard that was a
common desire, in your Army. You don't share it?'

Jamie sighed. 'Rob, I am sick of war, and I don't believe we'll ever
have peace as long as Charles wears the crown. I don't care what
becomes of the man, so long as he stops troubling England! But we
won't agree on this, we both know it. I am grieved to the heart about
Nick; I am sorry for your poor little Georgie. For the love of Christ,
I beg you, let's not quarrel!'

'We have all sinned,' Robert said sadly, 'and this war has been our punishment. If your choice turned out badly, poor Nick's served him even worse. Man is born to trouble, as the sparks fly upward.'

Robert had never been given to pious sentiments in the past. He'd changed, Jamie realized; the horrors of the war had scarred even those who'd stayed at home and tried to remain neutral. 'If I'd known how it would turn out,' he said, suddenly able to speak unguardedly, 'I would never have gone to war. Not just because of *this*,' he waved his bad hand at his scarred face, 'but because I was deceived. I fought for our rights and our freedoms, but those who led us only wanted to throw the King's men out of the saddle and mount up themselves instead.'

Robert stared at Jamie through the dusk, began to smile in surprised agreement – then frowned as he remembered. 'And yet you're part of this levelling faction?'

'That's *why* I'm a part of it!'

'I've heard it's a design against property,' said Robert warily. 'That you would do away with *mine* and *thine,* and make men have all things in common.'

'It's a lie. I've heard it said, as you have, but only by our enemies.' Jamie drew a deep breath, searching for more words. They wouldn't come. He'd often argued with his family in imagination, but even there he'd doubted his ability to convince them. Faced with his brother's sceptical attention he despaired.

We have no design against property, he could say, and *We want to dissolve the present corrupt Parliament and hold fresh elections for a new one. As for the church, we believe that each man should be free to worship God according to the dictates of his own conscience.*

He remembered a summer before the war, when his father had joined with some other landowners in a scheme to drain a piece of fenland. The people who lived in that fen, threatened with the loss of their whole way of life, had opposed the scheme violently, threatening the Dutch engineers brought to survey the land, tearing down fences and levelling hedges. George Hudson had been furiously indignant. *'The land is waste, a stinking bog good for naught but wildfowling! Drain it, and it will produce good wheat!'* That the fenmen would be turned out to beg, that his own family was already far richer than anyone he wanted to dispossess – that hadn't troubled his conscience in the slightest. His business was to get as much as he could from his land; those who obstructed him were lawbreaking ruffians, and deserved to be hanged.

Jamie had often been wildfowling on the contested fen, and hadn't been able to shut his eyes to the fact that draining it would ruin the inhabitants. He'd tried to argue their case with his father. George Hudson had been outraged by his son's disloyalty: he'd struck him across the face and commanded him never to speak of the matter again.

He cleared his throat. 'What became of Father's drainage scheme?'

'The war put a stop to it,' replied Robert. 'Such enterprises need peace.' He blinked. 'So this levelling business is the same? Justice for poor wretches?'

'Rob, I wish I could make it plain to you that it *would* be justice, in a world where injustice and oppression cry out to Heaven for vengeance! But I've no skill in speaking. I have writings, though, which could supply what I lack . . .'

'None of your poxy pamphlets!' Robert suddenly reached over and clasped Jamie's shoulder, looking him earnestly in the face. 'Jamie, we two are now all the sons of our father's house. This cruel unnatural war has done hurt enough. Let's have peace between the two of us, at least!'

Jamie's first thought was, *He means, give over fighting for what you believe in.* His second thought, though, was *He's the only brother I have left.*

He thought of Nick, rotting in an unmarked grave; the anguish was so intense that it almost blinded him. He reached up, caught Robert's wrist in his good hand and clasped it tightly. The muscles and tendons shifted under his fingers, blessedly alive. *All I need to do is to keep silent.* 'Amen to that,' he whispered. 'I should like nothing better.'

Two

Lucy stood by a bookstall in the churchyard of St Paul's cathedral and pretended to look at its stock of religious tracts. At the other side of the bookstall, Cornish Jenny, a 'mercury-woman' or news-vendor, was gossiping with what appeared to be another of her trade. Her strong sing-song sounded clear against the other woman's softer questions. 'Nay, indeed, I know not! Oh, it came in a bundle with some others . . . from an old man by the 'Change.'

Lucy picked up a volume of collected sermons and moved closer, holding the book up so that it concealed the direction of her gaze. The woman Jenny was talking to was about fifty, with a reddened face and hands and shrewd brown eyes. She was stout – which was very uncommon in a mercury-woman: they were generally rake-thin and ragged, like Cornish Jenny. The stout woman's woollen gown was of unusually good quality, too, and her cap and apron were clean.

'I've heard it sells well,' said the stout woman.

Cornish Jenny laughed and shook her head. 'Not so much *well* as *dear!*' She held out the piece of merchandise they were discussing: eight pages of smeared type on cheap greyish paper. 'There's plenty will pay *sixpence* for this, smudged as it is!'

'This old man by the Exchange,' said the stout woman. 'Do you mean Peterkin Evans?'

'Oh, not he!' replied Jenny easily, and launched into a description of a – completely fictitious – old man who could supply the newsbook.

'But who's the printer?' asked the stout woman, giving up on the old man.

'How should I know?' Jenny didn't so much as glance at Lucy – who was, in fact, the printer. 'It's no one licensed by the Stationers, that's certain, else it would be cheaper!'

The stout woman took the newsbook and wrinkled her nose in disgust. 'Phew! You know what this trash is?'

A less canny woman might have paused and looked sober; Cornish Jenny just laughed again. 'How could I, when I cannot read a line? I do but *sell* newsbooks, to earn a few pennies for myself and my poor fatherless children.'

The stout woman tossed the newsbook into the dirt of the church-yard. 'You'd do better to keep to the *Diurnall*!' she said severely. 'Your "poor fatherless children" will go hungry if you're caught with this one. It's seditious, a mouthpiece for the malignants. Parliament hates it above all its kin, and would pay good money to shut it down. You could be whipped for peddling it.'

At this Jenny did look sober. She stared at the newsbook and wiped her hand on her ragged apron. 'I didn't know.'

'You know now,' said the stout woman. She strode off.

Lucy put down the book of sermons and went round the stall. 'That was more than I expected,' she observed.

Jenny snorted. She bent down and retrieved the copy of *Mercurius Pragmaticus,* brushed off the dirt and set it carefully back in the voluminous pocket of her apron. Dirty as it was, it would still sell for four or five pence – which was four or five times as much as a licensed newsbook, and, more to the point, what she'd paid Lucy for it. The profit she made on each copy was the main reason she took the risk of selling *Pragmaticus* – but Lucy knew that she sympathized with the politics as well. The husband who'd left those children fatherless had been killed fighting for the King.

'So that was Parliament Joan, the great she-spy!' Jenny said, and shook her head in wonder. 'I'd never have guessed it. She looked like an alderman's housekeeper!'

Lucy shrugged. Parliament Joan had gained some notoriety among the Royalists of London: she made her living by informing on them. She'd been known to use the trick of pretending to be a vendor of unlicensed newsbooks to smoke them out. When Lucy had heard reports of an unusually respectable-looking mercury-woman asking questions about *Pragmaticus*, she'd decided to get a description to give to her vendors. Despite this, she felt some sympathy for the spy. 'She was willing to give herself away to warn you about the dangers,' she pointed out. 'She thought you were an innocent involved unwittingly.'

Jenny spat. 'Why should she worry about giving herself away to the likes of me? It's easy charity that doesn't cost a penny! She has a quarry in view that would bring her forty pounds. "Parliament would pay good money to shut it down." Indeed it would! It's *you* she's after, you and Prag. And if I'd be whipped just for selling it, what do you think would happen to you? You take care, and tell Prag to do the same!'

'I'll tell him,' Lucy promised. He'd be pleased, she thought sourly: any evidence of how much *Mercurius Pragmaticus* annoyed the authorities brought a smirk to the face of its author. 'Thank you, Jenny. You have a care of that woman henceforth, for you won't fool her again.'

'Go teach fish to swim!' said Jenny scornfully. 'Have a care yourself, girl!'

The retort, *I'm not a girl!* rose to Lucy's lips. She swallowed it. She took her leave politely and headed west, up Ludgate Hill, walking quickly and keeping an eye open for anyone following her.

She should not feel so angry, Lucy told herself. It didn't mean that Jenny doubted Lucy's claim to be married – and even if she did, that didn't mean she thought ill of her. Any lone woman would pretend she had a husband, in the hope that it would keep the predators at bay.

Sometimes Lucy herself doubted that she was married. Marriage, after all, was supposed to be a transformation: from girl to woman, from dependent child to guardian of her husband's house and honour. Lucy, however, was still living with married friends, sharing a bed with their young daughter like an impoverished relative, supporting herself by printing a newsbook whose politics she despised. The handful of nights in her husband's bed seemed like something from a dream.

The memory of her wedding night returned to her with a tingle. She'd been sick with fear beforehand: her only experience of sexual congress had been a bloody and brutal rape. What she'd discovered with her husband, though, had no more to do with rape than singing had with screaming. Jamie had been infinitely tender and reverent, and she'd felt as though her whole body was bursting into flower.

I want him back! she thought fiercely, and bit her lip. She wouldn't get him back any time soon. Indeed, since he was tangled in the war – that great blind wrecker of lives – she might not get him back at all.

Always, always, every misery and grief in England seemed to flow from the loathsome war. For six years now it had plagued the country, and even a resounding victory by one side hadn't been able to end it. The King's fault, Lucy thought angrily. He'd been offered fair and reasonable settlements, but he'd been unwilling to accept any constitutional limits to his own power. Instead he'd engaged the Scots to begin the war all over again — and he probably intended to doublecross them, too. How could *Mercurius Pragmaticus* call for that bloodyhanded man's restoration to the throne? Why in the world did so many people want to buy it? What on *earth* was a Leveller like Lucy doing printing it?

She had no answer to the first two of those questions, and a short, disreputable one to the last: money. It was hard for a lone woman to find work that paid well.

By the time she reached Convent Garden she was in a foul temper, furious with the King, his supporters, and herself, for printing weekly salvoes in his defence. She turned north from the paved space of the plaza, then followed a muddy alley between narrow houses whose upper stories overhung the path, shutting out the light. It stank: neighbours had emptied their chamberpots into it. Lucy kilted her skirts up and picked her way gingerly along to where the alley ended in a housewall. There she paused, checking that there was no one behind her. The alleyway stretched dark and empty to the road. She took a key from her pocket and unlocked the door on her left.

When she started on *Pragmaticus,* the press had been in the kitchen of an empty house to the south of Convent Garden; after two months it had been moved to a warehouse by the Thames. This — a disused storeroom — was its third home. She didn't know who owned any of the premises: that was the business of her employer. He had the other key, and even as she closed the door behind her the scent of tobacco told her that he'd used it to let himself in.

'There you are!' Marchamont Nedham exclaimed cheerfully. He knocked ash from his pipe and got up from the table where he'd been writing out the latest instalment of the week's news. He was a short, swarthy man; his long black hair and the gold earring in just one ear gave him a piratical look. He advanced on her with outspread arms and she hastily backed against the door with her hands raised to shove him off.

He halted. 'It's naught but a friendly salutation!' he said, sounding hurt.

She gave a snort of contempt. 'And do you salute your men friends thus? They must think it strange!'

'You're no man,' he said, with a leer. 'God he knows, I'm willing to be a very good friend to you indeed.' He hadn't gone back to his table, so she stayed where she was, back to the door. If she stepped forward he'd be sure to deliver his 'friendly salutation' and a good grope.

'Oh, you call that "being a very good friend"?' she asked tartly. 'And to think that in Leicestershire we called it "fornication"!'

'You're a cruel woman, Lucy,' Nedham said reproachfully. He went back to his table.

Lucy advanced cautiously into the room, then sidled past the writing table and over to the printing press. It was standing idle, the canvas tympan resting on the bed. Sheets of inked paper hung on lines all around it. Lucy checked one, but it was not yet dry. 'Where's Wat?' she asked. Thirteen-year-old Wat was her assistant at the press.

Nedham waved a hand vaguely. 'I sent him to market.'

Lucy made a face. Whatever errand Wat had been sent on, he'd take his time over it. The streets were far more interesting than inking.

'Well, he could hardly work the press on his own!' Nedham said reproachfully. 'Where've you been?'

'Taking measures to protect your business,' Lucy replied at once. 'And *you*, little as you deserve it! There's a pretended mercury-woman nosing about for the printer and author of *Pragmaticus*, and I asked our people to send to me if they saw her. Cornish Jenny sent, and I went to St Paul's and listened while they talked. The woman wanted to know where to find us. Jenny pretended not to know, so the woman warned her off, saying that Parliament would pay good money to shut us down. I've no doubt that she was Parliament Joan, the she-spy. She's searching for you, Mr Nedham.'

Nedham blinked – then, as she'd anticipated, smirked. 'Not all those who seek will find! You had a good look at her?'

'Aye. A stout red-faced woman of about fifty, too well-dressed to be a true mercury-woman. Jenny said she looked like an alderman's housekeeper, which is not a bad likeness.'

Nedham sniggered. 'So. Parliament Joan unmasked!' He looked down at the sheet of paper on his writing table, then dipped his pen in the inkwell. 'Have care of a fat woman,' he muttered, writing, 'aged about fifty, by name Parliament Joan . . .'

'I doubt it's her real name,' said Lucy.

Nedham crossed out. '. . . her name I know not, she is called by many Parliament Joan. The old bitch can smell out a loyal-hearted man as soon as the best bloodhound . . .' He paused suddenly, looking up. 'The mercury-women. Will any of them betray us?'

Lucy wrinkled her nose. 'They earn too much by selling *Pragmaticus*. Besides, the reward money would have to come from Parliament, which means it wouldn't be seen for months, if at all. They all know that.'

Nedham smirked again. 'It's astonishing how Parliament can never find money for its servants when it has plenty for its members' expenses. Well done, my girl! We'll print this warning. That'll put a stop to her tricks!'

Lucy said nothing. She suspected that she had more in common with Parliament Joan than with Nedham . . . not that Joan would see it that way, of course. Any meeting between the two of them would end with Lucy flogged at the cart-tail and thrown into prison – as a Royalist, which would be unbearable! Well, this public exposure ought to make the spy look for a less wary quarry.

'You say the mercury-women earn a lot by our efforts?' Nedham asked, his tone not quite one of idle curiosity.

Lucy snorted in contempt. 'If you want to increase our charge, you can find yourself another printer! Their profit is our safety.'

'Hear the child!' Nedham exclaimed in irritation. 'Thinking to instruct her master!' He gazed up at the sheets of newsprint for a moment, undoubtedly calculating how much profit he was losing to the mercury-women, then sighed. 'You'd not leave me, anyway.' He gave her a sly look. 'You like me too well.'

Her temper snapped. 'I would gladly leave, if I could earn elsewhere even half what I earn here!'

He merely smirked. 'Your husband, of course, cannot provide for you.'

She glared. 'How could he, when Parliament won't pay the Army?'

'Oh, come!' Nedham got to his feet. 'This husband of yours is an invention. You never said aught of him when I hired you. I've never seen hide nor hair of him. He never had any house or lodgings that anyone has heard tell. He's a word – a prayer you say like a child at its bedside, hoping it will protect you against the night's dangers. I've told you before, I don't believe in him!'

'He's no invention,' Lucy said grimly. 'He's with the Army in the west. He stands a good head taller than you, and he's a deadly swordsman. But I don't need a word like "husband" to protect me against *you,* sir, for there's another word would do. It's *"Pragmaticus",* and all I'd need would be to whisper it to the Licensor.'

'You won't, though,' Nedham said confidently.

Lucy gave a snort of contempt. 'I hate your malignant politics – *and* your lechery!'

'You like my wit,' replied Nedham.

It was, unfortunately, true. Nedham was the cleverest of all the London newsmen, the most inventive, the one everyone else imitated. Lucy could thoroughly enjoy delivering his wit to an eager audience – when his target was somebody other than the Levellers. To be fair, that was usually the case.

'I'd like it better in a better cause!' she managed at last.

He looked at her with unusual soberness. 'I was of Parliament's party in the first war, as everyone knows. I marched to the tune of "England's Freedoms" until I found myself less free under Parliament than ever I was under the King. You Levellers think that if you keep on marching to the same tune you'll eventually come to paradise, but I say you'll end up mired in war with the wolves of anarchy howling all around you. When you've lost your way the safest course is to retrace your steps.'

'So you changed your coat purely from a belief in the virtues of the King's cause?' Lucy asked sarcastically. 'The *very large salary* he offered you had nothing whatever to do with it?'

Nedham smiled. '"Money, thou soul of Men and Wit, but yet no Saint of mine!"'

It was a piece of doggerel he'd written himself. Lucy gave another snort. 'I think you were more sincere in the rest of it: "Thou art Religion, God, and all that we may call Divine."'

He laughed. 'You have it by heart! I'm deeply touched! Ah, Lucy, let's be friends!' He swept forward and took her in his arms.

She turned her face away from his kiss and kicked his ankle hard. He yelped and let her go, then bent and rubbed the ankle, glaring. 'You didn't need—' he began.

'I'm not your whore!' she spat. 'I told you that when you hired me! I've told you again at least once a week ever since! When will you believe it?'

'It was only a kiss,' he said, glowering. 'A man gives the like to his friend's daughters!'

Her eyes stung. She was so tired of this! 'Aye, if they're pretty maids, and their father isn't watching! You touch me again and you'll have to find another printer this very afternoon, for I swear I'll walk out and not come back!'

He went back to his table sullenly. 'God damn all Puritans, all Levellers, and all chaste women!'

Lucy's face tingled where he'd kissed it, and she could feel the imprint of his body on her breasts. An undesired thought strayed across her mind: *Thank God he always tries to conquer by storm. A loving siege would be harder to fend off.* She pushed it angrily away. She was married, and she loved her husband! She wiped her face with the back of her hand and went back to the printing press. She lifted the tympan, took out the forme with the previous day's news, and went round the other side of the table from Nedham to clean and set the type for today's story.

It was late in the evening by the time she finished printing. Wat had trailed back to the printworks shortly after Lucy finished her typesetting, and between them they took down the still-damp sheets, sprinkled them with sand, and added the new columns of print. Nedham left as soon as the press began its *scrape-creak-scrape*. He said the noise made it impossible to concentrate, though Lucy knew he had no trouble concentrating in noisy taverns.

With the sheets of newsprint once more hung up to dry, Lucy picked up the wicker basket she'd stowed in a corner when Cornish Jenny sent to her. She locked the door of the printworks behind her, picked her way through the alley, and trudged eastward. The long June day meant that, despite the late hour, there was still plenty of daylight left. The streets were noisy and crowded, as they always were in London: throngs of men and women jostled along the Strand, never looking one another in the face; beggars cried for alms on every corner; street vendors howled their wares; horse-hooves and iron-shod cart wheels rattled on the cobbles. The occasional coach sailed past, its windows shuttered, the coachman flicking his whip at the rabble to urge them out of its way. Lucy followed the Strand until it became Fleet Street, then continued onward across the stinking sewer that was the Fleet River. The dark bulk of the Fleet Prison loomed on her left. She turned up the street that ran beside its blank wall. The stench of the river was thick on the air, and she breathed through her mouth.

There was a single window set into the front of the building, and it was covered with an iron grate. Behind the grate a ragged prisoner sat intoning hoarsely, 'Charity for a poor prisoner, for Jesus Christ's sake, as you pray for God's mercy, charity for a poor debtor . . .' She put a ha'penny in the slot of the iron box set into the grating, but he continued his pleading without a glance. His face was glassy and his eyes were fixed a thousand miles away. He would have been begging all day, she knew. When dusk came he would be locked up again, and tomorrow a different prisoner would be given a chance to sit in the window. This poor wretch was undoubtedly contemplating how long he could subsist on the pittance he'd garnered this day. She turned into the archway just beyond the window, and rang the bell beside the heavy oak doors.

A grated window in the main door opened, and the turnkey looked out. He grinned, showing blackened teeth. 'For Major Wildman, aye?' He unlocked the door, then opened it with a bow and stood aside.

She set sixpence into his outstretched hand, and he grinned again – as he should, she thought sourly. Only a year before she'd been delighted to earn sixpence for a whole day's work, and this man got it simply for opening a door! She drew the cloth off her wicker basket without being asked.

'Strawberries!' the turnkey exclaimed in delight. He picked up the little punnet of folded paper she'd set on top, then inspected the rest of the contents of the basket: more strawberries, two loaves of fresh wheat bread, a wheel of cheese, a cake, some spring onions and fresh herbs, three bottles of wine and a pouch of tobacco. He snagged one of the bottles of wine, lifted out the slice of cake she'd cut for him, and nodded cheerily.

It always galled her to provide delicacies for the turnkeys, but she was resigned to it. If she hadn't set some aside, the turnkey would have taken everything. She walked stiffly through into the courtyard of the prison. It was a cheerless place: a stretch of barren dirt, frowned upon by galleries of cells, and crowded with dirty, bedraggled men. A couple of pie-sellers who'd paid to be allowed in were hawking their wares. The stink of the Fleet River smothered the scent of the pies completely. Given their usual quality, that was no loss.

A couple of the prisoners came over, leering. 'Looking for someone, sweetheart?' one asked.

She ignored him and strode on into the yard, even though she didn't know where she was going. Talking to whoremongers only encouraged them.

She eventually spotted John Wildman on the north side of the courtyard. He was arguing with another prisoner in front of an attentive audience. She noticed as she came up that his coat was clean and that his long hair and small pointed beard were neatly trimmed; that was a relief. Of course, he had enough money to buy what comforts the prison could provide – he was infinitely better off than the poor beggars in the window! – but it was, still, always a relief to see him looking clean and neat. Prison broke men, reduced them to shuffling, filthy, red-eyed wrecks, but it hadn't broken John Wildman yet.

'But don't you see?' Wildman was demanding. 'If he must swear in the coronation oath to grant laws for the people, then it follows that the *people,* not the King, are the source of law!'

'The people have no right to meddle in law-giving!' replied his opponent hotly. 'That—'

'Why not?' Wildman interrupted. 'All of us here have been obliged to *receive* the law, and, as scripture says, it is better to give than to receive.'

There was an appreciative laugh. Wildman glanced around, acknowledging it, and spotted Lucy. 'Ah!' he exclaimed, with pleasure. 'Mrs Hudson!' He started toward her.

His opponent grabbed Wildman's arm. 'See your whore later!' he ordered.

Wildman jerked his arm free. 'You insult a godly gentlewoman!' he declared angrily. 'This is the wife of my good friend Mr James Hudson!' That emphatic 'Mister' was to make it clear he was speaking of a gentleman, not a lowly tradesman.

The other man was abashed. He muttered an apology – to Wildman, Lucy noted with annoyance, though *she* was the one who'd been called a whore. Wildman accepted the apology and extricated himself. He came over, his eyes fixed eagerly on her basket. His appearance of neatness was less convincing close up: his linen was stained, he was painfully thin, and his eyes were shadowed. He'd been in the Fleet five months now. He'd been arrested for promoting a petition for the reform of government, but he hadn't been formally charged with any offence – which meant there was no knowing when he'd be released.

'How do you do?' she asked anxiously.

He grimaced. 'Well enough, in the circumstances.' He glanced around. Quite a few of his erstwhile audience were also eyeing Lucy's basket. There wasn't much he could do about that. In the Fleet, the only privacy was in a locked cell – and men paid extortionately to be allowed out of them. Wildman did the best he could, however; he gestured his friends back and escorted Lucy over to the wall, where they at least had privacy on one side. 'Do not stay long,' he told her in a low voice. 'There's fever here. Two men died last night.'

She winced. 'Shall I bring you some of Dr Read's water when next I come?'

'I have little faith in it, but I suppose it's better than nothing. Aye.' He looked at the basket again.

She handed it to him. 'Find a good place to unpack it,' she said in a low voice. 'Strawberries.'

His face lit. 'Bless you!'

Prisoners were expected to pay the jailers for their food, but what they got for their money was barely edible – and certainly never included strawberries. Wildman turned to one of his audience, a scrawny wretch who was still hanging about hopefully. 'Hopkins,' he said, 'fetch the old basket from my room, and you may have a share from this one.'

Hopkins at once dashed off. Lucy would take the old basket home and bring it back full in a week's time. That saved unpacking the strawberries in public and drawing the attention of the yard-full of half-starved men.

'Anything in the old basket?' Lucy asked hopefully.

Wildman shook his head. He was known as a pamphleteer, but for months now there had been nothing he wanted smuggled out. 'Anything in here?' he asked, hefting the basket.

She shook her head. 'There's been nothing new since Tuesday.' Tuesday was when another of Wildman's friends visited the Fleet.

Wildman sighed. 'It seems an age since I held anything worth reading!'

'You seemed to have found someone willing to argue with you, though,' she said hesitantly.

Wildman dismissed his erstwhile opponent with a contemptuous wave of the hand. 'No one amusing. Ah well! You're well? Have you heard from Jamie?'

'Nay,' she admitted. 'Not since May.'

'It means nought,' he assured her. 'I'm sure he has writ you, and the letter gone astray.'

He said the same thing every time she had no letter to report. The repeated reassurance was beginning to grate. Did he think she didn't *know* that letters went astray? Did he expect that knowledge to quell her uneasiness?

'I saw Parliament Joan today,' she said, to change the subject.

'What, the spy? I would have thought she was dangerous company!'

'I merely watched as she spoke to one of my mercury-women. She was asking about *Pragmaticus.*'

Wildman frowned. 'You should leave it.'

'I'll be safe enough, Major! Nedham has set down a description of her, boasting of the matter. There's nothing so deadly to a spy as recognition. She'll be in haste to find easier prey.'

'Nedham's a knave,' Wildman said instantly. He scowled, as he always did when Nedham was mentioned. 'A mercenary bawd. It frets me that my friend's wife should work for him. I wish you had employment elsewhere.'

'If I did,' she replied at once, 'I'd be too poor to visit you.'

He frowned. 'You're an experienced printer. You should be able to . . .'

'Experience means nothing, Major! Nor skill! When first we met you yourself proclaimed there was no need to pay me a man's wage, because it was my family's task to support me.'

That brought an irritated look. 'I never will be permitted to forget that, will I?'

'It's not reproach!' she objected, exasperated. 'If you thought there was no need to pay a woman as much as a man, why should you suppose all your fellows think differently? Last month Mr White came asking if I wanted work, and said he could offer sixpence a day and my dinner. That's a good wage, for a woman, and I might have accepted – if it left me with anything over after I paid the rent.'

Wildman frowned. 'How much does Nedham . . .'

'Ten shillings a week,' she said, not waiting for him to finish.

'Ten?' asked Wildman in surprise.

'It was six,' she admitted, 'but he raised it after *The Levellers Levell'd.*'

The Levellers Levell'd 'an Interlude', was both clever and nasty. Nedham had published it in December, shortly after Lucy started working for him. She hadn't known about it – his previous printer had had the manuscript – and when she saw it she'd tried to resign. Sometimes she wished she'd succeeded; she'd be poor, then, but at peace. Instead she had ten shillings a week and a guilty conscience.

Wildman shook his head disapprovingly. 'So he offered more to keep you by him? I like that even less!'

Lucy bit her lip, wishing she hadn't mentioned it. Wildman often seemed to feel that he ought to be keeping an eye on his friend's wife while Jamie was away, and she hated that. 'Why?' she demanded angrily. 'Do you think me dishonest?'

'Nay, nay!' Wildman said hastily. 'But you should not depend for your support on a rogue like Nedham! Jamie should ask help for you from his kin.'

Jamie had told her very little about his family. She hadn't even known that he was the son of a landowner until after he'd proposed to her. There was clearly an estrangement of some sort, and she very much doubted that his hasty marriage had improved matters. Whenever there was a long gap between letters she wondered whether he regretted marrying her. 'Oh, that would be a fine introduction to them!' she said. '"Good day, sir, I am your new daughter-in-law, and please can you give me ten shillings a week!" That would make them love me!'

Wildman looked mulish. 'And does Nedham love you?'

Nay, he lusts after me, she thought irritably. She couldn't say so, of course. Wildman would insist that she quit at once – or worse, he might tell Jamie. Her husband, she was quite certain, would be absolutely furious if he knew about Nedham's 'salutations', and never mind it was the sort of treatment working women put up with all over England. She gave Wildman a hard look, then – once again noticing his shadowed eyes – relented. 'I do mean to leave *Pragmaticus,* Major, as soon as ever I can.' The sooner the better, she added silently.

Wildman, too, relaxed. 'When you have your own press, you mean.'

He knew she was saving up for one. 'Aye,' she agreed. 'I've *ten pounds* already!' Most of that, it was true, was from a legacy – but she *was* managing to save a couple of shillings a week. 'Mr White said he might sell me an old press for eleven pounds ten.'

He glanced down at the basket in his hands. 'You'd have it sooner without buying strawberries for a poor prisoner in the Fleet, I think.'

'If it helps keep your spirits up, Major, it's money well spent.'

*   *   *

Walking home from the Fleet she wondered why it annoyed her so much that Wildman was trying to keep an eye on her. He was only doing what a friend was supposed to do. After all, men were *supposed* to guard and guide their womenfolk as they did their children.

Of course, it was ridiculous for John Wildman to try to play guardian when he was in the Fleet Prison, and *she* was looking after *him*. She wondered, though, if she'd feel any different if he were free. She didn't *like* being regarded as a weak and wilful child.

She sighed, silently admitting to herself that one reason Wildman's attempts at guardianship annoyed her was guilt. Jamie would *not* like it if he knew what she endured from Nedham. If she were a good wife she would find other employment. Many of the other employers she'd worked for, though, had been just as bad. The only way she could be sure of avoiding lecherous employers was to be her own mistress. For that she needed a press – which she could buy with just another one pound ten.

Three shillings sixpence a week rent – paid to her friends the Overtons, and gladly. She knew they were using it to pay off debts incurred and replace household goods lost because of their own time in prison. A shilling and a half to visit the Major and keep him supplied. A shilling a week to the Leveller common fund, to support printing for the cause, and the families of those in prison. Then there were the incidental expenses – she bought dinners as cheaply as she could, from cookshops and street-corner vendors, but it still added up, and every week there was always *something*: pins, a new pair of stockings, the latest pamphlet. Even at ten shillings a week it would take her until autumn to amass enough savings.

Jamie might be back by then. She often imagined what it would be like when Jamie came home and they set up house together. Usually her imaginings were happy daydreams: a little house, Jamie working at a forge, herself at her press. Sometimes, though – as now – they turned dark. Jamie was her master now, and everything she possessed was his. What if he took all the money she'd been saving for a printing press? He was entitled to, and if he spent it on his own business nobody would even disapprove – but it would, she was sure, destroy any chance of happiness for her, because she would hate him for it.

She pictured Jamie to herself, as she always did when the fear struck. A big man, slow to speak but quick to defend his friends. A man with a strong and natural sense of fairness. He would *not* rob her, she told herself. A part of herself whispered, though, that she didn't really know him very well. After all, she hadn't even known he was a gentleman. What else might he have kept from her?

She wished miserably that she could see him, and talk to him; that she could hold him close with her arms and let him kiss her fears away. Useless and pointless longing! She might as well wish the world at peace.

Three

Lieutenant Isaiah Barker did not improve on closer acquaintance.

He took eight days to return from Pembroke, rather than the week he'd promised. When he did arrive back in the salvage camp on the Severn, he was cursing the Welsh: their ignorance and poverty, their incomprehensible language, bad inns, barren mountains and, above all else, their abominable roads.

By then Robert Hudson was well on his way back to Lincolnshire. The great guns had all been salvaged from the mud, and were being dragged back to Bristol – three or four at a time, since the troop didn't have the horses to move all of them at once. The latest news of the war was that the remnants of the Kentish uprising had been thwarted in an attempt to enter London, and had fled across the Thames into Essex. The New Model Army – including Commissary-General Ireton – was in pursuit. Barker was eager to rejoin his master; however, he still intended to take Jamie with him. 'We're short of blacksmiths,' he informed Jamie. 'We'll travel light, and you'll hold yourself subject to my orders on the road, or I'll see you whipped.' He smirked. 'I have that authority!'

Jamie nodded curtly. What couldn't be avoided must be endured. 'Am I to take my tools?' he asked.

Barker shook his head. 'One saddlebag. I can requisition horses for you, but none for your baggage. You'll have to find yourself new tools when you arrive.'

Jamie was glad to get away from the inadequate forge – but after the first morning on the road with Barker, he wished himself back in the smoke. Sulphurous vapours were easier to cope with than the lieutenant's taunts. 'They say that when your famous chief John Lilburne was arrested last, he hid behind his wife to escape the soldiers. They say your bold lawman Wildman is now suing for a chance to sit in the window of the Fleet and beg.'

Jamie considered correcting Barker, and decided that that was what the man wanted: an argument which would let him pull rank and assign punishment to a mutinous Leveller. He bore the taunts in silence and spurred his horse. The lieutenant was tired enough from his journey across Wales that he eventually shut his mouth and concentrated on riding.

They made good time. Barker was authorised to requisition fresh horses from the garrisons along their way, and the long summer days meant they could start early and continue late. It rained on and off, but there was sun and wind enough to dry the mud. They reached Reading in the afternoon of the third day after leaving the Severn, and for once stopped before nightfall – to Jamie's intense relief. He wasn't used to spending so much time in the saddle. The local garrison commander informed them that the latest news had the royalist rebels in Colchester. Lord General Fairfax had tried to storm the town, but had been repulsed with heavy losses, and was now settling his army for a siege. Commissary-General Ireton was with him.

The most direct route to Colchester lay through London. Jamie's hopes had been rising with every mile they travelled toward the capital, and the next morning he was eager to set out, despite his weariness and aching muscles. About noon, however, Barker turned north off the main road.

Alarmed, Jamie spurred his horse forward until he was riding knee to knee with the lieutenant. 'Where are we going?'

Barker sneered. 'Colchester.'

'But—'

'You hoped for London, did you? For a chance to confer with your troublemaking friends and collect the latest seditious pamphlets? Fortune has failed you. I never travel through London unless I must: it's naught but dirty roads and slow traffic. We'll go round by St Albans and Chelmsford.'

The words 'I wanted to see my wife!' hovered on Jamie's tongue. He swallowed them: mention Lucy, and he gave this jeering enemy the key to his heart. In bitter disappointment he contemplated challenging the other man to a duel; his hand itched for the weight of his sword. He dismissed the idea: Barker wouldn't fight a man who was under his orders. '*I'll see you whipped.*' No, a challenge would only provide Barker with the excuse he wanted.

He considered turning his horse about and deserting instead – but that was no good. Ireton knew where to find him – or, worse, knew where to find his wife. Jamie was not entirely sure what Lucy was printing now, but he was sure that it hadn't been licensed. He dared not attract attention to her.

What couldn't be avoided must be endured. He checked his horse and fell back, riding in silence because he couldn't trust himself to speak.

Another day of hard riding. They reached St Albans in the afternoon, paused to collect fresh horses, and rode on as far as Hertford by evening. Next morning they took the road out of Hertford through Ware.

Jamie remembered the mutiny there, half a year before; remembered his arrest by the Army he now served. He thought again of Nick, dying in agony at Maidstone, and wondered angrily why he had ever agreed to re-enlist. He knew the answer, though: he had wanted to get out of prison and marry his sweetheart.

Barker slowed to ride beside him. 'I too was here last November,' he said conversationally.

Jamie gazed between his horse's ears and said nothing.

'I helped gather up all the copies of *The Agreement of the People* after the soldiers threw them away. We used them to light fires all the way to Windsor.'

Jamie looked up, once again tempted to challenge Barker; the man's avid expression killed the impulse. 'Why do you hate us?' he asked instead.

'You would plunge the world into anarchy,' Barker replied at once. 'If all men would be masters and none will serve, what other result could there be than perpetual strife?'

'So why did you fight for Parliament?' Jamie asked in disgust. 'A dutiful servant would have supported the King!'

Barker flushed. 'King Charles was a Papistical tyrant!'

Jamie stared. The opinion was common enough, but Cromwell and Ireton favoured religious toleration: their own religious opinions were among those Parliament wished to suppress.

'I'm not one of those who oppose toleration!' Barker said defensively. 'But Papistry is another matter. The Papists want nothing more than to subjugate us all, and plunge us back into superstitious darkness. They—'

'Anyone would think that Charles Stuart had signed over his kingdom to the Pope!' Jamie interrupted. 'In truth, though, as you well know, he was never anything but Protestant. His crime was to persecute Puritans – and now they're persecuting in turn. Did we go to war only to replace bishops with presbyters?'

Barker seemed at a loss for an answer. 'I went to war to maintain our ancient form of government,' he said at last, 'which the King had sadly abused. You Levellers, though, would destroy it altogether, and in its place set up this foul *democratic* Commonwealth!'

'How can you accuse us of wanting to destroy a thing which was torn to shreds before ever we began to speak out? At least we *have* a proposal for the government of this nation! What would you do? Restore a king who's refused to agree any limit to his power? Submit to a Parliament which abuses all who disagree with it – including its own Army? Crown Cromwell?'

Barker went red. 'Better Cromwell than Lilburne!'

Jamie snorted. 'First you complain that we would set up democracy; now, that we would make Lilburne king! It cannot be both.'

Barker glared, but hadn't thought of a reply when a farm cart in the road before them forced him to spur his horse aside, and ended the conversation.

The lieutenant tried several times to start the argument again, but Jamie refused to respond, and took a certain satisfaction from the other's anger. They rode on along the rutted country roads, and reached Chelmsford late in the afternoon.

Chelmsford was in disarray. The local militia had joined the rebels and gone to Colchester. Men from London had been hurriedly drafted in to provide a garrison, with a few officers from the New Model to provide stiffening. Jamie and Barker arrived at the guildhall to find it crowded with supplicants come to beg the release of townsmen who'd been arrested for their part in the militia's defection. Barker shoved past them impatiently. He was now in a great hurry to reach Colchester, and, to Jamie's dismay, when he at last reached the garrison commander he demanded fresh horses to set out again at once.

'We've scarce horses enough for our own!' complained the garrison commander.

'You've the ones we rode here from St Albans,' Barker said. 'They'll be good enough after a day's rest.'

The commander scowled. 'If they'll be good enough after a rest, then give them a rest, and take them on to Colchester tomorrow!'

Barker sneered and held out his letter of commission. 'Shall I tell General Ireton you denied me?'

They were provided with fresh horses.

It was nearly six o'clock when they set out again. Exhausted and desperately saddle-sore, Jamie shifted his weight from one stirrup to the other, trying to ease his aching rear. He longed for a chance to stop and lie down – though he had no intention of looking weak in front of Barker by saying so.

They'd picked up the main road from London to Colchester, and with the fresh horses they made good time, travelling nearly ten miles before the light began to fade. Just as Jamie was beginning to fear that Barker meant to ride all night, the lieutenant drew rein at a crossroads where there was an inn.

It was a good-sized place, stone-built with a large stable; the smoking chimney promised hot food in the kitchen. Barker dismounted and led his horse into the yard, calling 'Boy!' imperiously. A middle-aged ostler appeared from the stable and stared at them stupidly. Barker handed the man his mount's reins. 'We'll stop the night. Walk them up and down before you water them. We've just rid from Chelmsford, and they're hot.'

The ostler looked frightened. 'Sir,' he said hesitantly, 'the house . . . you should not . . . I fear the house is . . .'

'If it's full, someone can sleep in the stable!' Barker said impatiently, and strode on towards the inn. Jamie met the ostler's eyes and shrugged, but the man was goggling at his scars. He dismounted stiffly and followed Barker.

The din of voices from the main room of the inn died down as Barker entered; Jamie, following, found himself confronting a room-full of startled faces in a deepening silence. The inn was dark and crowded, and it was hard to make out details, but it seemed that the customers were not local farmers: there were some good broadcloth coats there. The certainty of danger struck Jamie before he could grasp the reason for it, and his hand dropped to the hilt of the cutlass at his side.

One of the men got to his feet – and yes, he too had a sword at his belt, and a hand on its hilt. 'Who are you?' he demanded.

Barker, too, had realized that something was amiss, but had no idea what. He stared blankly, his mouth hanging open.

'Roundhead spies!' said a voice from the back of the crowd, and a tremor went through the room. *Cavaliers,* Jamie realized; either a foraging party from the forces in Colchester, or deserters trying to make their way home. Either way, the red coats he and Barker wore had marked them as the enemy.

Jamie caught Barker's shoulder; the lieutenant jumped. Jamie gave the shoulder a jerk, then turned on his heel and strode back out of the inn. The ostler was still in the yard; he had unsaddled Barker's mount, but Jamie's stood waiting, reins looped loosely about a hitching post. Jamie started toward it. Somebody grabbed his arm; he glanced round, hand raised to fend off an attacker, and found that it was Barker. The lieutenant's eyes were wide and his teeth gleamed wetly in a gaping mouth. Jamie paused, startled and confused. Barker's face convulsed suddenly in loathing. He pivoted on a heel, and with all his weight flung Jamie back toward the door of the inn. Jamie staggered into somebody else, and suddenly everything was shouting and fists. He blocked a blow with his bad hand and tried to draw his sword; somebody knocked his hand before he could get the weapon free of its sheath. He dropped to the ground, still trying to draw the sword – then, as a booted foot stamped savagely at his fingers, gave up, and simply curled his arms over his head and huddled up as a flurry of kicks battered him. A pistol went off, and in the momentary silence that followed the shot he heard horse-hooves galloping away.

Somebody swore. A final kick landed in his ribs. Another pistol went off. Somebody yelled, 'Musket, fetch the musket!' and somebody else replied, 'Too damned late!' Then a strong authoritative voice asked, 'What became of the other one?'

'Here,' said somebody. Rough hands grabbed Jamie and hauled at him; he let them pull him to his feet, and found himself in the middle of a crowd of armed and angry cavaliers. One of them twisted his arms behind his back with a jerk; fingers questioned his iron brace, then gripped hard. He stood still, shocked and unresisting. A hard-faced man in a green coat shouldered his way through the mob, sword in hand.

The sword rose. Jamie had faced death before – but then he'd been fighting for a cause he believed in. To die like this, at some nameless crossroads, so that *Isaiah Barker* could make good his escape – 'Mercy!' he cried desperately. 'Please!'

Greencoat paused, lowering the sword a little. 'Answer me some questions, then! Who are you?'

Jamie swallowed, suddenly sick with hope and fear together. 'James Hudson. A blacksmith.'

'Christ, what a face!' said somebody.

'An *Army* blacksmith,' said Greencoat harshly.

'Not by my choice,' Jamie replied. 'I swear before the throne of God Almighty that I'd much rather be home with my wife!'

Somebody laughed, and Greencoat's mouth quirked. 'Who was your friend?'

'No friend of mine,' Jamie replied at once. 'His name's Isaiah Barker. He's a lieutenant, a dispatch rider for Commissary-General Ireton.'

That got a reaction. 'A *dispatch rider?*' Greencoat repeated. 'For *Ireton?*'

'Aye. He was sent to Lieutenant Gen. Cromwell at Pembroke. He collected me on the way back, because Ireton wants blacksmiths.'

Somebody whistled. 'You were coming *from Pembroke?*' asked Greencoat. 'Why did you stop here?'

'It's dusk,' Jamie pointed out. 'We were tired.' Even as he said it he understood that he and Barker had been mistaken for scouts from a troop that was hunting the cavaliers. 'We were but two,' he said breathlessly, 'and we were riding *east*. If there are patrols near, Barker knows nothing of them. He must ride to Colchester to raise the alarm – or else back to Chelmsford, I know not which is nearer.' His arms hurt; he shifted, and the iron brace knocked against some piece of metal on the man behind him with a muffled chink.

Greencoat noticed. 'What's that?'

Jamie glanced back at the man who was holding him. The pock-marked profile scowled, but Greencoat nodded, and the man's grip loosened. Jamie eased his mutilated hand free and held it out for inspection. The dusk had not yet given way to dark: it was still easy to see. Greencoat stared a moment. 'Clever work,' he commented. 'You made that yourself, did you, blacksmith?'

'Aye,' Jamie agreed. It *was* clever work, and had grown steadily more so since he first fitted it. It had a pin now that could hold the thumb-piece in place to avoid tiring his stump with long gripping, and the finger-pieces, initially just two iron spurs, had become a slot that could be used to secure objects. He sometimes thought such cleverness was in reality very stupid, because it attracted attention – but he liked having two hands.

Greencoat looked back at Jamie's disfigured face. 'Were you a gunner?' he asked.

He'd seen the like before, then. Jamie shook his head. 'Pistol misfired.' He remembered Naseby – how he'd dismounted, laid the pistol across his saddle and sighted along it at the fleeing royalists. He did not remember the explosion – only waking, blind in a horror of pain, with John Wildman leaning over him and saying, 'Easy, easy!'

'Not *just* a blacksmith, then,' remarked Greencoat.

Jamie met the other man's eyes. 'I enlisted to fight for our liberties. You need not tell me we've not won them. I've no wish to fight more, I swear it to you before God.'

Greencoat snorted. '"The multitude now have found their error, and repent that e'er they trusted to a Parliament."'

Jamie blinked. He'd heard those lines before, though he couldn't remember where.

'Well,' said Greencoat, turning to his followers. 'It seems we're in no immediate danger, but 'twould be better to depart. Go fetch your dinners, gentlemen. We'll finish our supper on the road.'

There was a chorus of groans.

'What?' demanded Greencoat. 'You thought we might stop the night? Here on the *London road*? Count yourselves lucky to have hot food in your bellies!' He turned back to Jamie. 'That's your horse there?'

Jamie looked at the dappled gelding still held by the ostler. 'It was Barker's,' he said. 'He took mine.'

Greencoat's eyebrows rose, and he went over to the horse and picked up the saddlebags sitting beside it. He undid the buckles and shook out the contents into the mud of the yard: a couple of shirts, some stockings, a book. He picked up the book, then grimaced and tossed it down again: it was the Bible. Jamie was mildly shocked at this contemptuous treatment of the Bible – though he suspected that Barker's own use of it was just as bad. He had never seen the lieutenant *read* that book, and it was likely that its presence in the luggage was meant to impress his masters.

'He kept the dispatches on his person,' Jamie said. 'And the money.'

Greencoat nodded resignedly. 'Put that back on the horse,' he ordered the ostler, indicating the saddle. 'We'll take the beast.' He came back to Jamie and inspected him a moment. 'Take off your coat.'

Jamie at once began to slip it off, and the man who'd held him finally let go to allow it. Greencoat took the garment and draped it over an arm. Jamie had no doubt that an Army coat would be very useful to a party of fugitives, but it seemed a good exchange for his life.

'Your sword, too,' said Greencoat, 'and your purse.' Jamie unbuckled his belt and handed it over, sword and purse still attached.

'My thanks,' said Greencoat, quirking another smile. 'Go in peace, and sin no more!'

Ten minutes later the cavaliers were gone, riding out of the innyard into the growing darkness. There were, Jamie saw, fifteen of them in all, with nineteen horses and a mule; three of the men were double-mounted to leave horses free to carry supplies. They had a quantity of these – sacks of grain, barrels of beer; a couple of live chickens hanging upside down from a pack saddle. They were a foraging party, clearly, and intended to bring those goods back into Colchester under cover of darkness. He hadn't asked where they were going, though. The men had left him horseless and penniless in the middle of nowhere – but they'd left him alive. He was grateful, and would prefer not to imagine facing them again on a battlefield.

A man in an apron emerged from the inn and scowled at the departing royalists. 'God damn them!' he exclaimed bitterly. He turned the scowl on Jamie. 'If you and your friend hadn't come, they might at least have left the crockery! God damn you all, King and Parliament!'

Jamie made a placating gesture. It was almost dark now, and the exhaustion he'd felt back in Chelmsford had crashed down overwhelmingly. His ribs and arms burned with bruises he'd collected from Greencoat's men and hadn't noticed while his life hung in the balance; his saddle-sore muscles ached miserably. He felt that at any moment he might break down shamefully in tears, and he longed for somewhere quiet to lie down. 'Sir, may I have a bed for the night?' he asked, unable to think of any better way to come at the question.

The innkeeper spat. 'And are you able to pay for it? Nay, for they took your money! How am I even to serve my guests now, with scarce a dish to hold the meat? Ah, but I have no guests, nor am like to, with the roads full of soldiers! God damn you all! How am I to replace what I've lost?'

'Sir,' said Jamie, ashamed of the roughness in his voice, but desperate enough to continue anyway, 'Give me a bed for the night, and I'll give you work to the value of it, I swear.'

The innkeeper glowered at him a moment, then spat again. 'You're a blacksmith, you told them. Can you forge me some good strong bolts for my doors? Very well. You may have a bed for a night, and something from the kitchen, though those rogues have left little enough behind. When your friends come, you be sure to tell them that I've been robbed, and I never served the malignants willingly!'

A little later, lying down in the quiet of an upstairs room with a slab of stale bread, Jamie began to shake. If he closed his eye he saw Barker's face convulsed in hatred, and Greencoat's sword raised. He imagined Lucy in London, smiling as she wrote him a letter. Would anyone in the Army even have bothered to let her know that he was dead?

For the first time, he wondered whether his reconciliation with his brother might provide a means of escape. Lucy would be safe if she gave up unlicensed printing and moved to Lincolnshire. Would she be willing, though, to leave London? Would his family take her in? Jamie could imagine his father's disdain. He fell asleep, muzzily trying to imagine what Lucy would say to it.

When the soldiers arrived from Colchester about noon the following day, he was at work. The innkeeper had a sort of small forge, as did many of his kind – a coal stove with a bellows, with an iron plate hammered on to a log for an anvil. It was good for shaping horseshoes, and not much else. Jamie had, after considerable effort, cajoled the fire into producing enough heat to let him beat out some door bolts and bolt-plates, but it was fiddly work. Even his best efforts got the iron only just hot enough to be malleable; there was only one hammer, the tongs didn't grip properly, and he was trying to shape the bolts from a broken pitchfork and the plates from an old piece of wheel-cladding. He did, however, manage an ugly but sturdy improvisation, and he was squinting over the last bolt-plate when the innkeeper came in cringing. 'Here he is, sirs!' he cried. 'He'll bear witness for me!'

Jamie straightened, resting the hammer on the anvil. Behind the innkeeper stood a party of grim-faced men in the buff-coats and pot-helmets of the New Model's cavalry. 'And who might you be?' their officer demanded belligerently.

'James Hudson.' Jamie loosened the pin in his thumb-piece so he could let go of the hammer. 'I was with Lieutenant Barker yesterday. He rode off on my horse.'

The officer shook his head in amazement. 'Praise be to God! He reported you dead.'

'I've no doubt he expected me to be. As it happened, the malignants were content to beat and rob me.'

'You should thank God for your deliverance, fellow! Those were bloody-handed men.'

'It was Colonel Farre that led them,' said the innkeeper. 'I recognized him at once.'

The officer gave him a savage look, and the innkeeper fell silent. Jamie tried to remember why the name Farre was familiar. Chelmsford, that was it. Farre was the militia commander who'd gone over to the Royalists and taken his men with him. All the supplicants at the guildhall had been denying that they'd ever liked him.

'They killed a dozen of our people, night before last,' said the officer, 'and slipped out of Colchester. Barker said he only 'scaped because they paused to butcher you.'

Jamie swallowed a surge of rage. Perhaps he dared not desert, but at least he could revenge himself on Isaiah Barker! 'That they did not is no thanks to him! Barker turned on me and flung me into their path, to delay them so he could make his own escape.'

All the men stared in surprise. The officer looked uneasy. 'Be that as it may, I am glad you are safe and well. We have need of blacksmiths. You should have reported in at once.'

Jamie stared a moment, then turned aside and carefully replaced the hammer on its hook on the wall. 'Whence come you?'

'From General Ireton, in Colchester.'

'Which is – what, some twelve miles hence? And you say that last night I should have set out to walk it in the dark? Bruised as I was, and weary from a long day in the saddle?'

The officer had the grace to look embarrassed. 'You might have set out this morning!'

'Aye, but I needed to pay for my night's lodging.' Jamie indicated the bolt-plate on the anvil. 'Even if I'd had the right to demand free quarter, I'd've had no stomach for it, with the innkeeper there lamenting his losses and crying out that he had not the means to replace what the malignants had stolen.'

The officer shot a glance at the innkeeper, who looked gratified and nodded emphatically. 'They emptied the storehouse and the larder!' he said. 'And they rode off with a score of my best dishes! What I am to do to replace my goods, I know not, for trade there is none, nor has been this . . .'

'Very well!' interrupted the officer impatiently. 'You were robbed – as many another has been, these six years. Complain to the malignants, not to me!' He dismissed the innkeeper with a wave, then glowered at Jamie. 'You must to Colchester now. I'll lend you a horse, and send a man with you. For myself, I must follow after the malignants, if I can.'

The Army's headquarters were at a small village called Lexden, on the road about a mile west of Colchester itself. As they approached it along the road, Jamie grimly noted the signs of a siege. Trees were being cut down, for timber and firewood; the fields had been stripped of livestock; farmyards were deserted. He and his escort had glimpses of the city as they drew nearer: high stone walls, strengthened with bastions to absorb cannonfire. 'How strong are the malignants?' Jamie asked his escort unhappily.

The man grimaced. 'Perhaps four thousand men, perhaps more.' He shook his head. 'Near enough our own numbers, if you discount the Suffolk militia – which we must, because they'd as soon join the malignants against us, if it would keep the war out of Suffolk. It will be a long siege.'

His escort brought him to a fine brick building – local lordling's house or civic hall, he didn't know – on the north side of the village. There were sentries posted at the door; the escort stated their business, then accepted a dismissal and went off with the horses. Jamie himself was admitted to the house and instructed to wait.

The entrance hall was flagged with stone, and dark; an iron candle-holder was fixed to the wall, but the candles on it were unlit. A portrait of a man wearing the stiff ruff of two generations before smirked down on the mud tracked over the floor. The murmur of voices sounded from behind a door at the top of a flight of stairs. Jamie stood for a while, wondering if he should announce himself. If that murmur meant the general staff was in conference, it seemed better not to. He sat down gingerly at the bottom of the stairs.

After perhaps twenty minutes, the voices rose, and there was a scraping of chairs. Jamie got to his feet.

'. . . *nothing* regarding the cavaliers!' said a nervous voice, as the door at the top of the stairs opened, admitting light from the room beyond. 'What I said, sir, was on behalf of the *town*. It is a *loyal* city, Your Excellency; it has always been steadfast in its adherence to Parliament, and . . .'

'It is occupied by a cruel and insolent enemy!' another voice interrupted. 'Oh, Christ!' This last was an exclamation of pain.

'Your foot?' asked a familiar voice sympathetically.

There was a grunt of agreement. 'I take for truth all that you say about the townsfolk,' the pained voice continued. 'But to spare them we would be obliged to spare the enemy. That were no mercy to the kingdom.'

'But Your Excellency . . .'

'Enough! I have offered terms, *generous* terms. We must hope that our enemies decide to accept them!'

A civilian Jamie didn't know came out on to the landing, so he stepped back, out of the way. The civilian started down, but stopped halfway and looked back to where Lord General Fairfax had emerged on to the landing. Jamie recognized him at once. He had often seen the general when he reviewed the troops – though the Lord General on the landing was not much like the armoured Olympian on a white horse. He was dressed in an old coat and breeches, with no boots; his right foot was swathed in bandages, his hair was dishevelled and his face was flushed and sweaty. Gout: he was known to suffer from it, though he was still under forty and the dark hair that had given him the nickname 'Black Tom' was without a trace of grey. His authority was unmistakable, however, even in his stockinged feet. Commissary-General Ireton, who stood supporting him, seemed shadowy beside him. Ireton's, though, had been the voice Jamie recognized. It was painfully familiar from the time of his arrest. Henry Ireton, Cromwell's son-in-law, the Machiavelli of the Army.

'I beg Your Excellency to remember the parable of the tares!' pleaded the civilian. 'If our Lord God spares the wicked to preserve the innocent, then surely we should . . .'

Fairfax gave an impatient hiss and struck the banister; the civilian hastily ducked his head and clattered on down the stairs and away. Fairfax took a deep breath, then, slowly and heavily, began to descend the stairs, leaning on Ireton's arm and hopping to spare his gouty foot. He was almost at the bottom before he noticed Jamie standing in the darkness at the side.

He recoiled. 'Christ!' he exclaimed, staring.

Ireton also looked at Jamie. 'Oh!' he exclaimed in amazement. 'It's a blacksmith I sent for. I was told he was slain on the road.'

Fairfax gave Jamie a look of alarm, as though he might have come from beyond the grave. Jamie bowed. 'Your Excellency, General Ireton. I was set upon, but escaped.'

The Lord General's eyebrows rose. 'Praise be to God for his merciful dispensation! By your looks it is not your first narrow escape, neither. Where got you that scar on your face?'

'Naseby, Your Excellency.'

The memory of that famous victory cheered the general. He smiled a little and leaned forward to clap Jamie on the shoulder. 'An honourable wound, then. Happier times than these!'

'You go on to your dinner, Excellency,' Ireton broke in impatiently. 'I'll speak with him.' He helped Fairfax on to the bottom of the stairs, then beckoned Jamie to follow him back up again.

The room behind the door was lit by large windows and smelled of tobacco. Ireton sat down in one of the carved wooden chairs and leaned an elbow on the table. He was a short, neat, slight man in his late thirties, so unremarkable in looks that people coming away could not even remember the colour of his hair, and described him as dark or fairish, depending on the light. 'Mr . . . Hudson, is it not? Lieutenant Barker told me you had been murdered.'

'We stopped at an inn,' Jamie said formally, glad of the opportunity to tell the whole story. 'The ostler tried to warn us that we should not go in, but Barker brushed him aside. Inside the inn we discovered a troop of malignants, who were robbing the place. The innkeeper said he recognized their commander as Colonel Farre, of Chelmsford.'

Ireton let out his breath in a very small snort of recognition and nodded for Jamie to continue.

'I was behind Barker going into the inn, and before him coming out, but he caught hold of me and flung me into their hands as they followed us. He took my horse and rode off, leaving me at their mercy. If he reported me dead, it was because he hoped there would be no one to report his own cowardice and malice.'

Ireton sat silent a moment, regarding Jamie with eyes that did not match the rest of his unremarkable appearance: intense eyes, cold and dark. 'Why did they spare you?' he asked at last.

Jamie's face flushed, but he met the gaze unflinchingly. 'Because I begged for mercy. I have faced death before, as you know. In a good cause I would accept it willingly – but I do not see why I should die for Isaiah Barker.'

Ireton sighed. 'Lieutenant Barker was carrying dispatches, Mr Hudson. His duty was to keep them out of the hands of the enemy at all costs.'

Jamie set his teeth. 'An *honourable* man would have found some other way to fulfil that duty!'

'You are not friends, I perceive.'

'No. He thinks that I ought to be content to serve my masters humbly – and he reserves to himself the right to decide who those masters should be.' He did not add, *He thinks they should be you and Cromwell*. Ireton undoubtedly knew that already. 'You are in agreement with him, are you not?'

Ireton grimaced. 'In the name of God, why this enmity? Do we not have trouble enough, with malignants rising against us to the west and to the east, Scots in the north preparing to flood across our borders – and Parliament unable to decide whether they or its own Army are the greater foe?'

'Perhaps,' Jamie said bitterly, 'this "enmity" I feel has to do with being unjustly cast into prison, then obliged to swear to serve you before I could get out again.'

Ireton let out his breath in a long sigh of exasperation. 'Should we have tolerated mutiny?'

'It was no mutiny! The Council of the Army had agreed . . .'

'The Council of the Army was party to the mutiny! Do you truly believe your *Agreement of the People* would have been tolerated by anyone *outside* the Army? Your precious *People* want the King back; to them you Levellers are rabid dogs! You stubborn fools! Your best hope was my own *Heads of the Proposals*. It would have given you most of what you wanted!'

'We were not the ones who rejected it,' Jamie pointed out.

Ireton frowned at him a moment, then, surprisingly, inclined his head. 'A just rebuke. And, truly, God has punished us for making an idol of the King. Because so many clamoured for his restoration we believed there could be no peace without him – but we should have perceived that God had declared against him. It is lack of faith which has brought us this bitter trial, to fight the war again.' His cold gaze again sought and held Jamie's. 'We have much common ground, you and I. I believe, as do you, that England must have a settlement based upon common right; that there must be new elections on a more equitable basis; that there must be religious toleration. We are beset by enemies who oppose all these things. Can we not fight as allies?'

To answer 'aye' would be foolish. Ireton and Cromwell had allied themselves with the Levellers before, only to betray them at Ware. On the other hand, to answer 'nay' would be equally stupid. Ireton was right to say that he and his supported most of the Leveller programme, while the royalists and the Scots were opposed to everything about it.

'Why do you ask?' Jamie demanded. 'I am under your orders. Do you ask a servant to be your "ally"?'

'In the days ahead we will need willing hands, not forced labour.'

'Then you should have taken pains to recruit the one rather than the other!'

'Well,' sighed Ireton, after a long silence, 'Colonel Rainsborough is not so stiff-necked. I will assign you to his regiment. Perhaps you will obey him more readily than you do me.'

Jamie straightened in astonishment. Rainsborough was a Leveller, the highest ranking officer to hold such sympathies. He had been appointed Vice-Admiral of the Navy the previous winter, but had been expelled from the position by a mutiny in the fleet. Jamie hadn't known he was at Colchester.

'I would be happy to serve under Colonel Rainsborough,' he said. Even as he said it, he wasn't sure that it was true. Some part of his mind was disappointed because now he had lost his excuse for deserting. It disconcerted him: he hadn't been consciously aware of making up his mind to leave.

Ireton nodded. 'I will give you a note for him.' He took paper and pen from the table, wrote quickly, then folded the paper and handed it to Jamie.

Jamie took it and bowed. Ireton got to his feet.

'There is one other matter, sir,' Jamie said quickly. Ireton gave him a look of impatience.

'Lieutenant Barker rode off on my horse, with my saddlebags,'

Jamie said. 'I want them back.' He had letters from Lucy in the bags, and the thought of Barker reading them was intolerable.

Ireton gave a small huff of irritation. 'Go report to Rainsborough. I will send someone to retrieve your baggage and bring it to you. I think it better if you and Lieutenant Barker do not meet.'

Four

At the beginning of July, Lucy returned from work to find Parliament Joan waiting for her.

She didn't register the visitor, at first. It was pouring with rain, and when she entered the house in Coleman Street, she was busy trying to wipe water out of her eyes with a sopping shawl. 'Here she is!' said Faith, who was nine and the eldest of the three Overton children.

Lucy wiped her face again and finally made out Parliament Joan standing by the kitchen fire. She froze; a part of her mind frantically calculated whether she ought to brazen it out or run off into the rain.

Joan made a *tch* noise. Mary Overton, mistress of the house, gave Lucy a reassuring smile – she was at the kitchen table, chopping onions on the few inches of tabletop not covered by newsbook pages. 'Mistress Alkin heard you were looking to buy a press,' she said.

Brazen it out, then: this was probably a fishing expedition. Lucy gave the visitor an uneasy look, but went back to the door and wrung out her dripping shawl over the doorstep. 'Mistress Alkin?' she repeated.

The stout woman responded with a good-natured smile. 'Aye, and christened Elizabeth! By your look, Mistress Hudson, you know of me by another name!'

'A mercury-woman pointed you out to me,' Lucy admitted warily, 'and said that you were Parliament Joan.'

Elizabeth Alkin sighed. 'That malignant rogue *Pragmaticus* has caused me no end of trouble! Never fear. I'm an enemy only to the King and his friends. If the Licensor's content to wink at what you print, so am I. As your friend said, I've come because I've heard you named as one that wants to buy a press.'

'Aye,' Lucy agreed readily. She'd made enquiries enough that she couldn't deny it, and anyway there seemed no danger in the admission. 'Have you one you mean to sell?'

Mrs Alkin hesitated. 'I *know* of one. Myself, though, I'm in need of a printer – and, I confess plainly, I'd much prefer another than the lecherous old rogue employed by my partner.'

Lucy regarded the spy with a frown, trying to spot the trap. 'And who told you I was a printer?'

'Oh, several people, but the one I took most note of was Mr Mabbot the Licensor. He said he had employed you himself for a time, upon *The Moderate;* he says he found you honest and hardworking, and that he only let you go when your family called on you to care for a sick uncle.'

That was one way of putting it; another was that he'd hired somebody else without telling her, at a time when she'd desperately needed money. Still, if he was willing to give her a good reference, she was willing to go along with his version of events. 'That's so,' she agreed. 'My poor uncle died, but he left me a small legacy, which I hope to spend upon a press of my own.'

'My partner is all of a sweat to sell me a press, if I will not use his printer,' Mrs Alkin replied. 'He says going to a strange printer would be fatal, that my business would continually take second place to whatever else the printer was engaged in – but I've no wish to plunge all my savings into printing until I've seen how well it pays. This will be a new venture for me, Mrs Hudson. My hope is to find a printer who wants a press, who'll buy the machine in the knowledge that there'll be work waiting for it. Those I asked said you might be such a one – and, I confess, I'd be pleased to employ a woman, not some man who'd puff himself up and think he knows better than me just on account of his sex.'

It was beginning to sound as though this might actually be a genuine proposal! 'Who is this partner?' Lucy asked suspiciously.

'Mr Henry Walker.'

'Of *Perfect Occurrences?*' Mary Overton interjected, and Mrs Alkin nodded.

This was reassuring. Henry Walker was one of the best established newsmen in London: *Perfect Occurrences in Parliament* was licensed and cautious and had been coming out every Wednesday for years. Walker had, moreover, shown a willingness to partner other publishers on new ventures, though none of these had been much of a success. It was entirely believable that he'd agreed a partnership with Mrs Alkin.

'He's offered me help in setting up a newsbook,' Mrs Alkin confirmed, 'and says we will divide the profits. This press he wishes to sell me was given him by a printer in payment of a debt. He wants ten pounds for it.'

That was a bargain, but credible, for a press collected in payment of a debt and offered to a new partner. Lucy didn't have to think whether or not she could afford it: she knew every penny of the ten pounds, two shillings and five pence in the box under her bed. She felt her face flush. 'You've seen this press? What condition is it in?'

'It works,' Mrs Alkin said cautiously. 'Mr Walker gave me leave to try it, and it seemed to me in good order, though I know little enough of such machines. It's of interest to you, then, this proposal?'

'Aye!' agreed Lucy. Then she bit her lip, reminding herself that this could still be a trap. 'Though I must see this press, and speak to Mr Walker, and . . . and see if the terms suit.' Her heart was beginning to beat hard. Her own press! Her own press *now*!

Mrs Alkin smiled. 'Speak to Mr Walker, by all means, and to any other you please! They will tell you that I am an honest widow-woman, that I love our liberties and hate the malignant wretches who would rob us of them. I recently came by a little money, and hope by spending it thus to spread the truth about that wicked man Charles Stuart, and perhaps earn a small profit to support myself.' Mrs Alkin paused, then – with a twinkle – added, 'The press and all that's printed on it must be properly licensed, of course.'

It was the twinkle which made Lucy certain that the spy had not the slightest suspicion that she was talking to the much-sought-after printer of *Mercurius Pragmaticus*. Parliament Joan believed – as the Licensor did – that Lucy was employed on an unlicensed *Leveller* press. Perversely, the older woman's trust gave Lucy a queasy stab of guilt.

'I should be glad to have some order in my work,' she said truthfully, 'and print only what's licensed.'

When Elizabeth Alkin had gone, Mary Overton gave Lucy a thoughtful look. She scooped the chopped onion into the pot of peas simmering on the hearth and wiped ink-stained hands on her apron. 'Ten pounds is a good price,' she remarked. 'Yet, I wish this offer had come when you had more savings in hand!'

Lucy frowned. 'You cannot think I should reject this!'

'I think you should be careful of the details before you accept,' said Mary. 'Any new newsbook is a risky venture, and Mrs Alkin made it plain that she'll pull out quickly if she doesn't make a profit. Then you'd have a press and nothing to print on it – and with no savings to tide you over, you'd have to sell up.'

'Even if I did, I'd likely make a profit!' protested Lucy. 'I'll not see such a bargain again.'

'*If* the press is sound,' warned Mary.

Lucy made a face. 'I'll be sure of that before I buy.'

'Be sure of the terms, too!' Mary insisted. 'I'd not see you shouldered with paying rent on a shop for a year, if this newsbook fails within a month!'

Lucy bit her lip: she hadn't thought of that. Mary was right to urge caution, and yet . . . her own press! She could say goodbye to Nedham and his groping and his vile malignant politics; escape the nerve-racking hazards of unlicensed printing, and still earn enough money to support herself and help her friends and the Leveller cause. 'I'll take care,' she promised. 'But I pray God it's what it seems!'

Mary smiled. 'Well, I hope it may be all you want, then!'

Lucy went over to her friend and hugged her. A less generous woman than Mary might have been resentful: Mary's experience in printing was longer and more extensive than Lucy's. The Overtons had once had a press of their own – but it had been confiscated by the Stationers, because of the 'scandalous and seditious' pamphlets printed on it.

'She might have offered the press to you,' Lucy acknowledged anxiously. 'I wonder that she did not. You're not vexed?'

Mary gave a snort of amusement and waved a hand at the print-strewn kitchen table. The pages were for the next edition of *The Moderate,* the Leveller newsbook to which her husband contributed and which she helped to print. 'I have work aplenty – and Mistress Alkin took good note of it! She doesn't want the likes of me. She wants an eager, pliable young printer, who will devote herself to her business and follow orders. Besides, she knows that if she took us from *The Moderate* she would anger Mr Mabbot.' Gilbert Mabbot owned *The Moderate* – and, since he was Licensor, no newsbook editor liked to offend him.

'But if you had your own press again . . .'

Mary sighed and shook her head. 'Lucy, dear, I've no doubt that we'd lose any press we bought soon as we bought it. Dick would print something the mighty ones of England detested, and they'd be

glad of the excuse to arrest him.' She made a face. 'Honest John in
the Tower, Major Wildman in the Fleet – for sure they'd send Dick
back to Newgate!'

Richard Overton was one of the Levellers' most forceful pamphlet-
eers, and had spent time in Newgate before. 'He still *writes* what the
mighty ones detest,' Lucy pointed out.

'Aye, but at least now the babes and I are clear of it!' exclaimed
Mary, her plain, pock-marked face losing its usual good-nature and
becoming bitter. 'God knows, I've no wish to revisit Bridewell.' She
had been imprisoned there for months; her children had been left to
the care of neighbours and relatives – except the youngest, the baby,
who'd been too young to leave his mother, and who'd died in a filthy
cell, covered with lice and fleas.

He might have died anyway, of course – babies died all the time,
particularly in London – but Lucy knew that Mary still ached with
guilt for that death, and for the suffering of her three older children
during her imprisonment. She hugged her friend again.

Mary hugged her back. 'You're welcome to Mrs Alkin's business,'
she said, trying to smile again. 'I'll ask about this press, though, shall
I? It may be somebody knows whose it was, and what its condition
is. And, my dear, think twice and thrice before you buy! If your
venture fails, you'll be worse off than when you started.'

The press turned out to be sound. Lucy felt uncomfortable when
gossip relayed that Mrs Alkin had 'come by' the money for her venture
as a reward for trapping John Crouch, the Royalist editor of *The Man
in the Moon*, but the terms offered for the new newsbook were very
good. When Lucy raised Mary's caveat about having to pay rent
whether or not the venture succeeded, Alkin's partner Henry Walker
offered the first month's tenancy free in a building he happened to
own. The price set for printing would cover paper, ink, and the wages
of the employees Lucy would have to hire to assist her. True, there
wouldn't be much profit afterwards, but the initial order was for five
hundred copies. If that number rose, so would the printing costs. If
it didn't, Lucy could find other customers. She spent several evenings
rushing around London making arrangements, and at last – with more
reluctance than she wanted to acknowledge – gave notice to her
employer.

Marchamont Nedham did not take the news well. '*What?*'

'I have agreed to buy a press,' Lucy repeated. 'Mr Henry Walker will sell it me for ten pounds.' They were in the storeroom near Convent Garden; Lucy's assistant Wat stood by the secret press holding an inked dab in either hand and gaping.

'You ungrateful wretch!' exclaimed Nedham furiously. 'I came and offered you a good wage, when you were cast out of house and work . . .'

'I *was* grateful!' she said indignantly. 'But I've *earned* my wages! To keep a press like this secret, and yet supplied with paper and ink; to get women to sell it, and have none betray us, to risk discovery and flogging and prison – if you find another to do that for *less* than ten shillings a week, I'll be astonished!'

'Very well, then!' snapped Nedham. 'Fifteen shillings a week. Take it, and give up this notion of your own press!'

She blinked, startled and taken aback. Fifteen shillings a week was three times what she'd be taking home from her own venture, once she'd paid her costs. For a moment she found herself thinking, *I could pay two shillings a week into the Leveller common fund, and give one to the Major, and still save . . .*

Then she asked, *save for what?* She'd been saving for a press, and now she would have it! Why on earth would she put it aside? She loathed *Pragmaticus,* loathed the King and all his works, hated Nedham's lecherous assaults . . .

She'd miss him, though. He was clever, and funny, and brave. He made her laugh.

God forgive me! she thought, in dismay. It was *definitely* time to go. 'I thank you, but no,' she said.

Nedham groaned angrily. 'You think you can manage a press on your own, do you?' he demanded, changing tack. 'A silly girl, a Leicestershire dairymaid, you think you can outman all the knaves in London?'

'Aye,' she replied levelly. 'I've managed here.'

'This is no printshop! This is . . .'

'Mr Nedham, I doubt, truly, that licensed printing is *harder* than dodging the Stationers and managing secret deliveries to a back alley!'

There was a silence. Nedham blinked at her resentfully. 'Another press will be heavier than this,' he said at last. 'You'll not have the strength to work it.'

She cast a regretful look at Nedham's press. It was, indeed, much lighter and easier to operate than the one she'd agreed to buy: it had originally been an army press, and was designed for easy transport. Her new press was an ordinary one, its sturdy bed made even heavier by the flat stone that made an unyielding rest for the formes of type. She *could* operate it on her own, but it was quite true that she couldn't keep it up all day. 'There are plenty of men in London who want work,' she said resolutely. 'I'll have no difficulty hiring help.'

Nedham grimaced. 'Aye, and what will he think, when he sees a pretty woman set over him?'

'I expect he'll think what you do, Mr Nedham – only, being under rather than over me, he'll be more careful in what he does about it.'

Nedham winced. 'I've never done you any harm!'

It was true. Nedham never seemed to believe she meant *no* unless she backed up the word with some sort of blow – but he'd never tried to force her and he'd never hit her back. He didn't grant her respect, let alone courtesy, but she wasn't afraid of him.

'I would sooner have my own press,' she said resolutely, 'and print no more defences of the King.'

Young Wat finally set down the dabs. 'Mistress,' he said excitedly, 'my Uncle Simmon needs work; he'd . . .'

'God *damn* it!' exclaimed Nedham. He jumped to his feet, came over and seized her by the arms. 'God *damn* you, woman, you know I like you *well*; why must you be so obstinate?'

She tried to pull free, but he was holding tight, and his hands were strong. 'Let me go!'

His only answer was to kiss her. She turned her face away, but he pushed her back against the wall, lips crushing hers against her clenched teeth. His grip on her arms was painful and the smell of him – of ink and dirt and stale wine – filled her nostrils, almost suffocating. She kicked and drew in a breath to scream.

Nedham let her go. 'What ails you, woman?' he asked irritably. 'Are you made of ice?'

'You let me be!' she gasped.

His face creased. '*Damn it!*' he said again. 'God *damn*! Very well, then: marry me.'

'*What?*' she cried, aghast.

He gave her a furious glare. 'If that's the only way I can have you, then that's what I must do.'

She didn't know whether to laugh or scream. 'Mr Nedham, I am married already!'

'I don't believe in this invisible husband!'

'What you believe is nothing to the point! I am married.'

He stared in angry disbelief.

'I was married at St Dunstan's in Stepney,' Lucy told him. 'To Mr James Hudson, as I told you, last January. If you go there you may read our names in the register.'

The disbelief ebbed slowly. 'You're truly married?'

'Aye. I cannot marry you, even if I wished to.'

'God *damn* you!' Nedham cried, in furious exasperation. 'Why did you not tell me sooner?'

Wat, who'd watched all this with his mouth open, tittered. Nedham spun about and clouted him across the side of the head. The boy was knocked to the floor. He sat up, holding his ear and sobbing.

'Keep a civil tongue!' Nedham snarled. 'Who pays your wages?' He turned back to Lucy. 'This husband . . .'

'He's with the Army,' she said. 'He serves unwillingly, but he was obliged to enlist after he was taken up at Ware. When the war is over, then we'll be free to make our lives together.'

'He has no kin who might support you?'

She felt herself flush. 'I support myself. There was no need to go to them and beg.'

Nedham let out a *huh!* of understanding. 'Married you without their blessing, did he? Well, I've no call to blame him. I would have done just the same.' He grimaced, then shook his head. 'God damn him to hell, the rutting son of an Egyptian whore! Likely he's done me a favour.' He gave Lucy a glare of resentful desire. 'I would have wed you.'

With astonishment, she considered the possibility that he really did love her, in his way – and felt ashamed of the way she'd treated him. 'Sir,' she said slowly, 'you've paid me a high compliment, and I am sensible of it, and sorry that I must disappoint you.'

'Huh!' he said again, morosely, and glowered. 'When do you leave, then?'

'I told Mrs Alkin and Mr Walker I needed a fortnight to set things in order. I hope that will give you time enough to find someone to take my place.'

'Small chance of that!' he said bitterly. 'I'm going to get a drink.' He stamped out of the storeroom, banging the door behind him.

Lucy went over to Wat and helped him to his feet. The boy cast a filthy look at the door and said, 'I won't stay here to work for *him!*' He rubbed his ear and turned hopeful eyes on Lucy. 'I'll come with *you,* Lucy! I'll ink, and Uncle Simmon will work the press, and we'll have the merriest printshop in all London!'

Five

The warm evening of Jamie's arrival at Colchester was the last good weather for a long time. He woke up next morning – on the floor of the makeshift shed that served the regiment as a forge – and found that a puddle had soaked the edge of his bedroll, while rain hung in a streaming curtain over the doorless entry. He was lucky; he had a roof over his head. In the camp beyond the doorway, damp men huddled under canvas, or crouched in makeshift shelters of brushwood, cursing the heavy skies. The fort intended to shelter them was still no more than a series of ditches, ankle-deep with mud and rapidly filling with dirty water.

The fact that Jamie had a dry place to sleep was a sign of exceptional favour and importance. Colonel Rainsborough had been delighted to get him. 'We have urgent need of your services, Mr Hudson,' he'd said the evening before. 'We need to shut up yonder city in a ring of iron – and we are short even of nails! I am obliged to General Ireton for sending you to me rather than another.'

Jamie bowed his head and muttered, 'I'm happy to serve, sir. My friend John Wildman esteems you above any man in this Army.'

Rainsborough was a tall, powerful man with a lively, changeable face. At this his eyes brightened in sudden attention. 'You're a friend of John Wildman? He and I were much together during the debates at Putney, and I love him dearly. He is a very honest, outspoken gentleman, of much wit and learning. His arrest was a great piece of wickedness. Have you heard aught of him since then?'

'My wife visits him every week, sir, in the Fleet,' Jamie replied. 'When I last had word from her, early in June, she reported that he was well, and that his sufferings had not broken his spirit.'

'God keep him so!' exclaimed Rainsborough vehemently. 'I pray he is soon free of that place! You have a wife in London, have you? She sends you news of him, and of our other friends?'

Jamie noted that 'other friends': there was no doubt at all it meant 'Levellers'. He wondered if he should have kept quiet about his friendship with Wildman – then felt ashamed. Why should he be reluctant to admit to his allegiances? 'Aye,' he agreed. 'She's a printer, and lodges with her friends, the Overtons.'

'Richard Overton? Of *An Arrow Against All Tyrants?* That writes for *The Moderate?*'

'Aye, and his wife Mary, that prints it.'

Rainsborough beamed. 'The very head and fountain of honest news! You'll find yourself much in demand whenever you get a letter!'

After that the colonel had introduced Jamie to all his staff as, 'Our new blacksmith, a friend of Major John Wildman; his wife helps print *The Moderate!*' Jamie was embarrassed to correct his superior, and let the error stand. Rainsborough's men shared their colonel's sympathies; Jamie was welcomed warmly. He accepted the treatment with as much grace as he could manage, and tried to suppress the feeling that every kindness was another bolt on his prison.

The regiment was not the one which had fought under Rainsborough in the first war. It was new, recruited in London the summer before, to guard the Tower after Parliament and the Army fell out; it had lost its previous colonel in the initial assault on Colchester the week before. Rainsborough, ejected by the navy mutiny, was a good match for it. He was recognized as something of a specialist in siege warfare, and the Tower regiment possessed more than the usual number of engineers, gunners, and – ordinarily – blacksmiths. Of the four smiths who'd served it in London, however, two had managed to get themselves excused from leaving the city, and another had died during the same assault that killed the first colonel. The remaining smith would have struggled to deal with all the regiment's work even if there hadn't been the siegeworks to do as well, and he welcomed Jamie with open arms. He was a short, wiry man with a shock of dirty brown hair, Samuel Towlend by name, and he did everything he could to make the newcomer comfortable. He found Jamie a bedroll and a new coat, both from men killed in the recent assault, and gave him his pick of the dead blacksmith's tools. That first morning, though, Towlend began heaping coal on the forge fire even before showing Jamie where to get breakfast. 'We've much to do,' he said; and when the two of them had fetched their bread and ale they went straight to the forge and set to work making nails. The men of the regiment were eager to build themselves a fort and get out of the rain.

They were still making nails mid-morning when a man arrived with Jamie's saddlebags. He tossed them down on the dirt floor of the forge with a thump, then stood watching as Jamie picked them up, unlatched them, and carefully inspected the contents. The sheaf of Lucy's letters was still there amid the dirty shirts and stockings, but the ribbon that tied the bundle together was missing, and the papers were shuffled and bent. He stared a moment angrily, imagining Barker jeering at Lucy's endearments – then decided not to make an issue of it. The letters could have been disarranged by somebody checking what the pack actually contained. He touched the sheaf to his lips, then set it gently back in its place before turning to thank the messenger.

The man nodded stiffly, frowning. 'I was given those by Isaiah Barker. He told me I was of a height with the owner, who'd been killed upon the road.'

Jamie straightened, looking at the other more closely. They were indeed much of a height. Barker, shorter and stouter, would have found the shirts a poor fit. 'I am sorry to disappoint you.'

The messenger brushed that aside. 'I am not so poor as to grieve for a few shirts! I . . .' He stopped.

He was uneasy about Barker, Jamie realized. The lieutenant clearly *had* taken another man's property, and left this man the awkward task of returning it. Barker, however, was presumably a friend or troopmate, and the messenger didn't want to think ill of him.

'He thought you dead,' the messenger said at last.

'Aye,' agreed Jamie, 'for he rode off on my horse, never expecting that the malignants would show me any mercy. He was a brave bully on the road, when I was under his command and could not raise my hand to him, but when we met up with the enemy he was in such haste to run away that he threw me to them as a man might toss a bone to a pack of dogs, to delay them. He is a coward and a knave.'

Barker's friend stared, anger and doubt mixed on his face. At the forge, Towlend had set down his hammer and was staring as well. Jamie saw that he'd committed himself further than he'd intended. He did not regret it.

'I will tell him you say so,' replied the messenger, at last.

'Do so! If he wishes to dispute it, he knows where to find me.'

When Barker's friend had gone, Towlend gave Jamie a look of concern. 'He won't fight you.'

Jamie shrugged. 'I spoke no challenge.'

Towlend flattened the head of a nail and tossed it into the waiting case. '"Coward and knave"?'

'Let him challenge *me,* if he chooses.'

Towlend raised his eyebrows. 'He's a lieutenant. You're a common soldier. He's more likely to horsewhip you.'

Jamie shook his head. 'He missed his chance of that upon the road, when I was under his orders. Now he must fight me or make his peace. My blood is as good as his!'

There was a silence, and then Towlend asked cautiously, 'You say you're a gentleman?'

Jamie hesitated. He'd been open about his family when he first enlisted. He'd looked like a gentleman's son then, though – a handsome impetuous twenty-year-old in a fine coat, sword and pistol of the best, mounted, God help him, on a good horse. Naseby had wrecked him and killed the horse. He'd kept quiet about his family after that: he'd told himself that it was to avoid embarrassment over money, but he now admitted to himself that it had been because of his disfigurement.

'I am a gentleman's son,' he now said defiantly. 'Lieutenant Barker knows as much, too, for he's met my brother, who's heir to the estate.'

Towlend puffed out his breath in a long sigh. 'Well!' After a moment he added, 'Then you're right. He must either explain himself or fight. If he fails of it, he accepts the name of coward.' He snorted, picked up his hammer again. 'I doubt this comes to a meeting.'

Jamie eyed his workmate a moment warily, suspecting that Towlend meant to report the matter to the colonel. Duelling was never legal, but the Army frowned on it more heavily than did the Law. It was bad for morale, and blacksmiths and dispatch riders were too useful to be thrown away on affairs of honour. He wondered whether he should swear the other man to silence. No: the demand might sour things between them, and if Towlend refused to swear what could he do about it?

He *wanted* to fight Isaiah Barker and finally wipe the sneer off that proud face. All the taunts along the road still stung, and the memory of the look on the lieutenant's face at the inn burned like a brand. He was confident he could beat the man. He'd learned to use a sword when he was a boy, and had always won most of his bouts. It was true that he was out of practice, and that he was blinded on the right side – but Barker hadn't struck him as a fighter.

Jamie abruptly remembered that Barker was Ireton's man. Kill or injure him, and there would be a price. Maybe it would be better if Towlend *did* report the matter to Rainsborough. He was immediately ashamed of the thought. He wondered if he himself were the real coward; he'd begged Greencoat for mercy, and now, it seemed, he was afraid of Henry Ireton.

Wondering and worrying was no use. He would fight Barker, or he wouldn't. He would die, or live with the consequences. He took a deep breath, gave Towlend a nod, and went back to work.

Barker's answer to the charge of cowardice came that evening. A Lieutenant Russell arrived at Rainsborough's encampment asking to speak to Mr Hudson. Jamie left the campfire with him. It was still raining, but he didn't dare take Russell to the forge, which – because it was warm and dry – was crowded with cold wet men eating their suppers. Instead he led the other man to a spot among some supper-emptied tents. The rain drummed on the wet canvas all around them.

'I come from my friend Lieutenant Barker,' said Russell formally. He hesitated. 'For my own part, I deplore the errand. We are all enemies to the malignants in the city yonder. We ought not to fight among ourselves!'

Jamie inclined his head courteously. 'I am willing to live in peace with any man.'

'Then you will apologize?' Russell asked eagerly.

'For what offence?'

Russell let out a slight hiss and peered at his face through the darkness. 'For the names "coward" and "knave" you flung at him!'

'Your friend treacherously threw me to the enemy and galloped off leaving me to die. I know no word for that but cowardice.'

'You might call it "duty",' replied Russell. 'He carried dispatches. He was obliged to keep them from the enemy at all costs. Come, apologize and make peace! We are all soldiers in the same Army: to fight among ourselves is no better than mutiny!'

'If your friend truly wants to make peace, I am willing. Let him apologize for the insults he heaped on me all our journey together, and let him explain his conduct the other night. I would hear him. If all he wants, though, is for me to beg *his* pardon – then, no, I will not. I have done no more than speak my mind about his conduct. It is up to Lieutenant Barker to defend his own doings, if he can.'

There was a silence full of the steady beat of the rain. Jamie understood, without a word said, that Barker would not and could not apologize. Even his friends had doubts about his conduct: to apologize would be to confess. Russell sighed. 'He believes you to be a gentleman?' His voice made it a question.

'Aye,' agreed Jamie. 'I am the son of Mr George Hudson, of Bourne Manor in Lincolnshire.'

Russell nodded. Jamie wondered if he'd ever heard of the Hudsons of Bourne. It seemed unlikely. His status was being accepted because Barker was willing to fight him. 'If you are a gentleman,' Russell continued, 'you know that the title of "coward" is intolerable to any man of honour. If you will not apologize, you must give him satisfaction.'

'I am very willing to do so. Allow me to find a second and a sword, and I am at Lieutenant Barker's service.'

He didn't ask Towlend to be his second. He feared that this was because he wanted his workmate to be free to report the matter, though he told himself that it would be wrong to risk the regiment's only other blacksmith – seconds were sometimes called upon to fight alongside their principles. He went instead to one of the more outspoken Levellers he'd met, a skinny pock-faced ensign named Philibert Bailey. He explained the situation and repeated some of the things Barker had said on the road. Bailey was fiercely indignant and agreed to act for him. He went off with Russell that same evening to make the arrangements.

Finding a place for a duel, however, proved unexpectedly difficult. Neither Bailey nor Russell was familiar with the surrounding countryside, which was so full of soldiers that it was hard to ensure the necessary seclusion. The two were forced to agree to meet again in three days' time, and to keep their eyes open for a good spot in the interim.

Jamie arranged to borrow a rapier from one of Bailey's friends, and the next few evenings he sparred with anyone who was willing. He was indeed out of practice, but still won more often than not. Height, strength, and a ferocious left-handed attack compensated for lack of skill. He lost, though, every time an opponent managed to get on his blind side. He resolved to end the duel without giving Barker that opportunity.

He wrote a letter to Lucy, but was unable to tell her about Lieutenant Barker and the impending duel. It wasn't safe to mention such matters when the letter might be read before it reached its recipient. If the meeting turned out badly, she'd get the news all too soon.

He wondered how long it would be before he received a reply. He'd had no letter from his wife since early in June. He imagined her bent over a letter, a tendril of black hair, escaped from beneath her cap, brushing the curve of her cheek. The surge of longing was painful. It had been three weeks? Four perhaps, since he'd had any news from her.

His daydream turned suddenly and queasily into a vision of his old rival Ned Trebet leaning over Lucy, brushing the tendril of hair gently aside, and kissing her. He told himself angrily that Lucy would slap Ned's face if he tried any such thing – which he wouldn't: he was an honest man. Lucy was honest, too, true as steel. The absence of letters didn't mean she had forgotten him, still less that she was betraying him. It meant only that a letter had gone astray – and probably more letters after it were being used to light fires for his previous regiment, because nobody would pay to send them on. He would have to wait until she knew his new regiment before he could expect to hear from her again.

He pushed aside the miserable thought that if the duel went badly, he would not read her next letter, either. He was not afraid of Isaiah Barker. As for Barker's master – well, Ireton was unlikely to go so far as to *kill* him.

The next day, Philibert Bailey appeared at the forge, drew Jamie aside, and whispered that he and Russell had found a good place for a duel. The adversaries could meet next day, at the conventional time of dawn.

The place was about three miles away. Jamie thought of borrowing a horse, but decided against it: there were already too many people who knew about the encounter. Instead he and Bailey slipped out of the camp well before dawn – Bailey knew the password for the sentries – and set out on foot in the dark. It was still raining. They'd brought lanterns, but the weak light wasn't enough to let them avoid all the mud puddles. After the first mile they were both soaked to the skin and squelching. After the second mile Bailey began to swear steadily under his breath. Most of it was variations on 'God damn this rain!' but there was a fair amount of 'God damn duels!' as well.

The spot Bailey and Russell had fixed on was an empty barn to the northeast of Fort Rainsborough. Jamie and Bailey arrived just as the darkness began to ebb, and found the barn deserted. They went in, set their lanterns down on a clear patch of floor, and took off their boots to wring the water out of their stockings. Bailey's face was sour.

'I am sorry,' Jamie said awkwardly.

Bailey looked at him grimly a moment, then sighed. 'You're not to blame for the rain.'

They sat in silence, hugging themselves for warmth, their wet clothes getting colder and colder. 'You're father's a gentleman?' Bailey asked.

Jamie nodded and answered the implied question. 'I was his third son.'

Bailey nodded. 'My father was a younger son, too. He was reckoned a gentleman, but though I followed his trade I was never any such thing.' He snorted. 'Gentle birth's a strange mystery!'

Jamie grunted agreement.

'It can come and go,' Bailey continued, warming to his subject. 'A man may be born among the yeomanry, an old uncle dies, and *poof!* suddenly he's a gentleman! Or sometimes it depends upon place, for a man who's but a worthless younger son would be a lordly heir were he born in the next county, where they go by borough English.'

'Ireton,' said Jamie.

'Eh?'

'Commissary-General Ireton. They go by borough English in the part of Nottinghamshire where he was born: the youngest son inherits all. He's an eldest son.' He'd learned this detail while he was in prison, after Ware, and remembered it, as he remembered everything to do with Ireton. It explained something about the man, he thought. There was a sense of grievance there, a Leveller-like desire to change the world's rules, without the Levellers' commitment to making those rules bear equally on all. The Commissary-General's cold eyes were sharp in his mind. He wondered again what Ireton would do if Barker died.

'That I didn't know,' said Bailey. 'Eh! I'd wager you wish they did that in — where was it you hail from?'

'Lincolnshire. I've no wish for my brother's place.'

Bailey gave him a sceptical look. Jamie considered the question a moment, then said slowly, 'Robert always had to be young Mr Hudson. I had more freedom.'

'But less money, I'll warrant!'

'Aye,' agreed Jamie, then added, to quash any rumours that he was simply mean about money, 'and even less after I enlisted against my father's wishes. I'd not have done so, though, had I preferred money to freedom.'

'Ah!' said Bailey, as though this made sense. 'My father wasn't pleased with me, neither. My uncle had a Commission of Array from the King, and my father thought I should go join *his* troop. He always licked his brother's boots, and agreed with every opinion that pompous jackass brayed, though to my mind he was much the better man.' He was quiet a moment, then added, 'He was grieved to the heart when I went to fight for Parliament. I've not heard any word of him these three years. God grant he's well!'

'I saw my brother lately,' said Jamie. 'It was the first time since the war began. I'd thought he would be the same as he used to be, because he 'scaped the fighting – but he was much changed.'

Bailey grimaced. 'I think no one in England has 'scaped the misery of this war. I think truly there is nothing on earth so foul and unnatural as civil war.'

Jamie nodded.

'If no good comes of all this,' Bailey went on softly, 'if injustice and oppression are left in their old places, then I think we will all be damned. The evil we have done these last seven years will condemn us everlastingly, unless we have some good to set against it.'

There was a sound of horses outside. Jamie got to his feet, his good hand on the hilt of the borrowed rapier. Two men rode into the barn, ducking their heads under the lintel. When they straightened, the light of the lanterns they carried showed that they were indeed Barker and his second Russell. Barker glanced around, saw Jamie, and froze a moment, his eyes glittering. Jamie touched his hat.

Barker looked away, then stared at Jamie's feet, which were bare. Jamie waved a hand toward his lantern, which was draped with his soaked stockings. 'It was a wet walk,' he said.

Barker said nothing, only sat his horse stiffly. His friend Russell dismounted, led his horse over to one side of the barn, and tended it, slipping the bit out of its mouth and loosening the girth to make it comfortable. Barker, after another unhappy glance at Jamie, went to join him. Jamie did some stretches to warm up his cold muscles while he waited.

Presently Russell came over. 'My friend says that he is still prepared to accept an apology.'

'Will he offer one?' Jamie asked.

'Don't play the fool!' snapped Russell impatiently. 'This meeting should not be taking place. Our swords ought to be used on the malignants!'

'I have said I am willing to make peace,' Jamie replied mildly. 'I would forgive your friend, if he asked it.'

Barker tied off his mount's reins with a jerk and came over. 'I was carrying *dispatches!*' he shouted, glaring.

Jamie regarded him in silence.

The lieutenant flushed. 'I had no choice! I dared not let them take the dispatches!'

'Your duty *forced* you to be a coward?' asked Bailey sarcastically.

Barker spat. 'Easily said, by a man who was safe in camp among his friends!'

Jamie stirred. 'When we went out of that inn,' he said softly, 'we were before the enemy. Together we could have slammed the door shut in their faces, and made our escape while they broke it down.'

There was a silence. Barker started to speak, stopped, then spat, 'A pity you didn't think of that at the time!'

'I thought only of getting to the horses and away,' Jamie agreed. 'They were standing in the yard. That alone might well have saved us both. Sir, this is fruitless. I've said how I regard your conduct, and you have demanded satisfaction. I am here to give it you.' He took off his coat and hat and handed them to Bailey.

Barker stood still, staring, and Jamie saw that the lieutenant was afraid of him. He felt a warm rush of pleasure.

Lieutenant Russell came over and looked earnestly into Jamie's face. 'Sir, if you will not be reconciled, then I ask you, for the sake of our common service, to let it end at first blood. The malignants would be overjoyed to see us killing one another!'

It was Jamie's right, as the man challenged, to say whether the duel should continue to the death or end at some earlier point. He hesitated only a moment. He already had what he wanted: the sneer wiped off Barker's face. 'Very well. For the sake of our common service I am content to halt at first blood.'

Barker's face lit with relief, then reddened. He pulled off his coat and gave it to Russell, then unbuckled his sword belt, drew the weapon, and tossed the belt aside.

Jamie took off his own sword belt, his maimed hand clumsy on the buckle, and drew the borrowed rapier. Still barefoot, he strode to the centre of the barn, Bailey and Russell following with the lanterns. The light of dawn which now shone under the eaves was half-drowned by the rain, and insufficient for a duel.

There was the ritual inspection of the swords; the seconds marked out the ground, then stood aside. Jamie and Barker faced one another, swords in the guard position. 'On my count, gentlemen,' said Russell. 'One, two, *three*.'

There was a trick Jamie's fencing master had taught him long ago, a way of catching and binding an opponent's blade. If you did it right, it snatched the weapon clean out of his hand. You had to have a strong arm to make it work, but if you did have the strength it was hard to defend against even if you knew it was coming. Jamie's forge-trained arms had more than enough strength, and Barker had not the least idea it was coming. An instant after Russell said *three,* his sword was on the ground and he was staring at Jamie in horror. Jamie lifted the rapier and nicked the other man's chin. Barker leapt back, clapping a hand to his face. Jamie held the rapier up in the lamplight, letting both seconds see the shining red droplet on the tip.

'First blood!' cried Bailey exultantly. 'Oh, well done, well done!'

'Isaiah,' Russell said to his friend, a little breathlessly, 'honour is satisfied. Will you call pax?'

Barker's eyes, dark and gleaming with hatred, fixed on Jamie. Then he nodded. He bent, retrieved his sword, and without another word went back to his horse.

Bailey was grinning when he and Jamie trudged back through the rain in the wake of the horsemen. 'That was pretty!' he said softly. 'Oh, that was worth a drenching! Proud popinjay from headquarters, and he was out in *one stroke*!'

Jamie grinned back. Now that it was over, he felt buoyant, light as air. He had repaid Barker for his contempt, but he'd done no hurt worth Ireton's attention. 'It turned out well, thank God,' he said. 'Thank you, Mr Bailey, for your help.'

Bailey grinned again and slapped his shoulder. 'Call me Philibert.'

There had been no hint of interference with the duel. Jamie concluded that he'd been mistaken about Towlend. As they squelched onward, however, they noticed a couple of horsemen trotting toward them. They drew nearer, and Jamie recognized one of them as a member of Rainsborough's staff.

'Mr Hudson!' said the staff officer irritably. 'We are here to arrest you for duelling!'

Philibert laughed. 'You're too late, sir! It's all over with – the other fellow was out in one stroke!'

'You're under arrest, too, Philibert Bailey!' snapped the officer, and Philibert stopped grinning.

It was mid-morning by the time they got back to the camp. Rainsborough was in his tent, reading reports. He set the papers down when his aide led in the dripping duellists.

The staff officer saluted. 'Sir, I am sorry to say we didn't find the place in time – but Mr Bailey says there was no harm done.'

Rainsborough looked surprised. 'You made peace?' he asked Jamie.

Jamie shook his head. 'We ended it at first blood. Lieutenant Ruh – my opponent's second asked it, in respect of our common service.' No point in betraying the other parties to the duel. 'I agreed.'

Rainsborough let out a breath in relief. His eyes flicked over Jamie, noting the absence of blood. 'How is Lieutenant Barker?'

'I expect he's had worse cuts shaving.'

Rainsborough relaxed. 'Thank God for that! This is better than I feared – but still, it was ill done, Mr Hudson. A house divided against itself cannot stand.'

'Sir,' said Philibert, 'that should be said to Barker. He was the challenger. Jamie was willing to make peace, but this Barker would accept nothing but that Jamie should beg his pardon for being abandoned to the enemy. He is a great enemy to our cause, too. All along the road he reviled us, knowing that Jamie was under his orders and bound to endure it. He mocked Major Wildman in particular, saying he sues to sit in the window of the Fleet and beg. He boasted, too, that at Ware he gathered up copies of *The Agreement* to be burned.'

Rainsborough, as everyone knew, had been at Ware: he had tried to present a copy of *The Agreement of the People* to Lord General Fairfax, and had been brushed aside. He sat up straight again, his eyes flashing. He glanced at Jamie for confirmation, then set his teeth.

'Jamie disarmed him at the first stroke,' said Philibert softly.

Jamie saw that there would be no punishment. The colonel was not going to punish a man for doing what he would like to have done himself.

'Even so!' Rainsborough said half-heartedly, 'You should not have fought. I have given My Lord General and the Commissary-General my word of honour that until this storm is past, I will set our disagreements aside and be obedient to their orders. We cannot afford to fight among ourselves. If we lose this new war, Charles Stuart will ascend his throne again, and our hopes and our people will be utterly undone.' Then the colonel smiled. 'However, since there's no harm done, we'll let the matter be.'

Six

Lucy was hard at work printing Elizabeth Alkin's *Impartial Scout* when Mary Overton hurried in, leading a stranger.

It was the middle of July, and Lucy was in her new printworks. This was a single damp room in a dark, fish-scented building, on Thames Street near Billingsgate Fishmarket. Wat's Uncle Simmon – a lanky, simple-minded young man with stringy hair and a tendency to breathe through his mouth – was sliding the bed of the press in and out while Lucy turned the handle of the screw and Wat inked. It was heavy, tedious work, and Lucy was glad of an interruption – until she saw the look on Mary's face.

Mary hurried up and hugged her. 'Be brave!' she said. 'This gentleman is come from Colchester. He says your husband is hurt.'

Lucy felt no emotion that she could identify – only a sense that the whole world had gone still, leaving each detail around her unnaturally clear and distinct. She noticed an ink stain on Mary's cap; the gasp of alarm from Wat and the snuffle from Simmon; the cry of a vendor outside in the road; the surprised stare of the man from Colchester. He was a soldier, a dark round-faced man in mud-flecked boots and breeches.

'What happened?' Lucy asked him.

The soldier stopped staring with an uneasy smile. 'There was a skirmish two days gone. The malignants had sent up one of their great guns, a drake, in the tower of St John's, hard by the south gate. They fired upon our people and did great slaughter, and My Lord General wanted it brought down. Your husband was working on the approaches, crafting and fitting braces for the trenches, when a shot fell among the timbers nearby. He was much hurt by the splinters. It's feared he may not live. He is asking for you.'

Lucy swallowed, unable to find words. The soldier smirked and said, 'I do not wonder that he longs to see you. I had not thought you would be so fair.'

She felt a sudden savage loathing for him: that he could smile and say *that*, after telling her that Jamie might be *dying!* She tucked her ink-stained hands under her arms to stop herself from hitting him.

'I came hither to fetch you to him,' the soldier told her.

'I thank you, sir,' Lucy said unsteadily. 'You are his friend?'

Another uneasy smirk. 'Aye. My name is Philip Bailey. Perhaps he has spoken of me, in his letters?'

Lucy shook her head. She'd had two letters from Jamie since he was sent to Colchester, but they'd contained very little about his life there. He'd asked instead about people in London – and in the second one he'd also wanted to know all about her new printing press.

Bailey looked disappointed. 'Well, I am his good friend, and I promised him I would fetch you from London. I have a good horse at The Bell at Bishopsgate. If you come with me now, we can be in Brentwood by nightfall, and at Colchester tomorrow.'

Lucy swallowed and cast a despairing look at her press. The sheet they were printing would be the fourth in the first edition of Mrs Alkin's newsbook. If she abandoned it, she abandoned the previous three days' work – together with the wages she'd paid Simmon and Wat, and the money she'd laid out on paper and ink. She didn't have anything left over to replace that expenditure – and if she ran off *now*, would Mrs Alkin give her credit, and employ her again? It seemed unlikely.

Jamie was hurt, and asking for her. Torn by splinters cast by cannon-shot. Her imagination conjured a horrible ruin of blood, lying upon a rough pallet and whispering her name. Her heart was still numb, but her eyes began to ache with tears.

Mary caught her arm. 'Go,' she ordered. 'I will see to things here.'

'But *The Moderate* . . .' began Lucy.

'Dick will get help from his friends,' Mary said firmly. 'You must go to your husband.'

Bailey took her straight to the inn where he had stabled his horse. There was no point fetching baggage, he told her, since he had no pack animal. 'You'll ride behind me,' he said. 'You've done that before?'

She nodded. Women usually rode pillion, and she'd travelled all the way to London behind a cousin's servant. She didn't like it – it was uncomfortable, and doubly disagreeable if the man in front was unpleasant – but it didn't frighten her.

'Brave girl!' said Bailey approvingly. He put an arm around her for a hug. It should have been companionable and comforting, but wasn't. His hand eagerly felt her breasts. She stopped short and jerked away – then pretended that she only wanted to get out of the way of some traffic. He smirked at her, and she looked quickly away, swallowing her outrage. He'd ridden all the way from Colchester to fetch her to Jamie; she ought to be grateful.

Bailey's horse was a tall, powerful-looking grey stallion. When the ostler led it out into the inn yard to saddle it, it laid its ears back and showed the whites of its eyes. Lucy looked back at it unhappily. She didn't like high-strung horses, and there was no pillion cushion behind the saddle. She would have to perch uncomfortably on the animal's bare back. Bailey offered to lift her up.

She drew back, pulling her arms against herself protectively and shaking her head. He raised his eyebrows, but mounted up, then offered her a hand. She took it reluctantly, got a foot into the stirrup, and scrambled up on to the horse's rump. The horse promptly side-stepped, tossing its head and snorting angrily. Bailey grinned when she grabbed his shoulder to stay on; he turned in the saddle and put an arm around her waist. His hand fumbled at her thighs. She settled herself sideways, took hold of Bailey's belt, and eased his arm away. Bailey grinned at her over his shoulder. 'I shall be the envy of every man that sees us,' he told her, 'with such a pretty thing clinging to my tail!'

She did not reply. She was again battling the impulse to hit him. As they clattered out of the inn yard, she tried to reason with her dislike. The man was Jamie's friend, and he was doing her a kindness. She should not hate him because he paid her inappropriate compliments and groped her. There were plenty of men who felt compelled to play the gallant with every pretty woman they met, and meant nothing by it. She suspected that the real root of her dislike was the fact that he'd brought her such terrible news.

She tried to suppress the wretched, selfish, sinful thought that the terrible news had come at the worst possible time. Even if Mary was able to satisfy Mrs Alkin, there was no way she'd have the time to search out other customers for Lucy's press, a matter of some urgency if the business was to be secure. How, she wondered angrily, could she think of such a thing when Jamie might be dying?

It was a grey afternoon; the roads were ankle-deep in mud, and the clouds threatened more rain. The heavy traffic was even worse than usual as people swerved about the road trying to avoid the deepest puddles, and at first Bailey had to give all his attention to his horse, which snorted and put its ears back at every barking dog or fluttering chicken. Lucy sat in a daze, struggling to understand how her husband of six months could be snatched away before she'd even had the chance to get to know him. Her eyes began to ache again and she swallowed repeatedly. She told herself she would *not* cry here on the public street, where everyone could see her – particularly when Bailey might try to comfort her.

As they left London behind the way became less crowded, and eventually Bailey felt free to grin at her over his shoulder. 'You are not what I expected for James Hudson's wife,' he told her. 'I expected a pocky-faced inkster like your friend.'

Lucy stiffened, shocked. 'Mary Overton is a saint! Even now she's doing my work, unpaid, so that I can come with you! How can you speak of her like that?'

Bailey shrugged. 'Because she's a pocky-faced inkster, aye? I said naught regarding her character!' He smirked. 'I thought you would be another such. Your husband is no beauty, and no rich man neither. How did he win himself such a pretty little black-eyed poppet?'

Lucy set her teeth. He was Jamie's friend, she told herself again, and as such he ought to be her friend too.

Perhaps, though, he was not really a *good* friend of Jamie. Now she thought of it, it seemed unlikely that he was more than an acquaintance: Jamie had only been in his new regiment a few weeks. 'Have you known Jamie long?' she asked.

'Oh, aye!' he said.

'Oh,' she said, disappointed. 'You served with him before he joined Colonel Rainsborough's regiment, then?'

Bailey hesitated. 'We were together in the war. This is dull talk; how—'

'Were you with him in Colonel Okey's regiment?' Lucy asked – then bit her lip: that was a stupid question. Jamie had moved between regiments, but blacksmiths were unusual. If Bailey had been one of Okey's dragoons he'd be one still – but she was sure that Jamie would have mentioned it if his old regiment was at Colchester. He would have wanted her to pass on news of old friends to John

Wildman, who'd been one of Okey's captains. Bailey must have been in some other regiment.

'Aye,' said Bailey casually, surprising her. 'This is dull talk, and you never answered my question.'

Lucy frowned. 'What question?'

'Why, how did Cyclops Hudson get himself such a beautiful wife?'

'He hates that name!' she said indignantly.

'He's used to it,' said Bailey, with another smirk. 'And it's apt.'

She frowned. She could not believe that this smirking scoffer was Jamie's 'good friend'. 'Sir, I confess I'm puzzled. You say you're one of Colonel Okey's men, and I thought they were not at Colchester.'

He glanced back uncomfortably. 'Nay!' he said, after an awkward pause. 'I never said I was one of Colonel Okey's. I said I *knew* your husband then.'

'Of what regiment are you then?'

Bailey hesitated again, and she was suddenly certain that he'd been lying to her. She regarded that conviction with bewilderment: why would he lie?

'Of the Lord General's Horse,' Bailey told her.

Jamie had never mentioned any friends in Lord Fairfax's own regiment. Of course, he hadn't told her much about his time in the Army, but John Wildman had been more talkative, and from him she'd gained the impression that elite cavalry, like Lord Fairfax's men, didn't mix much with lowly dragoons, like Colonel Okey's – though the Levellers of different regiments had worked together regularly. 'How did you come to know Jamie?'

'He did some blacksmithing for me, and we struck up an acquaintance.'

Lucy felt giddy. 'Sir. I know not why you would make sport of me, to tell me lies, but I beg you to stop it!'

Bailey drew rein sharply and turned in the saddle. Suddenly frightened, she let go of his belt, grabbed the cantle of the saddle, and slid off the horse.

He stared down at her a moment, then forced a smile. 'Not so used to riding as you thought, eh?' he asked brightly, and held his hand out to help her up.

She didn't take it. 'Jamie was not a blacksmith when he was in Colonel Okey's regiment! You cannot have met him that way!'

He frowned. 'I . . . he . . . it was a slip of the tongue, girl! He's a blacksmith *now*. Come, we waste time by this!'

Still she didn't take his hand. There was something *wrong* with Bailey's account of himself, she was sure of it. 'Tell me first when and where you met my husband!'

'I left him *dying*!' replied Bailey. 'I swore to him I would fetch his wife – and you would have me recount the whole history of my dealings with him before you'll come?'

'Sir, I never saw you in all my life before today! You say you are my husband's good friend, but how should I know that's true? You've not spoken as his friend would!'

'Damn you for a cold-hearted bitch!' shouted Bailey, his face going red with anger. 'Come here!'

She backed away. He heeled his horse round, came after her, and leaned forward to grab her arm. She shouted and wrestled free before he got a good grip; he grabbed at her again and caught her cap, tearing it off her head. She screamed, lashing out at him. The high-strung horse was startled: it kicked and bucked, and Bailey had to pause to steady it. She turned and started running back along the muddy road toward London. At once the stallion's hooves were pounding after her. She ducked and dodged, aware of the mass of the animal almost on top of her. There was a cart coming the other way. She darted desperately to it and seized the footboard. The driver's startled face looked down at her; an old man, white-haired. His horse squealed as Bailey's almost knocked it down, and the cart came to a skewed halt in the muddy road. 'Help!' she pleaded.

Bailey loomed over her and bent to grab her shoulder. 'Let be!' he warned the cart driver. 'This is between me and my wife!'

'He is *not* my husband!' Lucy screamed, in incredulous outrage. 'He *lies*! He . . .'

Bailey flung her against the side of the cart. She struck her chin, and bit her tongue, and had to cling to the side of the cart to keep herself upright. Bailey grabbed her again and tried to drag her on to his horse. She screamed as loudly as she could, kicking and flailing her arms. Bailey's horse, now thoroughly unsettled, shied and reared, almost unseating its rider.

'Here, here!' said the old man, flapping his hands in alarm.

Another man on a horse trotted up, frowning. 'What's amiss?'

Bailey swore, loudly and savagely. He let go of Lucy, heeled his horse round, and galloped off.

Lucy clung to the cart, gulping and sobbing. Her cap was gone and her hair was coming down. She wiped her wet chin, and her hand came away red. 'That man . . .' she gasped. 'He said he was my husband's friend. He said my husband was hurt, and calling for me. But he lied, he lied!'

'This was some piece of villainy!' the old carter exclaimed. He sounded more delighted than disapproving.

The carter offered her a ride to the next inn; the horseman offered to take her back to London. She declined both offers: she never wanted to travel with a stranger again. She searched the road until she found her cap. It was in a mud puddle, but she picked it up, rinsed it and wrung it out as well as she could, and pinned it on over her straggling hair. A lone woman with her hair loose would attract attention everywhere she went, and she didn't feel she could cope with trying to explain herself. She began the trudge back to London, glancing over her shoulder nervously every ten paces to check whether Bailey was coming back. The only thing that happened was that it began to rain.

It was dark by the time she reached the Overtons' house in Coleman Street. She was soaked through, and her head ached, both from the bang against the cart and from crying. When she knocked on the door, Faith Overton opened it. The girl cried out, and her parents came running.

Richard and Mary Overton both exclaimed over Lucy's unexpected reappearance, but hustled her into the kitchen without asking any questions. Mary fetched a towel, and Lucy hugged it round her wet gown and sank down gratefully on a stool by the kitchen fire. She told her story in sodden gasps, pausing every now and then to wipe her nose. Mary made her a tisane of chamomile, to ward off fever, and gave her some bread and butter – the family supper of soup had all been eaten.

When Lucy had finished, Richard came over and crouched next to her stool. He was a short, scrawny, lively man whom she loved like a brother. 'Are you sure that he lied?' he asked, frowning.

'Dick!' protested Mary. 'Look how ill he used her!'

'Aye, but if he'd sworn to his friend to bring her, and she of a sudden refused to come, and he lost his temper . . . men that have been long at war can lose all sense of civil and lawful conduct.'

Lucy hunched her shoulders miserably. She was not sure now that Bailey had been lying. On the long trudge back to London that certainty had faded. What had seemed indisputable became ambiguous. Perhaps she'd imagined things, or misunderstood what he said because of her own shock and grief. Perhaps she had misjudged and provoked him, and now he would go back to Jamie and tell him that he must die betrayed, because his wife wouldn't come to him. That was the thought which had made her weep until her head ached.

'You may be right,' she told Richard. Then she looked up determinedly. 'So I must go to Colchester and find what the truth is! I will set out tomorrow.' She had thought about this, too, on her walk back to London. It didn't matter if she lost the press. If Jamie died calling for her the guilt would haunt her till her deathbed. She cast a pleading look at Mary. 'Can you – can you print Mrs Alkin's newsbook while I'm away from London? I will repay you when I can.'

'Of course!' said Mary warmly. 'But how will you get to Colchester? The coaches are stopped on account of the siege.'

'I will borrow a horse,' Lucy said.

There was a silence. They all knew that it would be very hard for a woman, unaccompanied and not an experienced rider, to borrow or hire a horse – particularly to go to a military camp, where the animal might be requisitioned. Richard looked uncomfortable, and Lucy at once guessed that he felt he ought to offer to accompany her, but didn't want to leave his work – particularly since his helper would be doing Lucy's. 'Never fear!' she told him. 'I know I can't take *both* of you from *The Moderate!*'

'But will you be able to borrow a horse, on your own?' Mary asked doubtfully.

'I think I know who might lend one,' Lucy said.

The horse-owner she had in mind was Marchamont Nedham. She had never actually seen his mount, but he had complained regularly about the cost of keeping it when he rarely used it. She did not like having to ask a favour of him, but anything was better than allowing Jamie to die thinking she'd refused to come. She rose at dawn, packed up a small bundle of things for the journey, and set out into the

still-quiet streets, hoping that Nedham was still in his old lodgings.
Like his press, he moved about regularly to avoid arrest.

She was in luck. When she banged on the door of the house, his
landlady told her that he was asleep.

'I need to speak with him,' Lucy said. 'It's most urgent.'

The landlady sniffed, gave Lucy a disapproving look, but went off
upstairs. Presently Nedham shambled into the parlour, barefoot,
hatless and coatless, with his shirt tails hanging down and his belt
undone. He stopped short when he saw Lucy – then grinned. 'Sweet
Lucy!' He hurried forward, took her in his arms, and kissed her
soundly.

She gave an uncomfortable jerk, but bore it. Nedham let her go
and blinked at her suspiciously. 'What's amiss?' he demanded.

'Sir,' she said nervously, 'I've come to ask a favour. I need to go
to Colchester, most urgently. I know you have a horse. I beg you, let
me borrow it! I'll return it and give you its hire as soon as I can!'

Nedham gaped at her, running a hand through his dirty black hair.
'What time is it?' he asked abruptly.

'About five o'clock, sir.'

He groaned. 'Christ save me from such a damnable hour! Why do
you need to go to Colchester – *Colchester!* A city besieged! – so
urgently you must needs wake a man in the middle of the night?'

She licked her lips. 'A soldier came yesterday with some very ill
news, but I don't know whether it is true. He said my husband was
hurt near to death and asking for me, and that he'd come to fetch
me to him. But when we were on the road he did not speak as though
he were my husband's friend, and I questioned him, and he . . . he
was offended. He tried to take me with him by force, and then he
went off in a rage.'

Nedham stared. 'Your face. He did that?'

She touched her chin where she'd bruised it when Bailey flung her
against the side of the cart. 'Aye. When I tried to run away.'

Nedham let out his breath with a little hiss. 'This fellow tried to
abduct you? When was this?'

'Yesterday afternoon. And I cannot say whether or no he meant
to abduct me. Perhaps he was honest, and simply angry at being
questioned. But he didn't speak as though he were Jamie's friend.'

'God have mercy!' Nedham put his hand through his hair again,
then scratched his neck. 'This smells of some jape or wager. Your fine

brave husband bet that you would be willing to cast all aside and come running when he whistles; this fellow is trying to ensure the bet's not lost.'

Lucy blinked. The idea that it might have been a bet hadn't occurred to her. She didn't believe that Jamie would play such a cruel trick, but she could easily imagine Bailey doing so. 'It might be so,' she said. 'And it might be that Jamie's dying. Sir, the horse?'

'The horse, the horse! What would you do with a horse?'

'Go to Colchester, to learn if my husband truly is hurt!'

'On your own?' Nedham asked incredulously. 'A pretty young woman, to a camp full of soldiers?'

'The Army is no rabble, and a camp should be safe enough. There will be officers I can ask help of.'

He scowled at her. 'Can you even ride?'

She flushed. 'I've done so. On my father's farm.' She didn't add that it had been when she was a child, and that when she grew up her father forebade it: *I'll not have you exposing your legs to the lewd gaze of every man that passes by!*

Nedham grunted in disgust. 'I won't be party to this! No, you may not borrow my horse. Send your precious husband a letter!'

She stared a moment, bitterly disappointed. 'Then fare you well!' She started for the door, trying to think how else she might get a horse. If the livery stables wouldn't hire her a horse, perhaps she could offer to buy one, and let them buy it back when she returned? How, though, would she get enough money for that at short notice? Who else did she know that had a horse? Wildman had, before his arrest. What had become of it?

Nedham ran after her and caught her arm as she started into the street. 'What will you do? Nay, don't answer! You'll ask the same favour of another, and ride off on this mad errand anyway.'

'Aye!' she agreed, hotly.

'Your husband's a careless knave, to set his treasure posting up and down the public road! God damn him and all his works! I see that I must take you to Colchester myself.' He began to smile. 'Now that I think on it, I'd do well to get out of London for a few days – and where better to go than Colchester? I should see this famous siege for myself.'

She was dismayed at the prospect of making the journey with Marchamont Nedham, but it would take time to arrange an alternative even if she could, and if Jamie really was dying she had no time to spare. She waited impatiently while Nedham went back to his room and finished dressing, then followed him through the city to the livery stable in Smithfield where he kept his horse.

The horse was a bay mare. Her fine head and slim straight legs indicated breeding, but she was small, and her muzzle was going white. Lucy doubted that she'd be able to carry two riders all the way to Colchester and back. So, apparently, did Nedham. He went to the owner of the stable and spoke in an undertone, occasionally gesturing at Lucy. The man stared, nodded, went off, and presently came back with a second horse, a pretty dapple grey mare fitted with a side-saddle.

Lucy had never ridden with a side-saddle: it was the sort of gear used by well-born ladies, not dairymaids. She thanked the man, however, hoicked her left foot into the slipper-stirrup, and pulled herself up. Getting into the saddle was easier than trying to fit in behind a man, and once she'd settled there she discovered that it was much more comfortable than sitting pillion. She was particularly pleased to have the reins in her own hands rather than Nedham's. The owner of the stable smiled up at her – then took off his hat and bowed his head. 'God speed your ladyship!' he murmured.

Lucy stared in surprise; 'Hsst!' exclaimed Nedham, and laid a finger alongside his nose. The groom at once replaced his hat, but gave Lucy a knowing smile and a wink. Nedham mounted his bay. 'We'll be back next week,' he told the groom, and turned his horse to the road. Lucy followed him.

The streets were once again crowded, and, this being Smithfield, there were cattle being driven to the meat market to contend with, in addition to all the carts, riders, and foot passengers. Nedham dropped back and offered to lead Lucy's mare for her.

'I thank you, no,' she said firmly. In fact, the mare seemed untroubled by the commotion around them. Presumably she was accustomed to Smithfield. 'What did you tell that man?'

He smirked. 'That my companion was a lady of quality whose husband has been wounded in Colchester.'

Lucy frowned at him. 'You made him believe me the lady of one of the cavalier lords *inside* the city!'

'He chose to believe that,' agreed Nedham, still smirking. 'He's a loyal subject of King Charles. The thought that his wife's mare is carrying a faithful lady to the aid of her loyal lord will make him happy. Where's the harm in that?'

Lies are of the Devil, thought Lucy disapprovingly, but she was glad of the mare, so she said nothing. Besides, she was a liar, too: she certainly hadn't told her new employer who her old one was.

It was sixty miles from London to Colchester. The post- and dispatch-riders would cover that distance in a day, but ordinary riders, who couldn't obtain a fresh mount when their horses became weary, had to travel at a slower pace. Nedham, however, pushed hard. They walked and trotted, walked and trotted all morning. Midday found them thirty miles from London. By then Lucy couldn't imagine how she'd ever thought the side-saddle was comfortable. Her right leg was rubbed raw by the pommel and saddle-horn, her back ached savagely and her seat was numb. When they stopped at an inn for dinner, her legs almost gave way when she slid out of the saddle. She had to cling to the leathers to stay upright.

Nedham came over with his arms out. She hastily pushed herself away from the mare and made her way unsupported to the inn, though her legs were shaking. Nedham sighed and lowered his arms with a reproachful look.

'Are you able to continue at this pace?' he asked her, when they were seated in the common room with a dish of roast capon.

She looked at him in surprise. 'Surely the *horses* can't keep it much longer!'

'I thought to leave the horses here. Hire fresh.'

She stared. She had been resigned to spending a night on the road with Nedham – and to fending him off when they stopped.

He grimaced. 'The master of that stable is a loyal man, but who knows about all the grooms? There's still a watch kept on horses taken out of London.'

She understood that. The week before there had been a Royalist attempt to raise troops for the relief of Colchester; it had failed, in part because somebody had noticed that the Earl of Holland, who led it, was collecting horses all over London.

Now that she thought of it, the Earl of Holland and his plot explained why Nedham thought it a good idea to get out of the city for a few days, as well as why he was in such a hurry on the road.

'And besides,' he said, cheering a little, 'I've no wish to take my sweet Honey into the camp of His Black Lordship. If horses are to be seized, let them be other horses!'

She looked down quickly. He'd named his pretty bay mare *Honey* and grown fond of her, had he? 'I am very willing to ride on, sir,' she said. 'But I fear I have not the money to hire another horse.' She was not sure what Nedham was paying for her to make this journey, but she was determined to pay it back. She didn't want to owe him any more favours than she had to.

He waved that off. 'I do. We can settle when we are back in London.' He gave her a sly look. 'I suppose your new press makes you a good living?'

She was determined not to give way before him. 'It would be strange indeed if it did, the fortnight after I bought it! But if you will allow me credit, I will repay you when I have the business on a better footing.'

He snorted, tried to sip his beer, and found the mug empty. He leaned back, caught the serving man's eye, and held it up. 'How's the old bitch's newsbook coming along, then?'

'The first issue will be out in two days,' she said, and bit her lip at the thought that she wouldn't see it off the press.

'And you left London?' Nedham asked incredulously.

'What choice had I?'

'Why, you might have stayed and seen to your duty!'

'Oh, and when you marry will you think *your* wife's duty is to her business, not to you?'

Nedham snorted. 'Indeed not! *My* wife will be loyal and obedient, for I'll not harbour a rebel!' The serving man returned the mug, full, and he took a deep drink, then wiped his mouth. 'I'll grant you your duty to this boasting tinker of a husband, though I fear he has abused your loyalty shamefully. Is the old bitch's newsbook any good?'

She hesitated unhappily. *The Impartial Scout* was clumsily written, vehemently partial, and short on news. 'Not as good as yours,' she admitted.

'Hah!' Nedham said triumphantly. 'Well, I'd be willing to have you back when it fails – on terms, of course.'

After the meal, and another pint of ale, Nedham negotiated with the innkeeper, who kept some horses for hire and was willing to stable the animals they'd ridden from London. Their destination, Lucy noticed, was not mentioned; instead, Nedham spoke vaguely of going 'north'. A price was agreed, and the side-saddle was shifted to a mangy chestnut nag. Lucy found it harder to mount up than it had been that morning, but she gritted her teeth and did it. Nedham gave a few more instructions about his precious Honey's care to the ostler, then climbed on to his fat roan and started back on to the road. He edged his horse close to hers.

'I've no wish to visit a New Noddle camp under my own name,' he told her in a low voice. 'From henceforth I will be Ned Wentnor, your cousin, come to help you on the road.'

She had no choice: Mercurius Pragmaticus could expect speedy retribution from the Army he'd satirized, and she could not let Nedham come to grief because he'd helped her. 'Of course,' she said. 'And I am grateful, sir, truly, for your help.'

He beamed, then kicked his hired mount to a trot. Lucy followed, setting her teeth against the pain.

They reached Colchester late in the evening. By then it had once again started to rain. Lucy was so sore and exhausted that she slumped doubled over in the saddle, blindly allowing her nag to plod through the steady drizzle behind Nedham's. Gradually, though, she became aware that the land on either side of the road was stripped and trampled, and then a voice ordered them to halt. She lifted her head to see walls of turf and timber ahead of them, and the smoke of innumerable cookfires. There were armed men in red coats in the road in front of them: they'd arrived at a sentry post.

The soldiers stared while Nedham spoke to them, gesturing at Lucy. One of the men came over to her.

'Your cousin says you've come to see your husband, who's wounded,' he said.

'Aye,' she agreed faintly. 'Jamie Hudson, a blacksmith of Colonel Rainsborough's regiment. I was told his life was in danger and that he was asking for me. We have ridden today all the way from London.'

There was a stir among the men. 'God bless a loving wife!' someone called warmly. She supposed that most of the men had wives of their own, and her loyalty touched them.

'There were many men hurt when we took the gatehouse,' the

soldiers' spokesman said, waving a hand vaguely at the drizzle behind him.

'The gatehouse?' asked Nedham, appearing at the man's side.

'The malignants set up a drake in the gatehouse of the old abbey,' the soldier explained. 'They called it Humpty-Dumpty, because it was a fat-bellied gun like a monstrous great egg; it fired on our people and did great mischief. Three days ago we brought the wall down under it, at some cost.'

'Humpty-Dumpty had a great fall,' said another man, with a snort of satisfaction, and another sang out, 'All the King's horses and all the King's men, couldn't put Humpty-Dumpty together again!' Several voices joined him on the end of the phrase: it seemed it was a popular new ditty in the camp.

'I was told something of this,' Lucy said faintly, her heart sinking. 'I was told Jamie was working in an entrenchment, and a shot fell among the timbers.'

There was a silence. She could see the pity in the soldiers' eyes. 'I'll send one of my people to escort you to Colonel Rainsborough's fort,' the officer said soberly. 'I pray God they have good news for you.'

They rode on with one of the sentries as an escort, through a small village, then northward, along the raw earth and timber circumvallation that enclosed Colchester. They reached a bridge, where their escort spoke to more sentries. The men smiled up at Lucy, and touched her horse or her foot when she was waved through. They continued on, past more fortifications, more sentries; it seemed to Lucy's exhausted eyes that the mud and the embankments stretched on infinitely, an endless landscape of violence and hatred. Eventually, however, they arrived at the gates of a fort. Their escort explained their errand to the guards there, then turned to go back to his post. He paused, though, as he reached Lucy, and looked up earnestly into her face. He was young, she noticed, not yet twenty. 'I pray God that you have not come all this way in vain, sweet lady,' he said.

'Thank you,' she said, touched, and he gave her a shy smile and touched his hat.

One of the gate guards led them on, into the fort. It was full of low, mean mud-and-wattle shacks; a few camp followers hunched over cook-fires, but most of the people were taking shelter from the rain. There was a single larger and more substantial building in the middle of the fort, and their guide showed them to its door. Nedham dismounted. Lucy kicked her foot out of the slipper-stirrup and slid down, clinging all the while to the saddle. The muscles of her legs were so battered that it was hard to stand; she didn't know whether she could walk. Nedham came over and took her arm with unexpected gentleness. 'Courage, sweet!' he said. 'Soon you'll know the worst.'

Seven

Jamie was eating his supper at the forge when a messenger arrived with an order to report to the colonel at once. He exchanged a surprised look with Towlend, but obediently set down his dish of pottage.

'Your wife's come,' said the messenger.

Jamie froze, staring, then jumped to his feet. 'Lucy? *Here?*'

The messenger grinned. 'If Lucy's your wife's name, aye – but if the sweet creature waiting for you chances to have some other name, I'd take her anyway and keep mum.'

Jamie stared at him wildly, then hurried out into the drizzle without replying. The siege of Colchester was grimmer than anything he'd imagined, and the prospect of seeing Lucy seemed as wonderful, and as improbable, as roses in a dungeon.

Rainsborough was in the main room of the fort headquarters, a long mud-and-wattle hall which served as the officers' mess and general meeting room; Jamie briefly noted the colonel's presence as the man sitting next to Lucy. She was pale, wet and weary, but she looked up as he came in, and her face lit. The next he knew, her arms were wrapped tightly around him, her face pressed against his chest and her fists clenched in his coat. 'Oh, Jamie!' she said thickly.

The feel of her body against his, the sound of her voice, made him feel like hot iron under the hammer. 'What's the matter?' he asked anxiously.

'Nothing, now,' she said, tilting her head back to look up into his face.

'She was told you were wounded near to death,' said Colonel Rainsborough. His voice was tight with anger.

'No,' said Jamie stupidly.

'So I told her,' said Rainsborough. 'And I have sent for . . . ah, Mr Bailey.'

Jamie glanced over his shoulder and saw Philibert at the door, damp from the rain and bemused. Lucy stiffened in his arms, stared a moment, then let go of Jamie and turned to Rainsborough. 'This is not the man!'

'You're certain?' asked Rainsborough. 'This is Philibert Bailey, a friend of your husband's.'

'He is not the same man, sir. The man who came to fetch me was stouter, and dark-haired, and smooth-faced.'

'Sir?' asked Philibert in confusion.

Rainsborough relaxed and sat back in his chair. 'Ensign Bailey. This gentlewoman is Mr Hudson's wife. It seems that yesterday afternoon a man sought her out in London and told her that he had come to fetch her to her husband, who was hurt near to death and asking for her. He said he was her husband's friend, and gave his name as Philip or Philibert Bailey.'

Philibert looked blankly from the colonel to Jamie. 'She says that I . . .'

'She has just said it was *not* you,' interrupted Rainsborough. 'Be glad of it. Else I would have you in irons. It was a cruel trick, if it was nothing worse.'

'I was *here* yesterday!' protested Philibert. 'Everyone knows I was here! Jamie, you spoke to me yourself about dinner-time! Captain Drummond will vouch for me!'

'You need not defend yourself!' Rainsborough said impatiently. 'We are agreed it was not you.'

Jamie looked at Lucy in alarm, and this time noticed the dark bruise on her chin: his paradise had been assaulted. He wanted to sweep her up in his arms and kiss the hurt away; instead he locked his hands together behind his back, good hand gripping the iron brace. She always hated being grabbed; if she'd just suffered an assault she would hate it even more. 'Lucy?' he said, struggling to keep his voice soft, despite his rising fury. 'What befell?'

A stranger, a man he hadn't noticed before, replied. 'Why, the wise child suspected from the fellow's speech that he was not your friend, and she challenged him to explain himself. At this he tried to take her away by force, and when he failed, fled.' He snorted, eying Jamie in an unfriendly fashion. 'After that nothing would serve but that she should rush to see whether he'd told her true. I advised her to make her inquiry by letter, but she wouldn't heed me.'

'I feared that you were dying,' said Lucy. She touched his arm again, very lightly, as though checking that he was real. He noticed the ink stains on her fingers; the memory of those same stained fingers touching him on their wedding night flooded him with desire and tenderness. He took her hand and touched it to his lips, and saw some deep tension leave her. Her fingers curled around his own.

'No such luck,' said the stranger in disgust. Jamie looked at him, then, questioningly, at Lucy.

'This is my cousin, Mr Wentnor,' she said. 'I am much in his debt. When I asked to borrow his horse to come here, he insisted on coming with me.'

Cousin Wentnor gave Jamie a stare of outright dislike – understandable, Jamie supposed, if he'd been dragged away from his business for a long hard ride which had now been proved completely unnecessary. Jamie bowed his head. 'I am much obliged to you, sir.'

Cousin Wentnor scowled. 'Your wife, sir, might have come to grief on the road without company! She has business in London, too, which can ill afford her absence. That business is, I believe, all her present livelihood, since she has *no* support from you.'

Jamie blinked, taken aback by the hostility. He couldn't remember Lucy ever mentioning a Wentnor cousin in London. Perhaps the man had been visiting?

Cousin Wentnor evidently felt that Jamie ought to support his wife – and, of course, he was right. A gentleman's wife shouldn't have to go out to work, particularly at something as dangerous as unlicensed printing. Her family were right to be angry . . . Jamie remembered suddenly that she'd just bought a printing press and undertaken to print a new newsbook, a *licensed* newsbook. He'd been immensely relieved that she was finally free from the threat of arrest. Now she'd cast aside her new business to come running to his supposed deathbed, and God knew what that would cost her. Cousin Wentnor's anger was entirely justified. 'I am most heartily sorry,' he said wretchedly.

Cousin Wentnor's eyes flashed. 'You boasted of your wife, did you not? Placed a wager that she would come running the instant you called for her?'

Jamie stared at him blankly.

An angry snort. 'My first thought on hearing Lucy's story was that this was some jape or wager!'

Jamie understood what he was supposed to have done. His face went hot, and his good hand dropped to his sword hilt. Cousin Wentnor took a step back, suddenly wary.

Jamie forced his hand away from his sword. 'Sir,' he said fiercely.

'It's true this war has prevented me from supporting my wife as I ought, but I swear before God that I would never use her so contemptibly! I . . .' In the middle of his protestation, he remembered the look in Isaiah Barker's eyes after their duel, and stopped.

'Ah, you recollect some foolish words!' Wentnor exclaimed triumphantly.

Jamie shook his head. 'I recollected an enemy.'

Rainsborough gave him a sharp look, and Jamie saw that this thought had occurred to the colonel, too.

'An *enemy*, is it now?' asked Wentnor scornfully.

'A gentleman who challenged me, and lost, and took it very ill,' Jamie replied. 'He is a dark, stout, round-faced man such as Lucy described. He knows Mr Bailey as my friend, because he was my second at our meeting, and he knew of Lucy, for he had my saddle-bags in hand for a time, with all of her letters.'

Wentnor stared at him. 'He stole your saddle-bags? And then you stole them back? And the two of you settled this question of saddle-bags at swords' point? Is this how the Army conducts itself nowadays?'

'No,' said Rainsborough sharply. 'Mr Wentnor, you are welcome here, but I will not hear the Army slandered! A gentleman of the Commissary-General's regiment challenged Mr Hudson over some terms he had used of him, and they arranged a meeting and engaged one another privily, as gentlemen will when their blood's up, but – in respect of their common service – they halted at first blood. Mr Hudson, I will have an undertaking from you to leave this in my hands. Your quarrel with Lieutenant Barker was overlooked once; it cannot be overlooked a second time.'

Jamie looked at Lucy, wondering what would have happened if she had gone off with Barker. A denunciation as a whore or vagrant in some town along the road? He could imagine the lieutenant sneering: *I hear that the wife of our levelling blacksmith has been taken up as a public whore!* He could probably even have escaped blame for it. Any report that reached the camp would be muddled, exaggerated, and detached from its proper time – even if Lucy hadn't tried to pretend such a shameful incident had never happened.

Or perhaps Barker would have raped her, and murdered her afterwards to ensure her silence.

'Mr Hudson!' Rainsborough repeated. 'Your word.'

'This man,' Jamie said tightly, 'feared to face me again, so like a cowardly rogue he went about to attack my wife. God knows what he would have done to her!'

'And I will go to the Commissary-General and complain of him,' said Rainsborough. 'I have many disagreements with Henry Ireton, but he would never support such villainy. You may be sure that if it was Lieutenant Barker who played this cruel trick, he will be punished – but I must point out that we do not *know* that it was Barker.'

Lucy pulled at Jamie's hand. 'Jamie? What's this? You fought a *duel*?'

'Aye,' he said, uneasily. He'd given no thought to her when he arranged the duel, but now that she stood in front of him he discovered that he'd known she would disapprove. Her Puritan family believed that vengeance belonged to God, and she loathed violence even in its official forms. Her face now held a look of disappointment and apprehension. 'It was only to first blood!' he said weakly, wishing he'd run Barker through.

'You must give Colonel Rainsborough your word you will not do so again!' Lucy ordered fiercely – then seemed to realize that she was publicly giving orders to her lord and master. She glanced round at all the men in the room and added defensively, 'If this Barker is the man who lied to me, then Jamie would be fighting him in *my* name. Surely I have the right to say I don't want him to?'

Rainsborough smiled. Jamie saw that, like many another man, he found Lucy's combination of dark-eyed prettiness and fierce determination utterly charming. 'If your husband is able to dispute it, Mrs Hudson, he must have a cheek of brass. Mr Hudson?'

Reluctantly, Jamie inclined his head. 'I give you my word, sir, that I will not challenge Lieutenant Barker, nor seek him out to confront him. I will leave this in your hands.'

Rainsborough accepted the promise gravely. 'I will speak to General Ireton tomorrow morning. Mrs Hudson, I hope you will be able to identify the man who tried to abduct you?'

'Aye, sir,' said Lucy.

'I am sorry that you have had a long hard ride, though glad that you've found a joyful surprise at the end of it. Let me offer you as much hospitality as our hard circumstances allow. You and your husband may have a room here in headquarters for tonight, and I will have my servant bring you the best supper we can provide.'

Cousin Wentnor gave him a very sour look, and Rainsborough

grinned. 'Never fear, man! We'll find a bed for you as well, and you can sup with me and tell me the news of London. Do you follow the news, sir?'

'Aye,' said Wentnor, brightening a little. 'I've ever had itchy ears.'

The colonel's servant showed Lucy and Jamie upstairs to the staff officers' quarters, then went off to fetch them some supper. Their room was a plain cubicle, with a floor of bare boards; the daub on the wattle walls was crumbling in the persistent damp – but it was private. It was furnished with a chest and a mattress. Jamie wasn't sure whose they were, but hoped that the owner was absent on business and unable to burst in with objections.

Lucy at once sank down on to the mattress with a sigh of exhaustion. It was night now, and the light of the single candle softened the outline of her face, touching her pale skin with gold. Jamie, standing at the door, found a lump in his throat. So beautiful, and so brave! She had dropped her business, rousted out this reluctant cousin, and galloped all the way from London to this wet Hell – for *him*! For Cyclops Hudson!

He went over and knelt down beside her. 'I'm sorry!' he told her, taking her hand tenderly in his own. 'I should never have left you alone and unfriended in London. Your cousin is angry with me, and I fear he is right to be.'

She sat up, leaned forward and kissed him. '*Unfriended*, Jamie? What a thing to say! The Overtons are the kindest friends anyone could wish for – and did you *mean* to insult Major Wildman, to leave him out of the reckoning? But as for my angry cousin, he's . . .'

'John's in prison,' Jamie pointed out. 'But of course I meant no insult, to him or to the Overtons. I know they've been very good friends to you indeed. It shames me, that they have done so much for you, when they have no obligation and I have the greatest that a man can owe.'

She smiled at him. 'I am scarcely the only woman that's lost her husband to the war. At least I can still hope to get you back *alive* at the end of it! I was so afraid that I'd lost you forever!'

He kissed her for that, and forgot the rest of what he'd meant to say. The colonel's servant knocked, then came in scowling with a tray and a bottle of wine. He set it down and left again without a word.

The tray held a dish of baked pigeon. Jamie was astonished. Supplying an army during a siege was difficult, and he and his friends had been living on thin pottages – barley-groats seasoned with a handful of herbs, cooked with a twice-boiled bone if they were lucky. He suspected that the pigeons had been intended for the colonel's own dinner – hence the servant's scowl – and he silently blessed Rainsborough's generosity.

They ate sitting snuggled together on the floor, and ended up in bed before the wine was finished. Lucy clung to him passionately as they made love, then fell instantly asleep. Jamie lay awake for a long time, holding her close, listening to her steady breathing and imagining her body – now so soft and warm – lying violated and dead in some roadside ditch, cold under the unceasing rain.

He had never understood why she'd chosen him over handsome, convivial Ned Trebet. He'd had wits enough, though, to seize a treasure when it was offered him. Why had he been so stupid when it came to preserving that treasure?

He woke late, but was still up before his wife. He left Lucy sleeping and went to find her some breakfast. Everyone he met grinned at him and asked after his wife. It seemed that the story had already spread about the camp.

When he returned to the room with bread and small beer, he found Lucy awake. She was sitting on the clothes chest in her shift, right leg bent over left, her skirt turned up above the knee. She pulled it down hastily when the door opened.

'Are you hurt?' he asked with concern. He thought he'd caught a glimpse of red on her upturned knee.

She made a face, then – awkwardly, still shy in his unaccustomed presence – she pulled the skirts up and showed him where the skin was rubbed raw on the inside of her knee. 'It was the side-saddle,' she told him ruefully. 'I'd never ridden with one before, and it's flayed me. And, oh, Jamie, I ache so!'

His own experience of that ache was too recent for him to smile. 'Aye, hard riding's a cruel trial,' he said sympathetically. 'I'm sorry you were put to it.'

She smiled up at him coyly. 'And I thought you were pleased to see me!'

The best answer to that was to set down the mug of small beer and show her exactly how pleased he was to see her. She laughed joyfully, and was his paradise again.

Lying on the mattress afterward he inspected the flayed knee. 'I'll find you some cloth to bind that,' he told her, tenderly kissing the inflamed skin at the edge of the wound.

She sighed contentedly and stroked his hair. 'Thank you. I dare not ride with it like this, and I should start home today.'

'Today?' he repeated, lifting his head in startled dismay. He had counted on at least one more night together. 'Surely you should rest first!'

'Jamie, I've left Mary Overton doing my work for me! I can't burden her with that any longer than I must – and I must do all I can to keep Mrs Alkin's business. I'll be in a hard spot indeed if I lose it.'

'Alkin?' he said vaguely.

'Elizabeth Alkin, who hired me to print her newsbook! I wrote you of it.'

'Aye,' he said, remembering. 'Only I forgot the name. Well, does it matter so much if she takes her business elsewhere?'

'Jamie! It's *licensed*, and it's *twenty-two shillings* a week!'

He was silent: she was being paid four times as much as he was, and, unexpectedly, it stung. He saw that he'd been thinking her work was the same as when he shared it. He'd known that she'd since taken positions which were more professional and better paid, but he'd only ever seen her banging out Leveller tracts for a pittance to help the cause. He told himself that he ought to be pleased that she could support herself so well, but what he felt had nothing to do with pleasure. Her success left him feeling shamed.

'It's but four shillings and sixpence for me, once all the costs are paid,' she said, understanding something of his silence. 'That's scarce enough to pay the rent – in fact, the Overtons are remitting me a shilling, so that I can keep up my visits to the Major. Truly, Jamie, if I don't get other customers besides Mrs Alkin I'll be a burden to my friends – but if I lose her business I'll have to borrow or sell the press. I've had no time to find any other customers. Sorry as I am to leave you, I *need* to get back to London!'

'Nay,' he said, suddenly irritated, 'You've no *need* to toil thus at all! You are my wife now, a *gentleman's* wife. You might go to Bourne.'

She stared. 'Lincolnshire? Why would I go there?'

'You'd be safe among friends.'

'So I am in London! Why . . .'

'London is the unsafest place in England! Those of our friends who aren't in prison now might be set there at any moment! And Lieutenant Barker knows now where you are!'

'Aye, and I know who *he* is, too! If he *is* the man who tried to decoy me with that foul lie, he'd be a monstrous fool to show his face again! Jamie, I'm safer now than I've been for a twelvemonth, and I've just bought a press! Why on earth should I go to Lincolnshire?'

'You are my wife,' he pointed out. 'I wrote you of my brother's visit. Now we're friends again, my family ought to do their duty to you – and they've never even met you!'

'Aye, and if they have any *wish* to meet me, they've been strangely slow to let me know of it!' She caught her breath, met his eyes, and went on resolutely, 'The truth, now: they were angry because you married me, were they not?'

He tried to think of a tactful answer, realized that his pause had given him away, and admitted, 'Aye. They knew naught of you, see, and my father was angry because I didn't ask his blessing. But I think Rob will have set them straight. Most likely they're curious to meet you.'

She let her breath out slowly. 'If they are, they should say as much. You said you're friends again – which means you weren't, before.'

He'd forgotten that he'd never explained that to her, and forgotten, too, the speed of the mind behind those bewitching eyes. He looked away, embarrassed. 'My father was angry that I went to fight for Parliament,' he admitted. 'It was . . . we never agreed well. He called me disobedient, and I suppose I was. When I went off to war he made it plain he'd have no more to do with me unless I returned to what he called my duty. But . . .'

'And you would have *me* go to him? The Leveller girl his disobedient son wed without his blessing? Am I supposed to forswear all and humbly beg his pardon on your behalf?'

He didn't know how to reply. 'All I want is your safety!' he said at last.

She gave a snort of contempt. 'Jamie, I've told you: I'm safe in London! No. I'll not go to Bourne. I'll start back to London as soon as I've seen this Lieutenant Barker of yours.'

He was deeply dissatisfied: he was her husband, and he was trying to protect her. She ought to obey . . . but now that it had been pointed out, he could see that he'd been a fool to think she might be welcome

at Bourne if she turned up there uninvited. His father would treat
her with outright contempt – God, the old man was perfectly capable
of making her work as a serving-maid, or turning her off as a vagrant!
He would have to write Robert first, and explain the situation.

There was a knock on the door. Lucy hastily picked up her gown
and pulled it on, just as Rainsborough's servant came in smiling and
told them that the colonel would be off to visit headquarters shortly,
and that they were invited to come with him.

Rainsborough's staff had found Jamie a horse. Nobody said anything
about Cousin Wentnor and Jamie, relieved, didn't ask. Lucy sat pillion
as they rode through the camp and across the Colne. The pressure
of her body against his back was like sunshine in the persistent rain.
He noted how the men of the regiment stared in surprise and admir-
ation, wondering how their one-eyed blacksmith had managed to get
himself such a beautiful wife. He sat straight in the saddle, smiling.

At the headquarters in Lexden Ireton was willing to see them; he
was not, however, able to be any help. It seemed that Lieutenant
Barker was away with dispatches, and was not expected back for at
least a week.

'When did he leave, sir?' Rainsborough asked politely.

'Three days ago,' said Ireton, looking from the colonel to Lucy
and Jamie. 'Why do you ask?'

Lucy curtsied. 'Sir. The day before yesterday a man sought me out
in London . . .'

Jamie, listening again, was very glad that she was there to tell the
story herself. Ireton might have ignored a letter with the same information. He could not ignore this simply dressed young woman
standing before him and recounting what had happened to her plainly
and without speculation. He was visibly troubled by it: he frowned
angrily, and his small neat hands clenched. When Lucy finished, he
inclined his head to her. 'It was an abominable trick, Mistress, to try
to turn a poor woman's love for her husband to her undoing! You
are to be commended for 'scaping the snare. But I presume from
Colonel Rainsborough's questions that he suspects Lieutenant Barker.
I pray he is mistaken to do so. Colonel, what grounds have you for
this suspicion?'

Rainsborough made a face and spread his hands. 'Lieutenant Barker
matches the description. The story Mrs Hudson was told referred to

our attack on the abbey gatehouse, which was taking place at the time he left Colchester. He knew of the gentlewoman and where she lodged from some letters which had passed through his hands, and he is a bitter enemy to Mr Hudson. He'd challenged him once and lost.'

'What?' Ireton straightened angrily. 'I knew nothing of this!'

'I knew little more, sir, until it was done. The engagement was ended at first blood, out of respect to their common service, and your man sustained no more harm than a scratch.'

Ireton waved that aside. 'Why did you not report this to me?'

'Because it was done with, and no hurt taken,' replied Rainsborough. 'And you and I, sir, are not on such terms that we could afford another cause of contention.'

There was a silence. Ireton regarded Rainsborough with narrowed eyes.

'You would have blamed my man,' said Rainsborough, 'and I would have defended him.'

'I hope, colonel, that we would both have had more respect for the law than to defend either party to a duel!'

Rainsborough gave a snort of amusement. 'Oh? So you never meant to fight Mr Holles?'

Jamie was astonished to see the cold and ruthless Henry Ireton actually blush. It was notorious that he and Denzil Holles, both members of Parliament, had engaged to fight one another after a particularly stormy session of the House of Commons. The duel had been prevented, not by second thoughts, but their friends.

'Holles would provoke a saint,' said Ireton, still flushed.

'You and I are in agreement on that, at least, sir,' replied Rainsborough. 'My only complaint would be that you didn't fight the man and run him through. My point, however, was that gentlemen will fight, whatever the law may say about it, and since in this case no harm was done, I thought it best to look the other way.'

Ireton still looked dissatisfied. 'I should have been informed. I have trusted Barker; I need to be sure he is trustworthy. You say that *he* was the challenger?'

Rainsborough glanced at Jamie, who stirred uncomfortably and said, 'I termed him a coward, sir, for his conduct on the road. You know my reasons. He demanded an apology. His second urged me to make peace. I would have been willing, had Lieutenant Barker been willing to explain himself.'

The cold eyes fixed him a moment – then Ireton sighed. 'I see.'
Jamie felt shamefully relieved. Ireton was not going to defend Barker;
at least, not while Barker's morals were otherwise in question.

The general drummed his fingers on the desk once, then fixed his
attention on Rainsborough. 'Suspicion is not proof. I am sorry that
Lieutenant Barker is away, and that we cannot settle this at once. Mrs
Hudson, I must ask you to remain here until he returns. I will see
to it that you have fitting accommodation until then.'

Lucy looked up sharply. 'What? Sir, it's not possible! I must start
back to London today!'

Ireton's eyebrows rose. 'Out of the question!'

'Sir, I have a printing business which is all my livelihood, and which
cannot long endure my absence!'

'This is a serious accusation against a trusted servant!' Ireton
protested irritably. 'You cannot make it, then go back to London leaving
Lieutenant Barker under such a cloud!' He glanced irritably at Jamie.
'Tell your wife she is to stay here until Lieutenant Barker returns!'

Part of Jamie wanted to do just that: the thought of having Lucy
at his side for a week was delicious. The sight of his wife's angry face
dissuaded him – and what right did Ireton have to order her about,
wrecking the business she'd worked so hard to create? He crossed
his arms. 'Sir. My wife has been deprived of support from me – as
you well know, since it was your doing. I will not suffer her to be
deprived of her livelihood as well.'

Lucy shot him a look of gratitude.

'In truth, sir,' said Rainsborough, 'I think it would be most unjust
to deprive the poor gentlewoman of her livelihood, merely to spare
Lieutenant Barker a "cloud". Why must she stay *here* to identify the
man who assailed her? If Lieutenant Barker denies guilt, you can send
him to London, together with a witness to report. He'll look no
different there than here!'

Reluctantly, Ireton agreed.

Rainsborough had regimental business to conduct with Ireton, but
before starting on it he borrowed paper and wrote a notice. 'Here,'
he said, smiling as he handed it to Jamie. 'You have four days' leave
to escort your wife back to London. Her cousin has asked to remain
here at Colchester a few days more, and I've invited him to do so
as my guest.' He turned the smile on Lucy. 'He's as witty a fellow as
I've met in all my life, and marvellous well-informed.'

Jamie took the pass with delight; Lucy, however, looked uneasy. She bit her lip, then burst out, 'Sir, you should have a care of my cousin. He's a great gossip and wine-bibber, and he has never liked our cause. Tell him a secret and next week you'll hear it in every tavern in London. To speak truthfully, I'd not have sought him out at all, except that I needed a horse.'

Rainsborough only smiled again. 'Have no fear; I'll tell him no secrets! Mr Hudson, I expect you back in camp in four days.'

Jamie gave no more thought to Cousin Wentnor until the man came to bid Lucy farewell as they prepared to leave camp. 'I suppose you are happy?' he asked sourly.

She straightened, chin lifting defiantly. 'Aye, sir, I am.'

He snorted, gave Jamie a glare, then brought out a packet of letters. 'You might deliver these for me, since you've brought me here for nothing. Here, this one is for the innkeeper of that place in Widford where we left the horses – will you cast an eye over my Honey, whilst you're there? See that she's well tended? This is for my liveryman in Smithfield – have a care that your husband changes his coat before you speak with him, or he'll feel himself ill used! The other two should be left at The Sun in Convent Garden. The landlord will know what to do with them.'

Lucy took the packet and stowed it in her tiny bundle of luggage. Her cousin grinned, then swept her into his arms and kissed her soundly. 'A kinsman's privilege!' he said, when Lucy looked flustered and Jamie frowned. 'Fare you well, sweet cousin! As for you, Mr Hudson – you have better fortune than you deserve.'

He swept off jauntily. Jamie helped Lucy up into the side-saddle of her rented horse, then mounted his borrowed one, and they set off.

It was raining when they crossed the Colne and turned their backs on Colchester, but Jamie felt as though the sun shone. He had four days free of the siege, two of them to be spent with Lucy! He watched her tenderly, wincing in sympathy when she jarred her bandaged knee, asking her whether she wanted to stop early, 'for we can do the journey in three days, if you please. I can ride hard on the return'.

'Nay,' she said, with a weary smile, 'two days will be well enough. We can stop in Widford tonight, where we changed horses yesterday.'

'Where your cousin wants you to check on his horse. I never knew you had a Wentnor cousin in London.'

She glanced about nervously; there was no one nearby. Still she lowered her voice when she said, 'I don't.'

Jamie frowned in puzzlement.

'That was Mr Nedham.'

Jamie reined in his horse. 'What?'

'Hush!' she said urgently. 'Jamie, he came here to *help* me. He dared not do that under his own name, and I couldn't let him be taken!'

'*Mercurius Pragmaticus?*' Jamie protested incredulously. '*Mercurius Pragmaticus* is Colonel Rainsborough's guest?'

'I *warned* Colonel Rainsborough!' Lucy said.

Jamie shook his head. 'Not strongly enough! We must go back and tell him the truth!'

'No!' said Lucy in alarm. 'They might hang Mr Nedham for a spy!'

'So? Likely he *is* a spy!'

'Nay, he's a *newsman*! And Jamie, he only came to help *me*. He does not deserve to die for that, surely!'

Jamie remembered Nedham's parting kiss, and the man's open hostility towards himself, and saw that he'd been made a fool of. Rage sickened him. '*Indeed* he came for you! He is all a-bubble with lust, and he hoped to find me dead, the malignant rogue, so that he might have his way with you!'

Her face flushed. 'Jamie, he's treated me fairly and with kindness, and he never did you any harm!'

'Kindness!' he spat. 'Altogether too much kindness, I've no doubt!' It suddenly struck him, though, that Lucy had told everyone from Ireton down to the camp sentries that Nedham was her cousin. If Nedham were hanged for a spy, what would the Army do to *her*? The mood in the camp was savage. She could not expect mercy just because she was young and beautiful. 'What were you doing, turning to such a man?' he asked in horror.

'I told you! He had a horse! I *wanted* to borrow the horse and leave the man, but he insisted on coming with me!'

'You should have borrowed another horse!'

'I didn't know anyone else who might lend one, and I was afraid you were *dying*!' There were tears in her voice now.

'Then you should have stayed home, rather than trust to such a man!' he declared furiously. 'He's a mercenary son of a whore! I thought you'd done with him months ago!'

'He had a horse!' Lucy said again. She was starting to cry.

'Aye, and did you let him ride *you* to get it?'

He regretted the words as soon as they were out of his mouth. Lucy gazed at him a moment, her face wounded and white with outrage. Then she turned away and kicked her mount to a trot.

He wanted to gallop after her and beg her pardon; he also wanted to pull her off the horse and shake her. Instead he drove his mount after her and grabbed the small package of luggage tied behind the side-saddle. She cried out and grabbed it back. 'Nay, I'll have his letters, anyway!' he told her angrily. 'I'll not have you carrying sedition for him!' Perhaps, he thought, the letters would contain some boast about Lucy.

She clung to the package, and he had to wrest it from her, almost pulling her out of the saddle before she would let go. Her horse snorted and side-stepped, and at last she gave a gasp of pain and grabbed the saddle instead. He tore the bundle open, and a cap and stockings fell out into the muddy road. Jamie ignored them and tore open the letters, one after another.

Two notes to livery stables, announcing a few days' delay in returning and promising to pay charges; a letter which sounded like one to a printer, again mentioning the delay and containing instructions for what to do with the previous week's sheets; a note to somebody called John rescheduling a dinner. There was nothing seditious, and no mention of Lucy at all. Rage ebbing, he looked up guiltily from the last letter. Lucy had dismounted to collect her belongings; she had the wet, dirty things under her arm and she was trying to get back into the side-saddle. There were tears running down her face. He felt a wave of shame, and dismounted to help her.

The look she cast at him, of fear and loathing, stopped him in his tracks. She turned her back on him and clawed her way up on to her horse, and he felt as though the gates of Paradise were swinging shut, leaving him outside. She tucked her muddy cap and stockings into the front of her gown, turned her horse and rode on towards London. Heart aching, he followed her in silence.

Eight

Lucy had been worried that Mrs Alkin would be angry with her errant printer, but when she went to speak to her employer, on the morning after her return from Colchester, she was surprised to find the older woman sympathetic.

'Of course you had to go to your husband!' she said. 'I told your friend Mrs Overton that I would have done just as you did. God knows, I would have rid through fire to be at Francis's side when he was dying!'

Lucy was startled. She'd never given a moment's thought to Mr Alkin, though she'd known he was no longer about. It was odd to think of this large, forceful woman as a devoted wife.

'The King had him hanged as a spy in Oxford,' Mrs Alkin said, in answer to the unspoken question. Her voice was bitter. 'They had no evidence, but they hanged him anyway. I was in London, and knew nothing of it until it was done. Were you in time?'

'I was deceived,' Lucy admitted, still nervous. 'When I arrived in Colchester, I found my husband safe and well.' And mightily displeased with me for coming, she thought wretchedly. Jamie had scarcely spoken to her after making that monstrous accusation. She'd spent the whole two-day ride having conversations with him in her head – indignant, furious, reasonable, pleading – but every time she looked at his grim face the words withered on her tongue. The night they'd spent on the road had been passed in the common room of the inn at Widford, lying stiffly back to back, and the following afternoon he'd started back to Colchester even before she'd returned the borrowed mare to the Smithfield stable.

Mrs Alkin beamed. 'God be praised! Had another injured man been mistook, then, for your husband?'

'Nay,' said Lucy, and told the story of the false Mr Bailey. Mrs Alkin listened with keen interest.

'You should have writ out a description of the horse,' she said, when Lucy had finished.

Lucy stared at her employer a moment, impressed. She'd expected a pious exclamation about the wickedness of men — or questions about why her husband had enemies.

'People often take more note of a horse than of a man,' Mrs Alkin explained, misunderstanding the stare, 'and even if your oppresser didn't use his own beast, still he would likely have borrowed or hired it in his own name.'

'That is excellent advice, Mistress!' Lucy said respectfully. 'It was a big grey stallion, very high strung, very noteworthy. I will write and tell them so. Thank you!' At least, she thought, it would give her an excuse to write to Jamie again; though probably he didn't want to hear from her.

That thought brought a fresh stab of pain and indignation. How *could* he believe she'd been unfaithful? Yes, yes, he was undoubtedly right about Nedham's motives, but the fact that another man lusted after her didn't make her an adulteress! She'd only turned to Nedham because she was desperate to reach him, her husband. How could he blame her for that? The unfairness was not just infuriating, but disturbing. She'd believed that fairness was one of his great virtues.

Well, she wouldn't see Jamie any time soon, and meanwhile she had to pay the rent. Lucy turned the conversation back to Mrs Alkin's newsbook. There were no complaints, which was probably a factor in her employer's sympathetic attitude. Mary Overton had finished the first edition on time, and had persuaded most of *The Moderate's* vendors to take a few copies. Sales hadn't been bad for a new title. The real test, however, would come the following week. Curiosity would only help a first edition.

Mercurius Pragmaticus had a page on the siege of Colchester that week. Lucy bought a copy, in dread, but it was better than it might have been. Nedham's first priority had been to encourage the King's supporters by exaggerating the strength of the city's defence. '*It is fair weather still at Colchester . . . they feare no storm, knowing that he that would do is not able. Nevertheless, they are provided for it . . .*' The precision of the circumstantial details was less striking in the general bombast, and Rainsborough wasn't even mentioned.

Lucy worked assiduously for several days, printing each instalment of news as Mrs Alkin delivered it to her. She sent off a letter to Jamie with the description of Bailey/Barker's horse, also saying that she was sorry she had grieved him – but there was no reply.

She also put up notices in booksellers informing the citizens of London that her press was available to print any licensable material they might wish to publish; something she should have done the week before. Her rent-free month at the printworks expired at the end of July, and she needed to find more customers by then or run into debt.

No one appeared to take up the offer, but four days after her return from Colchester the publication of her address did gain her a visitor. She was setting type, sitting in the shop doorway to get the light, when she became aware of someone standing over her. She looked up and saw that it was Marchamont Nedham.

She started up, then sat down again quickly so as not to spill the type. She put her hands protectively over the forme. 'I scarce expected to see *you* here, sir!' she hissed. 'What if Mrs Alkin comes?'

Nedham gave a snort of amusement. 'She's come already. You're setting type. She's not like to be back until tomorrow, is she?'

Wat came to the door, gave a strangled yelp, and backed away again. 'It's Mr Nedham!' he informed his Uncle Simmon breathlessly.

'Aye, it is,' agreed Nedham, 'and if you've a mind to inform on me, boy, be sure that I shall inform on you. Lucy, sweet, will you come with me to the Swan, or must we talk in the street?'

Lucy stood up, carefully supporting the forme on her apron. 'We can talk in the shop, sir.'

Nedham followed her into the dark dank room and looked down his nose at the press as she put the forme aside. He took one of the drying sheets from the line, inspected it a moment, then tossed it aside, smirking. 'I see I need not fear for my sales.'

Lucy hesitated, wanting to rebuke him, but not able to. *The Impartial Scout*'s second edition looked to be even weaker and thinner than its first. 'Are you here for what I owe you, sir?' she asked instead. 'I have not the money here, but . . .'

He waved it aside. 'I'm here, girl, to ask you who read my letters.'

Her face went hot. She'd left his letters at The Sun in Convent Garden, as he'd asked, but there'd been no hiding the broken seals and torn paper. 'My husband, sir, feared they were seditious.'

'*Loyal*,' Nedham corrected her. 'It's your husband who's guilty of sedition, not I – and a fine figure of a man he is, too!' He screwed one eye shut and clapped a hand to the right side of his face, pulling the skin grotesquely tight. 'He might play Sin in a masque, for he's ugly enough, and has one eye for delight, and the other blind to the consequences! He's a cursed ill-favoured wretch, and to see him clutch and fondle you turned my stomach. I wonder, truly, why you wed him.'

The outrage Lucy felt surprised her. She hadn't expected this hot impulse to defend Jamie when she was furious with him herself. 'I wed him for his virtues,' she said sharply, 'which you lack. Sir, I'm sorry he read your letters, but he feared you were involving me in *sedition*.' She repeated the word with some emphasis. 'What decent man would not wish to protect his wife from such danger?'

Nedham scowled. 'You told him who I am.'

'Aye, I did.' *And I wish I had not.*

'God damn you, girl! Did it never occur to you what would become of me if he spoke out?'

'He has wit enough to know it would endanger *me*, sir, since I lied to protect you! He would never put me in danger, and if I'd held my tongue, what would I have said to him, when he asked after my cousin Wentnor?' She looked Nedham in the eye. 'Confess it: you knew he might read the letters when you gave them to me. They would not have been entirely innocent else!'

Nedham laughed. 'Oh, sweet, you're wasted on that mumbling stump! Come, have a drink with me, and we can talk – about business, if you must!'

She shook her head. 'Sir, that would not be proper, and my husband would be very angry, did he learn of it. What business you have with me can be discussed here.'

He gazed at her, still smiling. 'You do owe me money. That journey was made at my charge.'

She'd thought that would be the next ploy, would even have been suspicious if he *hadn't* tried to use the debt to pressure her. She grimaced and nodded.

'Why not deal with one another ingenuously, as friends? You were happy enough to meet me in a tavern when first I hired you.'

'That was before . . . before we knew aught of one another.' *Before you proposed marriage, and before my husband grew jealous.* 'It would not be proper now. Sir, I am in your debt, I confess it, for your kindness as well as the money, but I am a married woman,

and I cannot do a thing which I know would much offend my
husband.'

That brought a ferocious scowl. 'Well, then! If you will not deal
with me as a friend, then you cannot hope for friendly terms! The
cost of the Smithfield mare's hire was five shillings a day, and you
had her three days; the Widford horses were a pound ten, plus sixpence
for our dinner . . .'

'*My* dinner was three pence! And *one* horse from Widford for two
days was eight shillings!'

'Aye, but I made that journey on your account, so it's fit you should
pay my costs!'

She gazed at him in incredulous indignation. 'Sir, the time to say
that was before we set out! I tried to refuse your company then, and
I would certainly have done so, had I known you'd expect me to *pay*
for it!'

He slammed a hand on the press. 'Must I suffer loss because I
helped you?'

'Was it such a hardship for you to sit at Colonel Rainsborough's
table and tell him lies? You seemed at the time to relish it!'

'A long hard ride in ill weather, and this is my thanks!'

'Sir, your haste to be away from London had nought to do with
me! And if your real hope was to console me in my widowhood,
well, I'm accountable neither for the hope nor its disappointment.'

'Curse you for a shrew!' he exclaimed resentfully. 'Your tongue's
as foul as your husband's face!'

She bobbed a curtsey. 'By my reckoning, I owe you one pound,
three shillings and thruppence. That is, fifteen shillings for the
Smithfield mare, eight for the horse from Widford, and three pence
for dinner. I might freely bid you whistle for the money, since you're
in no position to sue me for it, but I will repay, because I am an
honest woman, and grateful for your help. Only, as I said, I have not
the money here, so you must set me a time and place to repay you.'

There was a silence. Nedham grimaced. 'Damn the money! I didn't
mean to quarrel with you, Lucy.'

She crossed her arms, steeling herself. Nedham might say 'damn
the money!', but if he remitted it, she had no doubt he'd try to get
payment in another form, and while it was true that she could get
away without paying him in any kind, she did not want to be in his
debt. He made her uneasy enough as things stood. 'Then let us deal

as friends,' she said mildly. 'I am content to pay what I owe you, with my thanks for your help. You need only set a time and place.'

He sighed, then glanced round the dark room, grimacing at the fascinated faces of Lucy's employees. 'The truth,' he said. 'Do you *have* one pound three shillings?'

She flushed. She did not. 'I can get it.' She pushed aside the uncomfortable thought that she would get it if she sold her press. If *The Impartial Scout* failed, as she feared it might, that would be her only recourse. She told herself instead that she could borrow the money, using the press as security.

Nedham regarded her a moment thoughtfully, then smiled. 'Well, then, you can repay me at The Sun in Convent Garden. Meet me for dinner at noon on Saturday! No, stay, make that Saturday next. This Saturday I'm engaged already.'

She made a face. She'd walked into that. She agreed, and resolved to bring Mary with her.

The second edition of *The Impartial Scout* was completed a couple of days later, on Friday. Lucy worked hard to persuade vendors to take copies, then awaited the results with trepidation.

She had yet to find any new customers. The mood in London was fearful and subdued, the citizens all reluctant to spend on inessentials when they might soon need every penny simply to survive. Parliament was discussing reopening negotiations with the King, this time without preconditions. Everyone knew that if they did it would cause a breach with the Army, but many would welcome it. There were plenty, even in Parliament, who feared the Army radicals even more than they feared the King. It was not a good time to publish banalities, but it was hard to get a licence to publish anything else.

On Saturday afternoon the mercury-women trailed into the printworks one after another, returning unsold copies. 'Those that hate the King buy *The Moderate*,' one explained. 'Those that love him seek out *Pragmaticus*, and the rest wait for the *Diurnal* or its kin. None see the need for this new book, Mistress, and those that took it last week say it's sad stuff.'

Mrs Alkin arrived at about six. 'God have mercy!' she exclaimed when she saw the stack of returns. 'Did we sell *none* of them?'

'Some hundred, perhaps,' Lucy said unhappily. Even if there were no more returns – which there probably would be – the sales wouldn't even cover the cost of the paper the book was printed on. A newsbook needed to sell at least five hundred copies to break even.

'Well!' Mrs Alkin puffed out her cheeks and sat down heavily on the stool by the composing frame. 'I'd a notion from the mercury-women I spoke to in the city today that our success was poor, but it's worse than I thought! God knows, this business is harder than it seems!'

'It always takes time,' said Lucy. '*The Moderate* made a loss for months.'

'I cannot afford to prop up this newsbook for *months,*' replied Alkin. She frowned at Lucy. 'I'd persevere a bit longer, if I thought I'd win through in the end, but I much doubt that I will. Your *Moderate* can never have sold so few copies as this poor work of mine – and scribbling is hard work! Last week I had much I wanted to say, but this week I found I'd said it already. To go on saying it, and pay a pound a week for the privilege – no, I can't afford it. I didn't know how I'd thrive in this new business. Now I do. I'll pour no more good money after bad.'

'But . . .' began Lucy, then stopped, biting her tongue. She wanted to protest – no, more than that! She wanted to shout that Mrs Alkin was a false jade if she did not provide Lucy's press with the work she'd promised! The insult, though, would be not only pointless, but unfair. Mrs Alkin had made it clear from the start that she wasn't prepared to make a heavy financial commitment. That, after all, was the reason she'd offered the press to Lucy instead of buying it herself. The old spy *had* provided work, too, as well as she could. Blaming her for being a bad newswriter was like whipping a willing horse because it was too slow to win a race. The real fault was Lucy's. She'd been so eager to buy her own press that she'd barely considered what she'd print on it.

'I'm sorry, child!' Mrs Alkin said, with concern. 'I see that this is a blow to you. Have you no other customers?'

Lucy shook her head. 'I will try to find some.'

She knew where to look for them, too, but she hadn't expected her heart to sink so at the prospect. Hitherto she'd obeyed her employer and looked only for *licensable* material, but if Mrs Alkin gave up on *The Scout* there was no reason to keep to that restriction. It wouldn't mean going back to *Pragmaticus.* There were plenty of Levellers and religious nonconformists eager to appear in print. She found herself wishing, though – with a craven intensity – that she could find some legitimate business instead.

It was odd: she'd spent much more time in unlicensed printing than the licensed sort, and she'd thought she was used to the risks. Instead the very idea of going back to it made her feel as though she was faced once more with that horrible side-saddle. When she'd started printing she'd been ignorant and fearless; now she found herself remembering the starving misery of the Tower, the stink of the Fleet, and Mary Overton's dead baby. *Coward!* she told herself severely, but the insult failed to produce any sudden access of courage.

When Mrs Alkin had gone, Lucy closed the printworks and walked slowly back to Coleman Street, miserably considering her options. The end of the month was now only days away. If she had no new customers by then she would either have to sell the press or borrow money. She didn't want to borrow. She'd heard too many stories about debts spiralling out of control, and knew she risked losing her press and all the money she'd invested in it. Most of that money had come from the legacy left her by her beloved Uncle Thomas – and she found that the fear of losing that troubled her more even than the thought of losing the press. As long as her livelihood sprang from his gift it was as though she hadn't altogether lost him.

Well, as she'd told Mary, she'd acquired the press at a bargain price, and could probably sell it for more than she'd paid. If she sold it now she could pay off her debts and be no worse off than she'd been when she bought it. Then she could start saving again, and buy another press after she'd lined up her customers . . .

Except that she couldn't go back to working for Nedham – not now, not when he'd made his feelings so plain, and Jamie was so angry and jealous – and nobody else was likely to offer her ten shillings a week. There was no way she could save enough for another press if she was earning sixpence a day and her dinner.

There was Wat, too, – and his poor simple-minded Uncle Simmon, but she felt less responsibility for Simmon. Wat, though, had followed her from *Pragmaticus,* and she doubted that Nedham would take him back. She knew he relied on his wages, slight as they were. Trade in London was so bad that his father, a bootmaker, struggled to keep his family fed. What would he do if she sold her press?

She briefly wondered about going to her father. When she'd married he'd promised a dowry. He hadn't had the cash to pay it, though, and who knew whether he ever would? Even if he did, the money would go to Jamie, not to her. Besides, he was far away in Leicestershire, and she needed the money now.

She pushed aside a wistful thought that Jamie and his rich family might help. Jamie was angry with her, and had no money of his own anyway; as for his family, they'd never wanted her at all.

Well, she'd managed to climb back into that horrible side-saddle even after it flayed her, so she supposed she could go back to unlicensed printing. The next day was the Sabbath. The day of rest would give her time for solemn and sober consideration, and the opportunity to overcome her jittery nerves.

Borrowing enough to pay off Nedham was easier than she'd expected. On Sunday she went to visit her cousins the Cotmans in Stepney, as she often did, and at dinner after church she told them about her trip to Colchester – though she implied she'd been accompanied by a friend of the Overtons. The Cotmans abominated Royalists, and she'd never told them about her association with *Pragmaticus*. Cousin Hannah clasped her soft hands together and gasped when Lucy described her encounter with the false Bailey. She exclaimed, 'Thanks be to God!' on hearing that Jamie was in fact unharmed. Nathaniel, however, frowned, and said, 'It mislikes me, coz, that you turned for help to strangers instead of your own kin.'

It was a sensitive point. Many of the family felt that he should have taken Lucy into his own household after her uncle died, rather than let her lodge with friends. Lucy was as keenly aware of this as Nat, and she ducked her head humbly. 'Sir, forgive me! Had I run all the way hither to Stepney to ask help of you, I could not have set out before midday, and I was in terror that Jamie might die before I could come to him.' It was true, but she privately doubted that Nat would have done anything more than advise her to write a letter.

Nat grunted, not entirely mollified.

'I'd still be very grateful for your help,' Lucy said, seeing an opportunity. The Cotmans weren't exactly rich, but they were better off than most, with income from rent as well as Nat's mercer's business. 'I was obliged to borrow a pound and ten shillings to hire horses, and I'd much rather be in debt to my kin than to a stranger.' She felt a lurch of guilt at the inflated sum – but the extra seven shillings would keep the printworks running for another week.

'A pound ten shillings?' asked Nat in horror. 'Where did you hire this horse? Whitehall Palace?'

'It was *two* horses, sir. Else I could not have rid all that way in a day. Sir, I'd be most grateful, and I would repay you as soon as my situation allows.'

'Oh, Nat!' exclaimed Hannah. 'We must help poor cousin Lucy!'

'If she'd turned to us first, the matter might have been settled at less cost!' Nat grumbled – but he went to his strongbox and counted out a pound and ten shillings. Lucy thanked him profusely, secretly amused by the look of self-congratulation that crept over his face. She suspected that not only would he tell everyone he'd loaned her the money, but that within a few days he would almost have forgotten that she'd actually made the journey before he did so.

The following day she returned from questing after customers to find that a letter had come for her from Colchester. She took it from Mary eagerly, then frowned. The handwriting was not Jamie's.

Mrs J Hudson,

First, be at ease. Your husbonde is in no Danger, tho' he took a chill upon his riding back to Colchester, and fell ill. He was sent with other Sick Men to Quarters in Braintree, yet the Surgeon sayes he maykes a good recoverie and shd soone be returned to his Duties.

Lieutenant Barker returned yesterdaye from his errand. General Ireton charged him with his conduct; he at first Denyed, but at last Confessed it when told that he must goe to Lundon and Deny againe to your face. He sayes that he did Alle in Jest, and wd have Delivered you unhurt to your husbonde, had you not taken Alarm and quarrelled with him. He thus escaped Punishment, but yet has not come off unscathed, for the General frowns upon him, and will employ him no more. He had pinned all his Hope upon Ireton and Cromwell and their Faction, and cries out loudly against this Sentence, but to no avayl.

I pray you remember me to Maj Wildman and our friends, and to your witty cousin. God keep you in health.

Yr. Servant

Ths. Rainsborowe

'That is a very generous letter,' Mary commented, when Lucy showed it to her. 'Few men of his rank would even remember that you waited here, still less trouble themselves to give you news.'

Lucy nodded, but her attention was elsewhere. Jamie was ill? Was that why he hadn't answered her letters?

'You don't seem pleased,' observed Mary. 'It's true that this Lieutenant Barker deserves worse than General Ireton's frown, but . . .'

'I don't care a fig for Lieutenant Barker,' Lucy interrupted, angrily folding the letter. 'Jamie's lying ill among strangers – and Colonel Rainsborough may say he's in no danger, but it seems he's too ill to write to me himself, which . . .'

'The colonel knows him to be convalescing in Braintree,' Mary interrupted, quietly amused, 'where he would receive scant news – and I cannot think that he or any other of Jamie's friends would be eager to give him such news as this, and perhaps provoke another quarrel.'

'Oh,' said Lucy, and bit her lip. 'I'd not thought of that.'

'Would you have set out upon another ride?' asked Mary, still smiling.

'Nay.' Lucy sighed and tucked the letter into her apron pocket. 'I should not have made the last one. Only . . .'

'Only you fear for your husband's safety,' Mary agreed, 'as who would not? Disease has ever slain more soldiers than any malice of the enemy. But truly, Colonel Rainsborough's an honest man, and you can trust his word that your Jamie is making a good recovery. A *Chill*, he says; not *camp fever* or, God forbid, *plague*.'

Lucy sighed again. She took the letter back out of her pocket and read it over. 'It's a kind letter,' she admitted. 'I like that he remembers Major Wildman, too.'

She was worried about Wildman. She'd missed one visit to the Fleet because of her trip to Colchester; she'd felt obliged to go the following week, though the meeting had been an unhappy one. She'd been unable to afford any delicacies, and Wildman had been bad tempered in his disappointment, berating her for meanness and complaining about her absence the week before. When she'd explained about her journey he'd disapproved of it, even though she hadn't admitted whom she'd travelled with or how badly it had turned out. He'd apologized, though, when she took her leave – apologized with a frightened urgency. Looking at his thin face and shadowed eyes, she'd seen his terror that he would be abandoned in that horrible place. Others of his friends had ceased to visit him, unwilling or unable to deal with the cost, the filth, the danger of infection.

Lucy bit her lip. She'd promised she'd come again. This week, though, when she was living on borrowed money, how could she afford it?

'You could ask money from the common fund,' Mary said, understanding her worry. 'But perhaps by Friday you'll have some customers.'

'God send it!' Lucy exclaimed.

She did not visit the Fleet on Friday, however. On Wednesday – the second of August – John Wildman was released.

Nine

Jamie had come down with a flux the day he returned to Colchester. He'd spent a day running between the forge and the latrine, then collapsed with a high fever. The Army didn't like to keep sick men in the camps – disease spread quickly enough as it was – so he was taken to nearby Braintree on a cart, along with half a dozen others with the same disorder. A local merchant was required to provide free quarter for them.

The merchant was a wool-dealer. His business had suffered badly in the war, he was struggling to pay his bills, and he was utterly dismayed to be handed half a dozen feverish and dirty strangers and told that he was now responsible for their care. He put the sick soldiers in his warehouse, which was half empty, bedded them down on fleeces, and tried to keep his family well clear of their contagion.

The warehouse had no windows; the only light was what crept under the eaves. In the badly ventilated room the stink of diarrhoea was soon overpowering. The care the men received was scant and slapdash, and the soldiers complained among themselves that if it hadn't been for the regular visits from the regiment the wool-dealer would have left them to starve in their own filth.

Jamie disagreed. The wool-dealer brought them gruel three times a day and saw to it that they were warm and had plenty of water to drink. It was too much effort, though, to argue with the others. His illness, coming on top of such a pile of other miseries, had left him exhausted and depressed. It seemed to him that it would be much better to die than to go on living. He had taken up arms for the noble cause of justice, freedom, and common right – and here he was, short of an eye and half a hand, disfigured, lying in a dark and stinking warehouse, soon to return to the stifling hatred of a bitter siege. He was estranged from his family and home; his father had all but disowned him; his nearest and dearest brother had died in agony at the hands of his own side; and now he had bitterly offended his wife, and had no idea how to make peace with her.

He was lying on his fleecy pallet, staring at the wall, when the warehouse door opened, admitting a flood of light and a spatter of rain. There was a murmur, and then his brother Robert's voice cried angrily, 'Oh, Christ have mercy!'

Jamie rolled over and sat up. Robert saw the movement and came over, his boots loud on the wooden floor slats. 'Christ!' he exclaimed, gazing down at Jamie in disgust. 'Did you come to my door, the servants would turn you off for a begging vagrant!' He turned on the wool-dealer, who'd followed him in. 'How dare you, sir? My brother is a *gentleman!* I would not kennel a *dog* in this foul hole!'

'Had I a sunny courtyard I would lodge them there!' the wool-dealer objected indignantly. 'How am I to provide comforts for these when I lack for my own?'

'You have a house!' Robert said bluntly.

'Aye, and three small children in it!' replied the wool-dealer. 'Would you lodge men with the flux with your own sons?'

Robert glared. 'I'll have him from here at once!'

The wool-dealer glared back. 'You're welcome to him! Take *all* of them!'

Robert spat, then dropped to his knees by the pallet and took Jamie's arm. 'Come, brother! Can you walk?'

'Aye,' said Jamie, dazed by surprise. 'But, Rob, I can't go home, I'm . . .'

'We'll speak,' Robert said firmly, and pulled him to his feet.

Robert led him out and down the muddy street. It was another grey day; the clouds heavy with more rain, but after the dark warehouse the light was dazzling. They went to an inn. Robert led him upstairs to a private room, then went to the door and shouted for a servant.

The man who answered the call had a face familiar from another world – a world of farms and stables, of wildfowling expeditions into the Lincolnshire fen and winter nights storytelling round the kitchen fire. Jenkin Simons, that was the fellow's name. His family had a cottage half a mile from Bourne Manor, and he and Jamie had sometimes gone fishing together. Somehow the sight of an old acquaintance caught at Jamie's heart the way the sight of his brother had not, and suddenly he wanted desperately to go home.

Jenkin frowned at Jamie for a moment in puzzlement, then

recognized him. His expression changed to one of horror and dismay. Jamie looked away, his eye stinging. He had imagined that look a thousand times, on the faces of the friends he'd gone hunting with, the pretty girls he'd courted. He'd dreaded it so much that going home had come to seem impossible.

'Jenkin!' Robert snapped impatiently. 'Tell the servants we need hot water and a basin, and bespeak us a good dinner.'

'Aye, sir,' replied Jenkin. He gave Jamie another pitying glance and added, 'Never fear, Master James. A few good dinners will set you up again.'

'Jamie,' Robert ordered, as Jenkin went out, 'take those stinking things off. I've fresh for you. We'll dine together downstairs, like gentlemen.'

Jamie obediently began to take off his coat, though he protested, 'But, Rob, I cannot go home; the Army's not discharged me, and if I desert . . .'

'We'll speak,' Robert said again. 'Jenkin!' He went to the door and called it down the stairs. 'Jenkin, when you're done, fetch shears and a razor; my brother needs his hair seen to.'

Half an hour later, washed, shaved, trimmed and dressed in clean clothing, Jamie found himself sitting opposite Robert at the table of the inn, contemplating a dish of roast capon and a mug of ale.

'Eat up!' Rob ordered. 'God knows you need some flesh on your bones. You were a sorry sight in June, but you're worse now.'

Jamie thought of objecting to the tone – but in fact the clothes Robert had given him hung very loose. Besides, he was hungry. He helped himself to the capon and a slab of good wheat bread. 'Thank you, Rob.'

Robert waited to be sure he ate before starting his own meal. 'What ailed you, any gate?'

'A flux,' Jamie told him. 'It's common in the camp.'

Robert made a face. 'I suppose you've been eating nought but gruel, then.'

'Aye.'

Robert frowned at the capon. 'Is that too rich a dish for you?'

Jamie's whole body had responded to the first mouthful of chicken with an eager craving for more of it. 'I've been clear of the ill for a couple of days now.' That was true, though he'd eaten nothing but gruel even so, and little else than pottages even before the flux. 'Rob, what brings you here?'

Robert snorted. 'What do you think?'

Mouth full of bread and capon, Jamie stared at him, baffled.

'*You,* you great fool!' Rob exclaimed in exasperation. 'After taking so much trouble to seek you out, did you believe we'd forget you? When I told our sisters how you did, they set about knitting and sewing, and I was recruited to carry you a package. What do you think you've got on your back now?'

'I thought the clothes were yours,' Jamie said, glancing down at the clean shirt.

Robert shook his head. 'I don't think a week's passed these last seven years that Peggy hasn't said, "I wonder how Jamie fares." When I told her how I'd found you, and in what state, she shut herself in her room and wept. We've lost one brother this summer; we've no wish to lose another – and by the look of you, we might well have done!'

'I was in no danger,' Jamie said guiltily. Peggy was his younger sister, the only one still unmarried and at home. Their mother had died a week after giving birth to her; the loss had left him determined to look after his poor little motherless sister, so he'd spoiled her shamelessly as she grew up. She'd been fourteen when he last saw her.

'I should think every man put in that black hell-hole is in danger!' Rob said angrily. 'How can your Army use its loyal servants so?'

'We were dry and fed,' Jamie replied. 'That's the best that can be hoped for, in war.'

Robert scowled, and Jamie braced himself for a reminder of how foolish he'd been to go to war. What Robert said, though, was worse. 'Enough is enough!' he declared. 'Come home.'

Jamie put his piece of bread down and stared at his half-empty plate, unable to speak. He wanted, more than anything in the world, to do exactly what Rob urged, and he didn't see how he could.

'Send for your wife,' Robert said. 'I told Father what you said of her, and his rage is much abated. Make your peace with him and he'll give her grace.'

Jamie looked up again into his brother's earnest face. 'And to make peace with him I must do what?'

'Christ, Jamie, he *wants* to forgive you! If you repented your errors and begged his forgiveness, he would welcome you with tears.'

'How, though, if I did not repent and beg?'

Rob let out his breath in an exasperated huff. 'You know he's near as stubborn as you are. Give him no choice but to stand by his word and by it he'll stand till Doomsday! Yield, though, and he'll run to meet you. Come, you said yourself that if you'd known how things would turn out, you would never have gone to war.'

Jamie shook his head. 'Rob, such repentence as I could offer would never suffice him. He might welcome me with tears, but then he would pick at the matter and pick at it, and each time I gave way, he would press harder. If I didn't lose my temper, my wife would lose hers. She's no wish at all to go to Bourne as it is, and . . .'

'You've asked her?'

The rich food was suddenly very heavy in Jamie's stomach. He pushed his plate aside and put a hand over his eye. 'She . . . I wanted her out of London. It's no safe place, and it cuts me to the heart that I can neither protect her nor provide for her. She nearly . . . she was assailed, Rob; she might have been carried off, killed, even, if she'd been less wary. And she rode all the way to Colchester after, to seek me out, and all I could do was quarrel with her for her company on the road.'

'What's this?' asked Robert in bewilderment.

Jamie told him the story in a confused jumble, backtracking to explain one detail, then leaping forward to another. Robert was horrified. 'You are sure that Mr Barker did this?' he asked, shaken. 'He seemed to me a gentleman!'

Jamie had almost forgotten that Robert had travelled with Barker from Maidstone to the Severn. 'He is a scheming malicious coward!' he said hotly. 'It's true I've had no word of whether he's returned to Colchester and spoken to the charge against him, but I've no doubt that it's true! You say he struck you as a gentleman, but you must remember that on the road he told lies about me to set you against me.'

Robert looked doubtful. He still wasn't sure whether what Barker had said about the Levellers was lies. 'Why would he do so?'

'Because he is of Cromwell and Ireton's faction, and ambitious,' replied Jamie.

'What has that to do with anything?' Rob asked in bewilderment.

Jamie stared a moment, realizing for the first time that his brother knew nothing of the political situation in the Army – and that Jamie should never have expected him to. Robert hadn't gone to war, and in Lincolnshire news was scarce and confused. London newsbooks reached the county only sporadically, and nothing was printed there. 'Rob, his faction shed blood of ours at Ware last year!' Jamie pointed out. 'I and many another man were cast into prison so that Cromwell and Ireton might gain mastery over the Army! Then this new war arose, and they found that they needed our help. There is a truce between us now, but very little goodwill. Men like Barker hope to demonstrate their loyalty and win favour with their masters by slandering us.'

Robert blinked. 'By "us" you mean Levellers. I thought you'd agreed to quit that faction.'

Jamie had not actually agreed any such thing, but he knew he'd let Robert believe he had. He struggled to think what to say, terrified of damaging the still fragile reconciliation, but ashamed to deny friends and principles. 'If I choose to be reconciled with you,' he said at last, 'it doesn't mean that I hate the cause I fought for – only that I prize peace with my brother more.'

Robert gazed at him for a long moment, then nodded. 'Fairly said. I suppose, too, that Mr Barker would have had no notion of any change in your loyalties.'

'Aye,' Jamie agreed, deeply relieved. 'Rob, I beg you, believe me, for this is most true! I do not ask you to love the cause, only to believe that others *do* attack it for no reason other than that they are bound to suppress it if they would gain power themselves.'

Rob blinked again, frowning. He undoubtedly knew enough to see that what he'd just learned explained a great many things. After a moment he said, 'You say that because of this – this struggle within your Army – Mr Barker made himself your enemy. That he insulted and slandered you, cast you to the common enemy to save himself, and in the end challenged you because you would not endure it quietly.'

'Aye,' agreed Jamie. 'And, Rob, I have you to thank that he even troubled to fight me. Had he not known beyond doubt that I was a gentleman's son, I believe he would have waylaid me with four or five friends and horsewhipped me.'

Robert's jaw set, his eyes brightening with anger. 'The insolent prating cur! You fought and beat him?'

'I disarmed him at the first stroke, and then, as I said, spared him, since we'd agreed to end the affair at first blood. I wish now I'd killed him!'

'I thank God you did not! By what you say it would have gone ill with you if you had.'

Jamie almost responded that no, his new colonel was a Leveller and would have tried to defend him – but publicizing his continuing connection to the cause would not be helpful. Feeling guilty for both the implicit deception and the implicit denial of his allegiances, he sat in silence, all appetite now vanished. Robert frowned some more, then sighed. 'Well, there is nothing to be done but trust in God! I've not understood, though, why you quarrelled with your wife over this. From what you've said, she did bravely!'

'She did,' Jamie agreed at once, stabbed by fresh misery. 'She rode all the way from London – in a day! And when she came before Ireton she spoke with such honesty and fairness that he could not contest a word she said. But I was a jealous fool, and I quarrelled with her over her company on the road; she'd gone for help to a man who . . . who'd employed her for a time upon his printing press, whom I suspect as a base lecherous rogue.'

Robert was looking confused and troubled, and Jamie was suddenly afraid that his brother had drawn the wrong conclusion and would go away thinking there was a stain on Lucy's character. 'All she wished was to borrow his horse!' he explained quickly. 'She knew he kept one, and thought he might lend it, but instead he insisted upon coming with her. I do believe her that she allowed him nothing and would have had naught to do with the fellow at all, had she not been so afraid for me – and yet I was so angry that I spoke as though I thought otherwise.'

'Your wife was employed by this lecherous fellow?' Robert asked.

'As a *printer*,' Jamie insisted. 'And she left his employ as soon as ever she could. She has her own printing press now – and that's another grief, Rob! She had engaged to print a new newsbook, a licensed one, and published by a *woman*, but she cast it aside to ride to Colchester. She was in great haste to get back, for fear that the journey would cost her the customer, and with it her livelihood.'

There was a silence. 'I thought she was supported by her kin,' said Robert, and Jamie suddenly saw the source of his brother's confusion. 'You mentioned an uncle, a London mercer.'

'He died of the smallpox last November,' replied Jamie. 'Lucy's supported herself since. I've given her nothing but a name.'

'I see why you want her out of London,' said Robert, now shocked. 'A lone woman in such a bear-pit! By God, a *Mrs Hudson* in such a bear-pit!'

'She lodges with friends of her uncle,' Jamie told him, trying now to reassure. 'Richard and Mary Overton, godly people. And she works as a printer. I told you she was a printer.'

'Nay, you did not!' replied Robert. 'You said you'd met her working upon a printing press, but I thought it some . . . some project of your faction.'

'It was,' Jamie admitted, 'but she took the skills she learned and put them to such good use that she not only supports herself, but helps her friends and mine. Rob, she was to be paid *twenty-two shillings a week* to print this new newsbook!'

The amount had shamed him; it stunned Robert. '*Twenty-two shillings?*' he asked in amazement.

'It seems that left her but a small profit, once the bills were paid,' said Jamie. Suddenly the shame he'd felt vanished. Other wives bereft of support might beg for help; *his* built up a business. 'She hoped to do better once she had more customers. Only – as I said – her coming to me at such a time may have cost her the one customer she had, and ruined her business before she could get it well set on its feet. I know nothing, though, for I've heard nothing from her since I left her back in London. Even in my illness, not one letter. I fear I've bitterly offended her with my foolish jealousy.'

Robert frowned at him. 'You wrote to tell her you were ill?'

'Nay,' Jamie admitted.

Rob snorted. 'And would your Army have forwarded hither any letter she did write?'

Jamie hadn't thought of that. 'I . . . suppose not.'

Robert began to smile. 'So she may well have writ you! It seems to me, brother, that she's unlikely to be so offended with you as you think. Women are pleased when men are jealous.'

Jamie shook his head. 'She was not pleased. I made a foul, false accusation. I am ashamed of it.'

Robert's smile only broadened. 'Then all you need do is write her and tell her so. Say you were consumed with love and jealousy. Women ever adore such protestations! You only need fear that she keeps the letter ever after, and brings it out whenever you breathe a doubt.'

'Do you truly think so?' asked Jamie. His spirits began to rise. Robert, he reminded himself, had been married now for over a decade; he ought to know.

Robert shrugged. 'I've not met the wench. All I know is what I hear from her besotted lover – but if she loves you half so well as you love her, she will forget your quarrel at the first kind word, and if she rode clear to Colchester when she feared you lay a-dying, she loves you well indeed. I am more concerned about her situation in London. I had thought her protected and provided for by her kin, but you say she is not. This notion of a woman running a business – in London, in such times as these!' Robert shook his head in dismay. 'You say you wished to send her to us, and she would not go?'

Jamie's face heated. Robert was offering help without even having to be asked. 'We spoke of it. She said straightaway . . . that is, she feared she would not be welcome. She understood that there'd been a quarrel, though I swear I never said aught of it. She said she feared my father would not welcome the Leveller bride I'd married without his blessing – and, Rob, I could not tell her she was wrong.'

Robert winced. 'If she came back with you, though . . .'

'Do you tell me that I am wrong, and that Father would forbear to press me?'

There was a silence. Robert shook his head again, unhappily. 'I fear you are right, Jamie. I should not have urged it. Father would not let the matter go – not yet. He grieves for Nick, and if Nick is to be a sainted martyr, you must confess yourself a guilty sinner. In time he may take a fairer view – but not yet. Still, he that has no horse can go afoot. If I can't bring you and your bride home, I can yet do something for you both. You must stay here, at this inn, until you are well again – and I will ride to London, to visit your Lucy, and see what might be done for her.'

'God bless you, Rob!' Jamie cried, and caught his brother's hands over the table. 'You are a better brother than I deserve.'

They shared a bed in the inn that night. In the morning Robert set out for London with his servant. Jamie, ashamed at the trouble and expense he was causing, swore that there was no need for Robert to pay for him to stay at the inn – he was much better, and would return to Colchester that day.

He supposed that it was true – a night away from the dark stinking warehouse and a couple of solid meals had left him feeling stronger – but as soon as his brother disappeared down the road, he wished he'd accepted the offered charity. He dreaded returning to the siege.

He found an Army wagon that was bound for Colchester and got himself and his new sack of luggage – the clothing made by his sisters – on board.

Ten

Nedham was not pleased when he saw that Lucy had brought company to their meeting at The Sun in Convent Garden. 'Who's this?' he asked in dismay.

'This is my good friend, Mrs Overton,' Lucy informed him, looping her arm through Mary's. 'I lodge in her house, and she printed Mrs Alkin's newsbook for me, whilst you and I were away from London.'

Nedham scowled. 'Why is she here?' A sly look. 'Did you not trust yourself to be alone with me?'

'The reverse,' Lucy said shortly.

'I did but think to have a pleasant dinner!' Nedham protested, looking hurt. He scowled at Mary again. 'Mrs Over*done*, you cannot be accommodated here. I bespoke dinner for two, not three.'

'Then you must find other company,' Lucy said briskly.

He gave her a look of deep reproach. 'This is unkind! Surely I've deserved better of you than this!'

'Sir,' she replied in exasperation, 'I told you plainly that I could not sit and drink alone with you in a tavern, for reasons you well know and all the world would approve! Do you take me for a simpleton?'

'Would that you were!' muttered Nedham. He glowered at Mary.

Mary smiled back. 'Sir, if we are not to have dinner here, then Lucy and I must needs dine elsewhere, and quickly, for I've a pile of news to print ere nightfall.'

'I've brought the money I owe you,' Lucy added. 'And I am grateful, sir, truly, for your help.'

'Damn!' muttered Nedham. Mary giggled, and he gave her a look of indignant surprise. Lucy took out her purse.

'Nay, nay, nay!' Nedham exclaimed. 'Would you pay me off like a tailor? We'll sit and dine – the *three* of us, dammit!'

He'd ordered a private room at the inn, an upstairs one. A little table next to a window had been laid with the best linen, pewter and glass; two chairs sat across from one another, intimately close. Mary looked at them and raised her eyebrows at Lucy, who lifted her eyes heavenward. Nedham, scowling ferociously, ordered the Sun's serving man to bring another seat.

The dinner was, as Lucy had expected, perfectly sufficient for three, and very good – broth and green sallet; jellied eels and a stewed fowl – though when the serving man brought wine, Nedham snarled at him to take it away. Mary took the lead in the conversation, first commenting on the inn and the Convent Garden neighbourhood, then on the food. Nedham, still angry, replied in grunts and tried to fondle Lucy's knee under the table. She pushed her chair back, out of reach, and chatted pleasantly with Mary.

After the arrival of the main course, though, Mary began on *Mercurius Pragmaticus,* and the conversation became more interesting. 'My husband thinks you the wittiest newsman in London,' she told Nedham, 'but also the most foolish.'

'Foolish?' objected Nedham, stung. 'Aye, I suppose it *is* folly, to tell the truth in such an age as this!'

Mary raised her eyebrows. 'Mr Nedham, we are all of us here engaged in printing the news; let's have no posturing about *truth!*'

'Posturing?' demanded Nedham. 'Perhaps your husband postures, but . . .' He stopped. 'Overton? Of *The Moderate?*'

'Aye.'

It was, Lucy supposed, a sign of how disappointed Nedham had been by Mary's inclusion in the party that he hadn't picked up that detail before. He knew perfectly well that she lodged with the Overtons of *The Moderate*. 'He's a very clever fellow,' Nedham conceded, in a much more natural tone. 'A most devilish Leveller, but writes like an angel.' He smirked. '"The temporary sagacity of opportunity politicians" – I could not have put it better myself. He may consider me a fool for my love to the King, but he's a greater one, for believing that any good will come of trying to put power in the hands of the rascal multitude.'

Lucy broke in with a snort of derision. 'If those who don't love the King are fools, what are you? "Hell's barking cur, that every Monday spent his stick of spleen in venomous railing on the King and Queen."?' Nedham had proudly shown her that response to his previous newsbook in a pamphlet entitled '*Mercurius Britanicus His Welcome to Hell.*'

Nedham brushed the objection aside. 'I never favoured democracy!'

Mary pulled a copy of *Mercurius Pragmaticus* from her apron pocket and held it out for his inspection. 'When Dick calls you foolish,' she said, 'it's for the like of this. "*Seeing honest* John *is got loose,'twill not be long ere* Mr Speaker *and* Nol Cromwell *be both brought to the stake; for he meanes to have about them with some purpose, I can tell you; but especially with* Cromwell."' She tapped the offending words. 'That's a clever man's folly, to believe that all the world but himself is simple.'

'You think to instruct me in politics, do you, Mrs Overton?'

Mary only smiled. 'Nay, you need no instruction there; it's of Levellers that you're ignorant. Parliament voted to renew its addresses to the King and – on the same day! – to free Lieutenant Colonel Lilburne and Major Wildman. I've no doubt *you* understood at once that the second was to hinder Cromwell from interfering with the first. Why do you suppose us so simple as not to understand it too?'

Nedham hesitated, torn between a desire to hear more and reluctance to listen to this most unwelcome guest. He glanced irritably at Lucy. ''Tis a strange world! Loyalty to the rightful King is called treason, and petticoats think to instruct educated men in the ways of Parliaments! It would be laughed at, in a satire.'

Lucy shrugged. 'Why shouldn't you hear news from petticoats? You've sought it from serving-men and ostlers often enough!'

'I've sought it, aye, not had it thrust upon me!' Nedham said sourly.

'Then I'll say no more,' said Mary, putting the paper away.

'Nay, nay!' said Nedham hastily. 'I'll hear you out. You say Honest John will be a friend to Cromwell? After Cromwell left him to starve in the Tower all last year? After Ware?'

'*Friend* is too strong a word – but aye, he has writ Cromwell a letter promising that we will not move against him while he is engaged in the struggle for our liberties.' Mary nodded in satisfaction. 'Ned Sexby is to carry it north. There will be no hurly-burlies in the Army – at least, none of our making.'

'*Our* making, quoth she!' Nedham exclaimed. 'As though a London scribbler's wife might raise up and cast down armies!'

Mary only smiled. 'If by that you mean that Cromwell never feared us, Mr Nedham, then my husband is right, and you *are* a fool.'

Nedham grimaced. Everyone knew that Cromwell did fear Leveller influence in the Army; it was why the Leveller leader had been left to rot in the Tower. 'Well, I thank you for the news,' he said, 'though

I've no doubt that all London will be reading Honest John's letter to Cromwell ere the week's out.'

Mary and Lucy both grinned in concession; it was a hit. John Lilburne never hesitated to rush into print, and never said anything privately if he could distribute it among his supporters.

Just then the Sun's serving-man came in hurriedly and whispered to Nedham, who exclaimed, 'Christ!' and jumped up in alarm. His eyes flew uncertainly to the door.

'They may be out the back,' said the serving-man. 'I've not had time to look.' Nedham grimaced and went to the window.

'I haven't given you your money!' Lucy protested.

Undoing the catch on the window with one hand, Nedham impatiently held out the other to Lucy; she hurriedly fished out her purse and emptied the contents into his palm. It was probably more than she owed, but she wasn't going to make him wait while she counted the change. A few coins tinkled to the floor; Nedham scooped the rest into his own purse, then opened the window and looked down at the street. 'Matt,' he said to the serving-man, 'be a good fellow, and give me a hand.'

Matt at once went over and offered Nedham his hand. Nedham took it – then let go, caught Lucy in his arms and gave her a passionate kiss. 'I pray God your husband gets the plague!' he exclaimed. He went back to Matt, climbed out the window, and, with the servant's help, lowered himself full stretch, then dropped. Lucy, flustered and outraged – such a horrid and blasphemous prayer! – got to the window in time to see him straighten his coat and saunter off.

The door of the dining room flew open, and Gilbert Mabbot, Licensor of the Press and publisher of *The Moderate*, strode in. Close behind him was John Wildman. Matt the serving-man managed to slip silently out the door before it closed.

'Mr Mabbot!' cried Mary in astonished misgiving.

Mabbot gaped at her. Wildman rushed across the room and looked out the window, but Nedham had already disappeared into the crowd. The major turned toward Lucy, his face – still haggard from his time in prison – blotchy with anger. 'Nedham was here!' he said furiously. 'Do you deny it?'

Lucy was suddenly every bit as angry as Wildman. It was instantly clear to her that the intrusion was Wildman's doing, that Mary had said something about the meeting to her husband, who had mentioned it to Wildman, who had gone straight to Gilbert Mabbot. All those months she had visited him in prison, searching out delicacies and bribing the turnkeys, and as soon as he was out, he *attacked* her. 'Aye, he was!' she said recklessly. 'I owed him money, and he insisted I come hither to repay it.'

'Owed him money!' spat Wildman. 'A likely story!'

'Mrs Overton!' Mabbot exclaimed, still staring at Mary. 'What do you here?'

Mary only gasped in dismay. Her employer had just caught her dining with the Licensor's Most Wanted.

The awareness that she'd got her friend into trouble penetrated Lucy's armour of righteous indignation. 'I brought her!' she cried urgently. 'I had no wish to meet Nedham alone, for he's a lecherous knave, so I made Mary swear to say naught of it to you, and brought her with me. She has no love for him, you may be certain, but like a true friend she came rather than leave me to face him alone!' She turned to Wildman. The shame of having got Mary into trouble made her more angry, not less. 'What I cannot see, Major, is why it was any concern of yours!'

'You are my friend's wife,' replied Wildman. 'Should I not care when you dine with a man you yourself term a lecherous knave?'

'Oh, this is *care*, is it?' Lucy cried. 'To bring Mr Mabbot down upon me, and upon poor Mary, who scarcely knew who I was meeting, and only came out of kindness to me?' The full implications of his presence shook her, and she went on furiously, 'This is care? To convict me of a foul sin, without the least ground, without even making any inquiry first, that is *care*, Major?'

'But how do you know Nedham?' demanded Mabbot, more bewildered than angry.

There seemed no point in prevaricating. She could never come up with any lie that would convince him. 'I worked for him for a time,' she said, biting off the words. 'After you had turned me off *The Moderate*, in the middle of winter, when my uncle was newly dead and I had neither house nor money. Nedham offered me work, and I took it.'

Mabbot's jaw dropped. 'You? You print *Pragmaticus*?'

'*Printed* it. Formerly. You've no right to reproach me, sir! You claim to believe in the freedom of the press, yet took the position of Licensor as soon as it was offered you! Aye, and you've abused it, to advantage your own business! My need was far greater than yours, but, unlike you, I was never at ease with hypocrisy! I loathed every malignant lie I was required to print, and got other work as soon as I could. I do not print for Nedham now, nor never shall again. That is the truth, I swear it before God.'

Mabbot continued to look bewildered. He glanced at Mary. 'Knew you that she was Nedham's printer?'

Mary had recovered her wits. She and her husband had both known that Lucy worked for Nedham, and had been glad of the extra money coming into the household. To say so, though, after all the effort Mabbot had put into the hunt for *Pragmaticus*, would be an open affront. 'I knew she worked on a press that was unlicensed,' she said, carefully skirting the issue, 'so I took care to ask no more of it. God He knows that unlicensed printing has given me grief enough, without adding to it.' Mabbot knew that sad story.

'I kept it secret,' Lucy said quickly; she could at least protect Mary. 'Mr Nedham wanted naught to do with the Overtons, and warned me often against speaking to them.' That was true. She glanced at Wildman's blotchy face and added viciously, 'Major Wildman knew, but it seems he kept it to himself so long as he was in prison and relied upon me to bring him comforts – which I could not have done without Mr Nedham's money! Now that he is free, though, and has no more need of my help, what must he do but run to you crying, "If you would arrest that rogue Pragmaticus, Lucy Hudson is meeting him at The Sun!"'

Wildman flushed. 'I feared for your safety and your honour. You'd told me, aye, that you'd quit Nedham's newsbook, so when I gathered you were to dine with him . . .'

'With Mary!' Lucy spat. 'You knew I'd enlisted Mary's help or you knew nothing of it at all! Why would I do that, if I were bent on mischief? If I needed you to guard my honour . . .' She pulled herself up, heart pounding. 'Nay. Say what you mean! You think I have no honour, that I am a weak wayward fool who'll betray her husband for the sake of a dinner at The Sun! What cause did I ever give you to think so poorly of me?'

'Nedham is a malignant rogue,' interrupted Mabbot impatiently, 'and not to be trusted. You should have come to me as soon as you quit him.'

Lucy regarded him a moment with contempt. 'And is that your

notion of honourable behaviour? To take a man's coin, then betray him as soon as you've quit him?'

'He should have been in Newgate long since!' Wildman said hotly.

'For publishing a newsbook?' asked Lucy. 'I can think of no other crime he's charged with! When you call for freedom of the press, Major, you should add, "for us; but Newgate for our opponents"!'

'He is our enemy!' Wildman declared fiercely. 'His clever lies do our cause much harm!'

'So say our enemies of you, Major! Does that mean they were justified in shutting you up in the Fleet?'

Wildman flinched. 'Why did you meet him here? Only tell me that!'

'I've told you! God have mercy, you know I went to Colchester! You know it as well, Mr Mabbot, since Mary left you short-handed when she did my work. Did you think such a journey costs nothing? Or that I had the funds for it, when I'd just spent every penny I had on a press of my own? I went to Mr Nedham because I knew he had a horse, but, as it happened, he was unwilling to lend her, and instead helped me to hire at a livery stable. I was left owing him money, and he insisted I meet him here to repay it. And aye, I *did* suspect his motives. That was why I brought Mary!'

There was a silence. They could see she was telling the truth. Wildman scowled. 'Jamie is a gentleman*!*' he complained. 'His wife should not be in such straits! Lucy, you have kin of your own in London. Could you not have turned to them? Or to Dick Overton? Or to any other man than that knave?'

'I thought Jamie was dying!' Lucy said, then stopped, swallowing; her voice had gone shrill. 'I feared my Stepney cousins would urge me to wait and send a letter,' she went on, struggling to lower it, 'and I'd not time to run about the city begging. Dick and Mary don't have a pound in coin, so Dick would've been bound to pledge goods and come with me, and how could I take him from *The Moderate* when I was already taking Mary? You were in the Fleet. I went to a man I knew had a horse, and soon wished with all my heart I had not! I put myself in debt to him, only to find Jamie in health – and now Jamie is angry with me. I borrowed from my cousins and came here today so that I could pay Nedham and be quit of him. That is what you interfered with! Do you think Jamie will thank you for it?'

'Jamie *knows*?' asked Wildman in astonishment.

'Aye. As I said, he is angry with me – but I doubt he'll be happy with you!'

Mabbot gave Lucy a thoughtful look. 'You could send a message to Nedham.'

'He shifts his press and his lodgings frequently,' she said quickly. 'I've no notion where he might be found now.'

'You might, though, send a message,' said Mabbot. 'Through one of his mercury-women.' He began to smile. 'Invite him to another meeting, to pay the money you owe.'

'I paid it,' she said. 'Just as he left.' She pointed at the spilled coins, still lying on the floor. 'He dropped those in his haste.' She knelt down and began to pick them up.

'Find another excuse, then!' ordered Mabbot, looking at the remains of dinner on the table. 'He'd meet with you eagerly, I've no doubt; he obviously hoped to obtain more from you than money!'

'Would you have me play the whore?' she asked, looking up indignantly.

'Nay, indeed not! We would arrest him the instant he appeared.'

She got to her feet, slipping the coins into her purse, and faced Mabbot squarely. 'I have taken his coin, and he helped me when I was desperate. I will not betray him.'

'Mrs Hudson,' said Mabbot, attempting a stern, magisterial tone that suited him very badly, 'these nice scruples do you no credit. The man is an enemy of our cause, and of the State as well!'

'He is guilty only of unlicensed printing!' replied Lucy. 'If that deserves prison, then all of us here might keep him company!'

Mabbot looked alarmed. 'God forfend! Mrs Hudson, Parliament wants Nedham's head, Cromwell hates him, and our own people detest him. Why should you protect him?'

'I do not, and would not, protect him!' cried Lucy, fighting an urge to burst into tears. Mabbot was the Licensor, and could close down her press. 'I hate his vile *Pragmaticus*! But you are asking me to betray him, a man who has been my benefactor. How can I do that? It would be shameless ingratitude!'

'You should never have accepted him as a benefactor!' cried Wildman in exasperation.

'Oh, that is easily said!' she exclaimed, glaring. 'But, Major, those of us who are not gentlemen with a rank in the Army and a couple of hundred pounds a year find it less easy to pick and choose our benefactors! *You* were glad enough of *my* help while you were in the Fleet!'

Wildman – finally – looked embarrassed.

'So you will not help me?' asked Mabbot.

Lucy ducked a curtsey. 'I cannot, sir, in all conscience I cannot!'

'Well, God damn you!' exclaimed Mabbot, and walked out.

Wildman, still in the room, looked warily at Lucy. 'It is most strange that you should defend Nedham, when you claim to hate him.'

Lucy pressed the back of her hand to her mouth, still struggling not to cry. She had offended the Licensor. She had made an enemy of Gilbert Mabbot, and to engage in unlicensed printing was now out of the question. She would have to sell her press.

'It is most strange,' she choked, 'that after all the kindnesses I've done you, you should ruin me!'

'I've done no such thing!'

Lucy shook her head miserably. 'What will become of my licence to print? Where is my livelihood, Major?'

He stared in dismay. 'I . . . I was trying to protect you!'

Mary came over and took her arm. 'Come!' she said firmly. 'We must go home.' She nodded gravely at Wildman, and escorted Lucy out.

In the street outside The Sun, Lucy began to cry in earnest. Mary put an arm around her shoulders. 'Hush, hush!' she murmured. 'There's no ill here beyond bearing.'

Lucy wiped her nose with the back of a hand. 'I'm sorry,' she said thickly. 'Mary, I'm so sorry! I never thought any harm, but I've made trouble for you with Mr Mabbot.'

'He quitted me of blame,' said Mary. 'Now that I've had time to think on it, I'm sure he would always have been eager to, since he so much relies upon Dick for *The Moderate* – even if you hadn't cleared me by taking all the blame upon yourself.' She gave Lucy a hug. 'It's I who should be sorry. Dick and I *did* connive at your working for Mr Nedham, as you well know, but I let you tell Mr Mabbot otherwise. Oh, my dear! If it were not so grave, I could laugh! The look on Gilbert Mabbot's face when you told him he was a hypocrite!' Despite her assertion that the matter was too grave, she did laugh. 'And when you said we might all justly keep Nedham company in prison, oh, he was like a frightened bullock!' She stopped laughing, though, and went on soberly, 'I fear you're right, though, to think that now he will search out some reason to take away your licence.'

Lucy sniffed and wiped her face again. 'It won't be far to seek.' She'd found two potential customers over the course of the week, one with a treatise on the Book of Revelation, the other with a strange compilation called 'The Burning Bush', an incendiary mixture of religion and radical politics. Both would be called heretical by Parliament, and neither was remotely licensable. 'I must sell my press.'

Mary nodded. 'I fear you're right.' After a moment's silence, she went on, 'If you do that, though, it will satisfy Mr Mabbot; it may even make him a little ashamed – as he should be! He's not a wicked man. He'll pursue you no further.'

Lucy hadn't even thought about that. A really vindictive Licensor could make every printer in London afraid to touch her. She was lucky that Mabbot was only greedy and mildy hypocritical.

'It's a setback,' Mary admitted, 'but not an overthrow. You'll have your money again, and when you make your next attempt, you'll know what you're about and can avoid the pitfalls.'

'Aye, but how am I to save enough to make another attempt?' Lucy said miserably. 'Without I work for Nedham, which I will not do.' She thought, wretchedly, of bald Mr Pecke of the *Diurnall,* and slovenly red-faced Mr White, who owned the press on which Mary printed *The Moderate.* Both were just as lecherous as Nedham, but neither was willing to pay half as much.

'Good!' said Mary emphatically. 'Lucy, dear, even if you can save nothing from your earnings, there's no cause for despair! There are other resources. Your husband can help you, when he comes home from the war, you've a dowry unpaid, there may well be legacies. You should not suppose that you'll have no money unless you earn it!' She squeezed Lucy's shoulder. 'You've always been determined to owe nothing to any man, and I admire that beyond telling – but you're too impatient! Two years ago you'd never even seen a printing press; why should you suppose that if your first venture with one fails, all's lost forever?'

Lucy wiped her nose. There was a lot of truth to what Mary was saying.

'You're young,' Mary continued gently. 'You can afford to wait for better times; and they *must* come, in the end, after so much suffering!

Whatever you do, though, Lucy dear, you must not go back to work for Nedham.'

Lucy looked at her doubtfully, and Mary returned the gaze with a sober certainty. 'He is in love with you.'

Lucy looked away. 'I fear you may be right. He knows that I'm a married woman, but . . .'

'But he does not fear God's vengeance upon adulterers,' said Mary, 'having seen precious little of it, in this world, anyway. Yet it will come, of that I am certain.'

'He isn't an evil man, no more than Gilbert Mabbot,' Lucy said, wondering, even as she spoke, why she was still defending him. 'That is, aye, he sets his profit and his pleasure before his conscience, but there's no real malice in him. He tells lies about us, but, but he believes that he does it for the best. It's not just greed; he's seen the world turned upside down, these last seven years, and it's frightened him, as it's frightened so many others. I do not love him.' As she said it she recognized, with relief, that this was entirely true. The mixture of attraction and exasperation she felt fell a long way short of love. 'He's a mercenary rogue, and I'd no more trust him than a horse-trading gypsy! But he's done nothing that deserves prison.'

'It would be a hard woman that sent a man that loved her to prison,' replied Mary. 'I don't say you were wrong, to answer Mr Mabbot as you did. Treachery is base, and if you'd agreed to do as he wished it would have been false and ungrateful. But you should have nothing more to do with Mr Nedham, for your sake, and your husband's.'

'I know that,' Lucy said. 'I had resolved it already.'

A deep tension went out of Mary's pocked face, the lines on it easing, showing the underlying sweetness that her friends loved and strangers never noticed. Lucy understood that her friend had been afraid that her advice would cause a quarrel, but felt she was bound to give it anyway, because she was afraid that Lucy would be badly hurt.

'It's why I had to pay him off,' she explained.

Mary took a deep breath, then nodded. 'Of course. Forgive me. You'd already said as much. Well, then, I should only add that, what-ever becomes of your business, you need have no fear that Dick and I will ever turn you out. You will have food to eat and a bed to sleep in as long as we have them ourselves.'

Lucy hugged her friend tightly, too moved to speak. Mary was right. What had happened was no ill beyond bearing, so long as she had such friends.

They both returned to the Overtons' house in Coleman Street, though Mary intended only to check on her children before returning to the printworks two doors down. Nine-year-old Faith, who was in charge of her little brother and sister when her parents were out, met them at the door. 'A gentleman came to see you!' she told Lucy. 'Da's taken him to a bull-baiting.'

Lucy's first thought was that it was Nedham; that he'd wanted reassurance that she was all right. She flushed angrily. Couldn't he see that a visit would only make things worse?

'Did he say who he was, sweet?' asked Mary.

'Aye,' agreed Faith. 'He said he was Mr Hudson, but it wasn't true. He had both eyes and both hands.'

'What did he look like?' asked Lucy suspiciously. 'Was he short and dark?' Faith had met Nedham once, but only briefly, and it had been a long time ago.

'Nay! He was very tall, a handsome gentleman in a fine coat! He had a beautiful bay mare, and his servant stood holding her when he came to the door!' Faith liked horses. 'He asked did you lodge here, and I said aye, but you were out; and I fetched Da from the print-works, and they went off to The Whalebone together. Then they came back here, without the lovely mare, and Da told me there was to be a bull-baiting at Moorfields, and he and the gentleman were going to see it.'

Lucy abruptly remembered how Jamie had wanted her to go to Lincolnshire. Maybe the visitor really was a Mr Hudson. 'Did he look anything like my Jamie?' she asked breathlessly.

'Nay!' said Faith, as though Lucy were being very stupid. 'He had both eyes!'

'Is he your Jamie's kinsman?' asked Mary.

'He might be,' said Lucy, feeling a bit sick. She felt utterly unprepared to meet any of Jamie's family, especially now that she'd lost her business. If anyone had asked, she would have said she hoped for help from them; but she found the prospect accepting their help now, when her business had failed and she stood gaping like a silly fool, excruciating.

'I hope there's no trouble at the bull-baiting!' Mary exclaimed worriedly.

Bull- and bear-baiting had been banned in London since the outbreak of the war, but clandestine meetings still took place, their times and locations passed by word of mouth among those who fancied the sport. If the word came to someone in authority, the meetings were likely to broken up by the Watch. Lucy had always found the sport cruel, but Richard Overton loved it, and would chase rumours of a bull-baiting clear across London. She hoped, with Mary, that there was no trouble, and also that Mr Hudson – if the stranger really was a Mr Hudson – actually liked bull-baiting, and wasn't going along just to be polite.

She needn't have worried. Dick Overton, his guest, and his guest's servant, returned to the house at dusk, loud and laughing, smelling of beer and tobacco. 'And here's our Lucy!' Dick told the visitors as they piled in through the door. 'Lucy, this is your brother, Mr Robert Hudson!'

Lucy curtsied respectfully, staring at Robert Hudson in fascination. His face showed her what Jamie must have looked like, before the pistol. The jaw was a little heavier, and the nose a bit broader, but the family resemblence was unmistakable. It was painfully poignant to see Jamie as a handsome man.

Robert stared back; he seemed surprised. 'Mistress . . . Mrs Lucy,' he managed at last. 'You're well met.'

'Where's Mary?' Dick asked, glancing round the kitchen.

'Still at the printworks,' Lucy said, 'finishing the run.'

'I'll fetch her home,' said Dick, and went off to do that.

'Mr . . . Mr Hudson,' said Lucy, after an awkward silence. 'Pray be seated. I trust you will sup with us tonight?' She'd spent the afternoon preparing the meal.

Robert took a seat on the kitchen bench. His servant looked around uncomfortably, then went to stand by the wall, his hat between his hands. In a wealthy household, his master would have been seated in the drawing room and he could have taken his ease in the kitchen.

'Mr Overton has indeed bidden me to supper,' Robert told her uncertainly. 'He's welcomed me very kindly, and seems a good fellow.'

'The Overtons are the kindest friends anyone might have,' Lucy said warmly. 'I thank God for them every day.'

'I've a letter for you,' Robert announced, and began to look for it in his coat pockets.

Her breath caught. 'From Jamie? You've seen him? How does he do?'

'Very ill, by my reckoning!' said Robert, with disapproval. 'Thin as a starved whippet, and very low in spirits. He's been ill with a flux, it seems. Jenkin, where's the letter?'

'Back at the inn, sir,' replied the servant. 'I thought it would be safer there than at the bull-baiting.'

'Run and fetch it, there's a good fellow!'

Jenkin bobbed his head and set off.

The thought of Jamie 'thin as a starved whippet and very low in spirits' was painful. 'Poor Jamie!' she cried anxiously. 'But he's getting better? Colonel Rainsborough said he was getting better!'

'You knew he was ill?'

'Colonel Rainsborough wrote me last week about another matter, a complaint I had made, and said that I was not to fear, that Jamie had been ill but was getting better. I've writ to him, but he's not answered.'

Robert frowned. 'Another matter? This would be that fellow Barker, that Jamie says tried to abduct you?'

'He told you of it? Aye, about that. Colonel Rainsborough wrote, very kindly, to let me know how it had turned out. You say Jamie had a flux? Is he getting better? I've had no word from him for weeks!'

Robert looked at her a moment, then gave a snort of amusement, as though at some private joke. '*He* said he was much recovered. What did Colonel Rainsborough say?'

'That Lieutenant Barker had confessed the deed, and claimed it was naught but a jest.'

Robert frowned. 'When I saw Jamie, he knew nothing of this.'

Lucy hesitated. 'Perhaps his friends thought it unwise to tell him while he was ill. You may see the letter, sir, if you wish.'

She went up to her room and fetched it. When she came down, the Overtons had still not returned. She suspected that Mary was telling Dick all about the disastrous dinner at The Sun, and the couple were agreeing their strategy with Mabbot. She gave Robert Hudson Rainsborough's letter; he read it over, then, scowling, read it again. 'It's clear why the colonel would want this kept from Jamie!' he said, slapping it down on the kitchen table. 'Barker's 'scaped any worse penalty than his master's displeasure! Was it naught but a jest?'

Lucy hesitated, then answered honestly. 'No. Lieutenant Barker meant me harm. When I took alarm and ran away . . . he would have acted differently, if he'd truly been in jest – laughed, or called out to me not to fear, or some such thing. Instead he flew into a rage, chased after me and tried to take me away by force. But what he truly intended, none will ever know. I took no harm, and am content with that.'

'I thank God that you were so wise!' said Robert, scowling. 'Wiser than I was, I fear, for I'd met him and thought him an honest man.' He sighed. 'Jamie said that you took horse and rode to Colchester, to see if what he'd told you was true.'

She flushed. 'Aye. I thought Jamie might be dying, and that . . . that he might die believing me faithless, because Barker would tell him I'd refused to come. But it was a mistake; I should have writ a letter.'

'Jamie said he'd quarrelled with you over your company on the road,' Robert acknowledged. 'And I've never seen a man so sick about anything as he about that quarrel.'

She looked at him sharply, and her brother-in-law smiled. 'It's in his letter, I'm sure,' he promised. 'Lord, is that such good news? My brother is a lucky man.'

Buoyed by the knowledge that Jamie was sorry, she felt able to confront a delicate subject head on. 'I am very glad, sir, that you should think so,' she told him. 'Jamie has spoken of you in his letters, and I know that he loves you well and dearly wishes to remain your friend. I should be very sorry indeed if his marrying me caused a breach between you.'

'That is fairly said,' Robert told her approvingly. 'If we go on as we've begun, sister, I see no reason for there to be any breach at all.'

The Overtons returned from the printworks, Dick frowning, Mary cheerful, and the conversation became more general. It emerged that Robert and his servant were lodging at The Whalebone, not far away. Lucy wondered if they knew that it was a Leveller meeting place. She was trying to think how to ask this tactfully, when all such thoughts went out of her mind: Jenkin returned from the inn with Jamie's letter. Lucy took it aside to read at once.

> *My verie deere,*
> *I am most hartily sorrie that I should ever have been such a Foole as*
> *to quarrell with my deerest Friend, and I muche regret the hastie*

Wordes that greeved you. I have such firm truste in youre Honoure and Faith that I am sure you could passe thro Babel unstained, but I was Jalous. I was angrie, too, because you went to another for Help, and yet in Truth I know that it was I, not you, who deserved the Censure, for I have given you no Help from the daye we were wed. I beg you, forgive one that has been a Foole, but yet loves you with all his harte.

    Yr. Jamie

The impending loss of her press faded into insignificance. She remembered Jamie's grim silence on the road after their quarrel, and suddenly she saw that all that anger had been directed at himself. That was her Jamie: determined always to protect his friends and utterly dismayed that he'd not merely failed to do so, but had lashed out and hurt her.

He was still the man she'd fallen in love with; she still had his love and trust. It again became possible to imagine a happy future, Jamie home from the war, a forge and a press, and everything joyful. She kissed the letter, then looked up to see Robert Hudson watching her with a grin. She grinned back.

Eleven

Deerest Friend,

Your Brother gave me your sweet Letter, which broght me such Joye that nothing cd content me more, I am alle smiles. I am verie sorry that I greeved you, and much repent going to N. for help. Nothing cd make me Happier than to be Friends with you again. Major W. may write you; there was an angrie meeting betwixt us, for he heared I had Appointed to meet N. and mistook me, but he knows now that I met N. onlie to repaye the monie for the Journay, viz £1 3s, so that I shd not be in his Dett; and I broght Mary with me. My Cozens Cotman loaned me the £1 3s; I thoght to repaye them when I hadde solde the Press, which Alas I must, for Mrs Alkin's newsbook failed, but yr Brother has kindly taken that Cost upon himself, and offers besides to paye my Rent until I have Worke again. I hope, tho, to find Worke soone, and not trouble him; and Mary has sayed that I may lodge with them rent or no. Never fear, I will never again print for N. nor have aught to do with him. I went to him onlie to borrow a Horse. I have never loved anie man but you.

I pray God you are recovered from your illnesse, and that this crewel Warre is soon ended, so that you can return to yr loving
Lucy

Jamie finished reading the letter, then touched the paper where Lucy's hand had rested. *I have never loved any man but you.* He looked up into his brother's expectant grin.

'You'll not kiss it?' asked Robert, pretending surprise. 'She kissed yours.'

They were in the headquarters of Fort Rainsborough. Rob had made a detour on his journey back to Lincolnshire to deliver the letter. He'd met Jamie at the regiment's forge, but it had been too noisy there to talk, and anyway he needed a pass from the colonel to continue on his way. They were sitting at the table in the headquarters' main room, waiting for the colonel to return from a meeting of the general staff.

'Thank you, Rob,' Jamie said quietly.

'It's no doing of mine, I promise you! I told you you'd be forgiven at the first kind word, but I was much mistaken. She'd forgiven you with no word at all. She adores you, brother. God knows why.'

God knew why, indeed; Jamie certainly didn't. He looked again at the signature, the dashed *L* and the slanting *y*, imagining the pen in her small ink-stained fingers. The surge of desire was so painful he had to set the letter down, blinking at tears. She was in London, far away, and he was here in Colchester among the damned.

'She looked to be in health,' Robert went on briskly, 'and happily lodged. I'm much easier in my own mind, having met her friends.' He grinned again. 'I'd feared that they were mad levelling Puritans, but Dick Overton's a fine fellow!'

Jamie looked up in confusion. To the authorities, Dick Overton was the very epitome of a 'mad Leveller', and a heretic to boot.

'I'd scarce met him,' Robert continued happily, 'when in comes a friend of his, saying, "Dick! There's to be a bull-baiting over in Moorfields!" and at once he cries, "Mr Hudson, I can offer you some sport!" So off we went, very merrily. The first bull-baiting I've seen these seven years, and a monstrous fine one. There were two dogs killed, brave beasts! Mr Overton was the best of company, a very witty, learned, good-natured gentleman, and as kind a host as any man could wish. His wife, though, seems a sober, decent creature, and she and your Lucy are fast friends.'

Robert presumedly didn't know that Mary Overton had spent time in Bridewell, locked up among the whores. Jamie had no intention of telling him.

'She was not at all what I expected, your Lucy,' Rob went on. 'I'd imagined some proud beauty, accustomed to courtly flattery.'

'What?' exclaimed Jamie, startled out of his misery.

Rob shrugged. 'You'd praised her beauty and said she had many admirers. The fellow you mentioned that she refused – would he be the landlord of The Whalebone?'

'Aye,' said Jamie, surprised again. 'Ned Trebet.'

'I thought as much!' exclaimed Rob, with satisfaction. 'I lodged there – Dick Overton recommended the place, and indeed they made me very comfortable, but the ostler and a serving-maid both warned me not to speak of you to the landlord, because you had stolen his sweetheart.'

'I did not,' said Jamie stiffly. 'I stood aside for Ned, as he asked, and spoke no word of courtship to Lucy until she had refused him.'

'Very scrupulous of you, I am sure,' Rob remarked, raising his eyebrows. 'But tell me, what did Mistress Lucy think of it?'

Jamie shook his head. 'She forgave me.'

Rob gave a snort of laughter. 'Clearly she had her eye on you from the start, and Mr Trebet with his fine big thriving tavern was as nought to her. Nay, I thought to meet some playful little cat, always a-grooming and a-preening. Instead, I found a . . . a peregrine.' He smiled at the conceit. 'A black-eyed falcon, that will bate and bite if you offend her, and would rather have the air under her wings than sit hooded in comfort and ease. The to-do I had to get her to accept money! "Nay," says she, "I've no need of charity." "Come," says I, "'tis duty, not charity, for a man to support his brother's wife while he is at the wars!" "And what says your father to this duty?" says she. I fear my answer to that was halting, and so straightaway she said she'd take no money that had not Father's blessing. I shall tell that to the old man, and see what he says to it! At length we determined that I might justly pay the cost of her journey hither when she thought you were a-dying, as an expense even Father would approve. For the rest she would agree to rely upon me only if her own hands failed her.'

'I fear they already have,' Jamie said bitterly, 'but by my fault, not her own. She says here that she must sell her press.'

'What's this?' asked Rob, taken aback.

'I fear it's so. Here she says only that the newsbook she had contracted to print failed, but when I saw her she was very troubled that her absence would harm it.'

'I remember you said so,' replied Rob, troubled now. 'And now I recall that there was some talk of this at supper, but she made light of it, so I paid little heed.'

'It will have been a great loss to her,' Jamie said heavily. 'She'd put all her legacy from her uncle into it, and all her savings. She should have married Ned! I've brought her nought but loss.'

'I thought to cheer you up!' Rob cried in exasperation. 'I brought you a letter from your wife, who's as sweet a piece as ever I saw in my life, and all afire with love for you. That would cheer me, I promise you! Instead you are as gloomy as ever.' He eyed Jamie suspiciously. 'Are you fretting over Lieutenant Barker?'

'Nay,' said Jamie, quickly. An indignant Philibert Bailey had told him all about Barker's confession and dismissal, but in his depression and exhaustion the result had seemed only what might be expected.

Robert continued to look suspicious. 'You've no mind to revenge yourself? The man assaulted your wife, my sister, and claimed it was but in jest!'

'He's been sent north,' Jamie said.

Robert frowned. 'To Cromwell? I'd heard that he'd lost his place there!'

'Not to Cromwell. To Pontefract, where the castle is besieged – a much less honourable place than that he had.'

'You made inquiry,' Rob observed.

'Only to avoid him. I pledged my word that I'd not seek him out or challenge him. The colonel demanded it, and my wife seconded him.'

Rob grunted. 'Is that what's preying upon you?'

'Nay. I'm sorry, truly!' Jamie said guiltily. 'Rob, I know you've taken pains on my behalf, and I am deeply grateful! It's only that this is a foul place, and to be happy here seems an affront.'

Robert frowned. 'This Army of yours seems in good order!' he protested. 'Better than I expected. I was received very civilly.'

'The Army is in good order,' Jamie said gloomily. 'But—' He stopped; then, pressed by the sheer horror of recent events, went on in a rush, 'Yesterday some women came out of the city – civilians, that had been trapped there since the siege began. The commanders had expelled them, because they'd been clamouring for the city to surrender. They had children with them, sick, starving children, and they begged our leave to pass through the lines and find shelter in the countryside. They said that in yonder city *dead dogs* are sold for twelve shillings apiece, and these poor creatures had nothing left to buy even such foul fare as that! We sent them back to Colchester.'

Robert stared in confusion.

'God have mercy, Rob!' Jamie said, his voice cracking. 'What will become of England? They were women and children, and not even Royalists, but our own, poor starveling wretches that begged us to let them go to the parish poorhouse! The order came: no, they must not pass, lest their passage give ease and comfort to the enemy, and so they were sent back to die of hunger. Rainsborough had a woman that railed at the order stripped naked, to shame her and the others into silence. Rainsborough did that! A man that I'd esteemed above any other in all this Army, a man I know to be as fair and just as any man in England! What have we become? What has this everlasting war done to us? I say "God have mercy", but why should He? We had none!'

Rob was silent. There was a sound of feet in the upstairs corridor above their heads.

'I'd heard none of this,' Rob said at last. He frowned at his brother. 'Jamie, you should quit this Army. It's no place for any man of conscience.'

'Would God I could!' Jamie cried.

One of Rainsborough's staff officers appeared from the stairs at the end of the room, his face flushed. 'What's this talk?' he demanded angrily.

Realizing that they'd been overheard, Jamie got to his feet. 'Ensign Stanley,' he said levelly. 'I spoke to my brother, not to you.'

'Spoke mutinously against your commander!' replied Stanley, glaring. 'What would you have had the colonel do? Disobey the generals' orders? You may grieve for the suffering of Colchester, but those that caused that suffering, and have power to end it are within yonder walls!' He swept an angry hand in the direction of Colchester – a direction that all in the camps were aware of, night and day, however many walls stood in between. ''Twas they who seized the city, and they who've prolonged the siege past all conscience and reason! If the citizens are truly opposed to them, let them open the gates to us – and if they won't, why should we feed them? 'Twould be the same as giving aid to the enemy!' He turned the glare on Robert. 'Did I rightly hear you counselling your brother to desert?'

'Nay,' said Jamie quickly. If the Army believed Robert had been recommending desertion, it would feel free to requisition his horse and send him back to Lincolnshire on foot. 'My brother spoke only of what I should do when this war is ended. And, sir, I spoke no mutiny – unless it be mutiny to pity the wretched.'

Ensign Stanley glared a moment longer, then demanded, 'What do you here at headquarters?'

'My brother, who is visiting, wants a pass.'

Stanley snorted. 'That I can give you.' He went to the box of paper at the end of the table, wrote out a note, signed it, then stamped it with an official seal. 'Take it and be gone!' he ordered, handing it to Robert. 'I'll not have you spread this discontent through the camp.'

Walking back to the stables, Robert asked quietly, 'Have I made trouble for you?'

'No,' said Jamie. 'Rainsborough is not one to punish a man for speaking his mind – and I've no doubt he himself hated what he did yesterday. The orders came from the Generals – that is, from Ireton. Fairfax would never be so ruthless, and in any case, he's ill with the gout. The ensign will hesitate even to mention this to the colonel, in case it draws a rebuke.'

Rob gave a grunt of relief. They trudged on a few steps, and then he said, lowering his voice still further, 'You truly cannot desert, can you? They're sending me off in haste lest I make you discontented. You're of sufficient value to them that if you quit them they would send after you. It would make trouble for your friends.'

Jamie nodded soberly. Rob put a hand on his shoulder and squeezed. 'I am most heartily sorry.'

Jamie caught the hand and pressed it, comforted. 'The war will be over before long,' he said, to reassure Rob and himself. 'Even if we abandoned the siege today and marched north, we'd still be too late to join up with Cromwell before he fights the Scots – indeed, he may have met them already. If he gets the victory, then the war will be over, bar a few strongholds, and I can hope for a discharge.'

'But if the Scots get the victory?' Rob asked doubtfully.

'I doubt they do,' said Jamie.

Rob raised his eyebrows. 'They say Cromwell's ill-provisioned and heavily outnumbered.'

Jamie shrugged. He did not know how to explain that thrill that ran through the Army when Cromwell was there, the way ten thousand minds shifted under the impact of one man's fierce, exultant confidence. He hated the man, but he found it impossible to believe that Cromwell would lose. 'If the Scots do get the victory, I think Parliament will make terms,' he said, conceding the possibility. 'The King will have his own again, and . . . God knows what this Army will do.' Lord General Fairfax, he thought, would submit to orders from King and Parliament, but Cromwell and Ireton would not.

Nor would the Levellers. To fight so long, to suffer so much, only to have Charles Stuart – the man most responsible for all the horrors! – restored to the throne on the same terms as before?

*Oppression, injustice and cruelty are the turning stairs by which he ascends
to his absolute stately majesty and greatness,* John Wildman had written
before his arrest. Jamie contemplated the possibility with anguish.
Monstrous as it was, he still couldn't find in himself the slightest wish
to fight another war to prevent it.

'This foul war will be over before winter,' he told Rob, hoping
desperately that he was telling the truth. 'I can endure till then. You've
brought me much comfort with Lucy's letter.'

When Robert had ridden off, though, he sat in the stables for a
long time, holding Lucy's letter, trying to imagine a future with her
in London and instead seeing only the starving women and children
of Colchester.

Cromwell met the enemy at Preston on the seventeenth of August
– met the English Royalist rearguard first and smashed it before the
Scots even managed to respond. Most of the Scots soldiers were
conscripts, and had never been eager to fight for a King who was
widely expected to renege on his promises. They had no appetite for
a match with Cromwell and the New Model Army, and they fled
south in a retreat that quickly became a rout. 'They are the miserablest
party that ever was,' wrote Cromwell, reporting it. 'I durst engage
myself with 500 fresh horse and 500 nimble foot to destroy them
all.'

News of the victory arrived in Colchester on the twenty-fourth
and was greeted in the camp with delirious uproar. Lord General
Fairfax promptly sent the news to the Royalist commanders; eager
soldiers attached copies of the dispatches to kites and flew them over
the walls, so that the enemy's common soldiers could not be misled.
The city shuddered, and at last the Royalist commanders asked for
terms.

Early in the siege, the terms of surrender had been generous. Now
they were harsh. Common soldiers would be granted quarter – a
bare assurance of their lives. Officers weren't promised even that.
They must surrender 'at mercy', to live or die at the will of the
victors. The Royalist commanders deliberated unhappily, sending
repeatedly to Fairfax for assurances which he refused to give. Their
men grew increasingly angry and mistrustful. There had been a trickle
of desertions throughout the siege, with desperate men letting themselves down from the walls by night and surrendering: these grew

into a stream, then a torrent. The besieged found it far easier to slip away than it had been, for the besiegers had already begun to celebrate their victory.

Jamie had been as relieved as any man in the camp at the news of victory, but he could not share the vindictive glee of his fellows: he kept thinking that Nick would certainly have been in Colchester among the defeated, if he hadn't died at Maidstone. He had no stomach for the celebrations. In consequence he was alone at the forge and stone cold sober when Rainsborough sent for his blacksmiths.

It was the twenty-seventh of August, a cold wet evening. When Jamie answered the summons, he found the colonel in the general headquarters in Lexden, in the upstairs meeting room, along with Colonel Whalley, another senior officer. Rainsborough's expressive face was, for once, grave and reserved.

'Mr Hudson,' said Rainsborough, when an ensign showed him in. 'You are most welcome. Where is Mr Towlend?'

At one of the riotous victory parties, was the honest answer, and by now thoroughly drunk. 'Sir, I know not,' Jamie said, straight-faced.

'This is your blacksmith?' asked Colonel Whalley. 'Christ! Don't you have one with two hands?'

'He is a very skilled, steady and *sober* man,' said Rainsborough reprovingly. 'Mr Hudson, we've had some intelligence which suggests that the enemy may try to break out of the city to the east. Colonel Whalley has ordered measures to prevent them, but he needs smiths, and his man is missing. Pray go with him, and hold yourself under his orders.'

Fort Whalley lay to the east of Colchester, and commanded a bridge over the Colne, which bent southward at that point. Whalley's regiment had been celebrating as enthusiastically as Rainsborough's; the colonel had ordered a halt to the festivities, but many of the men had gone off to the neighbouring villages, where there were taverns and brothels. Because of this, the colonel wanted chains put up along the riverbank, to prevent cavalry from rushing across in the dark. A pile of chains had already been collected, but they were mostly short ones, from wagons and gun mountings, and needed to be joined together. Whalley's blacksmith was nowhere to be found, but the fire had been lit, and there were men to work the bellows. Jamie set to work.

It was about midnight, and he'd come out of the forge to rest a little, when two of Whalley's men turned up with another man held prisoner between them. 'Where's Jones the Smith?' asked one, staring at Jamie doubtfully.

'I know not,' Jamie replied. 'Nor does your colonel, who's borrowed me off Colonel Rainsborough to take his place tonight.'

At this the soldier sniggered. 'I'll wager he's in Molly Standish's house at Elmstead, a-drinking and a-whoring. Well, then, blacksmith, this fellow here wants clapping in irons. He was spotted letting himself down from the wall. He's from the enemy, and we think he may be an officer.' He raised his lantern and shone it over the prisoner, and Jamie saw that it was Greencoat – Colonel Farre, who'd once spared his life.

Farre recognized Jamie in the same instant: he raised his eyebrows and gave a twisted smile. *We think he may be an officer.* They didn't *know.* Jamie could tell them – or not. He felt a curious numbness, as though this were something that had already happened, to someone else. He nodded, went into the forge, and found a box by the wall that held leg irons.

'You!' the first guard ordered, giving the prisoner a shove. 'Take off your boots!'

Farre gave him a cold look, but started to obey, standing on one leg to do so. At once the guard gave him another shove, so that he fell sprawling to the ground. Both soldiers laughed. Jamie said nothing. After such a bitter siege, this was the least that could be expected. Farre, white-faced with rage, sat and pulled the boots off, one after the other. One of the guards picked them up. 'Very good boots!' he remarked appreciatively. 'You *are* an officer, are you not?'

Farre said nothing. The other guard, grinning, said, 'He must be. The common soldiers *ate* their boots last week!'

Jamie slipped the irons over Farre's legs and checked where the rivets should go. Whalley's men were cheerfully discussing whether there would or would not be an attempt by the cavalry to break out of Colchester that night; they thought not, on the grounds that all the horses must have been eaten by now. Jamie looked into the prisoner's face, then deliberately raised a finger to his lips. Farre's eyes brightened with sudden hope. Jamie showed him where the rivets ought to go, then moved each one to the next hole along. Farre began to grin – then bowed his head to conceal his expression from the guards.

Jamie went back to the forge, fetched the medium hammer, and secured the irons at the too-loose setting. Farre kept his head down, saying nothing and meeting no-one's eyes. Jamie finished, then offered the enemy colonel his hand and helped him up. Farre pressed the hand once before letting go, then looked at the guard who had his boots.

'Oh, no!' said the guard, understanding the look. 'These are mine now.'

'*Ours!*' said his friend indignantly.

'They're too fine to sell,' said the first man. 'You may have his coat all to yourself. You! Take your coat off!'

Farre hesitated – then, without a word, took off his coat, and, with a small bow, handed it over. The guard took it with a snort of laughter, and the two men swaggered off with their prisoner shuffling between them.

Jamie went back to the forge. He knew that he ought to feel guilty. Farre was undoubtedly an evildoer who had harmed hundreds of innocents. He'd betrayed his trust in Chelmsford, bringing trouble down on all his friends; he'd led the men of his militia into the horror of Colchester, and likely ruined every one of them; he'd been party to decisions that had caused enormous suffering to the wretched civilians of the town. He ought, by rights, be held to account – but Jamie had set him free, quite possibly to work more mischief. The rash act might well come back to haunt Jamie, too. He could defend himself to some extent by blaming faulty leg irons and an unfamiliar forge – but what if Farre entertained friends with the story? If the tale reached as far as the Army while Jamie was still in it, there'd be a heavy penalty to pay.

Yet Jamie couldn't regret what he'd just done; instead, he felt at peace.

About half an hour later one of Whalley's captains turned up. Jamie set down his hammer, expecting a sharp question about the prisoner's fetters. Instead, the man said cheerfully, 'You can stop that, blacksmith, and go to bed.'

'Sir?' said Jamie in surprise.

The officer grinned. 'It seems the enemy have had a change of plan. Their foot understood that those few who still had horses meant to gallop off, leaving them to suffer our wrath alone. One of them had passed word of the plan to *us,* and now, it seems, all the rest have lined up by the gates and are refusing to let the horsemen pass. The commanders have given in and sent to accept the terms of surrender. In the morning they will open the gates.'

The gates of Colchester were flung open at eight o'clock on the morning of the twenty-eighth of August, nearly eleven weeks after the siege began. The New Model Army marched in, Lord Fairfax and Henry Ireton at its head, and took possession of Colchester castle.

Jamie wasn't with them. He'd gone to bed on the floor of Whalley's forge rather than walk back to Fort Rainsborough in the dark. He woke up when Whalley's men did, but rolled over and went back to sleep. Nobody disturbed him.

In the morning, he set out back to Fort Rainsborough. With extraordinary and absurd aptness, it was a sunny morning. The sentry posts had all been abandoned, and the sound of gunfire had been replaced by the singing of birds. Jamie walked slowly, savouring the light, the green of wet grass and the clean-washed blue of the sky. The siege was over – and he had returned an act of mercy, across the chasm of war. There was still hope.

Twelve

The evening after Robert Hudson left, Lucy was sitting sewing by the kitchen fire with Mary when someone knocked at the door. She heard Dick Overton greeting him: 'Why, Johnnie! You're welcome; come in, come in!' The guest responded in a murmur; Lucy couldn't make out the words, but recognized the voice as John Wildman's. She thrust her needle angrily into the stocking she'd been darning and got to her feet. She did not want to speak to him.

She was too late. Wildman came into the kitchen behind Richard, holding his hat in his hands and looking sheepish. He ducked his head, first to Mary, then to Lucy. 'Mrs Hudson,' he said unhappily, 'I've come to beg your pardon.'

A large part of Lucy wanted to shout at him to get out. She couldn't, of course: it wasn't her house. Wildman was a friend of the Overtons, and had spent many hours sitting in this same kitchen, planning Leveller projects with Dick and with John Lilburne. She couldn't possibly keep up a quarrel with him while she was living here; and, for that matter, he was one of Jamie's most trusted friends. Wildman had cared for Jamie after he was wounded, written his family to ask for money for his support, helped him get work again. She ducked her own head tensely. 'You need not beg, Major. Of course I forgive a man who has been so good and true a friend to my husband.'

Her resentment obviously leaked through. Wildman smiled nervously. 'I see you are still offended. In truth, you are right to be, for I wronged you. I fear that the sudden release from prison corrupted my judgement. All I could think was that now I was free to do all those things I had wished to do while I was confined – and one of those things was to keep my promise to protect a friend's wife. I was so eager that I blundered foolishly, like a man that runs to snatch a teetering wineglass, and oversets the whole table.'

'Wait,' said Lucy, frowning. 'Jamie *asked* you to protect me?'

'When he went to the war,' Wildman agreed. 'Knowing the hazards he faced, and the uncertain situation in which he was obliged to leave you, he asked me to watch out for you and to help you at need. I promised it gladly – but instead of keeping my promise, I soon found myself reliant upon *you*. I was ashamed, that's the truth of it – bitterly ashamed of my own helplessness. I suppose that I leapt upon the first opportunity to prove myself honourable, little caring that in doing so I imputed dishonour to you. I am most heartily sorry for it; I truly do think that the foul air of that miserable place addled my wits, so that I was unable to think clearly.'

Lucy hesitated, still angry, but sympathetic despite herself. The Fleet *was* a horrible place, and to be locked up as Wildman had been, without charge and without any way to fight his sentence, would abrade any mind, let alone one as proud and energetic as his. She'd known that he was growing desperate; she could understand how, in the sudden delirious surprise of his release, he might rush into a stupid action out of sheer relief at being able to act at all. 'I forgive you then,' she said. 'Let's speak no more of it.'

'But we must!' he said earnestly. 'I fear that I have indeed cost you your press, which I know you had laboured long to buy – and with the press, your livelihood.'

'I hope to find other work,' Lucy replied. 'There are a great many presses in London.'

'I hope you will not consider Mr Nedham's!'

So for all his humble words he *still* suspected her! 'No,' she snapped. 'I will not. And, Major, I do not need any more of your *protection*. It's done harm enough already. I trust my own wits will serve me better than any effort of yours!'

Wildman winced and lifted a hand defensively. 'Forgive me! I only feared lest my folly drive you into the very danger you were seeking to escape. Please, let me make amends. Since I've cost you your livelihood, it's only fitting that I should offer you my support in its place.'

She stared in growing indignation. He practically accused her of adultery, got her – and Mary! – into trouble with the Licensor, refused to admit that he'd been mistaken on the spot, when it might have helped – and now he thought he could make everything all right again by offering her money? 'I thank you, no,' she said sharply. 'I can support myself.'

He stared, taken aback.

'Jamie said nothing to me about accepting your protection,' she said, finding a justification he couldn't argue with. 'From what you say, it seems to me that he wanted no more than for you to be a friend I could turn to in need. If I need your help, Major, be certain that I will turn to you – but as to making myself your dependent, it would be a disgrace to my husband were I to do any such thing!'

Wildman flushed. 'I didn't mean . . .'

'Johnnie, give over!' Dick Overton exclaimed, much amused. 'Lord have mercy, what are you thinking of, to offer our Lucy money after you've offended her? You'd have as much luck offering it to Free-born John!'

Wildman looked aghast. John Lilburne's furious scorn of anyone who tried to buy him off was legendary. Dick clapped his friend on the back. 'Let's go down to The Whalebone!' he suggested. 'Your trouble is you've spent too long fasting and fretting in the Fleet. You need some of Ned's good beer.'

When the men had gone, Mary, who'd sat in silence by the kitchen fire throughout, looked up at Lucy with a sly smile. 'And how long will it take before you forgive him properly?'

Lucy sat down beside her and arranged her half-darned stocking on her lap. 'A long time indeed, if he keeps trying to protect me from the likes of Mr Nedham!'

Mary grinned.

'I think he has never seen me as aught but "Jamie's woman",' Lucy continued angrily, threading the needle over and under the coarse wool. 'All those times I visited him in prison, and to him it was a debt to Jamie, which he must repay by protecting Jamie's wayward little wife. I never figured in his mind at all.'

'Most men are thus,' Mary said sympathetically. 'And, indeed, we married women are no more than our husbands' shadows, and have no separate existence in law at all.' Then she smiled smugly and added, 'Dick is unusual.'

'Aye, he is,' Lucy said warmly. She had never seen Dick Overton treat any grown woman as a child in need of protection and guidance. 'I hope Jamie heeds his example!'

Mary grinned again and turned over the child's shirt she had been hemming. 'You've two offers of support now,' she observed. 'Mr Hudson's last night, and now the Major's as well. I do hope you find work soon, or Dick and I will be short of rent.'

'I'm sorry!' exclaimed Lucy, mortified. 'I'd not thought of you. I . . . if I don't find work within the week I'll . . .'

'Oh, hush!' Mary exclaimed equably. 'I'm sure you will find work, as soon as you've sold the press.'

The following morning Gilbert Mabbot called at the Overtons' house. Lucy had been trying to earn her keep by some house-cleaning, and when Faith called her to the door she was dishevelled and clutching a mop. Mabbot recoiled in alarm. Lucy gaped at him, then hastily set the mop aside and stammered that the Overtons were both in the printshop.

'That I know,' said Mabbot, relaxing, 'for I've just come from there. They told me that you mean to sell your press.'

'Aye,' she agreed, flushing a little.

'It's in good working order? Where is it?' When she stared in surprise he continued impatiently, 'I need a second press for *The Moderate.*' Then he smirked and added, 'The one we have cannot keep pace with our sales.'

Pleased with the thought that her press might be used to increase the circulation of *The Moderate,* she took Mabbot to the damp shop on Thames Street. The press still squatted in the middle of the dark little room, a stack of unsold *Impartial Scouts* piled on the tympan. She threw them unceremoniously to the dirty floor, showed Mabbot the machine, and opened up the cases of type for his inspection. He looked everything over, tested the big handle, and finally said, 'Eleven pounds.'

'Twelve,' she replied at once.

They bargained, and eventually settled on eleven and six, with Mabbot responsible for moving the press to its new home.

'Very good!' Mabbot said, with satisfaction. 'There's another matter then, Mrs Wentnor – *Hudson,* I mean. Though you spoke to me very insolently the other day, I am prepared to overlook it, and to offer you a place working this fine press.'

Become a hireling on her own press? For Mabbot, who'd just obliged her to sell it? She gaped, and at last managed an honest, 'Sir, I am amazed!'

Mabbot smirked. 'Well, well. I'm prepared to let bygones be bygones. You're a poor woman with a husband at the wars, and times have been hard for you, I know. Major Wildman has pleaded on your behalf, and Mr and Mrs Overton have said that they'd prefer you to any other helper.'

'I am indebted to them,' said Lucy; then added hastily, 'and to you, sir, of course! What would you have me do?'

Mabbot shrugged. 'What you did before – set type, correct proofs, assemble the sheets and so forth. Mrs Overton will have overall charge of the printing, under Mr White; you will answer to her. I can offer you four and sixpence a week.'

Lucy remembered Nedham's ten shillings with a pang – then determinedly pushed all thought of them from her mind. Four and sixpence was a good wage for a lone woman. She could pay her rent to the Overtons and still have a shilling a week over. True, it would take her a long time to accumulate any savings at that rate – but, as Mary had pointed out, she had time. 'I should be very glad of the place, sir,' she said humbly. 'Sir? Have you anyone in mind to ink, or to work the press?'

'Why?' Mabbot asked suspiciously.

'For *The Impartial Scout* I had a boy to ink, and his simple uncle to work the press. They were content with but a small wage.'

Mabbot brightened. 'Aye? If they'll work for four shillings a week betwixt the two of them, you may hire them again.'

Wat and his Uncle Simmon had, in fact, been happy to work for three and sixpence a week. 'I'll speak to them,' Lucy said neutrally.

She went first to the printshop on Coleman Street. Mary was still setting type for the day's instalment of news.

'Mr Mabbot has just hired me for four and six a week!' Lucy announced.

Mary set down the composing stick and rolled her eyes. 'I told him he should pay you five shillings!'

Lucy burst out laughing and hugged her. 'Why would he pay me what he pays you? Mary, dear *dear* Mary, I am more grateful than I can say. I know this is thanks to you and Dick.'

Mary smiled. 'Only in part. Mr Mabbot has sufficient virtue to know that he had earned your rebukes. Now he can preen and tell himself that he is a forgiving and magnanimous man. But it's true that I told him that I should like above all things to have my sweet friend working beside me.'

Lucy hugged her again.

She wrote Jamie with the good news, then, after some thought, penned a second letter informing Jamie's brother.

Sir,

You were kinde enogh to offer Help and Supporte to mee if I cd not find Worke. I am happie to saye that I have founde Worke alreadie. I am to help my goode Friends Mr and Mrs Overton to print Mr Mabbot's newsbook The Moderate. *I am well pleased with the Worke, and in Especial with the Companie, for I think trulie there are none I hadde rather keep Companie with, excepting onlie yr Brother Jamie. I thank you againe, sir, for yr Kindnesse.*

Yr sister, Lucy

She sent the letters off, spending her first spare sixpence on the postage, then forgot about them, swept up in the news that had to be rushed into *The Moderate's* pages.

At first the war took up most of the newsprint: Cromwell's campaign; the siege of Colchester; the depredations of the Scots; the manoeuvres of the Royalist fleet and the loyal one. The Prince's ships sailed up the Thames as far as the Medway, and London feared an immediate attack – but the wind and the tide prevented a battle, and the Royalists were forced by lack of supplies to return to the Dutch coast.

Then came the news of the battle of Preston. The war was not yet ended, but from that moment the way it would end was inevitable. All the London newsbooks reported the outcome of the siege of Colchester. *Mercurius Pragmaticus* – which Lucy still read when she could, though it enraged her – was full of outrage for the 'martyrs', the Royalist commanders who were summarily executed the evening after the gates were opened.

Against the custom of War *they caused within 4 houres after the* surrender *that incomperable* Paire *of gallant soules (Sir* Charles Lucas *and Sir* George Lisle*) to be shot to death; an act so unsouldier- like, unworthy and barbarous, that it will heap eternal* Infamy *on the heads of their brutish* Executioners.

That 'imcomperable Paire' were the only two actually shot; the noblemen were sent to London to await the judgement of Parliament, while junior officers were given quarter. Even one of the men who had actually been sentenced to death, a Colonel Farre, was found to have escaped before the city fell. The two who were shot – Sir Charles

Lucas and Sir George Lisle – had both previously given their parole not to fight against Parliament, and broken it.

Many members of the Commons, and nearly all the Lords, had been in doubt whether the Army or the Scots was the worst evil. Their faction – fervently Presbyterian and fiercely oligarchic – was now determined to settle the new government before the Army was free to impose something more democratic. Eleven members who'd been impeached by the Army the previous summer were allowed to return and take their seats. They pressed forward with an ordinance establishing a Presbyterian state church; the resolution that no more addresses should be made to the King was repealed, and commissioners were appointed to negotiate.

Everyone knew the form of government the commissioners desired: King Charles restored to the throne with a Presbyterian state church replacing the old episcopacy, and Presbyterian ministers of state replacing the old aristocracy. And it was nightmarishly clear – to Lucy, if not to the negotiators – that any such agreement would be struck down in blood. The Army – independent in religion and Republican in politics – would never accept it.

Sometimes, as her fingers arranged the letters for *The Moderate's* latest instalment of news, she felt physically sick at what she was reporting. Did those idiots really think that men who'd fought for seven years in the name of freedom and common right, men who were in the process of cementing their victory in a second bloody war, would, if confronted by a treaty between Parliament and the King, simply lay down their weapons and go home?

No. The Army was not going to disband itself and surrender its power to Parliament. Lucy was not surprised when Jamie wrote to say that he had applied for a discharge, but had been denied.

Thirteen

Rainsborough's regiment was posted north, to the siege of Pontefract.

The castle had been seized for the King on the first of June, and for most of the summer the Parliamentary forces in the north had been too hard-pressed to take it back. By September, however, Pontefract and Scarborough were the only Royalist strongholds still holding out. A Sir Henry Cholmley had been put in charge of the siege earlier in the summer. First he was sent reinforcements; then, as the month wore on and nothing was achieved, Rainsborough was sent to replace him.

Rainsborough's men did not have the least desire to go. They were deeply aggrieved at being sent off to another siege, particularly with the autumn now drawing on. They also had an eye on political developments in London, and suspected that their own radical regiment was being got out of the way. The colonel, however, was firm. A settlement of the government of England must wait until the war was over, and the sooner they took Pontefract, the sooner that would be. Late in September they set off along the Great North Road.

The wet weather which had added so much to the misery of Colchester had improved, but there had been no repairs to the road since then, and it was a mass of mud, potholes, and deep wheel-ruts; the passage of the regiment's gun wagons did not improve it. Jamie, travelling with the regimental forge among the supply wagons, spent a great deal of time pushing wagons out of holes.

The forge had two wagons, one for the forge itself and the tools, another for the supplies of coal and iron. Each had four horses to pull it, with a soldier assigned to drive and look after the animals. Philibert Bailey managed to get himself put in charge of the little convoy, hoping it would be easier than marching, but was soon cursing himself for his stupidity. In theory the two drivers and the smiths could have sat on the wagons and watched the world go by; in practice they were constantly unloading the wagons to lighten them, helping to double up the horses, heaving and hauling with the rest, then loading up the wagons again. Whenever they arrived at the end of a

day's march, they had to set up the forge and get the fire going to
shoe horses and do the most urgent repairs of wagons and harness
so that the march could continue in the morning. When it grew dark,
Jamie would collapse on to his bedroll, tired beyond feeling, which
was about the only advantage he could see in his position.

No one had said a word to him about Farre's escape. Nobody had
even come to ask him about a nameless deserter who'd slipped his
shackles during the last night of the siege. All the elation he'd felt at
his act of mercy, however, had vanished, crushed under the disappointment of his denied discharge and the prospect of another siege
to come. As the days passed along the road he thought more and
more often of deserting, of running, and finding a ship that was going
somewhere far away, and sending for Lucy once he was safely abroad.
He was so utterly worn out, though, in mind and body, that the effort
required was beyond him.

In the event, Rainsborough didn't make it to Pontefract. When
they reached Doncaster, a day's march away, the colonel sent to Sir
Henry Cholmley announcing that he would arrive the following day.
Cholmley sent back saying that he had been given charge of the siege
by Colonel Lambert, and that to step away from that charge before
the castle fell would be dishonour to him and to the man who
appointed him – particularly if he was to be replaced by Rainsborough,
whose enmity to the ancient government of the land was notorious.
Rainsborough's cannon and engineers would be welcome, but only
if they were to be under Cholmley's command.

Rainsborough was by no means a meek and diffident man, but
he could not take over a siege without the cooperation of the people
maintaining it. The regiment stopped in Doncaster while he and
Cholmley fired off letters, to one another, the high command, and
even to Parliament. The town already had a full garrison of
Cholmley's men and many of Cholmley's sick and injured;
Rainsborough's regiment was obliged to squeeze in where it could.
The colonel and his staff, refused accommodation in the existing
army headquarters, took over Doncaster's largest inn; some of the
men were quartered in the town, and the rest distributed among
the neighbouring villages.

Yorkshire was groaning under the burden of the armies there.
Cromwell himself, with his own forces, was only a few miles away
at Knottingley. The supplies to feed all these men had to be extracted

from a region which had suffered badly in the first war, and Rainsborough's regiment was not welcome.

For the first couple of days in Doncaster Jamie worked steadily alongside Sam Towlend, dealing with the backlog of repairs that had accumulated during the journey north. On the afternoon of the third day, however, they'd completed all the urgent jobs. Jamie picked up one of the less urgent jobs – a dented helmet – but Towlend caught his arm, stopping him.

'Leave it!' ordered Towlend sharply.

Jamie stared at him stupidly. The shorter man frowned up into his face, then took the helmet away. 'You need your rest more than Ned Wilkins needs that pot.'

Jamie blinked, baffled.

'You're worn to bone and rags, man!' Towlend said impatiently. 'You've scarce said three words since we came to Doncaster. The first breath of sickness that strikes us will carry you away. Go on, be off! Have yourself a mug of ale and a dish of meat, if you can find any, and if you can't, have a walk along the river. For my part, I'll put the fire to bed and seek out a friend with a newsbook.'

Jamie bowed his head numbly, then put away his tools and walked out of the forge. He, Towlend and the two wagon-drivers had not been billeted on any of the townsmen. In the cramped and insecure quarters of the town they were obliged to stay with the forge and keep it safe from thieves. This was not really a hardship: the two forge wagons carried panels of wicker and canvas which could be placed between them to form a shed, and the fire kept them dry and warm. This makeshift smithy had been set up behind Doncaster's main church, near the river. When he emerged from it, Jamie found himself looking out at the stream of the Don, sparkling in the sunshine, and trees shedding the last of their russet leaves. The air was cold after the heat of the forge, with that peculiar October brightness that leaves each detail soft-edged and glowing.

He washed the soot off his hands and face with water from the quenching barrel, then followed Towlend's suggestion and set out along the riverbank. He felt heavy and numb; his mind was still at the forge, repeating the steps he had taken to repair a broken axle.

When he came to a bridge he stopped, then sat down on the low wall and stared at the water. He thought of Lucy smiling up at him, then remembered her tear-streaked face after their quarrel. He told himself that she'd forgiven him, but her letter seemed remote and ineffectual beside the memory of her tears. He'd heard nothing from her for weeks. That was only to be expected, while the regiment was on the move, but it left her last words to him hanging in a void, with the meaning slowly leaching away from them. He thought again of the starving women and children at Colchester, and of the one who'd run naked and weeping from the soldiers' jeers. A huge unformed anger seized him: he, who had gone to war for the sake of justice for the oppressed, had become one of the oppressors. He clutched the wall with both hands. The iron brace rang on the stone; he looked down at it in sudden loathing, then fumbled loose the catch and wrenched it off.

Almost he hurled it into the river – but his fingers remembered all the finicky work he'd put into it. He sat there, holding the thing, unable either to throw it away or put it back on – then looked up to see Isaiah Barker riding over the bridge.

He hadn't for a moment forgotten that the lieutenant had been posted to Pontefract. It had troubled him; he had given his word not to seek Barker out or to challenge him, but he'd doubted his own restraint if they ever again met face to face. Barker obviously doubted that as well. When he saw Jamie he reined in his horse sharply, his face paling. Jamie got to his feet.

Barker abruptly clapped his heels to his horse's sides; the animal snorted in alarm and broke into a gallop. Jamie shouted in wordless rage as horse and rider plunged past, then hurled his iron brace at Barker's retreating back. The brace hit, and Barker gave a yelp, but hunched over in the saddle and galloped on, townspeople and off-duty soldiers scattering before him with cries of indignation.

Jamie ran after him a few steps, then gave up and turned back. He searched the dirty street until he found the brace. It was covered in dung, but undamaged, and he took it down to the river, rinsed it off, and dried it carefully on his coat. His heart was beating fast, and he was aware of a surge of energy that felt almost like happiness – how the rascal had run!

There were flecks of rust on the brace, particularly about the hinge and pin, which were hard to dry. He should get some grease on it and let it soak in awhile before he put it on again. He slipped it into his pocket and headed back to the forge.

Towlend was gone, but Philibert Bailey was keeping an eye on the forge. He was seated comfortably on a tussock with his back against a wagon wheel, eating bread and cheese. He greeted Jamie with a smile, waving his bit of bread. 'Want a bite? There's a whole loaf, indoors!'

Jamie went into the forge and found the bread. It was cheat bread, the coarsest variety, made of rye and pease with a generous helping of chaff and mill grit – but it was fresh, and there was more cheese as well, only slightly green. He helped himself and came outdoors to sit with Philibert.

'Sam Towlend fetched it,' Philibert said, then grinned. 'He managed on his own somehow.'

Shopkeepers were understandably reluctant to accept the promissory 'tickets' which were all the Army could usually offer them by way of payment; Towlend normally had more success at overcoming that reluctance when Jamie hulked in the background. Jamie nibbled the bread – cautiously, because of the mill grit – then swallowed. 'You may be off, if you wish,' he told Philibert. 'I'll stay here the afternoon.'

Philibert shook his head. 'I've no wish to be off very far.' He waved an arm at the river. 'I've a mind to see if I can get us some fish for supper!'

Jamie was sitting against the wagon wheel a little while later, re-reading Lucy's letters while Philibert fished, when half a dozen soldiers marched up. Their coats were not the New Model's red, but a mish-mash of colours: they were garrison soldiers – Cholmley's men. Jamie saw them making their way across the church green towards the forge; mildly puzzled, he folded the letters and got up.

'There he is!' cried one who wore an officer's sash. The whole party ran toward him, drawing swords and pistols.

Jamie hurriedly shoved the letters into his coat pocket – and one of the pistols went off. There was a sudden burning pain in his upper right arm; he staggered back in confusion and disbelief.

'Hold there!' yelled the officer, and the whole party closed round him. 'James Hudson? You're under arrest!'

Behind their backs he could see Philibert running towards them. He waved him back, and found another pistol aimed at his head. He put both hands in the air. His arm was burning, and his sleeve was wet. 'What's this?' he demanded furiously.

The officer slapped him across the face. 'No insolence!' he ordered. 'Tom, Jack, get his pistol!'

One of the men promptly seized Jamie's arms and twisted them behind his back; Jamie cried out as the injured arm sent out a fresh blaze of pain. The other man searched his pockets, fishing out the letters and the greasy iron brace. He tossed them aside; the letters fluttered in the light breeze and began to blow away across the yard. Jamie cried out again, tried to struggle free and chase them, then gave up and stood gasping, defeated by the pain in his arm.

'Where's the pistol?' demanded the officer.

'Jesus Christ!' exclaimed Jamie. 'What pistol? My wife's letters!'

'You went for your pistol!'

'I have no pistol! I've not touched one since I was maimed at Naseby! Those are my wife's letters!'

There was a moment of uncomfortable silence. The officer stooped and picked up the brace, looked at Jamie, then tossed it aside. He wiped his fingers nervously on his trousers.

'God damn!' said the one holding Jamie's arms. 'You hit him. He's bleeding.'

'Shut your mouth!' ordered the officer. 'Headquarters can deal with it. March!'

They marched Jamie off with a man holding each arm. He looked back repeatedly; the letters were scattered around the wagons, and Philibert had disappeared.

When they reached the churchyard gate, however, Philibert reappeared with eight or nine others of the regiment. 'There!' he yelled triumphantly, pointing at Jamie and his captors.

Cholmley's men halted, bunching together protectively as the newcomers advanced on them. 'Give way!' cried the officer, sounding nervous now. 'We are arresting this man for an attack on one of our officers!'

'You sons of whores!' exclaimed Philibert indignantly. 'Look what you've done! He's hurt!'

The blood was by this stage dripping from Jamie's hand, and he was feeling faint and queasy; the situation, however, was now perfectly clear to him. 'I did not attack Lieutenant Barker,' he declared, with savage deliberation. 'The coward saw me and ran away. You are arresting me on a false charge. Colonel Rainsborough should know of this.'

'You're coming with us!' exclaimed the officer determinedly, hand on his sword-hilt.

'God have mercy!' Jamie snarled in disgust, 'I'd have come at request! Philibert, tell the colonel!'

'Aye,' agreed Philibert, and ran off.

The men he'd summoned, however, remained. 'You've no right to arrest him,' said one. 'He's none of yours.'

'Get out of our way!' replied the officer.

Jamie closed his eyes; his head was swimming. He felt that it was up to him to stop this before swords were drawn, but he had no idea how. 'For God's dear love,' he said desperately, 'let's not stand wrangling in the street! My arm hurts!'

There was a moment's silence, and then one of Rainsborough's men said decisively, 'He should see a surgeon.'

Rather to Jamie's surprise, the garrison officer abruptly gave way and agreed. Perhaps he saw the surgeon as a compromise, or perhaps his nerve failed. The whole party marched down the road to the riverside warehouse which Rainsborough's regiment had designated a hospital.

There were only a few patients at present, but there was a surgeon on duty. When the procession barged in, he tried to send it out. Cholmley's officer doggedly refused to leave 'the prisoner', and so Rainsborough's men refused as well. 'For Christ's sake, then,' the surgeon said irritably, 'wait outside! We have sick here!' He bundled them out the door, then helped Jamie off with his coat and shirt and examined the wound.

It was a deep, angry gash along the upper right forearm and it was still bleeding freely – but the sight of it filled Jamie with huge relief. The bullet hadn't lodged in his flesh, to be dug out, leaving splinters of lead and bone to fester and rot. It was only a graze. He would heal.

The surgeon was stitching the wound when there was a commotion at the door, and then Rainsborough stalked in, pale with anger, eyes dangerously bright. He paused at the sight of Jamie sitting shirtless and blood-smeared, and cast a look of question at the surgeon.

'A graze from a pistol shot,' said the surgeon, tying off the last stitch. 'With God's blessing it should mend.'

'I thank God for it,' said Rainsborough. 'Mr Hudson. Pray tell me what occurred.'

Jamie drew a deep breath and described his encounter with Barker at the bridge, followed by the arrest by the garrison.

'God give me patience!' Rainsborough exclaimed, striking the heel of one hand against the palm of the other. 'It is not to be borne! An armed band sent to seize one of my men, without the least enquiry made, no reference to the law, no word to me – I'll have him *cashiered!*'

There was another disturbance; a man with a captain's sash came in, closely followed by the officer who'd made the arrest. Rainsborough turned on the first before he could say a word. 'How *dare* you, sir? How *dare* you?'

'I regret that your man was injured,' the captain said sullenly. 'The lieutenant believed he was on the point of drawing a pistol. But let us be clear: your man had attacked one of our officers first!'

'Who says so?' demanded Rainsborough. 'Lieutenant Barker?'

The captain blinked, then nodded cautiously.

'Lieutenant Barker,' Rainsborough said angrily, 'quarrelled with Mr Hudson back in Colchester, lost the duel, and then, unable to stomach defeat, went roundabout to London and assailed Mr Hudson's wife. He says Mr Hudson attacked him?'

The captain scowled. 'I know naught of this.' His tone said he didn't believe any of it, either.

'Do you not? And yet, it was notorious at Colchester! Barker confessed it, and Commissary-General Ireton dismissed him for it.'

This, finally, shook the captain. 'He confessed it?'

'He went to Mrs Hudson, an honest gentlewoman, and told her, falsely, that her husband was hurt near to death and calling for her. He claims it was but a jest, and since she was too wise to do as he wished and go off with him, he was given no punishment worse than dismissal. It is open and acknowledged, I say; if you scorn to take my word, you may ask your own Colonel Cholmley, for I've no doubt that Ireton told him of it! It is scarce surprising that when Barker saw the man he'd wronged on Doncaster bridge, he set heels to his horse and fled in great haste – but that you should simply take his word for it that he'd been attacked, and order violence against a fellow soldier in his defence, without first making the slightest effort either to establish the truth or to settle the matter peaceably – that I should never have believed of any officer in this Army!'

'He was bruised and terrified!' exclaimed the captain. 'He said he was in fear for his life, that this man Hudson had sworn to kill him, and he durst not ride back to Pontefract while his enemy was at large and the town full of his enemy's friends! I thought I was bound to act, to secure the dispatches!'

'And therefore sent six men with swords and pistols against one unarmed blacksmith?' demanded Rainsborough. 'The wicked flee where no man pursues. Mr Hudson had in fact sworn, at my insistence, not to seek Barker out or to challenge him – and for that forbearance he has bled!'

'I'm sorry your man was hurt!' protested the captain, sweating now. 'Lieutenant Perry misjudged . . .'

'No more of that!' cried Rainsborough. 'I'll not hear such baseness, to blame your lieutenant the instant it's clear that the order you gave him was wrong! You, sir, sent him out, with such force, and, I've no doubt, orders to act swiftly against a villain, knowing full well that Mr Hudson is my man . . .'

'Aye, I did know that!' the captain wailed. 'And for that reason I thought I was bound to act swiftly, before you could interfere!'

'And also, it seems, before any magistrate could interfere!' Rainsborough replied. 'Pray, do you fancy yourself king, to order the arrest of a free-born gentleman without warrant? You have erred, sir; you have flouted the law, civil and military both, and by God I will see you punished for it! Where is Lieutenant Barker?'

'Rid back to Pontefract,' said the captain. 'I . . . he abused me! He lied to me! Had I known the circumstances, I . . .'

Rainsborough gave an explosive snort of contempt, and swept a hand in dismissal. 'Out! I'll not hear you longer!'

It was a measure of his force of character that the captain of Doncaster's garrison slunk out at once, head low and shoulders hunched as though he'd been whipped. Rainsborough drew a deep breath and turned back to Jamie. 'Let me see,' he said, his tone suddenly gentle. He took Jamie's wrist and inspected the freshly stitched gash on his upper arm, then looked into his face with sober attention.

'Forgive me,' he said quietly. 'I should have demanded justice against that knave Barker before, and I should have recollected that the man had been sent here. I obliged you to leave the matter in my hands, and then negligently let it slip. I can only beg your pardon.'

Jamie had no idea how to respond. Rainsborough commanded a thousand men, and his position as the Army's highest ranking Leveller meant that he was engaged in politics at the highest level. Jamie had never expected him to devote himself to the affairs of a blacksmith. He gave an awkward shrug with the shoulder of the uninjured arm.

'You asked me for your discharge from this Army,' Rainsborough went on. 'I, knowing not how to replace you, refused, though I had seen that your heart was growing estranged from us . . .'

'No, sir,' Jamie managed breathlessly. 'Not from you, nor this regiment, nor *The Agreement*. It's only that what we wrought at Colchester struck me to the heart. And my wife, sir, has been left alone and unprotected in London, where you know our friends are not safe.'

Rainsborough sighed. 'However that be, you asked me for your discharge, and I, like a hypocrite, refused it, though I have cried out to all my support for *The Agreement*'s demand that no man should be constrained to fight against his will. Well, that throve as it deserved: you will now be so odious to Cholmley's faction that I dare not keep you, besides you'll be unable to work for at least a fortnight. You may have your discharge, Mr Hudson. I will draw up the papers this evening, and see to it that you have money to support you on your journey back to London.'

Jamie stared, unable to believe it. Rainsborough's changeable face became stern, and he added, 'Let Lieutenant Barker alone. If you fight him now, his masters will claim it justifies their defence of him, and it will strengthen their hands. Leave him alone, and I will deal with him as with them.'

Jamie abruptly understood that the colonel meant to use the incident as a lever to dislodge Cholmley. The prospect of getting away, though, was so glorious that he was perfectly willing to leave Barker alone – and he suspected that, this time, the lieutenant would be punished. If that garrison captain were cashiered, he'd make sure that the cause of it suffered something worse.

The strange thing was, he was convinced that this time Barker hadn't even lied. He'd believed what he told the captain: he had genuinely feared for his life. He'd attacked Lucy because he was afraid to face Jamie again. He'd believed he could dodge responsibility for whatever it was he'd had in mind for her, and her trip to Colchester had left him exposed and terrified.

'I am content to leave him,' Jamie whispered. 'I'd sooner see my wife in London than that knave in Pontefract.'

The colonel's face softened again. 'Then go home to your lovely wife, Mr Hudson. You have spent blood enough for the cause; in future, you can help her to spend ink, and I hope you may both be happy.'

The discharge papers arrived at the forge that evening. Jamie was sitting by the fire with Sam Towlend, Philibert Bailey and the wagon-driver, when a regimental messenger delivered a letter formally stating that he was being discharged wounded, together with twenty shillings – a whole pound! – and a ticket for the rest of his arrears of pay. He fully expected the latter to be worthless, but its inclusion reinforced the fact that this was an honourable discharge. He read the letter over and over again by candlelight, unable to believe it, then folded it carefully.

The others were watching him, Towlend with misgiving, Philibert and the driver with envy. Jamie tried to suppress a feeling of guilt at abandoning them. 'He said what passed today would make me odious to Cholmley's faction,' he said defensively, 'besides that I'll not be able to work till my arm's healed.'

Sam sighed. 'No doubt he's right. And, to speak truth, I feared for your health if we were put to another long siege, this time in winter. But I pray God we can get another smith soon!'

Philibert also sighed, then took Jamie's good hand and shook it firmly. 'I wish you all good fortune! We must give you a proper send-off. Tomorrow night, perhaps, when your arm's less sore.'

There were no celebrations the following night, though. Very early next morning Jamie was drowsing on his bedroll, unable to sleep properly because of the pain in his arm, when he was woken by a sudden burst of shouting from somewhere in the town. The noise wasn't from nearby, but the horror in it made him sit up, listening intently. Drums sounded, and then the bells of the neighbouring church began to clamour the alarm. Jamie got up and pulled his boots on, clumsily because of his sore arm. The others had begun to stir and sit up, but he didn't wait for them. He draped his coat over his shoulders and headed out to see what the matter was.

It was still dark, and very cold; the setting moon was nearly at the full. There was frost on the grass, and his breath steamed. The bells were deafening, but he could still make out the shouting in the broken intervals between them. He pulled his coat closer and followed the noise, past the church, past the inn on the marketplace that was

Rainsborough's headquarters. Half a block further on towards the
bridge the street was blocked by a crowd of soldiers, their red coats
unnaturally vivid in the torchlight. Jamie caught the shoulder of the
nearest, and the man turned a frightened face toward him. 'What's
passed?' Jamie asked anxiously.

The bells were still clamouring. 'The colonel,' the soldier began
breathlessly, then stopped, drowned out, and tried again, 'The
colonel . . .'

Someone further towards the centre of the crowd gave a long
shriek of grief and anger, and suddenly men were pressing into one
another to form an aisle, recoiling from some as-yet-invisible horror.
A small group of officers appeared, their faces grim and wet with
tears. They were carrying something on a stretcher. Jamie, with his
injured arm, was among the last to make way for them, and so he
found himself in the front rank looking down at Rainsborough's body.

The colonel was dressed exactly as he had been when he spoke to
Jamie the afternoon before, but his lively, changeable face was still,
his eyes glazed. His head was thrown back, and there was a gaping
wound in his throat. There was blood at the corner of his mouth, and
more blood all over the breast of his coat. Jamie froze in horror;
around him several men cried out. The pall-bearers paced on steadily,
looking neither left nor right.

They marched back to Rainsborough's headquarters. The crowd
broke behind them and followed. At the inn, the officers carried the
body inside, but the crowd stopped at the door. It had grown since
Jamie joined it; it now numbered two or three hundred, almost all
of them Rainsborough's soldiers. More men were running up every
minute, wanting to know what had happened. The bells kept ringing,
making it impossible to speak normally, but phrases swept back and
forth in a clamouring counterpoint: *'The garrison let them in'; 'They
said they had a message from Cromwell'; 'The sentries weren't at their posts';
'Cromwell sent them'.*

There were a few garrison soldiers in the crowd, and suddenly the
rest were snarling at them. They began protesting innocence and
ignorance; Rainsborough's men jostled them, pushing them away. They
retreated hastily, struggling out of the crowd; Jamie thought for a
moment that some of Rainsborough's men would go after them, but
then somebody shouted, 'Rainsborough!' A moment later, everyone
was chanting it, drowning even the bells: 'Rainsborough! Rainsborough!'

One of Rainsborough's captains came to the door and held up his hands for silence. The crowd obeyed, but the bells rang on. The captain said something to one of his fellows, who elbowed his way through the press towards the church. Everyone stood packed together, like cattle in a market, their breath making one great fog. Jamie cradled his sore arm against the jostling. At last the bells stopped.

'Friends!' shouted the captain. 'I beg your patience! It is true – I would God it were not! – it is true that Colonel Rainsborough's been murdered . . .'

A groan, huge and angry; the captain held up his hands again. 'His noble spirit is now with God, who best can cherish it! Who murdered him we know not. Four men were admitted to Doncaster by the garrison. They claimed to be messengers from Cromwell. God forbid it should be true! It will be looked into, I swear to you all, without fear or favouritism . . .'

'Did they give the password?' somebody shouted; and somebody else shouted, 'Where are they?' provoking a vengeful clamour.

Again the captain raised his hands. 'They fled! It may be they have been captured by now, I know not – but if they have, they must be questioned. Those who would silence them are no friends to the colonel! As to the password, it will be looked into, I promise it. Those that are required now will receive orders; for the rest of you, there is nothing to be done by you this night. We have lost the truest and best commander in all England, and we all rue it, and shall do so more in future, I've no doubt. But there is nothing to be done. Go back to your beds. To work injustice upon anyone whatsoever tonight were no memorial for such a gentleman, who ever loved justice better even than his life. Go to your beds! There's nothing to be done.'

The captain went back inside the inn, closing the door behind him. Outside in the street, the crowd shuffled its feet, then began to disperse.

Jamie met up with Sam, Philibert, and the driver, just before he got back to the forge. They all went inside together. Sam lit a rushlight from the banked-down fire, then stood holding it while they looked at one another in silence. Jamie saw that the others were in tears, which was oddly comforting because he was in tears himself.

'God give him rest,' said Philibert, his voice thick. 'We will never see his like again.'

Fourteen

Hundreds of people, *thousands* of people; and all were wearing sea-green ribbons. Most women had theirs pinned to the breast of their gown, but most men had them tied about their forearms, like the tokens soldiers wore into battle to distinguish friend from foe. Lucy supposed that many were, or had been, soldiers.

It was the fourteenth of November, a cold blustery morning. Lucy and the entire Overton family had walked out of London as far as Islington: *The Moderate* had called for 'all the well-affected in London and parts adjacent' to meet the funeral procession of Colonel Rainsborough, 'the never to be forgotten English Champion' and accompany it to the interment. The green ribbons were in token of remembrance.

The circumstances of Rainsborough's death were still murky. It was claimed that the murderers were cavaliers who'd slipped out of besieged Pontefract, that they'd intended to take the colonel prisoner and exchange him for a prominent Royalist. Rainsborough had been killed, it was said, when he refused to come quietly. Questions however, abounded: how had the cavaliers managed to get out of Pontefract and into Doncaster unhindered? Why had the guard commander assigned to Rainsborough's headquarters that night been missing from his place? Why had the murderers claimed that they had a message from Cromwell? How had they been able to escape so easily after the alarm was raised? Levellers inside and outside the Army were pointing the finger of blame at Sir Henry Cholmley, or Cromwell, or both, and the colonel was being acclaimed as a martyr for the Leveller cause. All over London the presses banged out elegies.

Dick Overton had written the appeal in *The Moderate*, but confronted with fields full of green-ribboned citizens, he was as stunned as anyone. 'How many do you suppose are here?' he asked in amazement.

Mary shook her head impatiently – it was impossible to count them – her eyes following her children as they dashed off toward a pond. 'Johnnie!' Mary called to her youngest, who had reached the pond and was leaning over it with a stick. 'Don't! You'll fall in and catch your death!'

Johnnie ignored her. Mary gathered up her skirts and ran after him, arriving just in time.

'Forty thousand signed the petition,' offered Lucy.

There had been a great Leveller petition presented to Parliament on the eleventh of September, with much noise and commotion, but no violence. Parliament had refused to take any notice of it, so on the thirteenth the Levellers had presented a second petition, demanding that the House consider the first one; that time there'd been a riot. That had now been a month ago, though, and the bruises had faded – along with the burst of hope inspired by the House's sullen agreement.

'There's not so many here as that,' said Dick, scanning the fields. He wanted a number to put in *The Moderate*. 'Nor would I hope for it! It's a great deal easier to sign a name to a petition than it is to walk all the way hither on a cold morning. Besides that, we cast our net for signatures much wider than London. That field there.' He pointed to the area to the left of the road, where Mary was now attempting to interest Johnnie in anything other than the pond. 'You count from there to that tree yonder; I'll tell over the same distance on *this* side.' He turned toward the field to the right of the road.

They both counted. 'Eighty-three,' said Lucy.

'A hundred, more or less,' said Dick. 'Call it ninety each.' He proceeded to reckon up how many equivalent patches were covered by the green-ribboned crowd, then grinned. 'Nigh on three thousand souls! Thanks be to God! This is beyond anything I hoped for. You'd think it a hanging, not a funeral!'

Lucy made a face. Hangings regularly drew crowds numbering in the thousands, but she always hated them. Death, in her opinion, ought to be a solemn occasion – and she loathed rowdy lecherous drunks.

Mary returned towing Johnnie, who was now wailing. 'Has there been any word how long we must wait?' she asked, with an anxious glance at the two girls, who were chasing one another across the field.

Dick shrugged. 'Soon. Ten o'clock, I was told, and we were slow on the road—' He stopped abruptly, looking at a stirring on the hill beyond them. 'There!'

'I wanna *catcha fishie!*' wailed Johnnie.

His father scooped the little boy up and deposited him on his shoulders. 'I'll show you nobler game than fish, my darling! When you are a man grown you can tell them of the day you caught the burial of a hero with your own eyes. Yonder they come!'

Over the hill the procession came, marching steadily along the Great North Road towards London. First came a man in black half-armour – the dead man's brother – riding a black charger and carrying a drawn sword, the point reversed; behind him was the carriage with the coffin. Its black draperies were covered with wreaths of rosemary and bay: rosemary for remembrance, bay for victory. Behind it a groom led a riderless horse.

Coaches followed, carrying mainly the wealthier women and children who were following the body to its interment. Dick counted them as they passed; there were fifty-four. Behind the coaches came the men, first the horsemen, then the foot. The procession stretched along the road out of sight.

Lucy couldn't help searching the marchers for one familiar slouching figure, though she knew he would not be there. Rainsborough's regiment was still in the north, its fate undecided – and Jamie's fate seemed to be even more undecided than that of his fellows. Jamie had written to her, and she'd received the letter only two days before.

> *I have my Discharge from the Rgmt, but I am Commanded to a Court Marshall. I met Lieutenant Barker upon Doncaster Bridg, I spake no Worde to him, for he rid off in Haste, but he went to the Captaine of the Garrissoune and begged him to Arrest mee, the whych he did. Col Rainsborowe complayned of this, for it was the daye before his Murther, and soe there must be a Court Marshall to Judge of the Captaine's Right, besides that the Investigation into the Colonel's Murther wishes alsoe to Enquyre into this; for this same Captaine Rokeby allowed the Murtherers into the Towne and did Nought to hinder their Escape. And soe I know nott when I shall have Leave to Come to You, butt I beg you Beleeve I think of you Nighte and Daye, and long onlie to be on the Road to Lundun.*

Most of the letter had been about Rainsborough's murder, and said things she'd heard from Leveller sources already. She wished Jamie had said less about that and more about his own situation: she was very worried about him. It sounded as though he were under arrest, and she kept imagining him shivering in some freezing prison. True, it also sounded as though the court martial was to try this captain, Rokeby, not Jamie, but if it acquitted the captain, didn't that mean Jamie would be condemned? She wanted to ask Wildman about it – as a law-trained ex-Army officer he was sure to know – but he was involved in the Leveller discussions with the Army, which were taking place at St Albans.

Perhaps, she thought hopefully, Wildman had come back to London for the funeral. The last of the men who'd followed the coaches was marching past, and the crowd began to fall in behind them. She joined them.

They entered the City at Smithfield, an endless river of sea-green badges, then followed the main roads as far as St Paul's. Citizens came out of shops and houses and lined the streets to see them pass, whispering to one another. Some joined them, and the procession grew longer and longer.

At St Paul's the Overton children began to droop, their teeth chattering from the cold. Mary took them off home, but Dick and Lucy followed the coffin on, through the City, then out along the Thames to Wapping. Rainsborough had been born there, and there in the parish church he was buried. The preacher gave a sermon on the text 'Believers shall at last appear glorious'. Most of the congregation, shivering outside the church in the cold, couldn't hear a word he said, but when he declared 'Amen to the righteous sentence Christ shall pass upon all treacherous and bloody murderers!' the phrase was passed through the crowd in a ripple of whispers, and a sudden thunder of 'Amen!' broke out. The Tower of London – which was in the keeping of men from the Army – fired a salute, as though the dead man had been a prince.

It was dusk by the time Lucy returned to the house on Coleman Street. She was alone. Dick had met some other prominent Levellers at the church and gone off with them. The Leveller leaders had all been exhilarated. Forty thousand names on a petition might be impressive, but it was abstract, and many scoffed at it; that river of sea-green ribbons had made Leveller strength visible to all London. Lucy, too, felt profoundly thrilled, partly from hope and partly just because she had set the type that summoned many of those people. She was used to printing presses now, but sometimes they still seemed magical.

The cold day, though, was growing even colder as night fell, and a day walking about London in the wind had left her chilled through and very hungry. She opened the street door hurriedly – then froze. There were men's voices sounding from the kitchen.

She'd had no conscious anxiety that the Leveller show of strength would draw reprisals, but the awareness of that possibility suddenly showed itself as something that had underlain her thoughts all day. She stood motionless in the hall, hand still on the latch of the open door. What was her best course? To turn and run before anyone noticed her, so as to find Dick and warn him? Or to go on in, and give poor Mary all the help and support she could?

'Lucy?' came Mary's voice from the kitchen. There was no strain in it. She sounded serene and cheerful, and Lucy drew a deep shuddering breath of relief. Whoever the visitors were, they weren't enemies. She closed the door behind her. 'Aye,' she said, and went on in.

The men in the kitchen were Robert Hudson and his servant Jenkin. Rob got to his feet and welcomed Lucy with a broad smile. 'Sister Lucy!'

The smile she returned was flustered and a trifle forced. Her heart was still pounding from the moment of terror in the doorway. 'You are very welcome, sir!' she said, trying to make up for it. 'I hope you have not been waiting long?'

Rob waved that off. 'We settled ourselves at the inn, and came hither perhaps an hour gone. Mrs Overton tells me you have been at the burial of Colonel Rainsborough, that was Jamie's commander.'

Lucy nodded. Mary glanced at the closed door behind Lucy and asked, 'Did Dick meet with friends?'

'Aye,' agreed Lucy. 'With Honest John, and Will Walwyn and Max Petty. I think they were off to The Nag's Head.'

Mary smiled at Rob. 'I feared it would be thus, sir. My husband's defence must be that he did not know you would be here.'

Rob ducked his head. 'Indeed, mistress, I've arrived unheralded and uninvited, for which I can only apologize again. I pray you, let me make amends by buying supper for the household.'

'That's kind,' said Mary, with a warm smile. 'I've been busy all the day, and had no opportunity to cook anything suitable for a gentleman such as yourself. Faith! Show Mr Hudson's servant round to Tom Grady's cookshop.'

'I'd thought to take you to my inn,' said Rob, taken aback.

'But you're at The Whalebone again, are you not? They'll be run off their feet there tonight just to keep the beer flowing. I doubt they serve supper at all!'

'Indeed? What's the occasion?'

'Why, Colonel Rainsborough's funeral!' Mary's face lit, and she went on eagerly, 'But you must have arrived too late for that. It was a glorious sight. There were *thousands* to mourn him, and more than fifty coaches! Every well-affected person in London will want to meet together to talk of it – and many of them will be at The Whalebone.'

Rob looked confused.

'Did you not know that The Whalebone is one of our meeting places?' Lucy asked him.

'*Our?*' Rob repeated; then, frowning, 'Do you mean Leveller?'

The eagerness on Mary's face went back to surprise. 'That is what others call us. I thought, sir, that you knew. Did my husband never speak of it?'

'Nay,' said Rob. He hesitated. 'And was Colonel Rainsborough a Leveller, too?'

Mary and Lucy stared; even Faith stared, astonished by such ignorance.

'I see,' Rob said grimly. 'I knew that my brother was long of this faction, but he said he would give up his adherence to it.'

Lucy gazed at him in shock, not knowing what to make of this. 'Jamie promised you that he'd abandon us?' she asked at last.

Rob grimaced. '*Abandon* is a harsh word, and beyond question he has no intention of abandoning you, Sister Lucy. As for your faction, he made it plain he still believes in the justice of this cause, but he agreed to give over pressing it, so as to have peace with his kin.'

'He said nought of this to me!' Lucy protested. How could Jamie make such a promise? How could he make such a promise on her behalf? If he gave up fighting for the Leveller cause, his family would certainly expect her to do the same.

'I imagine the sight of you drove all such matters from his mind!' Rob said, with half-hearted gallantry, then sighed. 'I'd not known this, about his commander being of the same faction – yet I suppose he was required to serve where he was posted. I'm sure that if he'd been free he would have left the Army altogether.'

Lucy suddenly understood that Rob was trying to convince himself that Jamie hadn't lied to him; she hoped, savagely, that he had. 'He surely told you that I am a Leveller!' she said.

Rob nodded glumly. 'I had understood as much – but you're a woman. I am sure you will be obedient to your husband.' He hesitated again, then went on, with sudden resolution, 'He did say that all the ill I've heard of this faction was lies, and, indeed, from aught I've seen and heard he spoke truth! I've seen none of the evils that others cry out against. But our father will never be reconciled to such new-fangled opinions, never! And if Jamie wishes to be at peace with him, he must let this adherence drop.'

Lucy glared in indignation and fear. Mary took her arm and leaned over to whisper into her ear, 'Say nothing you'll regret!'

Lucy let out a breath and nodded slowly. It was clear that even Rob now had doubts about what this promise had actually meant. She should listen to what Jamie had to say about it before she spoke out. 'I know that Jamie greatly desires to be friends with his kin again,' she said neutrally. Her heart sank: that was certainly true.

'And they with him!' Rob said forcefully. 'Which, as it happens, is the matter I've come to talk about. But there's no cause to talk on an empty stomach; let's send to this cookshop you spoke of.'

He gave his purse to his servant with orders to accompany Faith to the cookshop; they went out and presently came back with good wheat bread, a pot of broth, and some braised kidneys. Lucy and Mary had meanwhile cleared the papers off the kitchen table and set out the good beeswax candles. They all sat down to the meal together. The children ate with relish. It was much finer food than they normally had for supper. Lucy, however, picked at her portion, despite having been so hungry earlier. Fear of what the Hudson family might be about to propose for her had completely killed her appetite.

When the meal was over, Rob leaned his elbows on the tabletop and smiled at Lucy. 'I must apologize again for arriving so suddenly. The truth is that it was my father's place to write to you, and I feared he might say something to offend. He's used to his own ways and slow to change them, and he is still deeply grieved for my brother Nick. He lashes out at all the parties he blames for Nick's death, and you were of a faction he numbers among them.'

It was only because Rob had identified 'Nick' as 'my brother' that Lucy remembered who he was. Jamie had only mentioned him once, briefly, in a letter months before. Killed at Maidstone, she recalled. Jamie hadn't said which side he'd been fighting for, and she'd simply assumed Parliament. Now she understood otherwise.

'He is not unkind, though,' Rob continued. 'I told him how you are situated, and what you'd said, that you would take no money that had not his blessing, and it shamed him. When I showed him your last letter, that said you had work with your friends, he fretted that you were obliged to rely upon their kindness rather than our duty. Then there was – well, I'll tell you of it later; what concerns is that at last he said that it was not fitting that his son's wife should be left unsupported in London, and he agreed that I should come hither and bring you home!' He beamed.

Lucy swallowed sickly. It was what she'd feared: she was supposed to leave her work and her friends, lose all her hard-won independence, and rely instead on the charity of Jamie's horrible old father – and be grateful for it! It was clear, too, that Rob had worked hard to get the old man to make this offer. Turning it down would cause deep offence. She might be able to shrug off their displeasure, but Jamie wouldn't.

She thought of the green-ribboned crowd she'd been part of that morning, and the exhiliration of knowing that she had helped to raise it. She remembered all the outrageous injustices Parliament had inflicted on her friends, and ached at the thought that in future she would be able to do nothing to help. She thought, too, of the money under her bed, the brief weeks she'd been mistress of her own press, her daydreams of being so again. What was there for her in Lincolnshire? Her life was here, in London!

Faith Overton, who'd been listening to this with a frown of alarm, exclaimed suddenly, 'You can't take Lucy away!'

'Hush!' said Mary reprovingly. 'Lucy is a married woman, Faith; she must do as her husband wishes.'

As her husband wishes. With a flood of relief, Lucy remembered that she had a way out, if not one that would please Faith Overton. 'But Jamie will be coming *here!*' she exclaimed. 'He's been discharged from the Army. Had you not heard yet?'

Rob sat up straight. 'What? No, I'd heard nothing!'

'I had the letter two days ago,' Lucy said. 'I'll fetch it.'

She ran upstairs, desperately glad of the worrying letter. Nobody could blame her for staying in London to wait for her husband! She pushed from her mind the fear that the reprieve was only temporary, and that when Jamie did arrive he would expect her to move to Lincolnshire with him. She could argue with him then. There was no point borrowing trouble from the future.

'Here it is,' she said, returning to the kitchen with the folded paper. 'I'm sure he must have writ you, too, but likely the letter missed you on the road.'

Rob read the letter over slowly, frowning. 'Barker again!' he exclaimed. 'By God, that rogue haunts us like an ill deed!' His jaw set. 'Is it true, do you think, that Jamie spoke no word to him?'

'I know no more than what he says there, sir,' Lucy replied, 'but I cannot think Jamie would have writ me a bare-faced lie.'

'No,' agreed Rob, embarrassed. 'Forgive me. So this sudden shameful arrest is down to what he told me of, a struggle within your Army between your faction and Cromwell's?'

'It must be,' Lucy agreed. 'Certainly all the world now knows that Sir Henry Cholmley hated Colonel Rainsborough. It's said that when they brought him news of the murder, he laughed.'

'Where does Jamie say that?' asked Rob in confusion.

It was Mary who answered. 'Every newsbook in London had an account, Mr Hudson. If you care to read of it, I have that writ by my husband last week.'

Rob shook his head. 'I am behind the times, it seems. If the matter's so notorious as that, then even Father must accept that poor Jamie was caught up in it willy-nilly.'

'I am very troubled about this court martial,' Lucy confessed. 'It sounds as though it is to try this Captain Rokeby, because he had no right to order Jamie arrested – but I fear what might happen if the captain's acquitted. And who will defend Jamie, with Colonel Rainsborough dead?'

'Who indeed?' asked Rob, now looking worried. 'You know no more than what's set down here?'

Lucy nodded. 'I hope to ask Jamie's friend Major Wildman, who will know how the law stands – but he's from London at present.'

'I remember a Captain Wildman, who writ us after Jamie was wounded,' said Rob. 'This is the same man? Is he still with the Army?'

Lucy shook her head. 'He quit it summer before last.'

'So Jamie has no interest in the Army he might call upon?' asked Rob.

Lucy blinked. She hadn't considered Wildman in that light. 'I . . . I should think he has friends in his regiment . . .' she faltered.

Rob snorted. 'They did little enough for him when he was ill! And when I saw him last, he seemed disaffected from all his officers but Rainsborough, while they had little trust of him. He says here he's been discharged. How likely is it that those who neglected him before will exert themselves on his behalf now?'

Lucy stared. She'd been worried before; now she was getting really frightened. 'He . . . he wrote as though he soon hoped to have leave to go!' she protested.

'He would be bound to put a brave face upon it for you,' Rob said dismissively. 'Any man will strive to keep his wife from fretting for him.' He thought a moment. 'What funds has he?'

The silence that greeted this was its answer. 'None?' asked Rob in dismay.

'Your father, sir, gave him an allowance,' said Lucy. 'I was very glad of it. The Army scarcely sees its pay one week out of twenty, and of late, I think, not at all.'

Rob swallowed. 'Father stopped Jamie's allowance after he rejoined the Army and . . . and . . . ahhh . . .'

'Wed me,' finished Lucy. Jamie had never mentioned that, but it was easy to guess. 'Oh, God have mercy!'

'God help him!' exclaimed Rob in horror.

Mary stirred. 'I cannot think he is without friends,' she said. 'Colonel Rainsborough's regiment is full of our friends!'

'But I had required him to break off his adherence to your levelling "friends",' Rob said unhappily. 'It's no good: he is certainly penniless, and probably at the mercy of his enemies. He may have written to me begging for help – I'd know nothing of it if he had!' He ran a weary hand through his hair. 'I will start for the north tomorrow.' He got to his feet. 'Sister Lucy, I had hoped to bring you back to Bourne with me, but it seems you must remain here a little longer.'

Lucy ducked both her head and a direct response. 'I am very glad that you can go to Jamie's aid,' she said instead. 'With all my heart I thank you, sir! I do not know how he does, but I am quite certain he will do much better for your coming.'

Rob gave her a tired smile and took her hand. 'The more I see of you, Sister, the more I approve Jamie's choice. God keep you well until we meet again.'

When Rob and his servant had left, Faith came over to Lucy and stared earnestly into her face. She was a solemn child, weighed down by her responsibility for her younger brother and sister, which had struck her cruelly when her parents were both in prison. She and Lucy shared a bed, though, and Lucy often succeeded in making her giggle with some titbit of news or an old country-tale. 'Do you want to go away?' she asked now.

Lucy hugged her. 'Oh, Faith, sweet! I love you dearly, but you know I am only here because my husband is at the wars.'

'Do you love him?' asked Faith.

'Aye,' said Lucy – though a part of her wondered whether it was true. The burning conviction with which she'd begun the marriage had cooled under the cold airs of distance and ignorance. A large part of her now wished that she could just stay with the Overtons – living as Faith's aunt and Mary's younger sister, working on the press and sharing her bed with no one but this solemn child.

'I married him,' she told Faith – and herself. 'Once he returns I could not stay here even if we continue in London.'

'But I want you to stay here!' cried Faith rebelliously. 'We love you, too! Why does his love matter more?'

'That's enough, Faith,' Mary said sharply. 'God himself joins man and wife into one flesh, and none may sunder them. Time for bed.'

'But Mr Hudson's done *nothing* for Lucy all this year!' protested Faith. 'We've been all her family! And she doesn't *want* to go; you know she doesn't!'

'Fie on you!' replied Mary severely. 'For shame, Faith, to wish an honest wife parted from her husband! To bed with you at once!'

Mary took Faith upstairs, settled her and the younger two, and listened to them as they said their prayers. When she came downstairs again Lucy was finishing the washing up.

'What will you do?' Mary asked quietly.

Lucy bit her lip. 'What can I do? For me to ride north would slow Mr Robert, and give no help to Jamie!'

'That was not what I meant.'

Lucy looked down; she knew what Mary meant. 'What *can* I do?' she repeated miserably. 'If he has promised to forswear the cause for the sake of peace with his father, and if he decides to take me back to his father's house . . .' She looked up. 'It would go much against my heart. I suppose I would beg him to think again.'

Mary let out a *huh* of acknowledgement and sat down at the cleared table. 'Did you ever meet John Wildman's wife Frances?' she asked after a minute.

'No,' said Lucy, startled. 'I know she and her kin were of the King's party, and it caused a quarrel.'

'She's a Papist,' said Mary.

Lucy goggled. Everyone she knew spoke of the Church of Rome as an oppressive, idolatrous tyranny – the Whore of Babylon, drunk on the blood of the saints. She'd never met a Papist, though, to talk to. 'Did he know what she was when he wed her?' she asked.

'Aye,' said Mary. 'And the troubles of the state had begun then, though it hadn't yet come to war. The Major has always been for toleration, of course, and I suppose in his eyes that justifies him – yet I think that if he'd told her and her friends plainly, "I am for Parliament and common right", there would have been no marriage. Still, she *did* marry him, and when the war began she could not understand why her husband must take up arms for the party that most hated those of her religion. She begged him to remain neutral, at the least, and when he refused, she was bitterly hurt, and went back to her kin. For this she has the name of a scolding shrew, but I met her once, when she came to see her husband on some business. She was a soft-spoken gentlewoman, and very sad.'

Lucy was silent.

'Men expect their wives to follow their opinions,' Mary said. 'A woman who presumes to disagree with her husband is condemned by all. Do you think I was a Leveller when first I met Dick?'

Lucy stared at her friend, now shocked.

'Oh, I am *now,*' Mary said wearily. 'And for that matter, Dick wasn't one when we wed, for there was no such thing. I walked beside him as he followed that road, and agreed with him at each turning of the way. If I'd known how much it would cost us, I might have dug my heels in – but I didn't, and here we are. What I mean to say, though, is, if your Jamie truly has given up the cause, you have no choice but to surrender it as well. Poor Mrs Wildman at least has wealthy kin who are willing to give her support and protection. Your kin, by all you've said of them, would straightway tell you to go back and obey your husband.'

'I . . . I could work . . .'

Mary shook her head. 'Where? Do you think Mr Mabbot would employ you against your husband's wishes? I promise you, he wouldn't; a scandal on his press could cost him his Licensorship. Dick *would* let you stay here, out of pity – and, oh, how we all would rue it! A married woman lodging with family friends while her husband's at the war is one thing; a woman who's left her husband to live in the house of a leader of the faction she adheres to – that's another. To speak plainly, they'd call you Dick's whore, and me Dick's cast-off. We would be spat upon in the street – aye, even the children would suffer for it!'

Lucy pressed the heels of her hands against her eyes, which were burning. Mary was right, of course. She had no choice but to obey her husband. For the first time she wished whole-heartedly that she had never married.

'Jamie's brother m-may have heard what he wanted to hear!' she stammered at last. 'I think he fears that he did. When I speak to Jamie, I . . . I may well find him of my mind!'

Mary nodded. 'It's likely true that your new brother heard what he wanted to. But it's a bitter thing thing to be sundered from your kin. Your Jamie has suffered much in the wars, and it's not to be wondered at if he wishes to have peace at last.'

'Peace at the cost of accepting injustice?'

'And was it *justice* that killed my baby?' Mary demanded, her voice suddenly cracking. 'The cost of *fighting* injustice is no pittance! I've paid it in flesh and blood – and so has your Jamie. If he feels he can pay no more, who are you to tell him he must? Don't quarrel with him, Lucy; for God's love, don't quarrel! By all means tell him your wishes, but listen to what he has to say, as well! If he wants to go home, go with him peaceably. Owning a press in London might be a fine thing – but it's not worth the breaking of your marriage or anybody's heart.'

Lucy began to cry. 'It's all *wrong!*' she said thickly. 'Why must I choose? *Men* don't have to choose!'

Mary suddenly hugged her. 'The world is full of wrongs. We fight those we can, but the rest we must endure. Our consolation must be that this sad life is but a vapour, and soon gone. The only things which endure are faith, and hope, and love.'

Fifteen

Jamie had intended to follow Rainsborough's coffin to London. This was only partly out of respect for the murdered man: the journey would be easier and much cheaper if he could make it in company, sharing food and quarters with others. The twenty shillings he had been given might be more money that most soldiers had seen all year, but it wouldn't pay his keep all the way to London. He went to the assembly point in Doncaster market on the morning the cortege set out – only to have the captain who was organizing it tell him he had to remain in the town.

'Sir,' Jamie said politely, 'Colonel Rainsborough discharged me from the Army, and it was my intention to follow his body to its burial.'

'You'll be needed to bear witness against that scoundrel Rokeby,' replied the captain. He frowned. 'Have you no wish to see justice done?'

'Sir,' Jamie said, more sharply, 'I have barely money enough to carry me home if I travel with these others. I have no more entitlement to free quarter, and until my wound heals I cannot work. Must I starve for the sake of Captain Rokeby's trial?'

'I'll see to your support until the hearing!' the captain said impatiently. 'But you must remain here. The Army may have discharged you, but it can still command your attendance in court.'

It was clear to Jamie that he couldn't tag along with the cortege when the man in charge of it forbade him to. Still, he knew better than to trust a mere verbal promise of support, and dug in his heels until he got a formal written order.

The order didn't produce any money, of course: the regiment had no money. Jamie was quite certain that the twenty shillings Rainsborough had given him had come out of the colonel's own pocket, and he was determined not to spend it on anything but the journey home. No, the order was merely to protect him from possible charges of theft for continuing to eat. He went back to the forge. His fellows commiserated, gave him his bed back, and shared whatever food they were able to extract from the wretched citizens.

It was not clear what would happen to the regiment. Nobody was so stupid as to suggest that it should serve under Sir Henry Cholmley, but without Rainsborough there would be no taking over the siege of Pontefract in Cholmley's place. Everyone expected that soon they would be posted elsewhere. Cromwell's forces at Knottingley made their own presence in the north redundant anyway. In the meantime they idled about Doncaster, feeding off the citizens, fighting with the garrison, and endlessly arguing about the circumstances of the murder.

There was, as promised, an investigation. It went quickly at first. The sentinel on the bridge had been pistolled; the servants at the inn, who had witnessed some of the events, confirmed that what had happened was a kidnapping-gone-wrong; the officer in charge of Rainsborough's own few sentries was found to have spent the night in a whorehouse – he fled before he could be questioned. After the funeral cortege left, however, the investigation stalled. No progress could be made without questioning Cholmley's people, but this was something Cholmley refused to permit. He offered to take charge of the investigation instead, and was indignant when Rainsborough's men angrily rejected the suggestion. The impasse was broken, however, after the letters sent post-haste to London resulted in Parliament voting to set Lieutenant-General Cromwell in charge.

Rainsborough's men were furious. Nobody had forgotten that the murderers had claimed to be bringing a message from Cromwell, and as far as the regiment was concerned he was one of the prime suspects. They were still discussing what to do when Cromwell descended on Doncaster like a hailstorm. He arrested Captain Rokeby, turned Rokeby's staff out of the town's military headquarters, stood down the garrison and replaced it with his own men, and ordered Rainsborough's officers to present themselves at once, together with all the evidence they'd assembled.

That took up the first day. The following morning, Cromwell sent for Jamie.

Jamie followed the messenger to the fine old mansion that had, until two days before, been the headquarters of Captain Rokeby. His escort exchanged a few words with the sentries, then led him into the stone-flagged hall. There were doors to each side; a murmur of voices came from behind the door on the right, and the escort knocked and went in, leaving Jamie to wait.

Jamie leaned wearily against the wall, cradling his wounded arm.

It was nearly two weeks now since he'd received the injury, but the cut wasn't healing. It was inflamed and leaked pus; it kept him awake at night, and he had little appetite. He had never recovered either the weight or the strength he'd had before the bout of flux, and his exhausted body lacked the resources to heal. He ached to get this miserable business over with so he could go home.

At last the messenger who'd fetched him came back, nodded, and held open the door.

The room beyond was a dining room or hall. A dozen officers were sitting around a heavy oak table; most of them were unknown to Jamie, though he recognized the two that were Rainsborough's. He also recognized the man at the head of the table, though they had never spoken. Lieutenant-General Cromwell was a solid jovial man, with a blunt red-nosed face that might have belonged to a country squire, except for the intensity of those clear grey eyes. A sheathed sword lay on the table in front of him.

Captain Rokeby was sitting stiffly on a chair at the far end of the room – not at the table with the others, but against the wall. He looked altogether wretched. It was his sword in front of Cromwell, Jamie realized. The court martial was already under way.

'Mr Hudson,' said Cromwell briskly. 'We must ask you some questions under oath.' He picked up a Bible, which lay next to the sword. 'Pray place your hand on this and swear that you will tell the truth as you hope for the mercy of Almighty God.'

Jamie stepped forward and stretched out his left hand. Cromwell drew back the book with a frown, then offered it again, to Jamie's right.

'My arm was grazed by a pistol shot, sir,' Jamie said hoarsely, but he eased his bad arm forward and gingerly set his mutilated hand on the cover of the Bible. The iron brace was in his pocket: there seemed no point in wearing it when he couldn't use the arm.

Cromwell looked at the missing fingers, then up at Jamie's face. 'Misfire?' he asked.

'Aye,' Jamie agreed. 'At Naseby.' The magic name brought the usual flicker of appreciation around the court. He pressed his palm against the leather and swore to tell the truth.

He did not really suspect Cromwell of being an accessory to the murder, though he thought it possible. The cavaliers at Pontefract were known to be ingenious, enterprising men: a daring strike into an enemy stronghold was exactly the sort of thing that would appeal to them. He did suspect that Cholmley had, at the very least, known that an attack was underway and declined to interfere with it – but even if that suspicion were capable of being substantiated, doing so wasn't within his power. The one thing he owed God and this court was to tell the truth of what he himself had seen and done.

He began by recounting his meeting with Barker on Doncaster Bridge and what he knew of Barker's response to it, speaking simply and plainly. One of Cromwell's officers, who appeared to be acting as Rokeby's advocate, tried to catch him out: Why had Barker accused him, if they hadn't even spoken? Ah, so there was bad blood between them! Come, if Barker really had assailed his wife, he must have longed to revenge himself! What gentleman would meet his wife's attacker face to face and turn the other cheek?

Jamie shook his head. 'He rode off in haste. I threw my . . . I threw a piece of iron after him, and I think it struck him, but it did him no hurt.'

'So you did attack him!' cried the advocate triumphantly.

Jamie shook his head. 'Only in throwing at his back what I chanced to have in my pocket, and that was no weapon, nor capable of doing him any harm. Those in his way were in more danger. It's a mercy that none of them were hurt, for he rode down a busy street at full gallop.'

'But what was it you threw?' demanded the advocate.

Jamie fished the brace out of his pocket. 'That.'

The advocate regarded it in bewilderment, and Jamie continued evenly, 'I use it, sir, in place of the fingers I lost at Naseby. It's true that Lieutenant Barker could not have known what it was, but neither could he have known that it was thrown by me. As I said, he galloped off down a busy street. Men were cursing him right and left, and likely others threw things, too. I am on oath, sir, and I tell you that I did not attack him. I might have done, had he not fled, and certainly he *feared* that I would – but what he told Captain Rokeby was false. I did not attack him, nor had I any plan to follow after him or lie in wait to do him harm. I had given my word to Colonel Rainsborough and to my wife that I would neither seek him out nor challenge him, and that word I've kept.'

'Your wife asked this?' inquired the advocate, raising his eyebrows and somehow managing to imply both that he thought it unlikely any such request had been made, but that if it had, no proper man would have complied with it.

'Aye,' agreed Jamie stolidly. 'She would not have me put myself into danger on her behalf when she had taken no harm – and she believes vengeance belongs to God.'

'A sensible and godly woman,' Cromwell said approvingly.

'So you returned peaceably to your smithy?' coaxed another of the officers, who seemed to be the prosecutor.

'Aye. I was having a bite to eat and reading my wife's letters when they came to arrest me.' Jamie glanced at Rokeby, resentment flaring in him for the first time that morning. 'My wife's letters were scattered, and many are lost.'

The prosecutor's lips quivered. 'They also shot you, I believe.'

Jamie nodded and gave a bald account of how he had been shot; at the prosecutor's request he reluctantly took off his coat and rolled up his sleeve to show the weeping wound. Cromwell looked at it, then at Rokeby.

'This is Lieutenant Perry's fault!' Rokeby burst out. 'I only ordered him to arrest the fellow!'

Jamie glanced at the captain again, then turned his gaze soberly to Cromwell. 'The captain said this before, to Colonel Rainsborough. The colonel said he would not hear such baseness, to blame the lieutenant the instant it was clear that the order was wrong.'

A ripple went through the room.

'I was abused by this man Barker!' Rokeby protested. 'He was a dispatch rider, he said he'd been attacked, that he feared for his life! I was bound to believe him!'

'Without first making any inquiry whatsoever?' asked the prosecutor. 'You must know that by rights you should have sent to Colonel Rainsborough, and asked *him* to act.'

''Twere unjust to blame *me* because Colonel Cholmley made such an enemy of Colonel Rainsborough that I durst not go to him!'

'You durst not even *inquire*?' asked Cromwell mildly.

'I feared Rainsborough's malice!' Rokeby said hotly. 'I was bound to protect the dispatches!'

'Was there any matter in these dispatches that you feared to let Colonel Rainsborough see?' the general persisted, his voice gentle.

There was an abrupt silence, the whole court martial realizing in the same instant why it was being held in the middle of a murder investigation. Rokeby went pale and shook his head. 'It . . . I . . . 'twas but the principle of the thing!'

'What was in the dispatches, then?' coaxed Cromwell.

'Merely . . . merely reports on our troops.'

'And on Colonel Rainsborough's?'

'Aye,' Rokeby admitted.

'Such as information as to where his companies were quartered, and how his sentries were disposed?'

'Sir!' gasped Rokeby. 'It was no such thing as you imagine! Aye, I informed my colonel as to his rival's doing, but . . .'

'Including the information I spoke of?'

'Aye. Aye, but such is commonplace! You yourself must have the like!'

'Then why was protecting these dispatches a matter of such importance that you must needs order out half a dozen men armed with swords and pistols?'

Rokeby stammered, groaned, and at last cried, 'It was naught to do with the dispatches! One of Rainsborough's had attacked one of ours! Or, or, so I believed!'

'Wrongly,' the prosecutor put in quickly.

'Sir,' said the advocate, cautiously reproaching Cromwell, 'this strays from the case.'

Cromwell sat back in his chair and looked benign.

'Mr Hudson,' the advocate went on, 'by your own account, you were wounded more by accident than design.'

Jamie sighed. 'Sir, I had believed that the charge against Captain Rokeby was not that he gave orders that led to this injury, but that he had no right to order my arrest at all.'

'But in the unhappy circumstances . . .' began the advocate.

'The circumstances were made no happier by Captain Rokeby's folly!' snapped the prosecutor. 'Mr Hudson, what did Colonel Rainsborough do when he learned what had passed?'

'He was angry and indignant,' said Jamie. 'He came running to the surgeon's while my wound was being dressed, to inform himself fully as to what had happened. When the captain arrived, shortly after, he rebuked him, telling him he'd flouted both civil and military law, and that he would see him cashiered for it.'

Cromwell stirred and leaned forward again. 'Is that so, Captain?'

Rokeby shrank under that calm grey gaze and muttered, 'Yes. Sir.'

'So you had strong motive to wish the colonel out of the way,' Cromwell said quietly.

Rokeby stared, aghast. The advocate bit his lip, then again complained that this strayed beyond the case.

There were a few more questions after that, but Cromwell sat through them in silence, toying with his pen. When Jamie's account was finished, the general said pleasantly, 'Thank you, Mr Hudson. That will be all for now, but I will want another word with you later. Mr Piltry, see that this man is taken to Dr White to have that wound dressed, and give him something to eat.'

Jamie's escort saluted and led him out.

Dr White was Cromwell's own surgeon. He cleaned the pistol graze – an excruciating process – then anointed it with a strong-scented balsam and covered it with a clean bandage. When he was finished, a servant appeared and led Jamie off to the kitchens, where he was given the best meal he'd had in months. He was cleaning the plate when Piltry, the escort, returned and beckoned him.

The hall was now empty except for Cromwell, who sat alone at the heavy oak table, going over some papers. He looked up when Jamie was shown in. 'Ah. Thank you, Mr Piltry,' he said, then dismissed the escort with a wave. He linked his hands together and regarded Jamie, who stared back in silence.

'Captain Rokeby will be publicly cashiered,' Cromwell said, 'though – to my great sorrow – Colonel Rainsborough will never see it. I trust, though, that his brave spirit is beyond all such petty concerns, and now rejoices in eternal bliss.'

Jamie said nothing. He wondered what this was about. Cromwell surely *knew* that Rainsborough's men suspected him of involvement in their colonel's murder.

'The colonel discharged you after your arrest,' the general continued, after a moment. 'Why did he so?'

'He said that I had become odious to Cholmley's faction,' said Jamie, 'besides that I'd be unable to work for a time. He also knew that I was very eager for my discharge. I had applied to him after Colchester, but he refused me.' He met those clear eyes and added deliberately, 'I was obliged to enlist for this second war against my wishes. I was taken up at Ware, though I was a civilian, and Commissary-General Ireton gave me the choice between re-enlisting and prison.'

Cromwell lifted a finger in silent objection. 'We have made peace with your faction since Ware. Colonel Rainsborough agreed with me on the necessity of making common cause against common enemies.' He waited, looking at Jamie expectantly. Jamie, however, had no intention of getting into an argument with a general, and did not reply. Cromwell snorted, then went on briskly, 'Why should Colonel Rainsborough care whether you were odious to Colonel Cholmley's faction?'

'I think he meant to use Rokeby's folly as a lever to shift Cholmley,' Jamie replied honestly, 'and he was bound to employ Cholmley's people after. He warned me against pursuing Lieutenant Barker; he said it would tend to justify Rokeby's actions.'

Cromwell let out a breath, then nodded. 'So it would.' He gazed at Jamie thoughtfully. 'I am aware of your dealings with Lieutenant Barker; my son-in-law wrote me of the matter, since we'd both reckoned Barker trustworthy and employed him frequently. To be candid with you, I was intrigued to encounter the man who'd occasioned his disgrace.'

Jamie set his teeth. 'Lieutenant Barker,' he said softly, 'deserved worse than dismissal.'

'It cannot be proven, Mr Hudson,' replied the general. 'No more than it can be proven that Sir Henry Cholmley was accessory to your colonel's murder, with the connivance of this sorry wretch Rokeby. The law of this land presumes innocence where proof of guilt is lacking, and for my part I will never seek to overturn that presumption. It seems to me that your wife is wise, to rely instead upon the certain vengeance of Almighty God.'

There was a pause. Jamie was startled by the reference to Cholmley. Did Cromwell really think him an accessory – or was he trying to shift the blame?

'Lieutenant Barker,' Cromwell resumed, 'was certainly a man unworthy of his trust; and yet I should be sorry to see him – or you – come to grief because of the ill-will betwixt you. What do you mean to do, now you are discharged, and the reasons for the injunction to let Barker be no longer hold?'

'I mean to go home to my wife,' Jamie replied without hesitation. 'I would have followed the colonel's coffin to London, but I was told I must wait on Captain Rokeby's trial. I want no more of war; and as for Lieutenant Barker, I will be best pleased if I never see him more. Am I free to go now, sir? Or must I wait upon your investigation?'

Cromwell smiled. 'The record of the court martial will suffice the investigation for your part in all this, Mr Hudson. You are free to go, and I pray for God's blessings upon you and your godly wife.'

Jamie walked back to the smithy feeling light-headed, incredulously debating whether he should set out southward in the morning, or give his arm a couple more days to heal. The sensible course was to wait. Sleeping in barns and haystacks, as he'd have to do, wouldn't be good for an infected cut – but he didn't know whether he could bear any more delay. He wanted the hundred and fifty miles between London and Doncaster to become a single step, so that he could vault it and be there, taking Lucy in his arms and telling her, '*I'm home, I'm home and never never never will I go to war again!*'

Sam was at the forge, mending a cooking pot. He set down his hammer and looked at Jamie in surprised question.

'I'm free to go home!' Jamie told him rapturously.

With the prospect of another siege receding, Sam was resigned to losing his partner. He smiled broadly, shook Jamie's hand, asked about the court martial and Cromwell, and frowned over the general's hint on Cholmley.

'A letter came for you,' when they'd exhausted the subject and he was about to return to his work. 'It's there, on the big anvil.'

Jamie seized it greedily: it was the first letter he'd received since they marched north. He saw at once that it was from Rob, and he opened it expecting questions or condolences on Rainsborough's death.

> *Brother,*
>
> *I pray God you are in health, and have food enowe. Our Sisters send their deerest love. We have hadde here an upsett whych has done much to reconsile our Father to you, for Sir D. of the Countie Committee came hither and sayde that because Nick had gone to fight for the King at Maydstone, we might be reckoned as Delinquents; and that if we wished to scape this Fate we must obtaine a Certificate of the Countie Committee, i.e., Sir D. In short, he demanded that we give him £200 or suffer the Threat of Sequestration. Father was in such Furie that he scarce cd Speak, but Kate prevayled upon him to goe to his Studie and*

*let me deal with the matter. 'Sir,' says I, 'tis true my brother Nick fought
and dyed at Maydstone, but my brother Jamie is even now fighting
'gainst the Cavaliers at Pomfrett, after serving all Summer before
Colchester, besides sufferingWounds at Naseby in the firstWarre. 'Twould
be a shameful thing indeed, if he shd return from theWarres and find
his House Sequestrated for Delinquencie!'*

*At this the Rogue was throwne into Confusion, and he asked three
Severall times if it were true; and I gave him manie Particulars of your
Service, and showed him your last letter, wherein you sayd that yr Rgmt
wd goe North. Att length he saw that his Trick would not Serve, and
sayd, 'Well, he hadde not knowne it, and he was glad to learn that the
Hudsons had so Loyall a sonne,' and off he slunk like a whipt Curre.*

*When I went to Father and told him of it, he knewe not what to
saye, he had never thought yr Service cd be so strong a Shield. I told
him that you served now onlie to Shield us, since you longed to leave
the Armie but durst not until you obtained a Discharge, since without
that they wd pursue you and afflict us. I told him besides you wd most
gladly make Peace with him, but that you feared he wd nott Let be,
but pick at the Quarrel ever and anon; and I sayde I feared that too.
He was much Afflicted, and at length sayde that he hadde never intended
to be so Uncharitable, and that for his Part he wished you at home.
Then I reminded him of yourWife, whom you had Perforce left unprotected in Lundon, but who preferred working with her owne handes to
taking from us aught that hadde not his Blessing. This had shamed
him when first I reported it, and at last he yeelded, and agreed that I
might goe to Lundon and fetch her hither to stay at least so longe as
you are at theWarre. He sayes, tho', that he hopes when you do obtaine
yr Discharge you will come home, and he will strive to let old Quarrells
sleep.*

*I will soone leave for Lundon to fetche yr Lucie home; and I hope,
Brother, soone to see you beside her in your owne place.*

Yr loving Brother,

Robert

Jamie looked for a date, but there wasn't one. He read the letter over
again, with steadily increasing unease, searching for some clue as to
when it had been written. Post to and from Bourne was frequently
delayed. The post route ran along the Great North Road, and the
little town lay to the east of that. Letters usually stopped at Stamford,

and could languish there for days before a carrier took them on along the country tracks. Clearly, Rob hadn't heard the news of Rainsborough's murder, still less received Jamie's letter giving him the news of his discharge.

The idea of Lucy safe in Bourne was one he had contemplated many times, with longing, if always with some uneasiness. Now that Rob was offering to make it a reality, he saw it for what it was: bad. He tried to imagine Lucy sitting with his sister Peggy and sister-in-law Kate and doing embroidery. It was just about possible, but he couldn't imagine her smiling over it. He suddenly saw that when he married her she had acquired a double in his mind called 'my wife'. 'My wife' had the conventional feminine virtues of modesty and obedience; Lucy, on the contrary, was bold and outspoken, and he loved her for it. His father would not: they would quarrel, that was certain. His father would feel that his attempt at reconciliation had been thrown in his face, and would be hurt and outraged. Rob would side with their father. Lucy would – God knew! Walk out of the house, probably, and try to make her way back to London on foot, with who knew what terrible consequences? A wise man would have been determined to keep her and George Hudson as far away from one another as possible, but he, foolish Jamie Hudson, had wailed to his brother about how unsafe she was in London!

He read Rob's letter again, looking for some way to fend off the impending disaster. There seemed no way he could reach his brother in time to tell him *Whatever you do, don't fetch her to Bourne!* It occurred to him, though, that the letter he'd sent to Lucy might already have saved the situation. If she'd received it, she would tell Rob that Jamie had been discharged and would soon be home.

Letters, though, often went astray; he couldn't rely on her having received it. If she hadn't, would she really go home with Rob? He very much doubted she would want to, but she'd probably feel she had no choice. She might, though, ask for a delay, to set her affairs in London in order. Yes, she might well do that. That would mean he had time to write again, to her and to Rob, repeating that he was on his way home . . .

Home. He suddenly realized that that meant *Lucy*, that all the time he'd been planning his journey back, he had not once considered stopping in Bourne – only a few miles from his road. Instead, his entire mind had been fixed on Lucy, as though all the world were waste, and he a ghost, until she was in his arms.

He could walk to Bourne. It was half as far as London. If he pushed hard he could walk there in four days. He wouldn't even have to sleep in haystacks: twenty shillings ought to cover three nights' lodging. How utterly *stupid*, not to have thought of Bourne! Of course, he'd believed himself still banned from his father's presence – but he should have thought of stopping in Stamford, and sending a note asking his brother to lend him money and a horse. He supposed it was his cursed pride again. He'd been determined to make his own way, and he'd dreaded letting the people at home see his disfigurement. Well, pride be damned. He would set out for Bourne first thing in the morning, and hope that he arrived there before Lucy did.

It was still dark when he left Doncaster. He'd said goodbye to his friends the night before, and set his pack by the door of the smithy, ready for the morning. There wasn't much in it; he was wearing most of the clothes his sisters had sent that summer, in fat layers against the cold of late autumn. The pack contained only the odds and ends: one clean shirt; a pair of stockings in need of darning; a heel of bread and a flask of water; his discharge papers and a bundle of salvaged letters. His boots were sound; Sam had stapled up the split in the left upper and added some hobnails to protect the soles. He had a sword, too, a good plain serviceable hanger that had been sent to the smithy for mending and never reclaimed. Setting out on a long journey alone and unarmed was a bad idea even in peacetime.

The journey, in the end, was uneventful, and on the evening of the fourth day after leaving Doncaster he arrived in Bourne. The small marketplace was empty. Night was falling, and people were indoors by the fire. Jamie walked along the muddy street, his footsteps quiet on the soft ground, feeling like a ghost. There was the Swan and Bull, the tavern where he and his friends had so often met; there was St Peter's Pool, and the Wellhead; over there beyond the church was the long receding line of Carr Dyke, where he used to fish, with the fens black and silent beyond it. And here, here beyond the town proper – the manor.

He stopped in the gateway, swallowing, looking at the dark bulk of the house looming out of the dusk. Candlelight shone from a downstairs window. That was the dining room, so the family must be sitting down to supper. He stood watching for a long time, his feet growing numb with cold. Now that he'd finally reached his goal he wished he were anywhere else. At last, though, he made himself take the remaining steps forward and knock upon the door.

He recognized the woman who came with a candle to open it: old Molly, the butler's mother. She, however, recoiled at the sight of him, and slammed the door in his face. 'Be off with you!' she ordered from behind it. 'Trouble us and you'll get nought but a whipping!'

He set his good hand against the cold oak panel. 'Molly?' he asked hoarsely. 'Mrs Carlew?'

There was a silence, and then her voice said uncertainly, 'Who's there?'

He cleared his throat. 'Jamie. James Hudson. Is Rob . . .'

The door flew open again and Molly stared up at him, raising her candlestick. 'Dear God above!' she exclaimed. 'Dear God. Oh, Master James, what have they done to you?'

She was almost in tears, and he felt a strong desire to turn around and walk off into the night. Instead he stamped the mud from his boots and came in.

There was a flurry of footsteps, and another familiar face appeared in the hall: Alexander Carlew, Molly's son, the butler. He stopped at the sight of Jamie, his face hardening – until his mother cried, 'It's Master *James*, Sandy!' and the hardness was replaced with horror.

The door was still open. The draught through it was threatening to extinguish the candle, though, and Molly finally closed it; the *clunk* of the panel in the frame caused Jamie an irrational stab of panic. Then the door to the dining room opened, and his father appeared.

He'd aged since Jamie saw him last: his hair was mostly grey, his face was deeply lined, and he'd lost weight. Jamie was grimly certain, however, that however much the years had marked his father, they'd marked him more. A pretty young woman appeared at his father's shoulder, and after a moment he recognized his sister Peggy. Father and sister stared at him for a long moment, and he stared back. He knew that he should greet them and try to smile – but he couldn't.

'Jamie?' breathed his father at last.

'Aye,' he agreed, and took a deep, shuddering breath. 'I am sorry to . . .'

'Oh, Jamie!' his sister cried, and she ran forward and flung her arms around him.

She caught the sore arm, and he flinched and gave an involuntary gasp of pain. Peggy let go and stood back, gazing at him in dismay. His father staggered forward and clutched his arm – the good arm, fortunately. 'Have you leave to be here?' he demanded.

'Aye,' he said, struggling to force words from his tight throat. 'I was discharged.'

'Discharged?' asked George Hudson querulously. 'Rob said it was denied!'

'Last summer it was,' Jamie said. 'But the colonel granted it at last.' His father continued to stare at him, and he added, 'I've the discharge papers in my pack if you doubt my word.'

George Hudson opened his mouth and then closed it again. Another figure appeared from the dining room, a stout, stooped woman in a plain dark gown. Jamie had no time to work out who she was because Peggy tried to take his bad arm. He flinched back against the door. 'Please, Pegling! I've a cut there.'

'A cut?' asked Peggy.

'A graze. It's sore.'

'Oh Jamie!' cried Peggy, and shook her hands in the air, baffled in the need to touch him.

He was suddenly mortified to tears: his little sister had run to embrace him despite his disfigurement and filth, and he'd pushed her away. 'Oh, Peggy!' he said, and caught one of those hands with his good one. 'Oh, I am glad to see you again! And grown into such a lovely woman!'

She burst into tears and threw her arms around him again, this time avoiding the bad arm.

'Rob's gone to London to fetch home your wife,' said the woman who'd come in last, and Jamie finally recognized her as Rob's wife, Kate.

'I know. I'd a letter from him, five days gone,' he replied, ineffectually patting Peggy on the back.

'You truly are discharged?' asked his father.

'Aye. I'd meant to follow my colonel's coffin to London, but I was required as witness in a court martial.' The pressure on his heart was easing, and the words came a bit more readily.

'Your colonel's funeral cortege passed through Stamford last week,' sniffed Peggy, at last breaking away from him. 'There were a dozen coaches, and more than a hundred horsemen!'

'Colonel Rainsborough was a great man,' replied Jamie.

His father stiffened, and they looked at one another. Then George Hudson twitched his shoulders and asked, in a strained voice, 'Does your horse need stabling?'

'I came on foot,' Jamie told him, astonished and grateful.

'Clear from *Doncaster?*' asked his father, shocked. 'In five days?'

'Four,' said Jamie simply. 'I've grown used to hard marches. But I am very weary.'

'You look . . .' His father thought better of whatever-it-was he'd been about to say, and instead asked, 'Have you supped?'

They brought him into the dining room, sat him down at the familiar table and brought him soup and bread and butter – a thick, satisfying soup of bacon and barley, with soft wheat bread and sweet creamy butter, not like the stuff in the camps. He began to eat it slowly, relishing each mouthful.

'Rob told us of your maiming, and that you looked ill and starveling,' George Hudson said, watching him. 'But I'd not . . . I'd not . . .' He stopped abruptly, and pinched the bridge of his nose, then, voice cracking, cried, 'Dear *God,* boy, why did you not ask for *help*? I'd have sent more money, had I known!'

Jamie set down his spoon. 'I've not come to beg from you, sir.' Years of resentment bubbled up, and he went on defiantly, 'I'd not have come here now, but that Rob's letter led me to think you were willing to forgo your old demand that I submit my judgement to yours and condemn all I've fought for!' As soon as the words were out he regretted them. His father was trying not to quarrel; he ought to do the same.

George Hudson waved the argument away distractedly. 'I thought the King would *win!* I thought you'd be home within a year, with that cursed pride chastened, ready to heed your father and be a good dutiful son! I never thought . . .' He drew a deep breath, and to Jamie's shock and dismay there were tears in his eyes. 'I never thought it would go on so *long!* I never believed that the very world could contain all the grief and horror wrought by this terrible war!'

'Nor did I,' Jamie said truthfully. 'As for chastened, Father, I promise you, I am.'

His father seized his good arm again, pressing it hard. 'Oh, my poor boy!' he exclaimed, and wept.

* * *

Jamie slept that night on clean linen in his own bed. When dawn came he woke briefly, out of habit, then rolled over and went back to sleep. He was still asleep at mid-morning when his father burst into the room waving a piece of paper and shouting, 'What's this about an *arrest?*'

Jamie sat bolt upright, looked about wildly for his sword – then remembered where he was. He stared at his father stupidly.

His father stared back, paper frozen mid-flourish, face full of alarm. Jamie looked down to see what he was staring at, and saw only his own torso, the ribs painfully sharp under the pale skin. He'd stripped off his filthy clothing the night before, and the servants had taken it away to be washed.

'What's that on your arm?' asked George Hudson.

Jamie glanced at the bandage: it was sweat-stained and dirty now, spotted with blood where the constant chafing had rubbed against the stitches. 'I told you I'd been shot,' he said.

'Great God in Heaven, you did not!' cried his father, hurrying over to the bed.

Jamie was sure he'd said something about it, but the evening had lost all coherence for him after his father broke down in tears. 'It's but a graze.'

'Let me see!' snarled George Hudson, tugging at the knots on the bandage. Jamie gasped and jerked away, and his father stepped back, glaring. 'Tell me the truth, Jamie: have you been discharged or have you fled?'

'I offered you sight of the papers!' said Jamie indignantly. 'I am discharged wounded. Does my word weigh *nothing* with you?'

'Then what's this Rob says about an arrest?' his father demanded, picking up the paper, which he'd dropped.

Jamie grabbed the coverlet and hauled it up over his shoulders. There was no fire in the bedroom, and the November morning was cold. 'Give me leave a moment,' he said. 'Sir. I was asleep. Is Rob back, then?' A sudden thrill swept him, and he asked breathlessly, 'Is *Lucy* here?'

'Nay!' said George Hudson impatiently. 'Rob has sent us a letter from Stamford, saying that your wife had had word, *from you*, that you'd been arrested because of some quarrel between commanders in your Army. He sent this note in haste, on his way north to rescue you!'

Jamie blinked several times, trying to work out how Rob could possibly have got the idea he needed to be rescued. 'Oh,' he said at last. 'Aye. I *was* arrested, but the arrest was unlawful. 'Twas for that I was called as a witness in the court martial.'

'What court martial?'

'I told you I meant to follow Colonel Rainsborough's coffin, but was delayed by a court martial!' Jamie protested.

His father scowled. 'Perhaps you said something of it, but I could scarce pay any heed, with the surprise of your sudden arrival, in such a pitiful state! And I recall nothing about being *shot*! Let me see!' He made another move toward the bandage.

Jamie fended him off. 'Father, I beg you! It's mending, but the knots are stiff and the arm's sore. Let Molly take the scissors to it. I am very sorry that my brother will have a ride to Doncaster and back for nought, but I am at a loss to explain why he should think I needed rescue! I had writ Lucy – and Rob! – to say that I had my discharge, but that my return must wait upon a court martial to be held for a captain who had unlawfully ordered me arrested . . .' He trailed off. He couldn't remember exactly what he'd written, but he was beginning to see the source of the confusion.

'There's a letter from you to Rob downstairs,' said George Hudson. 'It came after he left for London. I didn't meddle with it.' He scowled. 'I'll have the whole tale from you – but first I'll fetch Molly to tend that cut. *Shot!* And not a word of it over supper!'

He went out. Jamie scrambled out of bed, found his pack, and put on his last clean shirt. He looked around for breeches, but saw none. He climbed back into bed just as his father returned with Molly.

The cut was a caked mess of dried blood and pus, mixed with smears of Dr White's balsam. Molly and his father both exclaimed over it in horror – though Jamie thought that after it was cleaned it didn't actually look all that bad; better than it had at the court martial, certainly. The family, however, seemed to regard it as potentially mortal. It was cleaned, anointed with Molly's best remedies, and earnestly debated, Kate and Peggy both coming in to inspect the injury and give their own opinions. That Jamie should rest in bed until it was healed was a foregone conclusion. The questions of what medicine he should take, and what his diet should be, were more vexed.

'It's weeks old!' he protested. 'It didn't hinder me walking all the way hither from Doncaster!'

'Aye, and much good that did it!' snapped his father. 'We should send for Dr Sidcombe.'

'It's had two surgeons already!'

His father glared. 'We delayed sending for the good doctor for poor little Georgie. We'll not delay again!'

Jamie had forgotten that Rob's only son had died from an infected cut. His family's alarm suddenly made sense. Nonetheless, he was very unwilling to suffer the attentions of Dr Sidcombe: purging, bleeding and a low diet would make it impossible for him to go to London. Lucy *had* had his letter: she would be waiting for him.

'I swear to you,' he said, 'it *is* amended from what it was a few days ago. Leave it, I pray you, at least until this evening: if it's worse *then* you can send for Dr Sidcombe.'

The family warily accepted this compromise. Now that he'd been reminded of her loss, Jamie found himself studying his sister-in-law. Georgie had been her first child; after that there'd been a stillborn daughter, and she'd been pregnant again when he left home. He'd assumed, without giving it much thought, that she had or would have more children. The laughing young mother of his memories, however, had been replaced by this slow heavy woman who moved as though her body pained her. The years had maimed her, too, and he doubted that there would be any more children.

Rob had told him that he himself was now the likely heir to the estate, but he hadn't taken it seriously. He'd always known that he'd never be Mr Hudson of Bourne Manor. The realization that eventually he might be turned all his world on edge.

Kate noticed his gaze and gave him a tired smile. 'We must cancel the dinner,' she said, with a sigh.

He gave her a bewildered look, and his father scowled. 'I had bid your other sisters and their husbands to dinner tonight, to welcome you home. Clearly, though, you'll not be fit enough for such rich fare as fatted calf. Molly, fetch him some milquetoast. Now, Jamie, you must tell us about this *arrest*, and how you came by that wound.'

Sixteen

Bourne Manor
17th November
My verie deere,

I feare I must have writ confusedly before, speaking of my Arrest, for they tell me my Brother Rob is on his waye to Doncaster to help me, tho' I needed no help and have alreadie left that Citie, as you maye see by the Super-scription. In Truthe, my Arrest was as Brief as Unlawful, and the Delaye was onlie for the Court Marshall of the Captaine that ordered it; and he has been casheered. As soone as the Sentence was given I was upon the Roade, for I wish above alle things to see you once more, yett I must tarrie here a little while. I suffered a Grayze from a Pistoll Shott in Doncaster, whych is slow to mende; for my part I cd Endure it, but my kin will not permitt me to depart until it is Whole.

I knowe my Brother Rob went to Lundun thinking to fetch you hither to Bourne. He did so out of Love and Care, but I feare it wd have turned out very ill had you come hither without me, and I am much to Blame for giving Rob to Understand other wise. I knowe it wd greeve you to leave your Worke and Friends in Lundun onlie to sit here in Idlenesse. My deerest Lucie, what we shall do I knowe nott, for my kin alle Expect me to remain with them here, but please beleeve that I will do No Thing untill I have spoken with you. It may be we can Discover some Settlement that will satisfie alle.

I count alle Houres wasted untill I see you againe.

Yr Jamie

'When I do see him again,' Lucy told Mary, 'I think I shall hand him pen and paper, and tell him he cannot kiss me until he's learned to explain himself properly in writing!'

Mary laughed. She lifted a hand from the composing frame and pretended to write frantically, then returned to snatching the letters she needed for the next line of newsprint. She and Lucy had taken to setting type together, sitting one on either side of a table that held the day's written text, calling out advice on spacings and line lengths.

'All the worry I spent on poor Jamie shivering in prison!' Lucy said in disgust. 'I *should* have worried about poor Jamie ill from a pistol shot! How did he come to be shot? Where was he shot? In the leg? The belly? His foolish head? He could best spare the last, I think, for he makes scant use of it!' She finished assembling a line on her composing stick, eyed it a moment, then slid in a couple of spacers to justify it. She slid the line into the forme and turned back to the composing frame. 'I pray God he hasn't fought another duel!'

Mary clicked her tongue. 'God forbid! The next line should end on 'expecting'.'

Lucy nodded and began to select letters, starting at the end with 'gnitcepxe'.

'Do you truly think he might have been duelling?' asked Mary, continuing the conversation as though the reversed sentences under their fingers were no more than stitches in a seam.

Lucy grimaced. 'He would have challenged this Barker on my account before, had Colonel Rainsborough not obliged him to forswear it. He gave no promise about what he would do if Barker offended him again. If there was a duel, it explains why he said nought of it in his last letter – though I suppose his silence needs no more explanation than his poor skill at letter writing!' She sighed. 'I never thought that skill would be so needful, when I wed him!'

'Indeed, it's a very scurvy letter,' Mary said slyly. 'Give it here, and I'll use it to clean type.'

'Indeed you will not!' cried Lucy, laughing. '*This* letter is a very fine one, and I shall keep it close! I make the next line end with "which", do you?'

The letter didn't remove the threat of removal to Lincolnshire, and didn't even address the question of what Jamie had promised his brother about the Leveller cause. And yet . . . it reassured her at some deeper level. *I knowe it wd greeve you to leave your Worke and Friends in Lundun onlie to sit here in Idlenesse* . . . He was *aware* of her, as his brother had not been; he understood that she had a life of her own. There might not be any arrangement that satisfied everyone, but at least he would try to find one.

In part her more hopeful frame of mind was due to nothing more than having had time to get used to the idea of leaving London. She'd found herself remembering the pleasures of the countryside where she'd grown up, and noticing all the things she hated about London: the noise, the filth, the beggars, the stench. There was something to be said, after all, for a move. Were there any printing presses in Lincolnshire? She'd never heard of one in Leicestershire when she was growing up, but she remembered the blackletter ballads she and her friends used to buy. They'd cost a penny new, and three or four girls used to band together to pay for one, then pass the sheet back and forth among themselves until the paper was thick and the words almost illegible. She had no doubt that there was a market for print.

She lost herself a moment in a daydream of owning the first printing press in Lincolnshire, of making regular trips down to London to see her friends and collect the latest ballads before returning to run off innumerable copies for the eager country customers . . .

Whether she could do any such thing would depend upon where Bourne actually was, and that she didn't know. If it lay far out in the wild fens she would . . . she would have to find something else to do. She needed to talk to Jamie. It had been so *long* since they had talked!

Or perhaps it was fairer to say they had *never* really talked. They had worked together on a printing press, and she had fallen in love, but he'd never been much of a talker. Probably she *was* a fool to have married him, a man she'd known so little about – a man she still knew so little about! She must make the best of it, and keep alive the hope that they could love one another and be happy.

'Lucy!' said Mary softly, and Lucy looked down and saw that the composing stick in her hands was full. She realized that she'd been sitting with it in her lap and staring idly at nothing for several minutes.

'Sorry!' she muttered, and went back to work.

Bourne Manor
24th November
   I write this in Teares. My deere Brother Robert is hurt, perhaps dying. He had rid to Doncaster, as you knowe, and it appears that when he came there and Enquyred after me, he was told all the Tale of my Arrest, and how Lt Barker had caused it; and he heard, too, that I hadde been shott, the Hurt done being made much greater in Rumoure than it was in Fact. He sought Barker out, but Barker having Choyce of Weapons chose Pistolls, at whych he proved more Skilled than he was at

Sword-Play, for he felled Rob with a shott to the Shoulder and fled Unscathed. Rob's servant was with him, and a Seconde he hadde founde in the Rgmt, and they brought him to an Inne and sent for a surgeon, and sent also to us. My Father is much stricken, but will goe at once, and so we ride in the morning, and I will leave this at Grantham to go with the Post South.

I beg you praye for my deere Brother, who was ever kinder to me than my deserving.

Jamie

Lucy had found the letter waiting when she returned from work. She had to read it twice before she could even take it in, the news was so shocking and so utterly unexpected. She remembered Rob saying wearily that he would start for the north, and her own warm approval.

She also remembered him asking her whether the attempted abduction had *really* been in jest, and his scowl at her reply. She had not taken note of that at the time, and she should have done – but then, this whole business of *duelling* was foreign to her. She wouldn't have understood that 'he sought him out' meant 'he challenged him', except for what followed. Why should a good man like Robert Hudson decide that he must risk his life for the sake of punishing a worthless coward? If you'd escaped the viper's bite, why chase after it with a stick? If Rob died, it would hurt Jamie much more than any arrest or pistol graze.

She began to cry. Mary, who'd been chopping parsnips, set down her kitchen knife in alarm and hurried over. Lucy flapped the letter in explanation. 'He says his brother Rob's been shot!' she choked. 'In a duel with that vile rogue Barker. He asks me to pray for him.'

'Dear Lord Jesus!' exclaimed Mary. She took the letter, looked at it, then caught Lucy's hands and drew her down on to her knees. Lucy had for some years found it hard to pray – whenever she tried, she found herself paralyzed by the religious doubts she usually managed to ignore. In this extremity, though, when there was nothing else she could do, she knelt beside Mary on the kitchen floor and prayed desperately for Robert Hudson.

For the next two weeks she lived in constant fear of another letter, announcing that Robert had died. None came. On the other hand, there was also no letter saying that Jamie and his father had arrived at Doncaster and found Rob on his way to recovery. The only news from the north was what appeared in the newsbooks: Col. Cholmley's regiment was to be disbanded, while Colonel Rainsborough's would return south, leaving the siege of Pontefract to Cromwell's men. Lucy was unhappily aware that the public news might well account for the lack of the private sort; a couple of thousand men removing themselves from a battlefield undoubtedly disrupted the post.

There was an abundance of disruption in London, too. The conflict between Parliament and Army had finally reached its long-threatened crisis. The Army had submitted General Ireton's *Remonstrance* to Parliament, but Parliament first deferred consideration of it, then rejected it, pressing on instead with negotiations for a treaty with the King. At this Ireton called for Parliament to be dissolved. Lord General Fairfax, who'd backed Parliament, found himself outvoted on his own council, and the Army marched into London.

The Army occupied London on the second of December. It kept good order and discipline, but the presence of so many armed men could not but be overwhelming. Soldiers set up camp on every green in the capital, and were quartered in every public building and many private ones; prices shot up and businesses closed their doors.

London was shocked and subdued – but the Levellers, for once, were happy. The Army Council had also voted to hold formal discussions with them on a settlement of government. Lilburne, Wildman, and Dick Overton were all on the committee to draft a new constitution. The Leveller leaders were wary, of course, but also elated: a new constitution! Based on *The Agreement of the People!* Dick bubbled with hope; Lilburne burned with determination; John Wildman blazed with enthusiasm. Lucy, however, found herself full of dread. The Army had occupied London before – but instead of a settlement there'd been months of wrangling, followed by the betrayal at Ware. Everything she heard now filled her with foreboding that the same thing would happen again – and in the meantime, the Army was *there,* on the street, an iron-clad presence that made any pretence of Parliamentary government a sham. What sort of democracy was imposed on a frightened and hostile populace by main force? She found herself unable to believe that Cromwell and Ireton, who'd used and discarded the Levellers before, intended to be honest partners now.

Mary shared her doubts. They did not talk about it much, but one evening when Dick was meeting late with the committee and they were sitting by the fire doing the mending, Mary suddenly said, 'If this turns out ill, might I send the children to you in Lincolnshire?'

Lucy looked at her friend's earnest face and swallowed the facile words of reassurance which had risen to her tongue. 'They would be welcome,' she said instead. 'Any or all of you would be, in any circumstances. You took me in when I had nothing, and you may call on me for anything I possess.'

Mary looked at her keenly a moment. 'Thank you. I pray God it never comes to that, but it eases my mind to think that if the worst happens the littles ones will be safe.' She sighed, then added, with forced optimism, 'Likely it will all turn out as Dick hopes, and I'm worrying over nothing. Still, I'm glad now that you're to leave London. It may well prove a blessing in disguise.'

Lucy could have replied that it was by no means certain that she *would* leave London – but she didn't have the heart. It was painfully obvious that Mary would gladly leave London herself, if Dick were willing to go. She reached out and caught her friend's hand. Mary squeezed it, gave her an unsteady smile, then resolutely resumed her sewing.

It was on the fourth of December, in the middle of this city bristling with guns and swords, that Lucy went to buy ink for the press and realized that she was being followed.

She hadn't consciously noticed anyone – but all the time she'd spent on unlicensed presses had left her instincts finely honed, and she trusted them. Of course, now that her work was legal she didn't need to worry, but still she stopped and pretended to check her purse while secretly glancing over the crowd. She was on Moorgate, near London Wall. The thoroughfare was bustling, even though every other man now seemed to be wearing a red coat, and it was hard to make out who . . .

She spotted her follower, a red-coated soldier leaning against a wall about half a block away on the other side of the street. He was slouching with his hat tipped forward, so she couldn't make out his face, but she could sense the direction of his gaze as he waited for her to walk on.

She slipped her purse back in its pocket and started on, amused. In the two days since the Army arrived in London she'd three times found a soldier trailing after her, but only two of them had worked up the nerve to speak to her. Those two had been harmless – and even if this one wasn't, he wouldn't dare do anything with so many people about.

She passed Moorgate and continued on into Moorfields: the ink-maker's was located outside the city wall, off the main road and at a little distance from neighbouring properties, so that their vile-smelling concoctions of soot and linseed oil would have space to simmer without suffocating anyone. The business was run by a family: old father, eldest son and wife, daughter and husband. The old man was not about today, and one of the couples was away as well, but the daughter and her husband were in the shop. They greeted her cheerfully and asked after Dick and Mary; she asked after their father. She was listening to their account of the old man's ague when Isaiah Barker marched in with a pistol primed and cocked in his hand.

She gaped, shocked but not seriously afraid. Surely he couldn't mean to attack her in the middle of a shop!

'Mrs Hudson,' said Barker. 'You will come with me. You,' the pistol described an arc between the gaping ink-brewers, 'will hold your peace.'

'Lieutenant Barker . . .' Lucy began – and he hit her.

It was a solid sweeping blow with his free hand; it caught her on the side of the head and sent her staggering into the shelves that held the pots of ink. The shelves shook, sending pots crashing. The ink-brewer daughter cried out and rushed to rescue her merchandise, then recoiled when Barker swept out his sword. He pointed the pistol at the ink-brewer son-in-law; the man raised both hands and backed against the wall.

'Get *back!*' Barker ordered the woman, jerking the pistol and hefting the sword. 'Be *quiet!*' She crept to her husband's side, sobbing.

Lucy was on her knees among the smashed inkpots, cradling her face where he'd hit it. The sword swung round and came to rest on her collar bone, and she looked up into the raw malice of Barker's eyes. 'Get up,' he ordered.

Her fingers groped at the ground, searching for something she could use to defend herself. All she found was a broken inkpot. The shards of cheap earthernware were held together by the thick paste of printing ink inside them.

'Get up!' Barker ordered again, and tapped the side of her neck with the sword, not quite hard enough to break the skin; she flinched involuntarily at the coldness of the metal. Bracing her elbow against the shelves, she pushed herself to her feet, folding the broken inkpot into the crook of her arm to hide it. It wasn't much, but it was the only thing she had. She wrapped her other arm around it, hugging herself.

'Now,' said Barker, 'come with me.' She hesitated, and he sneered. 'You will pay your husband's debts, sweetheart, but you can do it with both hands – or none.' The sword dropped and tapped her wrist.

Lucy looked at the ink-brewers, who both now stood with their backs to the wall, the woman crying, the man still holding his hands in the air. Barker looked at them too, and extended his pistol toward them. 'Beg them for help,' he told her, 'and you will be to blame for what happens.'

He would shoot the man, and use the sword to subdue the two unarmed women. Lucy shook her head. Still hugging the inkpot she walked slowly to the door. Barker followed her out sideways, pistol still pointed at the ink-brewers. He closed the shop door, then kicked a timber under the threshhold, jamming it.

Half-formed plans for escape flowed through her mind. She could run while he still had half his attention on the ink-brewers; she could hurl the inkpot into his face and run; she could throw herself to the ground and start screaming, hoping that *he* would run . . .

He wouldn't, though. He would kill her, and afterwards kill anyone who came running to help. This brazen daylight abduction was the act of a man with nothing to lose. She recognized, sickly, that it was the act of a man who was already fleeing a charge of murder. *Oh, Rob!*

When they were a few paces from the shop, Barker sheathed his sword and turned the pistol on Lucy, holding his arm close to his body so that the weapon would be less noticeable to anyone at a distance. There was nobody close by. Moorfields was an area of fruit and vegetable gardens, sprinkled with a few small cottages and businesses like the one they'd just left. She knew it quite well. She'd spent months working on an unlicensed press hidden in a Moorfields barn. It was a bright December day, about eleven in the morning. Frost sparkled on the grass, and the puddles had a rim of ice. There were plenty of people about, but they weren't crowded together as they had been on the streets of the city. Outraged and despairing, she contemplated her own stupidity.

She'd *known* she was being followed, yet she'd walked away from the crowded street and safety.

But who could have anticipated the *audacity* of this attack? In Moorfields, in broad daylight! Presumably Barker was preparing to flee abroad to escape a murder charge, and had paused to take revenge, but *surely* the ink-brewers would raise the hue and cry as soon as they got that door open!

'You go before me,' Barker said in a low voice. 'Take that track to the right, through the sheds. Quickly!'

She did as he commanded. Her face throbbed where he'd hit her, and there was a taste of bile in her throat. There was nothing mysterious in the order. He was getting them out of sight. When the ink-brewers worked up the courage to barge open the door, they wouldn't know which way he'd gone.

They passed the last shed. 'Now left,' he commanded, 'through the orchard.' She turned obediently under the branches of the winter-bare trees. She doubted he had any real destination in mind; he was simply taking her off towards a more isolated place, for the obvious purpose. She would not, *not* let him do it, she decided. He probably meant to kill her after raping her, so she would make her attempt at escape before he did. Then at least she'd be spared the rape.

'Straight on!' he ordered, when they reached the end of the orchard. They trudged on, going further and further from the city, walking along the edge of the vegetable beds, which were mostly bare brown mounds in this season, with here and there some green cabbages or yellow parsnip leaves. Barker's boots crunched the frost behind her.

She needed to get him off guard. She felt instinctively that challenging him would draw punishment, but that he'd relish it if she begged and pleaded. The thought of doing so was repulsive, but . . .

'Oh, sir!' she said thickly, not looking back. 'I *beg* you!'

He gave a snort. 'Do you now?'

'I've not been married a year, and I've spent scarce ten days of that in my husband's company! If he owes you debts, I know nothing of it. I *beg* you, sir, don't hurt me!'

'Your foul-faced husband,' snarled Barker, 'owes me my *life*, which he took from me.'

'But, sir, you are no ghost, how . . .'

'I'm no better than a ghost! Your husband stole everything from me. I had the trust and patronage of great men and the esteem of all my friends; he blasted my reputation, turned my patrons against me, and even when I'd been flung out to that wretched *Pontefract,* what do I find but Cyclops Hudson must come and wreck me even there! I was drummed out of the Army because of him!'

How can you blame Jamie for the result of things you did to hurt him? Lucy thought indignantly. What she said, though, was, 'I know nothing of this, sir! Please, please don't hurt me! I never hurt you!'

'You did me the worst hurt of all!' replied Barker, his voice rising. 'It was you riding to Colchester that turned General Ireton against me!'

She didn't try to argue; she just cried, 'I never meant it to! Have pity!'

He spat at her. She felt the gobbet of phlegm strike her shoulder, and flinched. 'That's right, you slut, beg me! You and your husband owe me everything you've taken, and you'll pay. That shed. Over there. Go to it.'

The shed was a small plain one, indistinguishable from dozens of others sprinkled across Moorfields to hold garden tools or livestock. Lucy walked up to it with her legs trembling and a cold sick weakness in her belly. It would be here. This might be the last sight she ever saw.

'Open it,' ordered Barker.

She put her hand to the latch and twitched it, then cried, 'It's locked!' She thought that might even be true.

Barker made a wordless sound of disgust and stepped forward to stand beside her. He gave her a glare and set his hand on the latch. She dropped to her knees, raising her hands pleadingly and crying out, 'Mercy, sir, I beg you!' When he glanced round in satisfaction, she lunged at the pistol.

She got both hands on it and jerked it away from him before he'd understood what she was about, but as she did the trigger was pulled or twisted, and the gun went off. There was a flash of fire from the jarred priming charge and a cloud of sulphurous smoke. The savage kick threw the weapon out of her hands again. She didn't dare look for it; she had no idea where the shot went, but it hadn't hit Barker. He was bellowing and drawing his sword. She grabbed her broken inkpot – dropped when she went for the gun – and hurled it into his face with all her strength; the thick paste plopped off again, but enough of it had got into his eyes to blind him. She jumped to her feet and started to run.

'You lying whore!' Barker howled, wiping frantically at his eyes. 'God damn you!'

She didn't look back, only hauled up her skirts and ran harder, listening, over the pounding of her own feet, for the sound of his coming after her. There was nothing, nothing, nothing – and then the crashing detonation of the pistol – and a scream.

She ran on: she wasn't even sure that the scream hadn't been her own, such was her heart-pounding terror. The cry was followed, though, by broken shrieks of agony. She looked back.

At first she thought Barker had vanished; then she saw his red coat flashing and bobbing on the ground before the shed. His shrieks became a moan, then ebbed into silence.

The sight had slowed her, and now she stopped and stood panting, staring at that red shape, already distant. She told herself that he might be feigning injury to lure her back – but she knew that those shrieks had not been feigned. Still, she could not bring herself to go and check. She turned instead toward the city, and made her way unsteadily back through the fields to the ink-brewers.'

There was a crowd in front of the shop, many of them carrying truncheons and hoes, a few with swords. The senior ink-brewer, the old man, was standing on an upturned tub gesticulating. He froze when he spotted Lucy, then cried, 'Mrs Hudson!'

Everyone turned towards her; several people cried out thanks to God. The ink-brewer daughter darted forward and embraced her. 'I thank the good Lord!' she cried. 'Did you escape him?'

'Aye,' said Lucy, and swallowed. 'I think he's hurt by his own pistol.'

She had to lead the whole posse back to the shed. They found Barker lying against the door, his face a red and black mask of ink, blood, and powder burns. Blood had made a puddle around him, but the dark soil was drinking it in, leaving only a red slick that steamed in the cold air. He was dead. The ramrod from his pistol had been driven through the side of his throat and up into the roof of his mouth. Lucy went to the nearest dung-heap and was violently sick over the stable-sweepings.

In ordinary times, the incident might have been reported in the newsbooks. 'Miraculous dispensations' were always popular items. Lucy was glad that the times were far from ordinary, and that Lieutenant Barker's death was passed over in favour of the Army's

purge of Parliament. Others might praise God's marvellous vengeance; she found herself filled with an unsettling rage. She had been
raped before; where had God's marvellous vengeance been then?

She dared not ask the question out loud. She knew the official
answer, having heard it in innumerable sermons and pious exhorta-
tions: the woeful state of the world was the result of human sin; God
was justly angry with mankind, but sometimes, out of his great mercy,
shielded men and women from the consequences of their own
wickedness.

The official answer did not satisfy her. Jamie's scars had taught her
something about pistols, and it was perfectly clear to her how Barker
had died. He'd tried to load the pistol in haste, while it was still hot
and without wiping it out first – something every man ever issued a
gun was strictly told never to do. Some fragment of wadding had
still been smouldering in the chamber, and when he rammed the
fresh charge home it had fired, shooting the ramrod into his face.

Of course, Almighty God *usually* worked through earthly chances
– but she also had the suspicion that if the pistol hadn't misfired she
still would have escaped. She'd been a good distance from Barker
when it went off. The ink in his eyes must have delayed him long
enough to give her such a lead that he'd known he couldn't hope to
catch her again. She thought she would probably have been out of
range of pistol shot even if he'd succeeded in getting the gun loaded.
She would have run back to the ink-brewers, who'd already raised
the hue and cry, and Barker would very likely have been taken and
hanged. So why was a miraculous misfiring pistol even needed? If
God wanted to work a miracle, why hadn't he done so the first time
she was raped, by those three cruel soldiers in her father's barn all
those years ago?

Questioning Divine Providence would shock and distress her
friends. Better to endure quietly, and let time and work wash away
the question and her anger. She found, though, that something in her
life was broken – some proud confidence she'd barely noticed, until
it was gone. She could not walk alone down a London street without
her heart pounding and a cold sweat starting; a lustful whistle or
catcall from one of the innumerable soldiers threw her into a rage.
Worst of all, the scent of ink, which for so long had meant *freedom*
to her, now made her queasy. The thought of leaving London became
more attractive by the day.

The incident did, however, make enough noise that, about a week later, one of *The Moderate's* mercury-women passed on a letter to her:

> *Sweete Lucy,*
>
> *It seems I 'scaped lightly. So often I tryed to engage you in Dalliance, and never once did I suffer Heaven's Vengeance. I'll be sworne 'tis because you've a liking for me: Matt at The Sunne told me how that hypocrite Knave Mabbot desired you to betray me, and you refused. Sweete, I am glad your Steelie Chastitie has been rewarded by Heaven, and you came off safely.*
>
> *Prag*

The missive annoyed her intensely, in many ways. How could he equate groping with attempted rape at sword-point? If he knew she'd refused to betray him, and what it had cost her, why he hadn't bothered to say thank you? Why did he consider that only 'Steelie Chastitie' could be behind her ability to tell him 'no'? Why on earth did he sign himself 'Prag'? Did he think she was fooled by his by-line's posturing? She longed to pen a really cutting reply – but anything along the lines of 'I do not like you!' would sound suspicious, as well as ungracious. She suspected, too, that he was better at cutting replies than she was, so she did not reply at all.

Seventeen

The journey north was a nightmare. There were three of them – Jamie, his father, and a servant – and they'd brought four horses, the spare to serve as a remount if one of the others went lame. They rode hard for two days, rising before dawn and stopping only when they could no longer make out the potholes in the road. George Hudson was white-faced with pain and exhaustion by the end of the first day, and Jamie was seriously concerned for his health.

Jamie's own health was much improved. Bedrest at home and as much food as he wanted had done wonders for the pistol-graze. He could not be pleased about it, though. His recovery seemed to mock Rob's decision to challenge Barker on his behalf.

They arrived at Doncaster at dusk on the twenty-sixth of November, less than a fortnight after Jamie had turned his back on the town. George was frantic to press on and find Robert. The letter with the news of the duel had included the name of the inn where Rob had been taken after he was shot, but Jamie had no idea where the place was, and it was not clear whether Rob was still there. He left his father to eat supper at a Doncaster inn and rushed around the town trying to find someone who knew what had happened to his brother.

The regiment had received its orders to return south, and was in the process of preparing to march. Everything was in chaos. Philibert and Sam were pleased to see Jamie, but not surprised. They knew of the duel and its outcome, but they had no news, and could only point him in the direction of Captain Drummond, who had been Robert's second – why him, and not one of Jamie's friends, Jamie had no idea. Drummond proved elusive. Jamie went from the regimental head-quarters to Cromwell's Doncaster base twice before eventually tracking the captain down in his quarters. Drummond was preparing his company to start south, but he confirmed that he'd left Rob at The White Swan, which was about eight miles north of Doncaster, on the Great North Road.

'It is a coaching inn,' said Drummond. 'A good-sized place, where a sick man may rest comfortably, if he has the money – which your brother does. He came north prepared to buy you out of prison, so he has ample funds for an inn. His servant is with him. The surgeon believed there was hope for him, and he yet lived when I last saw him.'

'When was that?' Jamie asked anxiously.

'Four days gone,' replied Drummond; then, defensive under Jamie's indignant stare, 'I've my company to concern me! I did what I could. Whether or no he lives is in the hands of God.'

Jamie went back to the inn where he'd left his father, hoping that the old man had bespoken a room for the night. It was dark now, and too late to set out again.

The innkeeper, hauled from his bed to answer the door, sullenly informed Jamie that Mr Hudson had taken an upstairs chamber and gone to bed – and he, the innkeeper, would like to do the same.

Jamie thanked the innkeeper wearily and decided not to disturb his father. He lay down on the floor of the common room, curling up against the warm chimney-breast. He was just drifting off when he heard steps on the stairs and sat up to find George Hudson coming down them with a candle. The old man was pale and dishevelled, but fully dressed. He recoiled at the sight of Jamie. 'What do you here?' he asked harshly.

'I had hoped you were asleep,' said Jamie.

George Hudson let out a huff of surprise and sat down on one of the tavern benches, setting his candle on the table. 'I *was* asleep,' he said, after a minute. 'I woke, and you were still not back. I was afraid for you.'

'Sir, you should go back to your bed,' said Jamie. 'We must be up betimes.'

'There is space for you upstairs,' George Hudson replied. 'You need not lie here like a servant.' He peered at Jamie anxiously and suddenly said, 'I know I have ever used you with less esteem than I did your brothers. I should never have apprenticed you in a mere mechanical trade; I should have seen you educated like a gentleman. I was much at fault, and I am sorry for it.'

Jamie did not know how to respond to that, either. He'd always been keenly aware of that lack of esteem, and bitterly resented it – even though he liked his 'mere mechanical trade', and rather pitied Rob's dusty hours struggling over Latin verbs. For his father to apologize, though, was unprecedented.

'You never thought I would be heir,' he said at last. 'No more did
I.' Then, with a pang of anguish for Rob, he added, 'And I pray God
I never am!'

George sighed. 'Even if Robert lives, I think he'll have no more
children. You saw Kate. If she died, and he remarried . . . but that's
an ill fate to wish on a poor harmless gentlewoman.'

'Then I pray that Rob keeps Bourne until my son can inherit from
him!' said Jamie.

His father smiled. 'Amen. You've shown yourself a loving brother,
Jamie. This journey has been good for that, at least.'

'I hope, sir, that it will be good for more, and that we'll find Rob
alive and nurse him to full health again.' He hesitated, then added,
'In the ruckus earlier I neglected to say that Captain Drummond,
who was Rob's second, gave me some grounds for hope. He says that
this White Swan is a good comfortable place, that Rob has Jenkin to
care for him, and that the surgeon had hope.'

George's big hands clenched. They both knew that wounds could
rot, and that shot wounds frequently did. 'I pray God he *is* better!'

'We'll know in the morning,' said Jamie. 'Sir, go to bed. You'll be
no help to Rob if you fall ill.'

His father stood. 'Nor will you, Jamie – and I think whether we
thrive here depends far more on you than upon me. Come upstairs.'

'I'm accustomed to hard commons, sir,' Jamie said. 'But I'd be glad
of a bed, if there is indeed room for me. Thank you.'

In the morning they set out before dawn. Early as it was, the
streets of Doncaster were full of men rushing about, of horses being
harnessed and guns secured on caissons. Bands of pikemen loomed
out of the pre-dawn grey like trees, musketeers like walking fence-
stakes. Even after they left the town they came across one band of
men after another, heading south from the villages and farms where
they'd been quartered to join up with the regiment for the march.
George Hudson watched them pass with troubled eyes. 'And all these
never even came to the siege?' he asked at one point.

'Colonel Cholmley wouldn't have us,' Jamie replied. 'Cromwell's
men must take Pontefract now.'

His father drew in his breath at this reminder that all the armed
men they'd seen had been only one regiment, and the Army had
another twenty just as big. ''Tis a strange world to me,' he said. 'I am
glad that you know its ways.'

The horses were exhausted after two days hard travel, but the distance they had to go was not great, and they arrived at The White Swan at about ten in the morning. It was, as Captain Drummond had said, promisingly large and comfortable-looking, a half-timbered building with a large stable. Leaving the servant to see to the horses, Jamie and his father hurried in at once.

When the innkeeper gathered who they were he beamed at them, and at once led them up the stairs. 'I gave him the best room in the house!' he announced proudly.

It was indeed a good room, with a window and a fireplace. Rob was sitting up in bed, propped against the pillows, his shoulder bandaged with clean linen and his arm in a sling. Jenkin Simons was sitting nearby, carving something from a piece of wood. When the door opened both men looked round quickly. Rob's face lit. 'Father!' he cried. 'Jamie!'

George Hudson burst into tears. He came over to the bed, sat down, and clutched the hand Rob held out to him. 'My dear boy,' he whispered, 'how do you?'

'Ill, but mending, as you see,' replied Rob. He looked beyond George to Jamie and said, 'I am sorry that I could not kill that scoundrel Barker for you. They told me you were wounded because of his lies.'

'It was but a graze,' said Jamie. His throat was tight, and he wasn't sure whether he wanted to weep, like his father, or howl with joy. 'I would sooner endure a thousand such than lose you.'

They stayed at The White Swan for twelve days, until Rob was well enough that even George Hudson agreed he'd take no harm from the ride back to Bourne. The bullet had broken his collar-bone, and ended up just under the skin above his right shoulder-blade. The surgeon had been able to remove it easily in one piece, which had helped reduce the infection which inevitably followed. Jenkin had been able to keep Rob warm and clean, and the fever and inflammation were already gone by the time Jamie and George arrived. George was profoundly grateful to the servant, and promised him the freehold on his family's cottage.

The innkeeper was very glad of their presence. He had suffered from the depredations of the Army – he had a thick stack of the worthless promissory tickets – and paying guests were desperately welcome, but there was more to it than that. The region was in chaos. In disbanding, Cholmley's regiment had filled the countryside with penniless soldiers; Cromwell's men were supposed to prevent them from turning to banditry, but had no resources to speed them on their way back to their homes. Men came to the inn two or three times a day, asking for food and frequently making threats as to what they would do if they didn't get it. The innkeeper gave them crusts and leftovers, but liked to have Jamie or Jenkin standing at his shoulder when he did, Jamie with his sword and Jenkin with Rob's duelling pistol.

The horses were in constant danger of being stolen. Jamie took to sleeping in the stables, a chain hung with old horse-shoes strung across the doorway; he was woken in the night three times by the sound of the barrier jangling as someone tried to creep in. He jumped up each time, drawing his sword and shouting, but was relieved that the would-be thieves simply ran off. The inn's ostler was a timid youth with a clubfoot, and none of the other servants were much better.

Then The White Swan started to run out of foodstuffs, as the regular orders of eggs, barley and fresh meat failed to arrive. Jamie and the innkeeper were obliged to go in person to the market at Knottingley – leaving Jenkin and the pistol to guard the inn – and protect their purchases of flour and pease with drawn swords all the way back. They still ran out of meat and eggs, but at least they didn't go hungry.

At Knottingley Jamie also went to the military authorities to complain about the missing supplies, and get letters exempting the inn from official requisitions. Cromwell himself wasn't there; he'd been summoned south by Lord General Fairfax. He'd taken only his Life Guard with him, however, leaving the rest of his forces to tighten the sieges of Pontefract and Knottingley, and his staff were now in charge. Cromwell's men weren't sure whether Fairfax expected him to rein in the Army, or whether the Lord General had been compelled to issue the summons by an Army Council which expected Cromwell to lead the overthrow of Parliament.

Rob wanted news of Barker, but all they learned was what they knew already: that Barker had been cashiered, fought a duel, and fled. Cromwell's men were much better informed when it came to the news from London: Jamie heard about the Army Council's vote to occupy the capital only three days after it was taken. He wondered how Lucy was coping. He thought of her constantly, worrying what she'd think of his continued absence, after all his promises to come at once. He had written to her with the good news of Rob's recovery, but he did not expect to hear anything back.

On the seventh of December, George Hudson conceded that Rob was well enough to start for home. The keeper of The White Swan was sorry to see them go, but no longer desperate to keep them. Cholmley's men had dispersed, and the disruption in the countryside was easing. He sent them on their way with blessings, and loud prayers that God would give them fair weather.

The weather was tolerable; it was cold, overcast and windy, but mostly dry, and when it did rain or snow they were able to find shelter. They journeyed in easy stages, so as to give Rob plenty of rest, never going more than fifteen miles a day.

Jamie had been perfectly content to stay with his father and brother while he felt he was needed, but as they rode south into areas clear of the worst of the war's disruption he became increasingly impatient. Lucy was expecting him in London. He had a great many things he wanted to say to her – and he couldn't help remembering that it was nearly a year since she first agreed to marry him.

On the evening of the fourth day of the journey, when they reached Grantham, he suggested that he leave the others and post ahead to London 'if you'll lend me the horse, Father, and money for the journey.'

His father was surprised. 'To London? Oh. Your wife.' He frowned. 'Will you not see your brother to his home first?'

'Sir,' said Jamie, 'my brother is recovering well, and you're but two days from Bourne even at this pace. You've no more need of my help, and I promised my wife I would see her in London as soon as I might. I promised it, sir, a month gone!'

George scowled; Rob laughed. 'You've done your work too well, Jamie,' he said. 'Now Father wonders how we'll manage without you.'

Their father flushed, and Jamie, startled, realized that it was true. George Hudson had started to rely on him, and by now depended on him to deal with all the troublesome things – Armies, wounds, discharged soldiers – with which he had no experience himself. He might not like or understand his son's political views, but that had become almost irrelevant beside the fact that Jamie's war record and experience were now a real advantage to the family. He had always been a pragmatist. Nick had ridden off to fight for the King, but George Hudson had stayed home and tried not to offend his neighbours.

It was very strange. Jamie felt that he ought to be indignant, to be valued at last only because he was useful and might become his father's heir. Instead, the simple fact of being valued, for any reason, was like a glowing fire in his heart.

'I must see my wife, sir,' he said defensively.

'Very well!' George snapped irritably. 'Go to the wench, and fetch her to Bourne. You may have your horse, and the remount, and money to keep you. We will see you at home, I trust, next week.'

Jamie hesitated a moment, then nerved himself and said evenly, 'Sir, even did I ride directly there and back again, it will take more than a week – and my wife has work and friends in London. For her to leave suddenly, without setting her affairs in order, would be a poor return for all their kindness. It will not be so simple as to ride in and bid her pack.'

His father glared. 'Then come as soon as you can.'

He arrived in London three days later.

It had been strange, riding down the road on a good horse, sleeping warm and dry in comfortable inns, welcomed everywhere by people who looked at the quality of his new civilian coat and the weight of his purse, and pretended to ignore his scars. He was uncomfortable with the fact that his father had loaned him the remount – he knew it was intended to whisk Lucy away at once, and he suspected she'd be reluctant to come at all – but he was glad of the extra animal, since it let him change mounts regularly and make better time. The winter days, however, were short, the roads were foul, and he was obliged to be careful with his father's horses. It was dark when he arrived in the City.

He stabled the horses at an inn in Smithfield. He felt unable to face going to The Whalebone, or some other place where people would know him. If he considered that reluctance it made him uneasy; had a new coat and his father's favour made him eager to shed old acquaintance? But he did not have much space for worrying about it. He was too impatient to see Lucy; his whole being was aquiver with the knowledge that she was only a mile away, and finally he would hold her in his arms.

Common sense warned him that he should wait until morning before going to find his wife. It was night, and she and her friends would be in bed. Common sense, however, had no more power to hold him than a rope of grass. As soon as he'd finished making arrangements for the horses, he set out to claim his bride. It was only when he reached Coleman Street and realized that he wasn't sure of the house that the doubts set in.

He did not know the Overtons well, and had been to their house only twice. He did not know how to recognize it in the dark. He was well aware, however, that they were Lucy's dearest friends – and that awareness, which he'd never questioned, suddenly revealed to him the huge gap between his wife's life and his own.

For a year he had been carried about England by the war, steadily losing faith in the cause for which he fought. He had walked in the shadow of death, and he wanted to escape it. The family that had rejected him now embraced him, and he wanted nothing more than to return to them, bury himself in country concerns, and forget politics.

For a year, though, his wife had been here, in the inky heart of radical London. She had started a business and seen it fail, paid and received wages, visited prisoners and signed petitions. Was she the same girl he'd married? He wasn't the same man.

He hesitated, wondering if it might, after all, be better to return in the morning. As he stood looking hopelessly at the darkened houses, however, a party of men and women with a lantern came out of a side road and began walking toward him.

'. . . pack of dissembling juggling knaves!' one man exclaimed loudly. 'God knows if they mean to hold elections at all!'

'But if you do not go back, they will settle everything among themselves,' a familiar voice replied.

Jamie suddenly realized who they were: it was a Thursday, and the Levellers of the City had just finished their weekly meeting at The Whalebone. Now some of them were on their way to Richard Overton's house to smoke and argue. And that shadowy woman on the edge of the party, listening . . .

He had no idea why she noticed him standing there in the dark, let alone how she recognized him. She stopped, though, very suddenly, then began to hurry toward him.

'Jamie?' she called incredulously; then, 'Jamie!' And the next he knew she was in his arms.

He held her tightly, as though he could press her into his own flesh and weld them together into one creature. 'Oh, my darling!' he choked.

'Jamie!' said the familiar voice, and he looked up to see that the others had come over with the lantern, and his friend John Wildman was smiling at him.

Jamie reluctantly let go of his wife and shook hands with his friend, then with John Lilburne and with Richard Overton. They were all full of smiles.

'A fine new coat!' said Wildman, surveying him. 'Lucy told us you'd been discharged.'

'Aye,' said Jamie, and cleared his throat. He did not want to talk to his friend or to any of them; he wanted to take his wife back to the Smithfield inn and straight to bed. Common civility, alas, precluded it. 'My kin have welcomed me back, strange to say.'

'God be praised!' said Wildman, beaming. 'And high time, too!'

'What . . .' began Lucy; she was still clinging to his arm. '. . . your poor brother . . .'

'I left him and my father at Grantham,' Jamie told her. 'They'll be home by now. He is much recovered, though the bone will take time to knit.'

'He's *alive*?' she asked, her face lighting.

'Aye. Did you not get my letter?'

'The last I had said he was shot, and you were to go to Pontefract!'

'Oh. Well. We went, and found him already much amended. We were obliged to stay with him for a time before he was fit to ride, or I would have been here sooner.'

'Oh, thank God!' cried Lucy passionately. 'Lieutenant Barker was so bold I feared he was fleeing the hangman's rope already!'

'What?' asked Jamie in confusion.

There was a sudden silence. He looked confusedly at the lamplit faces.

'This Barker came hither to London,' explained Richard Overton, 'and tried to carry off Lucy to revenge himself on you. But she escaped him, and he died by the misfiring of his own pistol.'

Jamie stared. His heart seemed to pause mid-beat, then resume with a giddy hammering. 'When was this?' he whispered.

'Not two weeks gone,' said Dick solemnly.

Jamie looked at Lucy: her eyes were bright with anger. 'You escaped hurt?' he asked anxiously.

She gave a tight little nod. 'I broke free of him. He tried to shoot me as I ran.' She paused, then went on, suddenly indignant, 'He set on me in *Moorfields*! When I went to buy *ink*! And oh, I was sure he would never have been so reckless unless he was already fleeing a death sentence!'

'I'd wager he thought he was!' Wildman said eagerly. 'A man who's felled his opponent with a pistol-shot, and knows himself disgraced and bereft of protectors, won't linger to hear how things turned out.' He beamed at Jamie.

'God has heaped a double blessing on you, my friend!' exclaimed John Lilburne. 'Your wife's life on top of your brother's!'

Jamie looked again at Lucy. He imagined coming to London and discovering that she had been raped and murdered two weeks before. Her survival, on top of Rob's, seemed suddenly too much good for an evil world. He caught her hand tightly, afraid that if he let her go she would slip away – that he would come to himself, and find that his friends had told him she was dead, and that the news had shattered his wits. 'But you 'scaped hurt?' he asked again.

'He tried to reload the pistol in haste while it was hot,' she replied. 'The ramrod went into his head.'

'Praise God for his righteous judgements!' said Lilburne with satisfaction.

Jamie swallowed, remembering sighting along his own pistol at Naseby. He wondered if that ruinous blast had somehow paid for Barker's death. Was it blasphemous, to imagine that bad luck could somehow *earn* good?

Probably it was. God gave, and God took away, and no human mind could fathom His reasons. Looking down into his wife's fierce dark eyes, though, he thought that if the one misfiring pistol had earned the other, he'd won a bargain. 'I thank God that you are safe!' he exclaimed fervently.

The anger in her face softened. '*I* thank God that you are come back safe from the war!'

'Praise be to God for his great mercies!' said the plain, pock-faced woman – Mary Overton, he remembered, Lucy's good friend.

'Amen!' said her husband. 'Let's not stand in the cold. There's a warm fire in my house, and we should make use of it.'

They all trooped over to the Overtons' house – it *was* the one he'd thought most likely – and into the kitchen. Candles were lit; Dick, with a sly smile, brought out a bottle of sack.

A young girl appeared in her nightdress as he was pouring it. She stopped short at the sight of Jamie. He thought that the look of dismay on her face was from his scars, until she cried to Lucy, 'Your husband's come!'

Lucy went to her and hugged her. 'Aye, sweet . . .'

The girl burst into tears and flung her arms around Lucy. Lucy gave Jamie a look of apology and kissed the girl's head.

Mary Overton came over and detached the child. 'Come, Faith!' she said gently. 'You should be glad because Lucy's husband has come home safe from the wars! Give thanks to God!'

Faith gave Jamie a murderous look. 'You mustn't take her off to Lincolnshire!' she exclaimed. 'She *wants* to stay here, with us!'

'Faith!' said Mary Overton sharply.

'I don't want her to go!' cried Faith, flinging her arms around Lucy again.

'Wicked girl!' exclaimed Mary. 'To make an idol of your own selfish wants! To bed with you at once!'

Faith turned tearful eyes to her mother, her mouth mulish. 'But who will look after us if they put you and Da in prison?'

Mary hesitated, stricken; her husband cried with forced cheerfulness, 'There's no danger of that, sweet! Come, leave off this foolishness, kiss Lucy goodnight, and go up to bed!'

Lucy took the child's face between her hands. 'You won't be left alone again, Faith, I promise it. I pray God you need not fear for your parents' freedom, but if ever they do fall into danger, I will look after you. I would come down from Lincolnshire to fetch you.'

Faith hugged her tightly and began crying again. 'I still don't want you to go!'

'Oh, sweet, life's full of partings! I didn't want to part from Jamie last year, nor he from me, but here we are well-met again at last! You and I will meet again, too, you may be sure of it. Go up to bed, darling. In the morning you'll be ashamed of how you carried on tonight.'

Faith kissed Lucy, cast a look of loathing at Jamie, and fled upstairs.

'Forgive her,' Mary urged Jamie anxiously. 'She will miss her bed-mate; and, indeed, she has been a troubled and fearful child of late, with the streets full of soldiers and the times so uncertain.'

Jamie cleared his throat uncomfortably. He felt like a robber – no, like a soldier, come to requisition something precious. 'She's but a child. Of course I am not angry.'

John Lilburne raised his cup of sack. 'Here's to your safe return from the wars, Mr Hudson! And may all our soldiers soon do likewise!'

They all drank to coming home from the war. The sherry was sweet, but with an acid edge that hurt Jamie's teeth. His joyous reunion had already become uneasy.

'Have you lodgings for tonight, Mr Hudson?' Dick Overton asked, when the cups were empty.

'I bespoke a room in Smithfield, where I left the horses.'

'Horses!' repeated Lucy in surprise.

'Aye. My father loaned me two.' At her look of alarm he burst out, 'You need not come at once! I told my father that you could not leave your friends suddenly, after all their kindnesses to you. There is time to . . . to make whatever arrangements are needed.'

'But you do mean to remove to Lincolnshire,' she said, watching him closely.

'Aye,' he said, and swallowed. Faith's *'She wants to stay here with us!'* echoed miserably in his mind. He was dreadfully afraid that the night would end with his wife in tears, begging to be allowed to stay in London. He had dreamed of returning to her so long and so desperately that he didn't know if he could bear it. 'I – my father wants me at home,' he said, struggling to get words out. 'We can talk over how best to manage it. I know that it will grieve you to leave your friends here in London, but I hope . . . I hope we can arrange matters so that you and I can be happy.'

'You're reconciled, then, with your father?' asked Wildman.

Jamie nodded. He felt he ought to elaborate, but his throat was clogged with all the things he wanted to say to Lucy.

'I'll hear the whole tale tomorrow,' Wildman said, slapping him on the arm. 'For now; I'm sure you'd prefer your wife's company.'

'I'll fetch you some things for the night,' Mary offered Lucy. 'Best you don't go upstairs just now; it will set Faith to weeping. Come back in the morning; we'll talk then about what is to be done.'

* * *

It was only a few minutes later that Lucy found herself closing the door of the house on Coleman Street behind her. She told herself that *of course* it wasn't for the last time – she would be back in the morning; she'd probably be coming back every morning for the next week, while her friends looked for someone to replace her on *The Moderate*.

She knew, though, that in an important sense it *was* for the last time. She would not inhabit this house again. She was stepping out into the darkness with a hulking near-stranger, and she wasn't even sure whether the giddiness she felt sprang from exhiliration or terror.

When she'd seen him standing in the street, a tall slouched form alone in the darkness, something inside her had seemed to shift, and all the resolutions about what she would say and do had gone out of her head. Running to him, having his arms around her, had felt *right* somewhere deep inside. The questions, though, were crowding back. What would she do in Lincolnshire?

'I'm sorry,' Jamie said awkwardly.

The Overtons had loaned them a lantern, which Jamie was carrying in his good, left hand; as he turned toward her the wavering light cast the scarred side of his face into shadow. Lucy frowned up at his half-profile, the single eye gleaming darkly under the brim of his hat. That face had changed since she'd seen it last: suffering had shadowed the eyes and drawn deep lines around the mouth. He was so *thin*, too! Rob had warned her, but still it had shocked her. 'For what?' she asked.

'I know you'd sooner stay in London than remove to a place unknown.'

She made a face. It was actually a relief, to know for certain that she was to leave London. She'd been unsettled ever since Barker's assault, and events since the Army's arrival filled her with dread. She was now more worried about her promises to Mary and to Faith than about the prospect of moving to Lincolnshire. If Jamie refused to give the Overton children house-room, what could she do about it? Even if *he* was willing to honour her promise, what if his father forbade it?

Of course, she might never be called on to keep that promise. Indeed, Mary wasn't really even threatened, this time – though she'd probably be glad of a safe refuge for the little ones even if it were only Dick who went to prison. Lucy hoped fervently that Dick, too, would be safe, but the Army's recent doings, and the Leveller response to them, made her queasy with apprehension.

'Your brother wished me to come away to Lincolnshire last month,' she told Jamie. 'It gave me occasion to accustom myself to the thought of such a remove. Pay no heed to what Faith said. She's but grieved to lose a friend. But . . .' Her heart sank. She shouldn't have made such a weighty promise without consulting him, so how could she explain that she *had* to keep it?

'But?' Jamie repeated, watching her with what seemed almost fear.

She burst out, 'What I promised Faith just now – Jamie, the Overtons have ever treated me like their own bloodkin. How could I treat them as less?'

His eye widened in surprise. 'Oh!' he said, as though he'd forgotten all about the promise. He smiled tentatively. 'I'd be most willing to receive Mistress Faith.'

'There are *three* children,' admitted Lucy.

That brought a frown – but only momentarily. 'They would all be welcome.'

'Truly?' she asked, scarcely daring to credit it. 'I know it's much to ask, but . . .'

He interrupted. 'Lucy, your friends have supported and protected you all this long year, while I could do *nothing* for you! It shamed me; I think it even shamed my father. Of course I would be glad of the chance to repay some of the debt I owe the Overtons!'

'But – your father? Would he . . .' She checked herself, then went on nervously, 'Jamie, one thing your brother said that troubled me very much was that you'd agreed to give up your adherence to the cause, and . . . and it seems to me that if your father understood whose children they were, he would not welcome them.'

Jamie looked sick.

'He'll forbid it,' she said, her heart sinking again.

He shook his head impatiently. 'It's not his affair. We will have a house of our own soon, I hope. It would never do, for you and I to squeeze into the manor alongside my father and brother and all. But . . .'

'We'll have a house of our own?' she repeated in relief. This was enormously good news. She would not have to become a humble dependent of Jamie's intimidating family!

'Aye,' he said impatiently, then continued urgently, 'But as to what

I promised Rob – Lucy, I only wanted not to quarrel with him! Nick was dead, and Rob was all I had; I thought we could be at peace if I only agreed to hold my tongue! I never meant to . . . to surrender! But he took it as meaning more, and now . . .'

'I saw how he took it,' Lucy said, when Jamie faltered again.

He swallowed. 'I haven't turned against the *Agreement*, Lucy. It's what we've fought for all these years, and it was worth fighting for. But, sweet, I am so *tired* of fighting!' Then he looked down and added, in a low voice, 'And I fear that whatever we do now, Cromwell and Ireton will win.'

That touched the heart of Lucy's own apprehensions, and she had no reply to it. 'But I can tell Mary that you agree to have the children, should they arrest Dick?' she asked at last.

'Oh, aye, gladly!' he exclaimed in relief.

She reached out and caught his hand. It was the bad hand; the iron was cold under her fingers, but the rough palm curved eagerly about her own, enfolding it warmly. 'Thank you!' she said in relief. 'I'd not have you think Faith is always as troublesome as she was tonight. In truth, usually she's too good and quiet for her own peace. That outburst was much unlike her, and I'm sure only came about because she's been so frightened, poor child. She's scarcely slept all week. She lies awake worrying. It was bad enough to have the streets full of soldiers, but now the committee's to be cast aside, and her father's on it. She's a wise child, she knows what's afoot.'

'What committee?' Jamie asked in bewilderment.

She peered up at him in surprise – then remembered that he'd spent weeks out in the country and on the road. 'Did you not hear that Free-born John, and Dick, and Major Wildman were asked to a committee with Ireton and some Parliament men, to draw up a settlement for a new form of government?'

Jamie stared a moment, then shook his head. 'There was some talk of this, before I left the regiment, but I didn't know it had come about. It actually met, did it? And it's to be cast aside?'

She nodded miserably. 'They *agreed* a settlement, Jamie! A settlement that was everything we've wanted all these years! But instead of being taken forward, all their work is now thrown to *another* committee, for *more* discussions – and meanwhile the real business is done in secret between Ireton and what's left of Parliament. The new committee is ignored. All everyone talks of these days is how there'll be a trial of the King. And this is after that treacherous purge! Did you hear of *that*?'

He winced. 'Aye. On the road south.'

She thought he must have: the furore surrounding the Army's purge of Parliament had been long and loud. The Levellers – and, to be fair, the Army leaders – had called for the *dissolution* of Parliament followed by fresh elections. Instead, Westminster had been surrounded by troops and all the members hostile to the Army had been excluded, leaving the rest in place. The House of Commons had become a creature of the Army, a rump representative of nobody. Cromwell, who'd been summoned south when the Army first marched into London, had taken a long time on the road, and managed to arrive in the capital the day after the purge was over, reaping the benefits while escaping the blame.

'Dick and Honest John have walked out of the new committee,' Lucy went on. 'Major Wildman wants them to come back. He says that though the new committee is an affront, yet to give over is but to surrender and let Ireton have his way.'

'Ireton will have his way whatever they do,' said Jamie heavily.

Lucy bit her lip. Lilburne had spent most of that evening's Leveller meeting denouncing Ireton as 'a dissembling juggling knave', and promising to write a pamphlet to lay bare all of the Army leadership's deceits. She'd listened, but privately feared that a pamphlet wouldn't be enough. Pikes and muskets were the only power in London now. 'Free-born John means to appeal to the common soldiers,' she said half-heartedly.

'Sweetheart,' Jamie said unhappily, 'we lost at Ware. Cromwell was too strong for us even then – and all this last year his power has grown and grown. All the glorious victories of the war were his. Lord General Fairfax spent all summer sat miserably before Colchester – it's no wonder he was thrust aside when the Army marched on London. It's Cromwell's Army now. Things might be different if we still had Colonel Rainsborough, but he's dead. Honest John's as gallant a gentleman as ever drew breath, but even he won't prevail now.' He gave her a desperate look and went on, 'Whether or not I hold my peace will not turn the scales by a hair – but it would cost me dearly. My family have welcomed me back, Lucy; my little sister Peggy ran and threw her arms about me when she saw me, for all that she'd not seen me since my maiming, and I was filthy from the road. And my father . . . my father *wept*. It would kill me to quarrel with them again!'

Lucy finally understood that he was afraid she would quarrel with him, forcing him to choose between her and his family. She felt a sudden overwhelming stab of pity. *If he feels he can pay no more,* Mary had said, *who are you to tell him he must?*

'Then don't!'she said impulsively. 'Peace is a joy, if you can win it. If Dick and Honest John agreed to hold their peace, their wives would thank God for it. I should not have said that! I beg you, never repeat it!'

He stopped, staring at her in astonishment. 'I will not. You're not angry with me?'

She reached out with her free hand and touched his chest. 'You are my husband, and you came back to me alive despite all this cruel war could do to us. How could I be angry?'

He set down the lantern, pulled her to him, and kissed her. 'Oh, my darling! I thought you would weep, or curse me!' He was in tears.

She reached up and stroked the scarred side of his face. 'Jamie, if removing to Lincolnshire is the worst grief I must suffer, I'll count myself blessed.'

He kissed her again. 'I thought of you day and night. Dear God, and even at the last I nearly lost you, and never knew it! I think if I had come here and found you dead, it would have driven me mad. I never want to part from you again!'

She leaned her head against his shoulder. She felt as though she, not he, had endured a long hard journey, but at last come home, into the circle of his arms.

He hurried her the rest of the way to his inn. It was across the road from the livery stable where Nedham kept his mare. That gave her a moment's pause, but then she turned her back on it and the memory. They went up to his room, and – because it was a cold night – climbed under the bed's thick covers before undressing, shedding shirts and shifts and stockings out from between the sheets. There they found paradise again, readmitted to Eden and to innocence after the long walk in shadow.

Afterwards, though, she got up and lit a candle. He groaned and buried his face in the pillow.

'We must *talk,* Jamie!' she said severely, getting back into bed and snuggling against him. 'Tomorrow I must tell Mary and Dick – and Mr Mabbot! – what I am going to do, so that they can hire someone to take my place on *The Moderate*. They will want to know when I'm leaving!'

'Aye, aye, aye!' he sighed, turning to look at her, and beginning to smile again as he did. 'Very well. When are we leaving, then?'

'When Mr Mabbot's found someone to replace me. But I also have a great deal to settle about Lincolnshire, and what we shall do there! I know not so much of Bourne as where it lies!'

'It's between Stamford and Grantham,' he told her. 'A pretty little market town a few miles from the Great North Road.'

'Near the North Road!' she exclaimed in pleasure. There would be coaches going back and forth to London, with passengers who might buy blackletter ballads – or cheese, if she decided to run a dairy. 'And shall we truly have a house of our own?'

'I'd scarce considered it,' he said, 'but, aye, we shall. My father has one married son under his roof already. If we stayed there as well, all the neighbours would shake their heads.'

'So we might have a house in Stamford or Grantham?' she asked. 'There must be plenty of call for blacksmiths on the Great North Road!'

He hesitated. 'As to that – I'm not certain that I . . .' He sat up in bed, gathering her into his arms and frowning down at her. 'There's . . . another matter. My brother Nick is dead, and Rob's only son died by mischance, and my father fears that my sister-in-law will have no more children.'

It took her a moment to grasp what that meant. 'You're now heir to the estate?' she asked incredulously.

'Aye. At present I am, after Rob. That carries weight with my father. He says now that he should never have had me apprenticed in a mere mechanical trade, and that he is sorry he used me with less esteem than he did my brothers. He now finds it convenient, too, to have a son who fought for Parliament. I . . . think he might not be happy to have me setting up nearby as a lowly blacksmith.'

'But what would you do?'

'Help manage the estate, I suppose.' He frowned again. 'Though as to that, if he expects me to help him drain fenland and turn the inhabitants out to beg, he should think again.' He sighed. 'Sweet, I know not what we will do – but I'm sure we will find something.'

Jamie was heir to an estate? For a moment Lucy was dismayed – then she told herself not to be foolish. Why should she be dismayed to learn that they would have more money and a better position than she'd expected? It was good news! It meant she could do more – run, not just a one-woman press, but a printing business which employed others, or a dairy that sold cheese all up and down the Great North Road. If friends needed help, she'd be in a position to supply it.

'You're most silent,' observed Jamie, brushing her hair tenderly away from her face.

The love shining on his face was like the sun. She understood suddenly that she had been wrong ever to doubt her choice, because what she had chosen was love, and there was nothing in all the world to compare with it. She cupped his face in her hands, wanting to hold that look for ever and ever, and whispered, 'I think we will be happy.'

What Really Happened
(and What Happened Next)

Imagine two contemporary historians sitting down to write a history of the war in Iraq; imagine that both are honest and painstaking, but one is an Iraqi academic, the other a former advisor to the Bush administration. Would you expect their two accounts to agree?

The English Civil Wars were and are just as contentious – but luckily for me I'm a novelist, not a historian, and the question I had to answer wasn't 'What really happened?' but 'What would my protagonists *think* had happened?' Was Charles I really a bloody tyrant, and were Ireton and Cromwell scheming ambitious hypocrites? Most modern historians think not. Did the Levellers *believe* they were? Undoubtedly! The history in this book is a Leveller view of the Second Civil War – as interpreted, of course, by a twenty-first century female novelist. For what it's worth, however, I've tried hard to be accurate. The big events all happened much as described, many of the characters are based on real people, and all the quotations from newsbooks, pamphlets and documents are genuine. The two main characters, of course, are purely fictional, as are their letters.

As in my previous Civil War novel, the language used for dialogue is a compromise between modern and seventeenth century, adopted because I wanted something that fitted in with the period documents but didn't completely alienate the modern reader. If it didn't work for you – well, I'm sorry!

King Charles I was tried and executed in January 1649, and over the course of that year the Levellers were crushed. There was a crackdown on press freedom in the autumn of 1649. (Gilbert Mabbot had been pushed out of the Licensorship before then.) *The Moderate* and *Mercurius Pragmaticus* were alike shut down, and the vast array of Civil War newsbooks shrank to one official mouthpiece: *Mercurius Politicus*. The editor? None other than Marchamont Nedham. He'd stuck with the Royalist cause until well after the King's execution, but when he was finally caught he bought his freedom by turning his coat. He exploited his monopoly on newsprint, married profitably, and supported the Protectorate with such panache that all the Royalists in exile hated him – but at the Restoration he was wealthy enough to buy himself a pardon.

John Wildman did not turn his coat, but his adroit dealings in confiscated lands made him extremely wealthy. He was a perpetual conspirator, first against Cromwell and then against Charles II and James II, but his wealth – coupled with some double- or possibly triple-agenting – allowed him to escape the consequences whenever he was caught. He was in the thick of the 'Glorious Revolution' of 1688, and was briefly rewarded with the position of Postmaster General, but lost it after he forged letters to discredit opponents.

Honest John Lilburne predictably fared less well. In the spring of 1649 he attacked Cromwell and his government in a pamphlet called *England's New Chains Discover'd*. He was arrested for this and other forms of agitation and was twice tried for treason: the jury acquitted him on both occasions, but he nonetheless spent most of the rest of his life in prison. He died in his wife's arms in 1657, during a brief spell out on parole, at the age of forty-two.

Just over a year later, Cromwell, too, was dead. If Ireton had still been alive at the time the history of England might have been very different – but Ireton had died of fever in 1651 while campaigning in Ireland. Oliver's eldest son, Richard Cromwell, inherited his father's title, but could not hold the Commonwealth together, and Charles II was restored to his father's throne in 1660.

The Overtons seem to have retreated from both politics and publishing and moved to the Netherlands before that triumph. Their voices, like those of so many others, disappear from history. Their ideas, however, are alive and powerful today, in constitutions all over the world, and in the minds and hearts of those who love democracy.